A FEAR AND A WARNING

William Foster Day

Printed by CreateSpace
Available on Kindle and other devices
Available from Amazon.com and other retail outlets

FOUR FRIENDS

By John James Jacoby

Book I

Preface

As I see it now, there are two types of innocence (innocence is the quality of existing without guilt), innocence within ignorance and innocence without ignorance. We are all born into the first type. Some don't want to awaken from this purity and remain innocent in their own unawareness - cows ready for the slaughter. Many become disillusioned by the awakening and refuse to search further: Life's bloody secrets are too much to confront, to justify and/or to handle. These people feel and fear they would be destroyed by truth. Their beings are, or they think they are, too fragile. They force themselves to become content with what they know and what they are doing. They refuse to reach out for knowledge: contentment ready for the slaughter. Some aren't destroyed or destroyable by the facts of their situation; yet refuse to act. They refuse to believe they can do something. They think they are too small in a too-large-a-machine. They place their faith and hope in the larger forces i.e. a company, the government and/or God.

3

These people also do nothing: resting in their faith, blind-hope really for the slaughter. Many other types of innocence rest in a bed of ignorance with either an inability or a lack of will to arise, but the result is the same: destruction by, or in, their dreams of life.

An extreme minority not only seeks the ignorance which exists and attempts to alleviate it, but they make amends for their share of guilt. It is to these few that a clarity of sight may exist. They are not confused by their own fears nor by the falsity which exists. By their deeds, they are again born into an innocence, but this time without guilt. They have shed their share of guilt. They walk their paths without the burdens of dread and remorse and with a continuing securable and secured freedom from these types of encumbrances. They realize their responsibilities to stop their share in guilt-creating events and to erase their culpability which already exists.

Yes, we are all born into many types of original sin for which we must make amends before we can share a guiltless path of knowledge and freedom; some sins come with just being human; e.g. we must destroy to survive or we can go against our natural instincts to survive, suicide. Some sins are the culmination of the crimes which our state, country, or nation has committed. Maybe some even exist because our family has committed sins, and we inherit them with our names.

Many horrendous acts have happened and are happening because people have said that they weren't or wouldn't transpire. We are all guilty if we just let

4

what we consider crimes happen. Of course, the main crime of which I speak right now is the unjustified war in which we are engaged. It seems we don't learn from the past but continue to force our will, our way of government, our values, our systems upon other people. We believe in choice for ourselves and then choose what is right for someone else and force our choice upon them.

The guilt which we are creating for our country is compounded by both those who are in position of guidance and control and/or by our innate want to remain innocent. This guilt is not only shared by persons perpetrating this war, or even by the ones letting it happen but will be shared by future generations.

What befalls us when our feeling of innocence is unveiled? We are forced to see our guilt: our unquestionable guidance disappears; we see through the systems which have deceived us, through the falsities and lies, reality awakens us into contrition, and we see that we have allowed what we consider crimes to happen (and yes, maybe then we will see through ourselves).

The responsibility for erasing this ignorance not only lies within the systems which are in some way informing us of events and in a sense creating a type of reality, but it rests within each one of us: to seek the truth, to take the responsibility not only for our actions but for the actions of the systems to which we give consent or even help to create, and to inform each other of the events which take place within the systems and the events which the systems affect.

This is but a single reason why I write. All of the other reasons for creating this manuscript are complicated and cannot be fully sorted even in my own mind, but I'm sure they will become translucent as this manuscript progresses.

My inexperience as a writer is apparent to me as it must be to many readers. I have rewritten those last paragraphs too many times to count and still can't come up with an inclusive, clear statement. Sections seem awkward and in many places, I question whether I have used the best words. I am not a writer by profession but a teacher. After teaching English for so many years, and after reading volume after volume, writing should be easy. But no, it isn't. And one reason it isn't is that my degrees have instilled a feeling that not only I, but all writers, must have a just cause to waste energy and demand time from a reader. After reading so much writing that has not justified its reason for existence, I feel that I must justify my work both to myself and the world.

Two nights ago I had a dream, one of those dreams which are so vivid and real that it consistently presses into my consciousness. Before the dream I had considered writing this manuscript but, of course, had done nothing, rationalizing that plenty of time exists. Then the dream transpired, and with every reminder of the dream, the obligation to tell this story increased until here I am at my computer. This was a real dream, as real as any dream can be:

It had come and gone. Not seeing it, not knowing what it was, I walked through the hamlet with almost a curiosity. I could see the devastation, its result, the empty hamlet, the broken windows, debris everywhere, an over-turned donkey cart, but I knew not what had caused it. On the other side of the village, my neighbors, the residents of this community, grouped together with sticks, pitchforks, axes, and other weapons in hand. They outwardly displayed courage, but knowing them as I did, I knew they were afraid.

I turned and walked back through the village. All the shops and houses were empty. Just small bands of people wandered the deserted streets.

I turned when a voice shouted hoarsely, "They went that way! That way." He pointed in a nebulous northern direction. Two groups of town's people were coming from different directions when he shouted. Everyone looked where he pointed, but only a few turned and began to move in that direction. The others stared with shocked blankness, or fear; some returned from which they had come.

I began to move in the direction he pointed but stopped as I saw someone throw a large book on the ground. It appeared to be a Bible. He seemed to be taking great pride in the loud sound it made as it hit the ground. Was that going to be a weapon? Insanity and fear predominated.

Small groups of people were heading in the direction the force had gone. I followed slowly until I could see their destination: a barren, light brown small dusty canyon where many were climbing the crumbly rock canyon walls with their weapons. They were preparing for the force's return. The preparation was being accomplished with a mood of excitement and even terror. People moved about chaotically. Nobody took charge. Nobody gave directions. Nobody even spoke a word.

I was wandering around, not approaching the ravine but trying to figure out how to help. What weapon should I get? A big boulder? I looked for one. But I did not know the force: what it was or how to stop it. A stillness spread over the crowd. The people on the canyon walls stopped climbing. Then I heard it, the roar, the screeching, the chaos. Now, panic and horror possessed all these people. Had anyone expected the roar to be so dense, so loud, so strong, so devastating? It was approaching. I realized that it was a huge mass of people running toward the gulley. Then I realized neither this gulch nor the people would stop those charging mass but just slow them. The people on the walls with their logs, rocks, spears, and clubs were not enough. I began to run. Others around me began to run, in all directions.

Knowing that the multitude would not gain on me, that they could not travel any faster than I could, I felt fairly safe just jogging. I had almost reached the hamlet when I heard the wave of people hit the ravine. The screaming increased to such a point that it seemed right behind me. Panic grabbed me, and I began to run faster. When I reached the other side of our small village, I was the only person running. Did those fools expect the hamlet to stop the masses? Were they hiding in their houses, under their beds? My increased pace lasted until the roar of anguished human beings seemed to lessen, and I entered the forest. Rays of sunshine penetrated the dense overgrowth illuminating sections of greenery, moss, trunks of gnarled trees. Everything seemed so beautiful, yet frightfully desolate. Knowing that the further I ventured into the forest, the safer I would be; nevertheless, I was hesitate in slowing my pace to a walk.

How many people who once fortified the canyon walls were now running with the masses? They had become a part of the threat and not its defiance. I laughed at myself. I had run. I had become them. I was just the tip of the chaos, the forerunner. But now I was by myself, isolated.

A clanging sound in front of me caused me to stop. Armored men marching in my direction frightened me again. Did I escape the masses to die here? I didn't have time to turn and run, so I slid behind a tree. The armored foot soldiers without taking notice of me passed on both sides of the tree behind which I hid. Almost all passed without giving me the slightest notice. Near the end of the procession, two men on horseback approached. They stopped on both sides of the tree. They spoke in a dialect which at first was hard to understand but finally what they said became clear. "From which direction were they coming?" I pointed in the direction from which I had just run. The two men dismounted and took me to a commander and a wizard who was dressed in a black robe. As we approached, the wizard was talking to the chief knight. The wizard's eyes rolled in his head as he waved an ax. When we approached they both stopped talking and turned. We three followed the chief and the wizard to a tree stump on which the wizard brought down the ax.

"Here we are. Now, show us where they are," commanded the Royal Chief. As I began to tell them everything I knew, I awakened.

I can see from the dream that I am the informant. It is my duty for I have seen the waste of human beings, not necessarily as in the dream but in that the people whom I have known to have the greatest capabilities, the greatest minds, have not been able to fulfill their potential in a constructive, useful way. Who is to blame for this tragedy; the present situation of the world, the systems which raised these people? Perhaps they themselves have to accept the blame. I guess all of us have to carry the burden of blame. I am writing not so much to place the condemnation but to prevent a continuance and a reoccurrence. As I have said I write also to make amends for the guilt that I have shared in these tragedies.

PART I

THE INNOCENT

Chapter 1

The title to this part "The Innocent" perfectly represents Thesus or at least did represent him until recently. He was innocent, but not without cause and surely not without effect. The depth of our hero's innocence extended to the point where he thought he knew what was happening and who he was.

When he was young, he was aware, sensitive to the extreme, intelligent, I would even say brilliant. But he believed in too much. He accepted what he was told; he believed people, too many of them, and he trusted humanity. Why shouldn't he? His parents are people who wouldn't have deceived him, and he thought that the world was in accordance also. When I indirectly confronted his mother, asking her how he had remained so innocent, she said that they never gave advice for which he wasn't ready but waited for him to question. Thinking about it now, I know she was innocent also. She didn't even fully understand my question or my indirect accusation of keeping him sheltered, making him almost gullible.

For years he did what he was told, not only by his parents but by his friends, teachers, probably even strangers. He obeyed, almost, to the point where when I first met him, I thought him submissive. He didn't see the full implications of his actions. He did what he was told because he didn't see the possible results. Also, I guess, he was reared to be obedient: his father being in the service and so strict. He always said, 'Yes ma'am; Yes sir' to everyone. But maybe this statement is unmerited to all concerned.

Let's say he was naive to what was really happening in the world. That would be more fair. Yes, his fault, if he had a fault, was not that he was a follower, a sheep, but that he was naive. He was acquiescent, without realizing it nor really knowing to what he was submitting. It wasn't that he didn't question. Indeed he sought the truth, even on a profound level; but he didn't ask the right questions. Maybe his fault was that he trusted himself too much. He presumed he knew what was important and what he needed to do without concern. It was a world where his greatest achievements were for the beautiful, the good, and the true. His was a young world, a precious world, and fragile.

As I was saying, our hero considered himself right, good, and just. People in his world viewed him as he regarded himself. He was a bit more curious and asked more questions than most. But even when I was his teacher, I reflected him as he perceived himself and so there was no reason for him to doubt. No, I guess, he was not totally to blame.

Then again, he wasn't and isn't spotlessly perfect. Though he probably thought, and still thinks, he is striving towards those goals (an example of naiveté?). Yes, he was striving for an idealistic concept of perfection. His ideals were created by the biographies and autobiographies of people he considered great. He learned all the "correct" words: courage, fortitude, perseverance, nobility, honesty, temperance, humility, inner strength, and he sought them within himself.

But maybe it was his striving for a perfection which kept him from seeing what was really happening. Oh, he saw other humans indulging in their vices. He was not naive to his or others' faults, but he thought that these people would bring harm on themselves. He expressed his belief as: "They had to live with themselves, and I have to live with myself." He believed in justice. He thought that those who cheated, cheated themselves, and would eventually have to pay. He believed that taking short cuts didn't pay, that the lazy person would have less experience with which to face the future.

He didn't believe that these people who wronged would be punished in the Great Beyond. No, even by eighth grade, he didn't believe in an omnipotent, omniscient God .... the Supreme Judge. Although at one time he told me that he, for a period of time, was waiting for instructions, a message to guide an inner decision.

When I first met him in school, he was more or less a pantheist, maybe without even knowing that term. He believed in what is here and now: mass, energy, the Universe. He believed in science, math, and all his studies, but his personal God extended far beyond what science could explain. When I first met him "It" was a feeling, an innate knowledge, that It - encompassed all that existed, and he was part of it.

13

The young man developed to the point where most youths get, questioning their own existence. Within a short time his beliefs evolved to the point where he rationally tried to disprove God's existence.

No, I am jumping ahead.

His first tirade to me about his beliefs began with the idea that that no God exists whose judgment dictates the final end of each human, but each human was his own judge. Each human held Heaven or Hell within. After people told so many lies, they would not know the truth. And yes, one would feel guilty (obviously another example of naivety) about his wrong doings and thereby would create his own Hell.

He did have his a morality. But he had too high a moral standard. For instance, upon realizing his transgressions, and many existed because of his unrealistic standards, he would try to prevent a reoccurrence by punishing himself. His chastisement would usually take the form an abstinence. If he realized his mistakes soon enough, he would try to make amends, but if he couldn't correct the wrong, he would dwell on his mistake until it would drive him almost crazy. Yes, it was perfection he sought. Again and again he fell from his standards, but never relinquished them. Again and again he would repent before persons who were not worthy of his humility because he felt he had transgressed. He believed in his philosophy and lived by it, and by living it, he made it real. This remarkable philosophy which approached sainthood was conceived and transpired in seventh and eighth grades. Yes, young and idealistic!

His philosophy was not the main aspect that separated him from the rest of the youth his age. On a battery of tests his intelligence was rated in the 99% plus category. His ability in reading, math, and science was the ability of a child over twice his age.

When left by himself, boredom was not a problem for he had a curiosity which kept him active. He would skip around in his studies, read books in class, become distracted by a problem, pursue that for a brief period, then find another topic worth pursuit. When his involvement extended into single regions of learning, he would not discuss anything but his preoccupation and within a short duration only an expert in that field could understand him.

He would become impatient and bored if you couldn't understand. Also he didn't have time to explain it (or in my opinion he did didn't have the communications skills); there was so much more to learn, to explore, and so off he would run.

During one of these periods of intense involvement, talking to him would consist of a lecture emphasizing the information he considered important. He had correct facts; this I can validate because when he delved into my field of literature, with only a slight leap in imagination, I could comprehend.

The reader may be questioning my relationship with Thesus; that is, how I knew my student so well as to make statements about his conduct, his thinking, his beliefs, etc. You see, I was this juvenile's seventh grade teacher, and a tutor for two years after that, then from that time forth, his friend and confidant.

When I began teaching, the school district was

poor and small. But when I finished three years later, it had grown tremendously, doubled in size. When I began, I was a seventh grade educator in one of the two junior highs in the immediate vicinity. The other teacher taught seventh and eighth. My class had about thirty maximum in the spring and about twenty in deep winter. Most of the students came from the farms. Some students were migrant workers and the remainder came from two small towns ten miles apart. Our hero was from a wealthy farm bordering on one of the towns. His father was a retired Captain from the Army, still active in the Reserve, and an insurance salesman. For a while his insurance deals included almost all of the property in the area. He also had some warehouses and grain bins to temporarily store corn and wheat which the government and others leased. It was seasonal, but when it all was rented, he made money. He also insured the bins. He grew corn, alfalfa, raised cattle, sheep, hogs, and the family had three goats. He also had land in the government experimental land bank, from which he was subsidized to grow specialized crops.

One year, or so the story goes, the government wanted to rid itself of some questionable corn which had been poisoned with the wrong type of fumigant. It contained a pesticide. The corn was unfit for human consumption. The government had sanctioned the experimental use of a preservant for extensive storage. Well, our hero's father was paid for the crop which he grew, was paid to spray the crop with fumigant, was contracted for the storage, and finally was paid for its disposal. His contract to eliminate the grain was inclusive of the whole county. Instead of burning the corn, he found a chemical which would neutralize or wash the poison. He bought a hundred and fifty head of cattle and pigs then feedlotted them for a year with the corn he was expected to have destroyed; if true, a real gamble in my mind, but "Best damn beef and pork we ever ate," said one of the locals. Then again I am not sure if this story is an exaggeration, but if true, I'm sure "The Captain" tested the beef for contaminates and enjoyed the beef as did everyone else.

It was these sorts of stories which were spread by the town's people who were jealous and never quite accepted the family. Many desired our hero's family to steal away in the night, depart as quickly and silently as they had appeared. Some of the locals always considered the family as outsiders: people of whom to be suspect. Even I, who had not been long in town, was more readily accepted. But then again, my role was a necessity to the community, and my acceptance by the students guaranteed my affirmation as a resident by its inhabitants in general.

I think their rejection of the family was derived from the manner in which our hero's father "came in and set himself up." In the space of three years he established himself financially with resources nobody knew he had. Then he started insuring everything in town with better rates, by representing many different companies and policies; whereas the other agent, who, from what I have gathered, had a monopoly on the business and only represented one company. This first agent was a "local boy who made good" and was reaping the benefits, but he had grown too big for the town and had moved. He flew into Denver from Chicago, hired a car, and drove out. Yes, our hero's father had found a jack-pot when he arrived. But at the onset nobody bought from him. This had also happened to a couple of other agents who had tried to get established in the county. But Thesus' father was established by other means and just "waited it out." The lower insurance premiums and the immediate payment for a couple of claims, eventually told the locals that "he was here to stay" and that they would be damn fools not to take advantage of the better rates. Then his insurance business boomed overnight. Since that time another local boy had returned from college and has started up another insurance operation. It has cut into the Captain's concerns. The father still has trade with most of the farms around the towns and with his Reserve buddies, but the local agent has all the commerce within one town's limits and almost all the production within the other town.

Our hero was one of four children, the next to the youngest. Each child in turn should have been more spoiled as the father grew in wealth. It is true that probably the later children gained more advantages than the earlier ones, but I would not say that any of them were indulged excessively. If the father and/or mother thought it was to the child's benefit then they consented. But the father still had worked too hard and knew too well the value of money and the results of spoiling a child.

It is true, Thesus as an adolescent had

advantages which no other child in town could claim. Private tutors started as soon as his curiosity became more than his parents could handle. Of course, each family member had the most current computer, of which the children had supervised access to anything they wish to know, but the parents did not encourage this. I thought it was a little reactionary, but they were paying me to accomplish what the computer could, so I didn't say a thing. It was only in late high school when Thesus earned complete control over his own computer. (Looking back, maybe his parents were more knowledgeable than I have given them credit.)

In the first year I taught him, he was absent from class almost a third of the time. His parents didn't make him attend when he didn't wish. Also he was always going to a doctor, an orthodontist, a private lesson of some type. He took music lessons; private swim lessons in the family's pool; riding lessons, which he hated; ski instruction; sometimes week-end skiing began Thursday afternoons, so he left school early. There was always something: a family meeting, a cultural event in Denver. His wrist phone computer would vibrate during class and I knew, after a couple of times, it was Thesus' parents preparing him or his personal calendar reminding him of some upcoming event, and to procure an excused absence. Subsequently, I discussed the matter with him and his parents and tried to put a stop to class hour calls and excused absences. This was before the school put a stop to all types of cell phone calls while at school.

His absenteeism prompted inquiry. His

computer records were filled with facts about his intelligence, his teachers' attitude about him and his tutors. My concern was mainly with his influence on the morale of other students. I was assured he was getting an education, but the students complained: if Thesus didn't have to attend why did they? I heard this twenty times during the year.

Yes, the town's jealousy of the family included our young man, but his aloofness prevented the jealousy from affecting him. It probably never occurred to him that they had anything but a friendly attitude towards him (another type of innocence for sure).

Chapter 2

My predominate feelings about the area when I arrived was a light blue-and-brown freshness. The altitude of the prairie towns must be in the four thousand feet range, and so the sky is a generally translucent blue. The almost always, light blowing breeze takes the dust from the fields and roads, and suspends it in the air subtracting the dark blue from the sky. The spacious fields are broken into squares by the specifically designated county dirt roads which create a straight line from horizon to horizon. In the early fall when I reached my new school district, the fields had been mowed; the wheat, corn, and alfalfa stored. On the specially treated, moisture-retaining soils, a selective hybrid of corn had been harvested. Stubble from all the crops had been ground and spread onto the acreage which mixed with the dust. The dry land was waiting to be plowed for the next planting, probably a winter wheat. A little further east was prairie, just plain uncultivated grasslands; I don't know why people call it "grass land"; it is weed land: sage, dry tumbleweed, some yucca, cactus, ragweed, and small durable brownish-green plants close to the ground, like dehydrated buffalo grasses.

The only obstruction to the light brownness was in the west: the three inch high, gray Rocky Mountains. The mountains seemed to grow as storms began to build over them, an illusion to which I always fell prey. I've never discussed this with anyone. When I first noticed it, I didn't understand. Then after a while, I forgot to mention it, or I thought, how mundane. The mountains at one moment, usually in the mornings, were a small, light gray bumpy line protruding on the western edge of the plains. Then at a second glance in the day, usually in late afternoon, they were larger and whiter. The clouds were indistinguishable from the mountains due, my theory, to the sun's proximity

A prevalent scene that comes to mind, which represents my feelings about the place, now ten years later, was standing on the L shaped porch of our student's family on a Sunday afternoon; I could see the second guest miles away, creating a dust plume on the open road. I thought this could be two hundred years ago, and that dust plume could be horseback riders coming to the ranch, although way too quickly. He was leaving a quarter mile of dust, blocking the view of the mountains, in the calmness of dusk.

Because he was late and exceeding the speed limit, he was taking a chance on hitting a wash board section. I kept thinking: he's a fool. These are designated dirt roads, intentionally left that way; he undoubtedly is driving a commuter car created to travel the wireless toll roads at a hundred and fifty miles per hours. As the new math teacher turned onto the ranch road, the brown cloud ceased its forward motion. The radio in the kitchen was playing Country Western, while Thesus' sister, Jenny, prepared the meal. When a hawk screeched, I looked up into the sky. The setting sun was still on its wings. Crying out again, taking a last look at the day, it was by itself. It was a solitary flight and song.

In spite of the blazing red sky and the anticipation of a very good home cooked meal, I was homesick. I was lonely; just plain lonely, and I had only been there for almost a year. God, what have I gotten into for two years in the middle of nowhere?

A telephone ring interrupted my self-pity. The open communicator buzzed, and Thesus' father answered. The teacher was in the ditch. The Captain pushed a button on his phone, "Did you hear? Yes. Take the truck …. the off-road four wheeler is rounding-up sheep on the east twenty. After pulling the car out, join Joe in separating out the non-pregnant sheep and get them ready to ship. Don't forget to record their tags in the computer, and I will figure-out which males will be joining this group.'

"'Dinner will be delayed while a ranch hand drives out to the accident and pulls the car back onto the road. Would you like to drive out and watch?"

The most exciting event for today in this Wild West. "No, I'll just help myself to a second drink," and mentally prepare myself for the up-coming days.

But as the second year transpired, there was no time for reverie, and very little self-pity. In fact, I began to enjoy my teaching experience so much, I signed a second two-year contract.

Thesus' mother's and father's ranch, and in fact, that whole family's existence seemed timeless. They preferred "the old ways"; maybe this is slightly inaccurate; they preferred the country life. This is not to say that they didn't have modern conveniences; they had everything, including a totally computerized barn and house. The barn was fascinating to me. It cleaned itself, maintained its own "healthy" environment in different sections for different animals. It even had a small area for milking, pasteurizing, and bottling milk for family and friends. With compartments for high priced bulls, milking cows, chickens, hogs, even turkeys, this family could have been totally self-sufficient. Which is getting to my point: they didn't want the "outside" world, or that was my impression.

But possibly it was more their manner, because when I think about their modernized mechanisms, it seemed as if they owned every available one: the most up-to-date computers, the cleaning robots, the solar heating and electricity, wireless communicators, and an entertainment room with access to film libraries, virtual reality head gear, games and games and more games: the ability to view athletic competitions in process, any place in the world; playing games with anyone in the world who owned a computer, in almost any tournament in the world.

So my perception of this family as timeless farmers was probably derived from their self-imposed isolation: their petition to keep their county road from being paved and definitely not computerized (this I did not know at the time); their self-sufficiency both materially and socially. Looking back, it was a new, refreshing experience, but back then, it was a lonely existence, and therefore this whole impression is obviously biased and partially a projection of my own mind.

I came to the district because it was my only job opportunity, and I knew I needed experience. The first year, I became Thesus' seventh grade teacher; my second and third, his tutor while still teaching seventh grade. In my first year's tutoring, many times the material I presented was so trivial for him that he became bored. In conjunction with teaching I began studying on-line and in Denver, as a means to escape the immediate feeling of desolation and the long term depravation of mental stimuli through personal social interaction. I worked on my Master's in English at the University of Colorado Extension and subsequently began teaching what I learned. In the second year of tutoring I gave him the same research assignments which I had. We would go into his home library together, access the Web or other libraries through his computer and find the material. We would discuss it, then both write the papers. Our discussions were sometimes more profound than my seminars, but his papers were terrible. They were either incomprehensible or so self-evident that both of us felt they weren't worth writing. Of course, I never expressed my opinion for how else was he to learn to write and express himself except through writing.

Before continuing, let me mention something important, I just remembered. When I investigated Thesus because of his absenteeism, I checked his file. I not only obtained information concerning his IQ, but what is more important, I found a note not to disclose the fact to the young man. The record stated that it was his parents' wish. But now I wonder if they even knew. I, of course, did not tell him. I could understand the request, and thought at the time, let him decide his own life without the qualification of a test with questionable validity.

Anyway getting back to the story, Thesus had a couple of friends, one whom he still sees occasionally. The other only remained a friend for a couple of years. He lived on the farm adjacent to Thesus' father. They used to build forts, play football, go camping, play tennis, ski, play golf, and all the other activities in which young men from wealthy families participate. He was a year older and bigger than my pupil; consequently, Thesus never won any of these physical contests or almost never won.

His other friend, a weak fragile boy named Adrian, was the only person his age who could challenge this student intellectually. Their original common link was they both were the only two in their classes who were not natives. They were forced together due to ostracism. This friendship began before I entered the county but didn't really become active until High School. They didn't "hang together" until then because they had to be transported by a parent. For a couple of years, their friendship was totally on computers. They lived too far apart. They would play chess, "go," and a million other games. They would recommend books to each other and then discuss them. In high school when they acquired cars, they "slept over" at each other's homes or had Bach parties. Our hero had a girl friend who was, of course, beautiful, and filled his mother's house with respectability. She wore the perfect outfit on every occasion. She said the correct phrases at the correct time. The fact that Thesus' father was only a Captain bothered her when either she or her parents realized the significance of the placement in the service. But his overwhelming local financial success helped the matter. Thesus was the only "really" eligible person in her social class. I always thought that they probably did more than listen to Bach all evening but maybe they didn't. I wouldn't have put it past them.... either way.

A main "glue factor" in this relationship was Thesus' mother's approval of her: "She is the right girl for Thesus, from a nice family," and even went so far as to invite her to dinners and other soirees without Thesus' knowledge or approval. Thesus said nothing and accepted it all without argument as his mother's way. She and Thesus "sort of went steady" the last couple years in high school.

One of the reasons I mentioned Thesus' friends was that with Adrian, our youth almost never won any games. Adrian was never athletic but would stay home all the time, read books, and study games. He had read all the books he could acquire on chess and "Go." He taught my pupil how to play bridge and within weeks they played well enough to beat their parents. I think Adrian is still active in many different tournaments and is a Master Player. Our hero didn't study games. He enjoyed playing them but did not take them seriously. Games were for enjoyment. Studying them would ruin the fun of playing, "You would be playing someone's format, sticking routines on set situations."

To make my point before going too much further, between not winning at sports and not winning at games, and being "put down" socially by his girlfriend, our hero was not egotistical; and between not getting straight "A's" and never being told about his intelligence, I don't think he ever realized his potential. I don't think his parents did either. Everyone knew he was intelligent but how intelligent I don't think anyone guessed.

Adrian graduated first in his class while our student came second. Adrian had straight "A's" while Thesus had some B's." I don't think as a student he deserved all "A's" because he didn't strive for them in comparison with Adrian who really did study and worked hard. In comparison with the rest of the students' work in his classes, he should have obtained the "A's." Another reason he didn't make the grades as he should was because he didn't satisfy the expectations placed upon him.

Some teachers were a little hard on him. Some were unjustifiably hard. He told me about a grade in eighth grade: a "C" in his first semester English course. I think he was graded on the subject matter of one paper rather than on the quality of his work. The paper in question was entitled, "Why a Pure Democracy Won't Work." He gave the paper to me when I questioned his grade. I guess it had caused a commotion in the school. Even reverberations reached the Principal who went into the class two days after Thesus had read it aloud and tried to get our hero to retract his thesis.

I confronted Thesus in the hall one afternoon about the whole matter after I had heard rumors. "I told him (the principal) I meant the paper, that unless human beings change, I don't know how a Democracy would work. We need to educate the public to teach them the importance of participation. He (the principal) said that I was young and had much to learn."

The principal debated with Thesus for a while in front of the class. After which our hero asked the principal if he thought Democracy in the United States was working. He turned and left the room as if he didn't hear the question. Nobody ever mentioned the paper again. Our young friend became a hero to his fellow classmates, but he privately told me that if he had known the effect of the paper, he would not have submitted it. Here is the paper below:

WHY A DEMOCRACY WON'T WORK

Our forefathers fought for freedom, for Democracy, to give us the right to choose. Their struggle was hard for it was idealistic. They believed that educated humans would be able to make the best choices. The reality of the situation was that they didn't have a chance of winning the war for freedom. England was strong, powerful, with armies at its disposal. America was weak, with no army, and its citizens were divided in their want for freedom. Many men didn't want to fight for the idealism and their independence. Only one-third of the population really wanted to revolt against England; one-third was undecided and one-third wanted to stay under England's control. This last group was undoubtedly the ones profiting from England's control. The rebels must have believed strongly because they fought and won. These founding fathers were not just dedicated but inspired for not only the chance of freedom, but for justice and equality. for it was their *perseverance which prevailed.*

This was many years ago. Now, the struggle is over; we have relaxed. <u>Laissez-faire</u> is the attitude everyone has assumed about politics. What are the polling statistics telling us? Less (fewer) than 45% of those who can vote, vote. We are secure and don't need to concern ourselves with the running of the government. Let other citizens do it.

It is human nature to be lazy and that is why a Democracy won't work. Everyone will struggle when there is a need to struggle but will fall asleep when the struggle is over, and it will be when we aren't paying attention or don't care that our freedoms will be taken from us.

In order for a Democracy to work, people must participate and care about what is happening. But people are lazy and don't care unless they are threatened.

I noticed the lack of solid facts, a lack of citations, which I hadn't taught him, and some punctuations problems, so I assumed that was the reason for the "C."

One evening when the paper was returned to him he handed it to me, saying he was embarrassed by it. The paper was simplistic and poorly written. He knows that our country isn't a pure democracy but a representative government, and that is why it works because we do let others govern us, and we don't govern ourselves. "I can laugh at the whole incident now, but I still don't know why there was such a fuss and the principal appeared in my classroom."

I have some more of his writings. I am presenting them here because they show the subject matter which occupied his time. They are not a true representation of his thoughts but an unsophisticated representation as I have said his thoughts far outstripped his ability to communicate in any medium.

To begin, I have two poems which were responses to assignments in his seventh grade class.

"NO TIME"
I don't have time for girls and boys
I don't have time for childish toys
I must grow up to help mankind
So they will have time
For girls and boys and childish toys.

The second semester he submitted this one.

"TO UNDERSTAND"
To understand,
To have tolerance in one's opinion,
To be able to place oneself in another's

31

footsteps,
To try to understand nature,
As it tests the people's endurance
With its torrent winds, its unpredictable floods
and its plagues;
To receive its calm seas, its cool breezes and
its serene sunsets as blessings from heaven,
To understand oneself
To control one's emotions, inwardly and
outwardly,
To understand even blinding religions, to
respect all beliefs as one respects his own
To understand other humans,
the aged and the youth;
the ignorant and the intelligent;
the friend and the enemy,
Should be the quest of all humans.

He prefaced the next poem with the ensuing comment: "The question this poem raises assumes that reincarnation exists and that humans advance to near perfect beings on earth by returning and taking different forms." When questioned further, he told me those "striving sum" may have come from the other dying species. It is less formal for I was tutoring him, and he just spontaneously wrote it and submitted it. There is no title.

Many may come and many may go
But towns and country continually grow,
From where do they come, all these striving
sum
And where do they go –
Yes, that is the answer to know.

He did submit one more poem, but it was sometime later in eighth grade. It was not an assignment but his own initiative. To me at the time it seemed so obscure that I asked him if he would like to discuss it and clear his thoughts, something I could not have done as his teacher with twenty other students. He said, "Yes," so we worked on it for a couple of weeks and produced another poem. The first poem doesn't have a title, but the second does.

The mid-morning sun is burning bright,
As my thoughts wandered and I fight
Because nobody will come.
The music turns into a monotonous sound
As body and mind go their separate ways
Because nobody will come.
The sun turns the wall into a crimson red,
As the void ends a perfect day,
Because nobody has come.

The statement "the void ends a perfect day" kept me wondering, and I questioned him about it again and again. He never could explain it to me adequately. My interpretation now is that he meant it ironically.

His revision is as follows:

"MY OWN PRIVATE FEAR"

Midmorning
When the concert began.
My mind was excited
By the sounds of the first pure notes.
All that I heard grew in my mind
And filled my body.
It would be so easy to compose music such as
this;
To leave society behind and create clean fresh
music for all to hear;
To compose the world into a single pure note;
It would be so easy.
But the sun climbed higher.
The music and words created a monotonous
sound;
Meaning and feeling were lost
And thoughts wondered:
"What soft brown hair she has.
How perfect she looks
Sitting with her tightly crossed legs.
But her face is society's face with artificialness
She sits combing her hair, not listening.
"No! Listen to the music.
Listen to the music"
Into the crimson sun, following her
As the music faded.
Now, my desires filled

But the music is gone
And in its place, the graying evening;
Awaiting the night
To end a perfect day.

For a while, I thought that Thesus would become a great poet but that was not the direction he took. I didn't encourage him any more than he wanted. Maybe this was a mistake. To my knowledge, he didn't write anymore after this last poem, and I didn't say anything.

Even though the four poems were written within two years, one can see growth. This rapid and expanding appeared in every field he attempted.

In contrast to the papers I will present an incident which I feel represented the complexity of his thoughts at this period in his life. Of course, it is an extreme example because I wouldn't have remembered it unless it remained vivid in my mind. I can't remember the exact words but only this facsimile. The substance is accurate, though the verbiage may be improved

I had come to tutor on a Saturday morning, midwinter. The roads were icy and covered with drifting snow. I had over compensated my time of arrival, arriving fifteen minutes early. When nearing the living room, I heard two voices and music. Having often questioned the content of their discussions when adults were excluded, I didn't enter the room but placed myself outside the door. They were sitting crossed legged on the floor; an unfinished chess game separated them. A Brandenburg Concerto was playing- I don't know which one; a fire was roaring in the fireplace, and they were sipping hot chocolate. Our hero was talking:

"If humans are progressing toward any goals such as becoming a pure rational being or any other attribute of God's...."

"Such as infinite," Adrian inserted.

"O.K. Let's say that, assuming infinity exists outside our conception of it. If God is infinite, all attributes are Its, and if we are attaining any of them then we are becoming: one," he raised a finger, "a god, equal in a quality or qualities with God; two," he raised a second finger, "humans are not advancing towards any goals but only think they are; or three, God is progressing; or finally, god is just a creation of mankind and that as humans advance, so does our concept of god.

"If we are assuming that God is the supreme or the absolute, or the infinite," he nodded to his friend, "how could It become more than It is, more perfect, more infinite?"

"And humans are mortal," answered his young friend, "We could never reach the infinite, never become God; like you can't stack a number of pennies to the infinite. You can't have an infinite number of pennies, or the time to stack time," he laughed.

"We could be coming back again and again, improving ourselves. Infinitely?"

"Reincarnation! But what if humans are not progressing but progress is only an illusion?" Adrian inquired.

"I can't accept that," our novice answered, "But oh, ... you don't mean in a personal way, you mean in a way to become equal to God, but still, if all attributes were Its', any progress would constitute becoming more equal. No, I can't accept that.

"So we still have two possibilities. What if god is a human's creation?"

"I don't think so," answered his young friend, "for how would everything have been created?"

"The question of the origin of existence, right? What if everything that is here has always been here? There was no beginning, and there will be no end. It is hard to conceive of an infinity existing in one direction: there was a beginning, and there would be no end. If there were a beginning, there must be an end and if there were no beginning there will probably be no end."

"Maybe!"

"But still if that were true then one, we are excluding the possibility that God could create a beginning and no end or two, that God could be a part of the whole or It could be the Whole, Itself, but still does there need to be an Originator?"

The music stopped and only the cracking fire made noise in the room. His young friend reached over grabbed the remote and said, "And we must reconsider the possibility of being godlike. For if there exists an infinity, either with or without God, we are in it."

"No, I want you to hear something else," then our young seeker sprang to his feet to change the recording.

Thinking the conversation was over for the moment, I entered the room. My young student's back was to me as he fiddled with the machine.

"I am probably discounting other criteria for God's existence," he said. "What do you consider the criteria of Its existence?"

"Hi," his friend said after he heard me and turned in my direction. I stood, waiting for Thesus' reply. I am sure my stare reflected my expectation because he said after an extended moment:

"Still we need an explanation for the existence of matter and energy, a prime force and/or maybe a continuing force." But his answer was forced, self-conscious; it was an answer to a quiz. I have speculated what his answer would have been if I hadn't entered the room. I was sorry I had. It was apparent that I was an outsider to him: at the time someone who graded him.

I thought to try to regain the unselfconscious atmosphere by stating my opinion but didn't because I was the teacher, a voice in a position of authority. My opinion meant too much. Also, in personal matters such as religion one should develop his own thoughts and attitudes. If questions occur to young people, naturally, out of their own intelligence, they will have the potential to answer them. If one person could imagine a question, I'm sure that person could find an answer. And in opportunities like this, if I expressed my attitudes which were based on many years of experience and questioning, in short more sophisticated, I may have thrown a wrench into this student's or his friend's evolution of thoughts; so instead, I accepted the role of teacher, and said, "It is good that you young men are expressing your thoughts for exploration. They should be expressed and explored for how else are we to know them. But I wouldn't get too involved in your own answers because they are bound to change and encompass more knowledge then you possess now."

This role of teacher has stayed with me with all my students, even to some degree with this fellow, although now it is only an occasional slip into formality. But even then he was more relaxed with me than his friend, and I don't think he thought my entrance had caused his friend to stiffen. But Adrian rose to his feet and he said, "I agree with you that one should express thoughts of belief no matter the inner conflict. Expressed and explored; express and explore. God, if It exists, would not punish exploration. It is a human trait, a natural curiosity, a want to know. Fear and guilt should not be a part of exploration." I had to smile, not only at the content of his statement but because his statement was so formal in its presentation.

I can see now, because of students like both of them, I was teaching and will continue to teach, if I ever get a job again. They had the potential to make change. I once told this young fellow; the only reason why I was the instructor, and not he, was years of education, experience and knowledge, but within a short period of time, he would surpass me.

I wanted to transfer to him all my knowledge and understanding because he was so willing to accept it, so able to assimilate and understand it, and that he could use it for the best possible purposes. He was a pitcher, an almost endless vessel, able to absorb everything poured into him and yet, contain it, to be poured out later with a more refreshing interpretation, and with new insights. Many times I have heard regurgitated, aged material which had become incorporated into his own thinking. This aged liquid usually had a better, deeper, more interesting flavor.

I, of course, felt the responsibility of teaching especially to him and hope I have not faltered, something I still question. I did the best I could at the time and that's all any person can do. In teaching I tried to stick to the facts or what I considered the facts. But I was naive also…well, I am being easy on myself … ignorant, is probably more correct. I still acknowledge the responsibility for my actions, for what I taught, and question whether I shouldn't have taught him more or at least made him question that which he was not questioning. Maybe I should have made him question more relevant information, made him read news releases, watch the news and question it. In short, we should have dwelled more in the 'political, economic and social realities' rather than on literary abstractions. But then again, maybe I shouldn't feel the responsibility that I do. I might have taught him my biases, my opinions and that is something I still think is wrong. My experiences are not sacred. My life and opinions about life should not be used as examples from which to teach. Let the students judge life for themselves, and I not judge it for them. Yes, if I would have pushed my beliefs on him, everything could have turned out worse because

40

I now realize that I didn't know politically what was happening either.

Anyway, as you can see from the conversation on that cold winter's day, our observer's thoughts were profound for his age but not always relevant to the here-and-now, to the direct physical and social realities which we confront daily. As I have said, he didn't know the questions to ask. He didn't even question the realities which directly concerned him; he didn't know what he had to control to master his political, social, and even physical destiny; yet, he thought he was in control, but maybe I am judging him again, something I don't want to do. Who knows one's potential to control one's life or how much one actually controls. He thought he was exploring important questions, and he was. But he thought that the rest of his........the world was under control.

Chapter 3

Thesus has had much to contribute, not only because of his intelligence but because of his innate ability to understand himself. Although his understanding of situations was limited, I think if left on his own and with a true knowledge of events, he could have understood and conveyed knowledge about life nobody has yet realized.

Yes, he could fit together other events, other combinations of actions, but he could not fit himself into the situations except on an abstract, philosophical level. He could not judge correctly his position in society nor other people's conception of him. But then again, maybe he knew but didn't care, so intense was he in his pursuits that he was oblivious of others' opinions. He didn't question others' conceptions or their effect on his life. In fact, he was naive to the effect the surroundings had on him. For, he ended in too many situations where he didn't want to be.

Anyway, not to belabor the bad but emphasize the good, he also had flashes of insight which would astound even the most educated and intelligent. A person would be talking to Thesus and he would only be half listening, expending his energies nervously fidgeting, but his face would lighten, and the person wouldn't be able to finish the sentence before he would expound his insights.

Once an Air Force personnel came to the High School. I thought he was going to recruit, directly, openly, but he talked about the space program, new fields of science and progress in the U.S. in general. He seemed to imply: join the Air Force and become part of it all. It was an up-lifting speech presented in an interesting, informal way and on a level where everyone in the auditorium could understand him. But even I could tell that his knowledge had been coached, that he didn't know his subjects first hand. In other words, I doubted whether he could have validated all of his information.

Our school was a perfect place to recruit because of our type of students. They would have joined the services just to leave the farms and go somewhere and fifty percent of them were not qualified for college.

So uplifting was the lecture that the applause

came like thunder. One girl even stood to initiate a standing ovation. It turned into a fight between her and the audience. Many probably wanted to give him a standing ovation but didn't want to join her. The audience refused to stand because she was standing, and she refused to sit just because everyone refused to stand. Anyway, the speaker came to her rescue by raising his hands, stopping the applause and asking if she wished to start the questioning segment. Still standing, the girl asked what she could do for our country "being only a student and all." After his answer, only one person raised his hand to ask another, and he jumped up before he was called upon. It was our hero.

He began to ask questions which the personnel officer couldn't answer: questions which went beyond the officer's knowledge of space travel, astronomical bodies, and the structure of the universe. When the officer began dodging our hero's inquiry, Thesus began to corner him, disproving some of his statements. Students who could understand began to laugh, and individuals began to applaud our seeker's statements. It was embarrassing. Thesus didn't share the embarrassment and probably didn't understand the laughter. He was getting at the truth and stating his thoughts.

At that moment Thesus became a hero to some people in the school. He was representing our school in the same way a winning basketball or football team would have.

After a while the officer quit defending himself, just assumed a fake smile, and let the juvenile talk.

Being unconscious to this fact, our hero, rather than becoming more cautious and factual, began speculating as to the answers to some of the questions he had asked. But when the officer was about to question the young man, our fellow would clarify his statements before the officer could verbalize. At least this is what I assume because the officer never pursued questioning.

Feeling even less defensive, our hero began flowing with thoughts, expressing his ideas, a persisting habit. He expanded some of the ideas the officer mentioned. Then he offered some possible fields of exploration such as to reinvestigate the possibility of an aether: a massless form of static energy. "From my studies, the probability of this speculation is good," he said. The officer knew enough to state that all previous experiments disproved the existence of an aether, but our interesting young man replied that because the aether could be positive and negative charged massless energy units that they are trapped by our magnetic fields, and there would only be "a relative movement where the earth's magnetic field dissipated ..... and then there would only be a slight displacement."

After the lecture, I looked up "aether" and found that it was a theoretical medium through which light traveled, but the need for the concept didn't exist anymore. I couldn't understand Thesus's interest in the concept nor all that he said concerning it. In fact, the existence of an aether was disproven in the early 1900s.

I thought I understood the discussion until I

have tried to reproduce it here. I was not paying close enough attention because of my fear of the embarrassment of all parties involved. The only thing I can remember - and it is not clear in my own mind - is the statement about an aether leading to a possible exploration of new energy sources. The shifting levels of the electrons which produce light is a non-depleting system, "a counter-entropic system" is the term I think he used. It is a system which gains in energy rather than loses energy. Thinking back now, I wished someone had taped the discussion and taken it to an expert in the field of quantum mechanics. Of course, no one in the auditorium could reply to his statements. The students became exasperated with him and started booing. One of the science teachers was very impressed by what our hero had said, and one science teacher thought this pupil didn't make any sense at all. I should have actively pursued an effort to record what he said or at least I should have done more research so that I could have asked him questions at a later time and recorded that. But then again, I am sure an expert would have had trouble understanding this student because of his inability to communicate exactly and precisely.

Anyway, the recruiting officer approached the young man after the lecture and began pressuring Thesus "to sign up." He promised Thesus all the time and space to experiment, something I doubt he could have delivered (unless he was given special authorization). He promised a complete free-ride to specific colleges, including the Air Force Academy, where he would have individualized instruction and at the same time, he would be free to pursue anything he wished if he joined the Air Force for four years.

Thesus said he would think about it. But, of course, it didn't stop there. Later, I was told by Thesus' sister, the Air Force even pressured Thesus' father; that is when Thesus excluded the possibility.

This incident is somewhat of a transgression, I was discussing his ideas. In the beginning, or should I say when I first met him, he would express his ideas freely. I told him he should patent the sellable ones and develop the others on paper and at least record them. But he said, "I am in no position to further the ideas, but they should be furthered, and so I communicate them in the best way I can, to whomever, in hopes that they are furthered."

One idea was to find plants which would consume the greatest amounts of pollutants and give off the greatest amount of oxygen. In Biology he began research to try and find a genus of moss or fungus with the idea of planting them on the north sides of large buildings in our most polluted cities. Basically, I thought it was a good idea and a good bit of knowledge to know but a little too far out, too farfetched for him to accomplish.

Another idea was to recycle water from the family garbage disposal: to water their garden with the liquid and use the condensed solid as fodder for livestock. He began to install a disposal the home, but it was never completed. Either his parents didn't like the idea of having a second sink just for this project or he found a more important task to achieve.

At the same time he was working on a crystal

battery with more than 1.5 volts. The Chemistry teacher was so impressed that he suggested that our student study Chemistry. He, the teacher, took the suggestion a step further by obtaining a potential scholarship to Denver U., but Thesus balked. He wanted to explore other fields before he made a commitment to his life's occupation.

Another idea was a fruit picking robot which used an electronic scanning device, laser, I think, to differentiate by color between ripe and unripe. It was light sensitive with filters of some kind. The whole machine was situated on a truck which drove up and down the rows of trees. A vacuum pump and a mechanical arm sucked the fruit from the branches then dropped it into a shoot which funneled the fruit into a water trough. The trough was skimmed and the fruit boxed. It was inventions like his fruit picking machine which he knew he couldn't develop so he sent the idea to different companies. He received a few replies, but nothing was ever manufactured that I know.

It was in college when he quit giving out his ideas so freely. He began thinking in terms of graduating and making a living. He tried to sell ideas after copyrighting them. But he discovered companies and individuals buy products, not ideas. He decided he would develop some. He worked on a ski-carrying case. It was made out of plastic in which the boots, poles and skis were pressed so they wouldn't warp. It was airtight so the ski's edges wouldn't rust. He worked out a rack for the top of the car and a rack for the ski area, both had locks, which he said were "break-in proof." The case had both wheels for dry land and if turned over, a ski or something which would slide on the snow. It could be produced with a plastic injected mold, very inexpensively and he could assemble it. He followed through by visiting ski shops to see if they would carry his product. Good idea but where would they store the large cases? He didn't follow through with it, even to patent it.

Of course, he had ideas dealing with every subject he encounter; as an example, one in math: how to circle a square.

"Wasn't that impossible, or was it to square a circle?" I asked.

"Squaring a circle, maybe, but to circle a square all you have to do is make each side of the square a function in a calculus equation where the number of sides approach infinite and their length approach zero."

"Is that possible?"

"I really don't know, yet. I need to take a calculus class. But listen to this: If that is possible, why couldn't one square a circle by starting with an infinite number of points and reduce them to four and expand their lengths?

"I can't wait so I am studying it on the Internet."

No, boredom was never a problem. But, at least to my knowledge, he never persevered. However, he did get a patent. His father paid for it. It was a game. Pieces moved around the board acquiring money; with the money one would obtain power by buying power cards, and when one had enough money and power, one could declare himself dictator. It was based on the political situation of a country in which the United States was involved. He quit trying to sell the patent after submitting samples of the game to various companies. Later he told me that the game company, M Plus 2, took his idea for folding the playing board so that it would fit into a small box but it did not want the controversial game. Why his father supported that idea by paying for the patent and not some of the others, I have no idea. Especially since this particular patent might have brought unnecessary attention. Or maybe the father was making a conscious or unconscious statement.

As the reader can tell, Thesus had plenty of ideas, more than I can record here or even remember. It was some time after college when he was so frustrated and discouraged that he quit thinking up ideas or at least quit communicating them. He had found that more than one of his ideas was imitated or borrowed. He gained nothing for generating the idea, neither money, nor recognition.

Even later in San Francisco when he was trying to get a job, he decided to suppress his ideas "Why should I waste time on things that aren't going to get me any place? I have immediate problems to worry about, and I am not even going to reveal my ideas at all because somehow the wrong people hear about them. Maybe I have miss chosen my friends .... but I don't mean you. Some people have taken some of my ideas and begun to use them. Who knows how they got them, especially the ones pertaining the government: my Welfare Reform Program, my

Criminal Rehab program, my Medical Insurance program, and some others. I guess I presented some of them at job interviews. It is not bad they use them; it is probably to the betterment of the society. But they (whoever "they" are) refused to hire me to positions where I could have helped develop the ideas nor did they give me credit or reimbursement."

I answered, "Maybe your ideas are ideas of the times, not your ideas alone but ideas which simultaneously occur to many people: the zeitgeist?"

"My ideas and attempts to further them are getting me no-place, and I will just quit recording them; then I'll see if they still are used."

Later the government did hire him, but not as an "ideas" person. It was during this period he quit having ideas all together. "My mind doesn't seem to create answers, to solve problems, any more. I don't know if it is because I am out of practice or I have changed internally."

It was also during this time period that we were looking at jewelry in the museum in Golden Gate Park, and I was commenting on the price of star opal. He said that it was too bad that we even had to consider money or how to acquire it. It was too bad the system functions this way, but what could he do? And yes, I can see it from his point of view: it is too bad he could not direct his ideas, thoughts, or energy to useful acceptable purposes. He thought that maybe something was wrong with him in that he could not adjust properly.

"I have been down so low that I have wanted to suckle the system, just get money any way I could.

I have applied for jobs which haven't even performed a service, jobs with only payment, and yet, I think I could produce positive change for the ....

"There have even been times when I have been tempted to just take what I wanted, not caring about the results."

After he had decided not to publicly express ideas that would directly help either individuals or systems, he decided he would only publicly express ideas which were beyond easy understanding and/or only applicable in a distant future.

The weirdest idea I can describe was a magnetic air car; a computerized car, which pulsated magnetic fields opposite to the local ones. This evolved into a car that would "know" the surrounding magnetic fields and counter them. As I can remember the engine consisted of metal bars rotating rapidly emitting the pulsations. By changing the angle of pulsation one could control the direction of flight. The computer would know the configuration of the local magnetic fields then control the up-down motion of the rotating bars and the speed of rotation. It would control the angle of emissions and the timing of emissions. In other words, it was the opposition to the local magnetic field which controlled the speed and direction of the car. I think I have that correct. But it sounds as if the earth needs a stabilized magnetic field. Does it have one? I always wanted to ask him about that.

But to finish my point ..... he told me he believed in the existence of a person in our society who hated people but loved humanity and therefore only thought about a future, possible world. I could list other ideas, but I can see his battle with the system, and I will not betray his trust by lessening his chances of winning that battle.

As one can see he became not only a confused, but an angry, young man who was shocked by the system which raised him, but he had not lost his idealism. He had become cynical and defiant, but he still maintained his hope. This situation was generated by, not only having his ideas stolen, not only being in financial difficulties, not only having all attempts at success thwarted, but by the systems categorizing and ostracizing him.

I have begun slipping into discussing San Francisco, and now I am talking about the present and haven't even finished the details of the past.

Chapter 4

In spite of the scholarship he was offered to Denver U. or an opportunity to matriculate at many other schools, he decided on Colorado University (C.U.). It was against the wishes of his parents, the suggestion of his instructors, and the request of his advisor. Most of them recommended other schools, smaller, well known, top named schools where he would have obtained more individual attention. He chose C.U. because it was large enough for him to explore what he wished, and he realized the possibility of examining different fields more freely, discovering himself more thoroughly, and meeting a variety of people. He wanted to know himself, his society, and why it all existed as it did.

"Every vacation my sister came home from college exhausted and changed. (She attended a top-rated eastern school for two years). I knew what awaited me if I went to one of those colleges everyone wanted me to attend. There would have been time to do nothing but study. I would have just been putting off the inevitable questions that must be answered."

When this fellow enrolled, it had been two years since we last met. I already had my Master's degree and had begun my Ph.D. in Boulder. I was also a teaching assistant and very busy, but as soon as he established residence in the dorms, we immediately resumed our relationship.

His parents had written me when to expect him and asked if I could acquaint him with the campus. He had missed being on campus with his oldest sister by a year. She had graduated and moved to San Francisco.

We talked constantly during the tour. At first we assumed the same relationship we had had when I tutored him. But before the conclusion of our first meeting, that relationship had changed. He continued to call me Mr. Jacoby, but it was only out of habit. We were on more equal terms. That isn't to say he wasn't a freshman, but that we were both students with common goals: the acquisition and communication of knowledge. He opened up to me as never before. He expressed ambitions, hopes, fears, beliefs, and doubts. The drives he communicated were the drives of almost any young man his age, not completely confused but not lucid in direction. Each of his hopes seemed to push him in a different direction. His ideas were scattered as they had been when he was younger; question upon question caused his thoughts to wander. He knew too much and too little to bring his knowledge together for a unity of direction. But I believed in him. I knew he would find his way and be very successful at whatever he attempted.

Contrary to what I believed, his academic beginnings were unsuccessful: he received poor grades. His mind was not on studying. His intelligence and education didn't carry him as well as I'd expected. I had thought that he could have mastered grades more easily, but as he said, "It isn't so much that learning is hard, but it is just hard to study. And no matter what I learn, I am never tested on that material." My first response to his statement was a remembrance of him not studying the subject matter taught in secondary school, but later I came to realize it was more of a different problem altogether.

At first he spent all his time reading in the library, then later began to play bridge constantly. Bridge games were generated in the dorms. He almost always attended classes in early afternoons then played bridge until next morning. For a while I thought he had been defeated by the results of a few tests and had given up. But he indicated he was passing and that was enough; bridge was all he wanted to do. By this time, the games had moved into the computer where professionals were playing. It wasn't the game itself that seduced our dupe, but the challenge of the other players. They were probably players of equal intelligence, the first he had ever met en mass, and they were more skilled at the game than he.

This period of bridge playing passed before his freshman year elapsed but not in time to rescue his grades. He had been encouraged to take all advanced courses because of his achievements in high school, and he thought he was passing until the grades were posted. His average was below a "C," and he was placed on probation. At first he was shocked but then became apathetic.

That first summer he retreated back home to discover inactivity. Adrian had not returned but had procured a job in close proximity to his school in the East. They had never written so this colleague didn't know of his friend's absence and was disappointed not to find him home.

After looking for jobs that would interest him, mainly in Denver, then on The Net, not finding anything, only word processing, our student went back to Boulder and attended the summer school's second session. He took two courses: one he thought he would enjoy; the other to help raise his grade point average. But within matter of weeks, he quit attending classes.

He obtained a fake ID and began to frequent local beer parlors. The people fascinated him. He found friends who were intelligent and were psychologically on the same level as he. They were all non-directed, mostly confused kids from semi-wealthy families. I thought it was another phase through which our advanced adolescent was passing, and he would eventually grow bored. It took longer than I expected, and the effect was more profound than anticipated.

"We are all looking for the same thing," he said. "For the first time, I have found people who are involved in the search for self, for a reason, for a purpose."

It was an intense time for him. He seemed more active than usual. He was constantly with his friends, drinking beer, socializing until two or three in the morning. I attended some of these "parties." Oh, their conversations were profoundly interesting, but they didn't seem to conclude in any activity, any action at all. Their insights shocked me. Questions were raised which had never occurred to me. In short, they were interesting discussions but impractical, too abstract. It was like advanced discourses in High School. They never discussed world events, nor even personal problems but discussed extensions of his high school philosophical questions. I attended more than some; for me it was a regular nightly habit after studying, during that first summer. These friends were from other colleges, enjoying the vacation, the summer school.

When the fall semester arrived, it appeared as if the people he saw were different from the summer school crowd. Our hero reflected the change. He attended meetings, political debates. He was on this committee and that committee - to organize this group or that group.

All of this took place within one semester. By the end of the fall semester of his sophomore year, he was well-known on campus. Part of this recognition was due to his predictable appearance: a black turtle neck jersey and blue jeans. He wore them constantly. A big bulky sweater was added in mid-winter, and in summer, his cowboy boots changed to sandals. His hair seemed clean but long and unkempt.

He told me he donned this combo from practicality. "It is easy to maintain; it doesn't show dirt and resolves those early morning decisions."

He never aggressively sought nor became the leader of any of these groups, but he was always one of the more active members. By the second semester his appearance at parties and meetings was in great demand. His grades again reflected his activity. They improved but not enough to secure a non-probation status. This second year he received either "A's" or "F's," but his overall average had only improved to a fraction of a point less than the required "C" average. He had to petition for re-admittance.

That spring semester he was always in trouble with the authorities. The trouble was never overtly linked with politics, but looking back, I think these activities precipitated trouble. I wish I knew more information concerning this fellow's affiliations. I was never interested in politics, so we didn't see a great deal of each other during this term. But political disturbances appeared to spout like wild flowers over the campus, and I knew he was always on the scene, and probably managed a government's list. For sure, he was on the local police's list.

His first "run-in" was extraordinary. Basically it was just an identification check: this older juvenile was making his way to class in broad daylight. Two policemen drove pass. He saw them notice him but thought nothing of it. He hurriedly began crossing a vacant lot. Halfway across, he heard a siren but was too intent in his goal "to study the situation."

The squad car screeched around the corner into the lot with sirens blaring, skidded to a stop in front of him. He thought something was happening behind him because the police jumped from their car with guns drawn. He began running towards the car, imagining he was endangered. A policeman grabbed him, thinking Thesus was attacking, threw him against the car, then down on the ground. He said he literally bounced off the car onto the ground. With that, the other cop pinned him down, slapped handcuffs on him, lifted him with his bound arms, smacked his face down on the hood, and frisked him. This caused a crowd to gather, and they began to jeer and threaten the police who bulldogged the anonymous young man into the car and drove away.

Thesus, still dazed, of course, was released after they failed to find any charges. It was fortunate he never carried his fake ID or marijuana, (an illegal substance on campus, but commonly used and readily available in colleges. Many have thought it has been kept illegal, for just such cases as these, a reason for arrest.) He was released from the downtown station and had to walk back to campus.

When I met him a day later, he was bruised and still upset. We talked for a while, and it calmed him. "It must have been a mistaken identity," I said. "Everyone is stopped for some silly reason, for an ID check, especially around campuses. Even I have been checked early in the morning after one of your parties." It was true and so common an occurrence, it almost transpired without my acknowledgment.

His second "run-in" was a little more serious. He was arrested for stealing eighty cents worth of soda cans. (The Judge laughed also.) As Thesus explained later, he was recycling an almost full plastic bag of pop cans as a favor for his landlady. He had placed the bag in his car and then ventured into a Laundromat to make a phone call. After the call, he saw four more cans. He secured them and started for the door, but before reaching it, he saw a police car drive past.

"Actually, I stopped and began questioning the moral and legal aspects of my action, then decided to leave the cans especially because of my previous problems with the police, and I didn't have time to sort out the situation. As I was about to get into my car, two uniformed officers came up behind me and grabbed my arms. They asked what did I do with those four cans I was carrying. I explained the whole story. They looked at the bag in the car. One stayed with me, and the other took my identification to the patrol car. When he returned he told me to come with them.

"They took me down to the downtown station and recorded that I stole eighty cents worth of pop cans but released me on my own recognizance after I promised I would return the next day.

"It could be that they were hoping I wouldn't return so they could really arrest me, but I told them to check my story with my landlady and left. The next day at the police station, a cop, one of the two from the day before, told me to follow him. When we entered the police car, I asked him where he was taking me. He said to the city jail. I asked, 'Why?' He said he had a witness who saw me steal the cans. He incarcerated me in jail until arraignment.

"I can't believe it's true," I said. "Did you find out why?" He shook his head to indicate he didn't believe it either but there it was. "Life is sometimes stranger than fiction."

"Were you dressed as you are now?" He was wearing the same old outfit. He nodded yes. "They probably thought you were a transient and should be chased out of town." I laughed, but he didn't smile.

"They could have checked to see if I were a student. Anyway, before arraignment I called home. My father asked me if I had done it. I told him no, and he called our family lawyer who called back within ten minutes. This shocked the policeman who I think could see his mistake.

"So maybe you are right. But now he had to go through with it. He took me up to see the Judge who smiled at the charge until I smiled back, and she became very serious. Later my father told me that our lawyer was head of the Bar.

I was released on bond, five hundred dollars. I couldn't help smiling when they read the charge: maliciously and feloniously carrying three dollars and fifty-six cents worth of soda pop cans from the premises of the Laundromat. I had several thousand dollars in the bank for college so the whole thing seemed absurd.

"That evening I got a call from the Deputy District Attorney. It seems I only had to appear at the trial, and they would drop the charges. I did show and made a verbal complaint against the officer for making-up a witness. Now I ask, what if I hadn't been who I was: if my father were poor and couldn't hire a lawyer? I might have had more problems. I would have stayed in jail for days. Hell, they might have convicted me of something I didn't do and placed the criminal band on me." (Ankle-bands are mainly used to locate and follow prisoners' movements and so was a little bit of an over exaggeration on his part.)

"Yes," I said, "it was probably a mistake. Just dismiss it."

Looking back, it made sense to say that those incidents might have befallen him because the local police wanted his finger prints and photo because of his appearance. But then maybe I was naïve.

Of course, his troubles with the police didn't end there. He began to be hassled for more subtle reasons than these apparent ones. The next occurrence after the stealing charge was dropped was the "booting" of his car, which means the police clamped a front tire of his car so it is impossible to drive. The boot was administered because of a parking ticket that was allegedly issued his freshman year. It took one hundred and fifty dollars to remove the boot and another fifty-five to pay the ticket. He complained that he had never received the ticket. "Why wouldn't I have paid it?"

His car seemed to be followed frequently. Sometimes he was stopped for a license check. The first time this happened he wasn't carrying a driver's license. He told the policeman that he had one and presumably the officer called for a confirmation. But, this time, the State Patrolman issued a ticket for driving without a license: he said there was no record in his computer bank. Our hero had to appear in a distant court, a two hour drive, to prove his innocence. He produced his license; the court recorded it; it cost him nothing except time and money for gas, but it made him angry.

For a month he was stopped approximately once a week. He took his car home and left it the rest of the semester. Shortly afterwards, a stranger approached him and asked if he were being troubled by the police. When our innocent said yes, the stranger told him that because of the verbal complaint Thesus had lodged against the witness-creating officer, the police agent had been suspended from the force. Just stay "low and cool" for a while and things would die down.

But the encounters didn't end. The next happened one night in the student union. A political organizer had arrived from the East coast to organize a campus strike or protest against something. An interesting side-light is that it was an activity in which our fellow student never participated. He stated that the reason for the strike was not worth the damage to the University and in fact, he fought against it. If the strike were effective, he reasoned that it not only could harm the school's efficiency but could affect its reputation for years afterwards. "Of course, I was against it. It was too extreme a measure for too minor an incident; a peaceful march would have been enough to demonstrate dissatisfaction. The campus could have been closed; people might be graduating without the needed knowledge or skills; our reputation as a university would be lessened. But still, I was in charge of the committee to escort the 'nationally-known figure.'"

It was the night before the strike, and the organizer and Thesus were in the Student Union. The professional activist had made a phone call to someone in New York, and while they were walking down the stairs to leave, six law enforcement agents approached from different directions including back above them. The police asked for identification which neither of them had. Then the police said, "Well, you have to come with us."

The organizer didn't move and said, "Am I under arrest?"

The police said, "No."

"Then I don't need to go with you."

On the other hand, our hero said, "Oh fuck, here I go again," and started to follow. Two officers grabbed Thesus and shoved him against the wall then frisked him.

Undoubtedly thinking our naive student was the activist because of his statement, the officers arrested him. By the time they discovered Thesus' "name, rank, and serial number," the organizer had left town, and the strike had commenced.

Another mistaken identity, another call to his father, another dismissed charge, but this time Thesus said nothing about the arresting officers. At the end of the school year, our pupil checked to reassure himself that his grades were above a 2.0 and decided to drop out of school when he was guaranteed re-admittance. Meanwhile he decided to hitch around the country and to visit friends he had met in college but with whom had lost contact. He phoned their parents, but they didn't seem to know where their children were or at least wouldn't tell.

Another "police action" was inflamed in South America, and so he dismissed their disappearance to dodging the draft. His theory seemed to be confirmed when within three months after dropping out of school, the draft board "called in" our innocent for a physical. Thesus assumed he was automatically deferred because he had been declared a "latent diabetic" by the arm services in a military hospital in Denver. Diabetes had forced his father into early retirement, and therefore at that time the whole family underwent glucose tolerance tests. He was fourteen when the government decreed Thesus a potential diabetic, and from that time forth he was placed on a strict diet. The family had opted against any of the modern procedures to "prevent" his condition from worsening, including the pancreas implant of stem cells

He was still on the diet when no abnormal amount of sugar was registered in his blood for the draft physical. Discovering this, he went to the military hospital for his records. "Lost in action, or should I say, lost in inaction." He laughed. He asked his father to inquire but with no results. Thesus decided to seek a private diabetic specialist.

Meanwhile, recruiters again encouraged him to join. Each and every branch approached him, not only with letters but with personal calls. Most told him he could study and become what he wanted.

He remained in complete compliance of a special diet for a week before taking another glucose tolerance test with the private physician, but all of the results were negative. The doctor couldn't understand the term "latent diabetic," "either a person has it or doesn't. Maybe it was confused with Type 2 diabetes, but I don't even see that. Look at it this way, your experience of not eating sugar and remaining on a diet for all those years was probably beneficial."

Immediately Thesus registered for the second semester summer school. While standing in a line, he was approached by a political activist who among other events told Thesus that the political organizer from the telephone booth incident had been killed in an automobile accident. Unanswerable confusion reigned then was replaced by anger. Since the Army was after him he focused his anger at the Services. He swore if they attempted to draft him, he would leave the country and applied for a passport. When it arrived, he reserved a ticket to Switzerland for the end of the summer, just in case. After acceptance for the fall semester, he asked the school to write the draft board for a confirmation of deferment. He even considered a quick trip to Canada and was prepared to travel.

It wasn't that he preferred not to fight in another unjustified war, but he thought that they were drafting him unjustifiably. They were trying too hard to get him, and to him that in itself proved something was wrong. What it was? He didn't know, but he wasn't "going in" no matter what.

His father, surprisingly, didn't advise him either way. Even when his father knew Thesus was leaving the country, he didn't say word "one." Obviously his father was aware of something and was doing his best to further what he thought was 'right,' but he didn't disclose what he knew. He told Thesus he would support him with any decision.

It was inconceivable to me then and now that the father didn't tell his son the political and social realities as he must have known. Maybe he knew too much. Maybe he was encouraging Thesus to leave.

Fall semester commenced without hearing from the government. He began school but was ready for anything. Three weeks later he received his student deferment. I don't think his father influenced the changed status. Looking back, I don't think his father was in "good graces" with the services, and therefore couldn't have exercised any pull.

At this point in time, my family as a pre-graduation present for my PhD passed the hat and raised some money for me. I used it to go to Europe to help me to prepare for the language comprehensives, to get away, and to see some places I had only studied: "to round out" my education. By the time I came back, took my comprehensives and had my advisors agree on my topic for the dissertation, Thesus was preparing to graduate. Since I took a couple of weeks break before my serious research, he and I had some time to talk. One of the most revealing discussions was right before his ceremony.

Thesus had just barely graduated, partly because his grades didn't improve and partly because he didn't declare a major until his final two semesters. For two years he was majoring in psychology and almost fulfilled the requirements but an experiment made him change his mind. Then he took nothing but philosophy classes for one whole year.

While sitting in the student union, drinking coffee, him wearing a cap and gown, he explained his circumstances. "It happened the second semester of my junior year, when you were still in Europe. For a requirement in a psychology course, I was forced to participate in a psyche experiment. If it hadn't been a requirement that would have been different but it was. I was a rat forced into a maze, expected to do something for what reason, I still don't fully understand. It didn't really make sense. Why would someone ask another person to shock him when he could rig up the mechanism to do it himself. I really didn't believe it all.

But then the cruelest thing I ever heard was his moan. If it was really happening, I was really shocking him, he should have never let me know. I mean, if he were crazy enough to really be testing what he said, the more humane thing to do was not to throw doubt into my perception, and not let me know I was, so I dismissed it as being real.

"When I was supposedly shocking him, these ideas popped into my mind. I became extremely angry at the thought of what they were doing, no matter what it was. What if he were really receiving the shocks? I couldn't and positively didn't believe it then and don't believe it now. But what if he were that stupid? Should I have said, I don't care; I won't participate; flunk me? Yes, maybe I should have.

I tested the shock on me, on the lowest scale; it was like a piano keyboard, and nobody could have taken that for any length of time. I was going to test it, on the highest scale, but the research assistant stopped me, almost jumping at me so I wouldn't. It was impossible that he was doing what he said he was; he would have been jolted to jelly.

"If I would have had more time to think about it and consider the consequences, especially whether I was willing to take the responsibility for my action, shocks or no shocks, but I was completely prepared to let the experimenter determine my moral and ethical responsibilities. I had put my trust in his authority. I never thought he would do harm to either himself or me. At least this is what I thought at the time."

"Exactly what happened?"

"At the time, I thought it was a test of aggressive behavior. First I was told to shock him while he was writing the alphabet backwards, hypothetically to test psychological abilities under electrical duress. Then he asked me to recite the alphabet backwards a couple of times, encouraging me to do better; other people had done it better, he said. I was doing very poorly, he said, almost to the point of badgering. That was the reason I thought it was a test of aggression,.... his irritation,... then he prompted me to shock him a series of times again. I thought at the time that this experiment was so obvious that I was going to play along and foul up the works. I was going to prove that I wasn't being fooled by this stupid test. No human being would intentionally hurt himself, but maybe this is giving him too much respect, thinking that he was human and not a machine, not thinking he was a masochist or maybe a sadist for putting me in this position."

Thesus was angry. His face had turned red and he was almost shouting. "That bastard! I wonder if he was the one who created that experiment? I pushed the buttons with the idea that he was not receiving the shocks. With the idea of proving human freedom."

"Couldn't you tell?" I asked.

"He was on the other side of a partition. What is this feeling I have now and have felt off and on since the experiment?" It is not total anger but another feeling, a sickening feeling." He paused to calm himself. He leaned back in the chair and took a drink of his coffee, then released himself with a deep, long sigh.

"I tested the shock on me ...... Another earlier required Psyche experiment in which I had to participate was to anticipate a combination of numbers. Numbers flashed on a screen in a set combination, and if I could have figured the sequence and predicted four following numbers, I could have left. Of course, the proctor warned, 'Your sequence could be a completely random pattern, which may never be found.' I spent two and half hours in that small room without finding a logical pattern.

"But I did use a pattern I had set in my mind

when I was presumably shocking him. A high scaled pattern was generated the longer I had to participate. I told him I did it for science, not believing I had done anything at all.

"Guilt," he said with a surprised voice. "A feeling of guilt, doubt, nausea that I would have participated in something that degraded human beings. I should have just refused to participate."

"Afterthought is always easier than forethought." I said, "Don't feel too bad. I also doubt if he were receiving those shocks and maybe if he were he deserved them...."

"What a horrible thing to say," he paused, thinking. "How many humans have been led into situations, told what to do and did them because they were told, as you said, trusted in the authority of the person in control, not really knowing what was happening."

"You were just another innocent victim, caught. And what can you do about it now?"

"I don't know. I am sure they were testing me and not the effect of those shocks. That is what I thought at the time, and I was just angry enough to go along with his stupidity. But still........" He paused again for a moment then laughed his first cynical laugh I had ever heard, "I failed the test. They did elicit anger from me and aggression, that's now, but then I swear I didn't feel either."

"It sounds as if the experimenter should be categorized ...... as what?"

"You mean an aggressive follower who would get even at any cost .... or just inhumane?" He began to fail psychology examines, ended up with a couple of "D's" in courses, then dropped from majoring in psychology.

(Now, looking back at those Psychology experiments, I don't think he failed them, I think he passed. "They" thought that he was controllable. Those experiments probably saved his life.)

In spite of his poor grades, his skepticism, his dislike of psychology, I think later he formed a synthesis of his knowledge. Mainly it came after he had quit rebelling against the concept of it. After his negative opinion of it ceased to dominate his thinking, a single insight which he expressed was the realization of his conditioned behavior: how many events and people had determined his identity. He questioned who he was underneath all of the conditioning, where were his freedoms: his freedom to become who he wanted, his freedom to determine his choices, and the unconditioned freedom to resolve those choices. He questioned how much he was himself; how much he was what other people and organizations had determined him to be; how much chance, environmental stimuli, had determined his identity. It was in San Francisco when he began meditating, to peel off the outer layers of his being, all those conditioned aspects of himself, all those beings which were fantasy, all those unwanted beings which grew like barnacles, the ones which he was because he conformed or because he rebelled. He tried to submerge deep within himself to find his innate being: a greater being with a greater knowledge beyond his conscious wisdom and knowledge. "It must be good, right, and just because it is good, right and just that existence exists." He believed that his innate being would lead him through the labyrinth, the maze of confusion in his life. His primitive being knew how to survive where as he was so confused, his conscious knowledge was so contradictory that he couldn't act. He had no basis for necessary decisions. He couldn't consciously comprehend the whole, but he believed his instincts knew. He was trying to discover the depth of true knowledge, sound his innate being and then surface into an understandable world.

When he first arrived in San Francisco, he lived his intuitions, and he said he thought it worked for a while; this was how he escaped the society's, the government's and his own labyrinths.

His sister saw him traversing this period of introspection, but she thought he was just withdrawing, trying to escape himself and the world around him, and she mentioned this to him. Usually when one speaks the truth, and it is the truth and it hurts, the person under attack responses vehemently, but her accusations didn't faze our hero. Her statements, her viewpoints would usually knock him off balance as much as any force could; this time he just dismissed her comments. He knew that something was radically wrong and had been amiss for some time. He believed in his method and himself, and I think it paid off.

I saw this period of his life as one when he finally became aware of nebulous forces, forces over which he had no control or even knowledge. His realization existed in an acknowledgment of domains, events, people beyond his understanding and his ability to govern: yet, realms which had a profound effect upon him.

Later in S.F., he did withdraw in a way. He was not as adventurous, not out-going. Unless asked, he wouldn't give his opinion about anything. He was insecure, off balance, unsure of himself. All he could do was try to protect himself. He had become an observer of life, defensive against the onslaught of chaos: degenerated beliefs, multiple realities rushing in on him, a shaken self-identity, and no power over any of it.

Part of his problem was naiveté. He may have revealed his true nature and a truth about a potential nature of human beings but he was only aware of nebulous forces over which he had no authority; forces which he titled destiny, fate. He was realizing that winds could blow from the wrong directions. Winds could arise from deep recesses to create chance occurrences. But he interpreted these winds as a test of his volition, and he would use them as a means to find his potential. He knew he had yet to find a more real power and control.

After those challenges was his cry as he charged down his inner being, slashing at his faults where he found them. Perseverance, fortitude, endurance became predominant reports in his speech, especially every time unexplained events occurred.

What he didn't realize was that he stood in an artificial wind tunnel: he wasn't dealing with natural phenomena nor even simple social occurrences. Yes, equilibrium was destroyed because trust, faith, belief were still too much a part of his thinking and vocabulary. He still maintained a belief in the good, the right, and the just; a belief in the potential of humanity, for mankind could and would manifest those qualities, make them prevail in spite of fate or destiny because we all seek them. "We have it within us." Humanity's purpose is to create virtue, (even if it is just a creation). One meaning that mankind gives to life is to make justice prevail, even if there may not be an innate justice, (naive, for sure).

Yes, for a while he thought his foe was an impersonal Universe, a universe with no god or a universe which god deserted. He thought that humans were united in overcoming if not defeating the "absurd," that we were united in giving this world and our lives meaning, purpose, and significance.

Even the thought that we could be united is naïve, in my mind; but of course, I don't fully know the Real Reality, so who am I to make comment. But one thing for sure, he was wrong. A far less noble reality loomed.

One possibility beyond his conception was that records could follow him. These records would be interpreted by people who never knew him, never really knew the real situation; yet judgments would be made concerning this information. Decisions would be made, actions would be taken, and his destiny could and would be changed. Yes, he saw that he was conditioned by the identity placed on him, but he couldn't completely comprehend how it was derived. He didn't see his effect either in high school or college. He couldn't understand his influence nor others' interpretations of it. He thought he was free to experiment with his life, discover what he wanted and what he considered important and become who he wanted. He didn't realize the results of the IQ tests in high school, that he caused a sensation in college, that he was well-known, too well-known, that many people had acted on his decisions, and even to some he had been an idol, to others he was a rebel, to others a criminal. In short, he underestimated his effect. He only thought he was exploring politics, learning about the system and testing it.

He also had no comprehension of other peoples' jealousy of him, of his intelligence and abilities and that they acted because of their jealousy by trying to demean him. Even this was obvious to me, but he just dismissed others' actions and motivation as not worth his attempt to understand. We are all equal, and he treated and respected others as equals: even their beliefs, even about him.

Nor did he recognize the control which systems could exert, either as a manipulation of an individual or as a fluke, an impersonal idiosyncrasy of the systems. He didn't know that a person's power would and could multiply if that person knew and could use the system. Also, he didn't know that sometimes systems were out of control, that sometimes they were without commanders , and that during these times, many innocent people could be and were hurt, that once machinery was set into motion, often it couldn't be stopped or diverted.

Chapter 5

After college, our fellow went home for a couple of months, sat around reading, waiting for the draft board to contact him: a period of incubation. I really didn't know his thinking because I was in New Orleans teaching English in a Community College. I did receive a letter from him, (an actual letter) questioning his destiny. Was the army his fate? "What was the difference between destiny and fate, if any? Can fate be determined by...... who or what?" Is destiny an inevitable event, events, series or otherwise - the total of all action. Then what is free will? He said that he doubted and hoped against "a predestined destiny," but he could see it as a possibility. "How much of my fate is determined by me, if any?" His letter was not really clear to me, and I thought at the time that it was typical of his vagueness and his inability to communicate, but now I see it as a brainstorming session, something I taught him. I am sure he had specific ideas in mind, and I made a point to remember to discuss them with him at some future date.

After a month, he decided to hell with it; he wouldn't let the Army destroy the immediate moment, and he decided to quit dwelling upon it. He wrote his sister in San Francisco asking if he should visit. His parents, knowing that he wasn't going to stay on the ranch, without at least exploring the "Outside World," encouraged his visit. Nobody knew, including Thesus, his ultimate action if he were "called up."

Maybe Margaret, his sister, could help him decide. Maybe she understood what was happening in the United States, where as his father wouldn't say or didn't know.

Then again maybe his father thought he knew what awaited Thesus and encouraged the visit so Thesus' sister could and would keep track of him, ... just in case.

I suppose his father gave him some advice, but I am also sure, "The Captain," couldn't tell Thesus what he really needed to know. Probably experience could be his only real teacher. Life had changed since his father was young. Situations, governments, the general type of people this young man would encounter had changed, and the father must have known it. Perhaps he didn't, or else knowing, refused to comment. But the fact remains, his son was unprepared.

No! I can't believe that Thesus' father didn't realize the total situation. He was a very intelligent man, and he must have known enough of life and the "powers that be" to at least protect and help Thesus more than he did. His father must have known the functioning systems and what was happening politically. I mean there must have existed a great number of reasons why he never attained a higher rank than Captain after twenty years of service, and why the family stayed isolated on the ranch.

But, maybe this harangue is unfair. Maybe he was so entrenched in the system, he could not comprehend the whole. Maybe he had been totally conditioned, or the powers that now control were constructed too subtly or rapidly. It was, or must have been, progressive, and if there were underlying currents while Thesus' father was in the service, he may not have realized the change. Then when he retired, he totally engrossed himself in the ranch and making money and must have been oblivious to the radical changes around him.

I am sure that Thesus necessarily received some knowledge and advice from his father. But how am I to know what information passed between father and son in those couple of months at home? How can any outsider know the intimacy or explain an intimate communication between close relatives?

From what I gathered later, Thesus boarded with his sister for a couple of weeks while seeking employment and a place to live.

He found a beautiful apartment and was still there when I arrived on the scene two years later. It was a perfect place and inexpensive. "Almost too good to be true," were his words.

Being an older apartment on Nob Hill facing the south and with high ceilings, it was bright and cheery. It had French doors which opened onto a sun porch and three steps down into a sculptured garden. A mysterious enchanted realm was created when fog mingled among the fuschia hanging from the deciduous trees. Mingling among the shubbery brought one face-to-face with a sculpture of the veiled goddess, Persephone, who was surrounded by evergreens and secret pathway. San Francisco was yards away but.... Then walking back up the stairs onto the sun porch, through the wooden doors into the apartment was like entering a spacious, white sphere. The shimmering San Francisco light was pervasive. The high white ceilings with white trimming around their edges, oak floors, and latched wooden, white windows which opened outward gave the effect of a Victorian house. Moistured intense light reflecting from these off-white walls and ceiling made the apartment glow more brightly than the diffuse ocean atmosphere of outside.

Once in a dream, in this apartment, I saw Margery, draped in a long white lace dress, kiss Thesus on the lips. He was also in white: suit, shoes, and hat. The blurry white scene shone surreal as they floated from the floor: two angels at a moment of transcendence.

But this is getting ahead of myself again; back to the direct situation.

His father had given him money to get started, a homestake as was, which within two months he had spent. He had to borrow from his sister for two more months until he finally obtained a job painting the other apartments in his building from his landlord: the only type of job he could take while waiting. It was a nice gesture on his proprietor's part, and a gesture which exemplified how everyone treated Thesus. Thesus, in turn, told everyone he was doing a favor for his landlord because his regular maintenance man couldn't do the work. But, of course, a veil had yet to reveal the true circumstance.

Our hero was very attractive. When he graduated from college, he still had the boyish face of a high school student. He had thought that his youthful appearance might hinder him from obtaining a temporary, construction-type job, so he grew a mustache. He thought that it worked and had helped him secure the apartment and later the job. The landlord and he worked together painting and fixing the apartments as the tenants left, but the owner became sexually aggressive: "made a pass" at our young friend.

The way the innocent described the advance, later, was without repulsion. It was presented in a matter of fact manner. He said he was sitting on the sideboard of the sink after having cleaned a stove. The proprietor had replaced some broken window shades and approached Thesus and began stroking the insides of his legs. This action so shocked his person that he quickly jumped from the sideboard. "Because I jumped the owner's hands went up my legs and caught me in the crotch. It caused pain, to put it mildly, but I tried not to respond to it. We began to talk about what he wanted, what he felt. I explained that I didn't have those feelings, and that what he was doing didn't excite me but made me feel uncomfortable. We talked a good two hours. I think I came to understand his feelings: a man could have sexual and other emotions for another man. I didn't nor still don't condemn him for this. Each of us has our preferences. 'To each his own; live and let live.'

"I think he left knowing how I felt, that it was not my way; it was not what I wanted. I think we could accept each other."

It was then I think that Thesus should have left the apartment, but he didn't. He didn't have the money. He had saved money from the job beyond canceling a payment of rent but not enough to leave. He still hadn't repaid his sister, so he could not borrow from her, nor had he repaid his father. These were self-imposed obligations but necessary to him. In his own mind, he was trapped financially, but at the time, he didn't feel entrapped in the apartment. Of course, he could have left. His father gave him the money, not lent it, and would have been happy to give him more, but I think back to all the times I have ensnared myself because of self-imposed commitments and think - no blame.

But then again, I am sure if he had had the money he would have moved. "It was somewhat uncomfortable living there after that incident. My landlord never asked me to do another job, and I never asked him. Besides that, since the diagnosis of diabetes was incorrect, I was waiting to be drafted. I knew it was a matter of time before they inducted me. I was surprised that I hadn't received a notice before then. Two of my friends from college had been called-up, and one left the country. I was ready to leave, but wanted to see what was going to happen. At that time, I had started listening to my dreams, and they didn't confirm to me going into the army, and I had some strong feelings against it happening. But I had already made a resolve not to go in and was prepared to leave the country because I had heard stories from high school friends who had come back. It wasn't so much their stories but that I had known them: who they were when they went in and who they were when they came out. One of them was a complete mental blank. He was a juvenile delinquent, rebellious as hell, before he entered and reemerged four years later, a complete vegetable. If they could do that to him, what would or could they do to me? Another friend, who had dropped out of college and was drafted, came back drinking heavily, so heavily he couldn't quit. They kept having to throw him into the hospital to take 'the cure.' An acquaintance came out of one of the services, got married and two months later beat his wife to death. I must admit that these were extreme exceptions, but everyone else I had known, who went in, came out .... how can I say .....different, confused.... docile, almost zombie-like, for sure, if not confused then, more conforming. It can change you, and I didn't want to be changed like that. I was beginning to realize I was not like everyone else and didn't want to be. I was having a hard enough time figuring who I was and who I really wanted to be. And besides, the army didn't need my manpower."

He still had his last card to play, wiring for money from his father and leaving. He cut his hair, found his passport, and was mentally ready to travel. But his intuition was correct. He never received a draft notice but instead a job acceptance letter. Nobody knew how much his father had helped arrange this, if anything.

Orders came through, from where nobody would say, but .... it was a position in the National Park Service at the administration level. It was an extremely high paying job for "doing nothing." Quite literally he did nothing. His boss didn't have an assignment for him and really couldn't say why Thesus was hired; and he wasn't the first either. Our hero didn't press the question but remained silent. He needed the job, or at least the money, and he felt that it was perhaps an alternative to service.

It seems very obvious now, not back then, a certain amount of categorizing and manipulation were occurring, even before this event. But our innocent didn't question their existences. Why would anyone or anything be taking a special interest in him? He was one of four hundred and some million in the United States alone. He had no illusions about his significance. In fact, he saw his ego, his feelings of significance, as detrimental. He visualized his self-importance as presenting a barrier which he had to overcome in order to alleviate his fear of death. Fear, for Thesus, was an obstacle to self-discovery and freedom. "If one could feel as if he were not important, then he would feel that the loss of his life was insignificant. Undoubtedly, other animals don't abstractly feel the impending loss of themselves and probably don't even feel fear, especially abstractly as humans fear."

Yes, as mentioned, his struggle was internal. It was a struggle to know oneself and to liberate one's potential.

He saw all the events in his life as unrelated. Fate, chance, luck had been against him in the past and now they (it was?) were turning. He had a simple explanation for every event; in the past, there were mistakes in identity, personal harassment from a police officer, another psychology test which he failed, one more bad grade. And now, he had gone through a bad period but events were changing. Luck was on his side: something good had happened. He had had trouble with the authorities: the police, the school, the army but finally he was "going to get a fresh start." His name had "come up in a computer someplace," and he was going to fill the slot.

It was the natural order of things. Natural selection prevailed in nature, and in society a type of selection could and would also occur. All he needed to do was find his niche: the field in which he could accelerate and thereby succeed and contribute to society in some meaningful fashion. He felt he had learned from his experiences, and "We will always progress if we can learn. At least I won't make the same mistakes twice." Yes, detrimental incidents had happened, but he was leaving them behind and only taking the experiences with him. But he still had a greater awakening awaiting. Yes he was right, his name had surfaced in a computer someplace.

His first assignment in his new position was to inspect parks and verify existing reports. The job kept him busy but was not important. The parks were not the major ones but smaller, the ones seemingly no one knew were the government's. One, he was appointed to document all the informational signs in the parks, he had a check list. If people were camping in the park, how many people, and he had to question each one: how long had they been there; did they enjoy it; would they make any recommendations: he had a survey. If the parks had pay containers for camping, he had to validate who was collecting the money, transfer that person's data to his computer, so that it could be compared with the personal information he had acquired.

Interestingly enough, he was order not to go to the main National Parks, nor even enter them without written consent. This revelation hit Thesus in a strange way, but at first he complied.

He spent as much time traveling as inspecting. Margery told him to be patient; it was an entry level position. This undoubtedly happened to many young adults because the Park Service employed over 3,500,000 at the time and to my knowledge, many had been placed without real assignments. Outside of the military, at the time it was the biggest employer in the United States. In spite of the computer input being monitored by his superiors, it seemed as if they soon forgot him until he began to investigate outside of his assignments. He was particularly interested in improving in The Golden Gate National Recreation Area. It was in San Francisco and he visited it on Sundays. Even in his computer, he not only hit brick walls of "non information," but he was re-assigned.

In my opinion at the time, he was relieved of his duties in the field because he became active in trying to change most of the parks after inspection. He proposed suggestions pertaining to environmental stability, safety improvements, and capacity increases. His proposals were not the main reason for his transfer, but because he began to get results. Obviously, over a million and a half young adults who had been placed to be reformed, or just to hold them in place, couldn't be encouraged to make changes.

The Park Service congratulated his initiative, gave him a raise, and a higher G.S. rating with a promotion to a main office where they could watch him more closely. His title was Junior Executive Director of Records. They gave him two secretaries, then took one away. The other quit within six months, and they didn't assign him a third. In my opinion, also in retrospect, one of those secretaries was intended to watch him, and the one who quit was really a secretary. This next job was to re-arrange and file obsolete information concerning the parks. He scanned old reports into a computer, then either had the computer verbally read them to him or he read them, then he had the computer classify and categorize them, but he had to confirm the placement of the reports into the files, and make a record where he had placed them. It sounds boring, and it was. A pace of activity had to be maintained because his input was again monitored. They really never forgot him; they just assumed they had him where they wanted.

He was thankful when he thought they "forgot him," overlooked him, because he had become involved with "a young lady." It was because of her that he had time to pursue a new method of logical thought. He had begun to develop a new form of logic, something he had conceived in college with no time to explicate it. While reading a philosophy book, instead of arranging files, he re-discovered it: A new mathematical system which he equated with a system of logic. He translated the math into symbols and then worked the symbols as if they were math equations. After he derived some good results, he began to compare his answers with other logical systems. In most cases he had to relearn the other systems. For months, he carried symbolic logic books with him. He had written a whole manuscript of logical progressions of his new method and compared them with established results. For a while he thought he had broken through into a new understanding of the Universe. He began a second book using only his symbolic language.

The day he conceived a possibility of how creation could evolve from a void, he called me. Of course, I really didn't understand. I didn't understand symbolic logic. But to paraphrase my understanding: in an infinity, the probability of extensions, of many dimensions, occurring in a progression manner was great. It was as logical as zero to the zero power equaling one, (something I never understood) and the three dimensions equaling exponential functions (something I may never understand).

I told him it was beyond me, but it sounds as if it contradicted his theory about an aether. After thinking a couple of seconds, he said no, not really. "I'll let you read my first book of logic, and I'm sure you will understand. In fact you can edit it for me." But within a week, the first book disappeared. He searched for it for four days straight with no results. He hid the second and only worked on it secretly. If that first book is lost permanently, only he has the secret to unlock the second. It was like a Rosetta stone.

Contrary to his "setbacks," in this period of his life he was in good spirits. He felt he was accomplishing great things with his life. He would find his misplaced book, and he was getting involved.

His girlfriend used to visit him at work. She didn't understand his job or his new theory but helped him fulfill his required duties. She did what he told her to do. After moving in with Thesus, she resigned her position as receptionist in a bank. He willingly supported both of them, which he was basically doing anyway, but she was doing his busy work.

For both of them it was their first real love. They couldn't live without each other for more than fifteen minutes at a single stretch. The relationship began when he invited her along to inspect a park with him. From the start, she used to travel with him. Everywhere they went they held onto each other. Nobody had to tell me this; it was still occurring when I arrived in San Francisco. I walked in on them a couple of times in the weirdest places making love.

They held each other constantly both physically as well as mentally. Theirs was a mutual security-afraid to let go relationship, afraid the dream would end, afraid of what they had sought for so long would disappear. Of course, still in my opinion, it was sexual gratification which neither had experienced. For both it revealed the mysteries that had existed since puberty. But maybe it was more; it was the newness of intimacy, the newness of discovering a person in depth, the uncovering of another human being and seeing your new self in relation to that being. To Thesus it was a "completing of opposites, discovering the other half of my being, seeing a mystery unfold, fulfillment of the Grand Design.

"Before I met her, oh, I wanted to know what it meant to be a woman, to know breasts that could nourish, to know a body that would complete me and could create another human being, to share a more complete world, to know another human in all of our complexities."

And at another time, "I had surfaced long enough in relationships. I had surfaced long enough within my own being. My basic being, the essence which drives all, sought this depth. The craving of which I wasn't even aware exploded and came to possess my being.

"But it is more, so much more. It is who I am with her. What she helps me become. In her I find a new communications. It is only through love that we can possibly break the incommunicable barriers both within our own beings and between beings. And when we touch, we are no longer isolated, or even hidden from ourselves. We can love: each other, ourselves, and life, itself. We can see life anew because it explodes forth in our beings. It gushes forth, flows, and we know."

"He thinks he is in love?" his sister said, "Don't worry about it, it won't last. Lust doesn't last. And he is way too idealistic; no reality could live up to his abstract fantasy."

"What worries me," I replied, "is that he doesn't know a thing about her: where's she from, in a very broad sense. He met her on the street in front of his apartment."

And of course, our harbingers did transpire. He thought new depths would always be within her to seek. Why shouldn't there be? Both she and he were changing, growing, and sharing their new beings, sharing their evolving worlds. But her respect for him became admiration, then devotion, then adoration, then worship and idolization. She finally gave all to him and had no more to share. She seemed to become him, in thought, gestures, and action.

He didn't see this happening. He was more complete than he had ever been before, freer, more able to pursue himself and his interests. He didn't have to fulfill requirements for school or work. He was also not driven by suppressed desires, not diverted by seeking that unexplainable something that he didn't have. For the first time, he had time to investigate what he wanted. He was swimming in this freedom and loved her for helping him attain it. But he didn't see her losing her identity to him.

When the excitement of discovery, the mystery of each other, and when those moments of sexual gratification were achieved, he began to know her too well, (of course, still my opinion); he began to see more objectively. He loved her but differently than before. She couldn't understand the change, became insecure, and wanted to marry immediately. She demanded marriage. He was no longer possessed by love. He loved her but no longer was in love with love as he once was. Her hold on him decreased considerably when he began to develop his ideas "for explaining the creation of something from nothing and how dimensions exist." He was involved in a world of the abstract, and she saw no other way of regaining or securing him except through marriage.

He began to encourage her to venture out and to meet other people. "To continue her growth so that we could have more to share, more to give each other. I wanted her to go out, get involved, develop and come back and share her development with me. I wanted her to continue to complete herself and keep growing. I trusted her. I wasn't worried about losing her. I thought that we had something great, a depth that couldn't be obtained except through our own unique communication. I thought we had a special, one-of-a-kind relationship. I thought of her as an extension of me, and I was an extension of her, and that through exploration, we would both become more than we were."

If she would have only realized that by letting go of him, she could have held him and that by letting go of herself she would have grown, but she was lodged in the vice of insecurity. She tightened her grip, held him closer, more tightly, began smothering him and stifling his growth. But eventually he succeeded in forcing her to find her way. He encouraged and paid for her return to school to finish her degree, something she repeatedly said she wanted. He put a stop to her working for him, knowing full well it would slow his research and writing. He would have to do his job again.

For a while it all seemed successful. At first they would work on and discuss her school assignments. And even later,
both come home at night refreshed by their day's experiences and would discuss the day's events with a glow of insight.

They were still living at his apartment. The price was good; probably the best in town. It was beautiful, light and airy, with just enough room so neither impinged on the other. After she moved in with much external and internal debate, he no longer felt uncomfortable about the incident with his landlord. Without ever questioning whether everyone would leave them alone, he easily became more friendly with them all. Why shouldn't he? He had not only stated his preference, but he was happy, and he shared his happiness with all he encountered.

He never forgot or mentioned the incident with his lessor but was not affected by it either. Everything was fine; he was in love, almost joyously; the world was good; life was beautiful. He still wasn't saving his money but was paying back his sister and father, plus sending his girlfriend through school. Many months she took care of the rent. (I wish I could remember her name but...) He bought a jeep-type van with a seven year guarantee. He had plans to begin saving as soon as the last payment was made - "An American Dream."

The only aspect of his life that was not perfect was his job. He still had years ahead of him - reading and filing old reports. It seemed as if this would never be completed. He spent most of his time transferring the material into the computer. Too much work needed to be accomplished. And he was constantly aware "they" had a means to check the amount of his "input," so he had to pace himself.

He applied for a transfer, stating: he felt he could be of more use in some other capacity, or that if he were given another secretary, he could devote his time to more important matters. He never received a reply but heard instead that a supervisor would call on him periodically.

For months he came home from work, watched TV, slept, arose, and went to work. During the weekends of this period, he and his girlfriend would awaken at eleven, go to the beach, lie in the sun, go to dinner, then maybe to a movie, then home to bed. After three months he realized he didn't and wouldn't get his transfer. He began drinking more and complaining that he was wasting his life. He felt a greater destiny awaited him, though he knew not what. He contemplated "striking" and just pursuing his own interests while the bureaucracy slowly turned and finally fired him. It sounded messy and tedious, and he couldn't motivate himself enough to stop working. Also he couldn't think of anything that he wanted to pursue. The logic system amazed him; it was beyond his comprehension now. He never found his first manuscript. He couldn't fully understand the second anymore. He couldn't see how he drew the conclusions he did, much less how to advance them. When he had begun working on this system, it was a spontaneous occurrence. He wasn't escaping his job, but an idea was sparked and a deep commitment to express that idea possessed him and drove him. Later after working for months filing, no ideas possessed him. Nothing drove him to do anything. Everything required more energy than he had. He began to get sick and stay home. While at home he tried to read and regenerate his imagination; but it was forced. No ideas came forth. He wanted that drive again, the commitment, an involvement that would make his life worthwhile. He wanted something to give his life meaning again, but authors and ideas which at one time held his attention, compelled him to think, sparked him, meant nothing now, nor were they even understandable and what was worse, he couldn't concentrate to try to understand.

Only TV and video games held his attention. He was hypnotized by them. The TV filled a void when he was exhausted and the games fulfilled his need of achievement, a pseudo feeling of accomplishment. He was good at them. On one Friday after work he bought one and mastered it over the weekend with continuous playing.

But it was as if he were drugged on sedatives or tranquilizers or an hypnotic drug if one exists. Looking back, it may have been true. I have seen on the Internet where the government was experimenting with drugs and giving them to their employees without their knowledge. But then again, it may have been the constant contact with the computer and TV which consumed him.

His sister told him that everyone begins a career by performing menial tasks. "Just be patient, and I am sure you will be reassigned soon."

His reply to her comment was something like, "I have done a good job, so far, except during the time when I worked on my theory, and even then the job was getting done, schedules were met. Nobody could have done it better or faster. Only time will determine whether I should have spent the time on that theory.

Why shouldn't I look for another job, look for something more interesting?"

This conversation took place after he had awakened to the fact that nine months had passed, and he had accomplished nothing. His girlfriend had finished a year of school. "She has changed, grown, but I haven't. Now, she is bored with me, and I don't blame her." She had joined some organizations and was getting involved with "what was happening."

Thesus thought it was only happening in her head, but he didn't say a thing. At first he attended some of the meetings with her but discovered nothing to them. They didn't interest him, and even worse, "they seemed nationalistic and even racist."

When she ventured out at nights, he watched "The Tube" or played his games. To him, their two worlds were separating wider than their communications could bridge. They quit discussing what they were doing, quit trying to share their worlds. What did Thesus have to share?

To her, our hero fell from divinity; he no longer interested her, was no longer worth her energy. She had no one to whom she could devote her life. She no longer had someone to whom she could sacrifice.

They began to fight. Our hero explained that the problem was mainly sexual. "Is it possible to go through a dry period? As sexual as I have been in the past year and a half .... maybe it has had its toll."

At the time, I began to question whether someone was physically harassing our hero, but I remained quiet. Later, I think his sister, finally, believed this theory also.

Our friend Ike Jacoby (no relationship to me as it turns out) explained to him that it was probably psychological. His job and his boredom that made him impotent. This made some sense to our hero.

"I still have the drive and the will, but nothing happens. We make-out; I want to make love to her but can't get an erection. I love her. I respect her, more than myself at the moment, but it isn't working because of this sexual thing. She thinks it's her; I know it's me. Maybe I am a latent homosexual and have been suppressing it?"

"Why do you think that? Do I turn you on?" Jacoby laughed.

"I am not sexually driven anymore. Is an itchy butt a sign of suppressed desires? Also I have diarrhea all the time."

"Sounds as if you should see a doctor."

. About a month later, his girlfriend left. In my opinion, I think she had already began cohabiting, that she had found a man who was "getting some place" and knew she could get him.

I had been in San Francisco a little over a year before their break up. In New Orleans, I had also been involved in a relationship which didn't culminate in anything but unhappiness, so I had great empathy for our young hero. In that this was his first, I knew breaking up was the worse. Whether it was a really "true," lasting type of love didn't make a particle of difference, he thought it was; he thought he lost his "one, true love," and he was hurting physically, emotionally, and mentally. As before and again, he questioned himself. It was his fault. Something was wrong within his being. Both Ike Jacoby and I knew that he needed company to occupy his time and thoughts so that the intensity of his loss would be lessened. We took it upon ourselves to help; for both Ike and I knew what it meant to have loss someone. Jacoby, of course, had lost Margery, our hero's sister, after five years of an intense relationship.

I hadn't obtained a job teaching for the Fall, and Ike never had a job of which I knew so we convinced Thesus to take a couple of weeks from work and go with us to Big Sur. As it all transpired, very little convincing was needed, just a mere suggestion.

Chapter 6

We three stayed at the Big Sur Cabin Inn for two weeks. It was a log cabin secluded in a ravine with six rooms for lodgers. Surrounded by large trees and underbrush, travelers had to know of its existence in order to find it. Originally we passed the turn-off twice before locating it. Because we were so distracted by the cliffs falling into the ocean, the blue Pacific, rolling with a somber blue depth, and on the opposite side of the road the abrupt hills, we didn't see the one-car dirt road jut from the hair-pin turn. Even after daily travel up and down the coastline, along the highway that seems to move like a black snake precariously positioned on a slight ledge, we would invariably miss the hidden dirt lane overgrown shrubbery while concentrating on the road which diverted the car from slamming into the mountain. After the third time, we accepted the missed discovery as "a given" rather than neglect the scenery.

During the days, we went as far north as Monterey or as far south as we could drive before dark and dinner. Every day we would find an accessible beach and walk it. At night, we sat around the fireplace in the inn or went drinking in local bars. The most monumental event was when Thesus began to awaken and live again. It was as if the ocean air, the long walks, cleansed our friend's mind, and he began to think anew.

One night near the beginning of our vacation, we all talk about our lost-loves. We three had drunk too much, and Thesus started the conversation by remembering an episode with his girlfriend. When Jacoby began to talk about his relationship with Margery, both Thesus and I felt extremely uncomfortable. Of course, she was our friend's sister, and one of the main reasons for me moving to the Bay area. So this was the first and last time our ex-girlfriends entered into our conversation. Thesus seeing his mistake ended the conversation by saying: "Isn't it strange how mankind has mastered or can master anything it sets out to achieve except on the human, personal level. One personal relationship can be or can seem to be more complex than all our technological achievements. I read in the newspaper that the man who master-mind our first human landing on Mars is getting a divorced. Neither of the couple can figure out what went wrong."

The rest of our conversations were inspired by

98

the scenery, the exhaustion of the climbs up and down the cliffs, our long walks along the rocky ledges above the shoreline. A couple of days the ocean was violent. The inn keeper told us it was this way every Fall. Massive waves would crash against the shear precipice shoreline with such power and energy that all three of us stood silently in awe the first time we saw the phenomenon. The ocean was so deep where it met the shore, the power of the waves hadn't dissipated. Huge swells, sometimes fifteen feet high, slammed against the boulder-lined shore with thunderous booms.

One time we climbed down the cliffs to stand in the spray of the exploding waves. It was after this excursion that our hero broke from his daze. Ike was talking about art, the only subject he ever discussed; I was listening, making references every now and then to some other author's view.

We had reached the car, raised the windows, turned on the heat trying to warm and dry us; and for the first time that day, both of us could hear Ike's dissertation above the roar of the waves. "There is no good or bad art," Ike insisted. "Each artist is walking his own path of development. He is only as far along in his chosen direction as he can be; one person cannot judge another person's development, so how can one say this is good art or this is bad? All humans are only so far in their development, progressing at the rate they can, given their situations, their personalities, and so forth. One artist cannot be and should not be compared to others."

I thought, go on and rationalize your failures, say

you stand alone and cannot be compared, but I just added to his statement with a quote from Benson, the painter, "An artist could never be considered a failure unless he quits working."

Surprisingly Thesus asked, "But shouldn't the goal of art not only to better one's self but to improve upon art, nature and mankind, … everything?"

"Is it possible to improve upon nature?" I inquired.

"Hopefully," responded our young awakening friend, "both in relationship to mankind and to nature itself. Humans have the power to create balanced systems. We already determine what lives and what dies; we help determine our and all life's environments."

I could see his gears starting to turn and was determined to give them a push. "But be specific. How can we improve upon nature?"

"By improving ourselves, (he smiled) and of course things like damming rivers, irrigating and growing plants where nothing was before; creating hybrids and other forms of genetic engineering, transplanting animals from one area to another, and generally repairing what we have thrown out of balance." His answer was impatient, hurried, not well thought-out or constructed. His impatience was an old characteristic surfacing. He felt caught in the obvious, in trivia, and in the inadequacies of the language. It was a sure sign that his mind was actively pursuing thought which he wished to communicate, and it was not only two steps ahead of what he was saying but that his spoken words fell short of what he wanted to say. It was a good sign. But Ike was totally unaware of this breakthrough and said.

"What may be improvement to me, may not be for you. So you may judge what I do as non-art, and yet it may be a great step for me, or with all humility, in the field of art. You as a non-artist may not see the contribution, the step forward, the exploration, the redefinition, the communication, or see the personal development that I made in achieving what I have. It is only through working, creating, that the artist becomes an artist. He is not an artist unless he is creating. He only changes his being by creating. He only takes that step beyond himself by creating. He can only take other people beyond their ordinary experience through making this step. This in where a betterment is created."

"If it is so personal, couldn't the step to the 'beyond' be the wrong step, a step that could make things worse, not better? And how would the artist know, if it just is subjective progress to him? How can he judge?"

Ike answered our hero without a pause, "O.K., but the art object will reflect the direction of the step whether it was good or bad. The viewer looking at the object will know and hopefully the artist re-viewing the object with some type of objectivity will also know.

"Look, many philosophies of art exist; my personal one is that if I create a better me, create of myself a greater person and an artist, then everything I create, no matter what medium will be a great work of art, because it will express that me."

Good luck, I thought, but our hero expressed it as "If you can control the medium and yourself to really express the 'me' you are…"

With very little pause and in my opinion littler thought, Jacoby interrupted: "Taking into account that what is expressed is representative of the person and his experiences, in some form or another, the greatness will be in the work, and I dare say, with or without the mastery of technique. It is not 'control of medium,' as you put it, that makes an artist, for if it were just mastery of technique anyone who is taught to master a craft is an artist. Right? Wrong! Artists create. There are many artisans but few artists. Artisans perfect what already exists; the artist adds to what exists. The artist takes himself one step beyond and therefore adds to humanity. And if human beings can keep one step beyond their destruction then our existence may be assured."

"Are you talking about creating something from nothing?" I asked.

He thought for a moment; "Yes and no, it must happen all the time, for from where would original ideas evolve? But specifically what I am discussing is experiencing something new or adding two things together and getting a new relationship, a product beyond what exists, a product beyond myself or should I say the artist? This is the artist's concern, to take himself beyond, to become more than he is, to improve upon himself."

"Give us an example," our hero insisted.

"Two words never placed together before, two medium brought together, two concepts…."

"But you know," I interjected, "Wallace Stevens would put a limitation on that, not necessarily on the method but qualitatively. He said in _The Necessary Angel_ that one must "create the unreal from the real."

"Very good," interjected our hero, "exactly my point. We all know of Icarus." His pause was interpreted as a lack of energy, so we didn't interrupt. "So you understand that one should create the abstract reality, for that is what art is, out of the physical, observable reality so others may relate to the creation, so that other people can see and maybe use the betterment to improve upon the existing reality, an improvement upon that which exists."

"That is discounting art for art sake, or from using art objects as the step-off stone, an abstract reality from which to begin the creations," Jacoby defended. "It getting dark, and I am hungry. Let's go."

"Yes, I'm starved," Thesus reiterated.

Placing the car in gear, I tried to continue, "Aren't the art objects things that exist?" but realized the question was redundant. Ike must have miss interpreted it for he responded, "Some of them represent things that exist, some don't."

Thesus, on the other hand, pushed forward, "But couldn't a person get so beyond himself that he loses himself and plummets into the ocean of mystery never to be found either by others or himself?" At the time I thought, there was a concern Thesus had about Ike that I hadn't seen before. Our seeker's pursuit of him was more intense than ever. Looking back it was probably this concern which was the partial reason

Thesus emerged from his cocoon, his daze. He kept questioning Jacoby about his philosophy, his reason for doing art. It seemed sometimes as if he were taking mental punches at Ike, but Ike didn't respond to the mental probes as if they were attacks but would absorb them as if his mind was jelly, and every jab would make an impression but made no difference. Jacoby's mind would form around the void left by the mental fist as if it never had occurred.

I once asked Jacoby if he felt threatened by this young fellow's questions, and he responded with one of his idealistic statements but without complete knowledge or belief: "No, Thesus wants to know. His questions help me grow. They make me question, change, and become."

And it was true that with every discussion of art, the foundations of Ike's philosophy of art would become more set, concreting, as were, and maybe this was our hero's fear, his struggle.

On our last day of vacation, we stopped in an art gallery which was south of the inn where we stayed. Ike didn't really want to waste his time visiting it because he didn't think anything would be worth his while. But Thesus insisted because of curiosity and to add something knew to our itinerary. We found sculptures, paintings, clothing, some of which were finely wrought, created with imagination and skill.

"You can't tell me that you don't judge some of these works as good and some as bad," I asked.

"I find some more interesting than others. I find some done with greater craftsmanship: maybe one, this one (he walked over to a bronze sculpture of what looked like a man pulling himself from a swamp) touches me to the quick. I would have liked to have done it. But to say this is art and that (he pointed to a large rock covered with metal and wood which to me was nothing in particular) is not art would be wrong. They may have been created by the same artist at different times. This one (the bronze) was or may have been created to express man's relationship to the Universe and that one was to explore the possibilities of different medium placed together. This bronze thing is figurative and that one is abstract. Almost everyone can see what is happening in this one, but maybe only those who have explored the use of wood with metal and rock can see what the artist was trying to do; only he, the artist, can judge whether he accomplished what he set out to accomplish. We, the viewer, must assume that he accomplished his goal for he quit working on it and put it on display."

I looked at the title of the multi-medium rock piece. "It was created by a woman." I smiled at our hero. He didn't see me. I looked at Ike. He was almost seriously angry, so I said with a little sarcasm, "Then art only expresses where the artist is at the time of the creation."

"It can't help but be," he answered, "but of course, that is not all art is--- it increases awareness, communicates knowledge, not as academic books but it can in a more innate knowledge way, a knowledge of the sublime … and then again that is not all art is."

With that comment we left the gallery and drove north, collected our luggage from the Inn and prepared for the return trip. At the first bar even before Carmel, Ike insisted on stopping and having a drink. Of course, he didn't have any money, and it didn't occur to him that he would be imposing on us by insisting on stopping so early in the afternoon nor in making us pay for his drinks. But we stopped, and our hero "picked up" the bill. He was the only one working, so I didn't say anything but had the cheapest drinks in the house, a couple of drafts.

On the way back to the car our hero said, "Artistic truth, both expressed and implied, can and should transcend nature, including human nature, is that your premise?" Ike nodded in the affirmative not knowing where are hero was leading him. But I thought I knew, so I added, "But it should not 'wantonly violate the laws which make the real world rational,' right?"

"Yes, the artist can himself transcend, transcend this transient world and be free to express that which goes beyond reason, not be confined by the intellect, reason…."

"But he can't contradict everything that has made him real; he cannot contradict the real, itself. It must be based in reality," I said.

Ike laughed and continued, "What in the hell is reality? It can't be someone's conception, our different individual predispositions, our individual perceptions."

It was at this point I could tell he was a little drunk. He must have had more than just the two drinks in the bar. I was in the back seat by myself and just laid my head back knowing there must have been

106

a transference of money when I was in the bathroom, and now there was going to be a long harangue.

"Is it the reality by which science and math has tried to order the Universe? We both know it isn't the symbols and words that express this "ordered" Universe. Is it the reality which philosophy and theology creates through projecting meaning, in my humble opinion, a created meaning? We have distorted reality, our perception of it, more than it is, by trying to measure it. It is probably infinite, but we have broken it down, something which can't be done unless we distort the concept of it. Maybe reality is not set; for change is in all. Maybe reality doesn't exist but is only a word in man's vocabulary to keep him from seeking something, he knows not what; it is a word created to help make mankind feel secure in that he thinks he knows what exists, we have a word for it, or if not that, that something does indeed exist even if it is beyond our grasp. If it is just a word then it is a limitation, a boundary that we have placed on ourselves; we say this is reality, or even, reality exists. I don't reproach those who seek it or invent it. I believe that man's only salvation is in this search and in his ability to create. The artist is either trying to explore, express, or create it. Sometimes he is trying to realize an ideal that is not intrinsic in nature and is trying to bring himself into a state of being that is this ideal and thereby bring the world along with him. If he succeeds then the ideal exists in the world, and he has created a reality.

"Like that sculpture we saw of a man trying to pull himself, out of the muck and mire, man must continue his attempt, but he won't succeed if he says, 'This is reality and we can't transcend it; we can't go beyond it; this is our limitation.'

"You were right that each work of art can only express where the artist is, his perspective, his interpretation of reality. An artist may see mankind striving forward with loud crashing symbols in a symphony, trumpet flares declaring mankind's newest victory over nature, death, chaos, or he may see mankind already doomed to hell and damnation unable to climb the mountain of forgiveness. He may see the world in solid bold sculptures able to withstand all the tortures sent from the skies or the world as absurd, 106 coke bottles standing side by side on a five hundred foot tall matchbox cover, and so where is the reality? These are all a comment about what exists, yet, now, create our reality, are part of it."

With a slightly slurred speech and beat pattern, I knew Ike was reciting one of his:

Man is the child of nature
Not some mistake
Growing into a god
A creation he makes.

"I see mankind as a creature who has the power to create a new world whether he wants to or not, a world excluding nature. Man is nature's child growing into a new nature. As children can and do transcend parents, we will transcend nature. Mankind already creates an order, meaning, and gives himself a significance which does not necessarily exist in nature, and he has had to do this by stepping away from nature. And if human beings can keep one step beyond themselves, their destruction, then their existence has a chance to continue forever."

Drunk for sure, he's repeating himself again.

"You mean by stepping on nature," I said. "You just wait until nature steps back. We'll see how great this mankind is. We will see if we can really transcend."

"Come now, boys," our hero laughed, "but yes, if mankind gets too far beyond and doesn't see on what we really depend, we could get into bad trouble. We don't want to limit ourselves unjustifiably, but we have to know our limitations. We don't want to destroy ourselves by attempting something impossible. All mankind, right now and maybe forever, is a mosquito on nature's butt, taking more than we give. We may be a parasite, a minor discomfort that with one explosion of the sun will swat us with one large hand. Reality, to me, is this (he pounded on something solid like the steering wheel). Reality is the communicator and the communicable, the common ground which we all know, share, and can confirm, but, of course, it is more than we know, it is the bases of what we know, that which permits us to know and that which we can know, no matter how distorted. You are probably asking yourself how do we know we share any commonnesses? As an absolute we don't, but on a functional, receivable, predictable level we do. On the level we know we don't know all, we do. On the level that we know everything is just probable, we know we know. We base our lives, our communications, on the probable and the more it works, the more we can communicate, work together, make predictions, know the results, the more probable it is as we think it is. For different people to a different degree, we all share this common ground upon which we dwell. We all share the life force or that which has promoted and continues to promote existence, the reason we can even question all of it."

Our hero's words didn't seem to affect Ike. They didn't seem to faze him or sink in. Maybe he wasn't really listening or he couldn't comprehend because he started off in another direction.

"Let me restate what I said the other day. It is clearer in my mind now. (I suppressed my laughter. There was no doubt he was drunk and must have a bottle in the front seat). Every human can be an artist of his own being if he could only realize it. (Ok, I met someone whose body is a canvass to tattoo and pierce.) And this makes it impossible to judge a man's work because each person working in his medium is a person standing on a path that extends from his own being outward. This path is a path of communication, exploration, and on and on.(Really!) This path is connected in his own being, not as a circle maybe but as a path inward, outward; it is connected and communicated, when the expression in the medium is the true expression of his own being, not an attempt to master the technique or style (what are you saying?). The further this connection goes into his own being, into the most primitive parts of his being,

110

the more Universal his art, for we are from this Universe. So this path leads both inward and outward, hopefully without obstruction. If the artist is traveling down the path of his own being then he must pass the involvement of the manipulation of the medium, pass the subjective expression of his own feelings and emotions in order to touch upon the main flow which is in all mankind.

"If he walks in the opposite, he must pass all the obstacles mentioned plus the ones reality imposes. All his art which is created along the way shows the direction and distance he has traveled."

"But they don't necessarily show these things to the viewer," said our hero. "For as an artist is walking he is not necessarily creating, and we only see products which are dropped here and there, and we can't always follow the development. (Yes you have defined Ike's shit. I suppressed my laughter again.) Therefore the communications link between the artist and the viewer is not always complete. The artist may think he has communicated, but did he?"

"In order for this communications to exist both the viewer and the artist must walk down the path that the artist traveled, passing all the obstacles and get to the point where the medium is so sensitive, so raw that it can carry the slightest impression, where the artist's own individuality, growth and primitive being are imprinted in the work."

"I agree with Thesus," I said. "Only when the path is cleared in both directions is the communicational link established. Only when we can see each step taken, as it is taken, can we follow, and the artist cannot be in a position to determine that, only the viewer can say if the art work has communicated anything."

"You, both, are living in a too rational, ordered world to see art for what it is: its true potential," he answered. "The steps are not that ordered or rational. There are leaps and bounds. The viewer must be able to make them in order to follow, or be able to accept an art object as an independent entity, a unique, created object."

We sat in silence for a while. I thought Ike might have passed out, so I slept the rest of the way back to San Francisco.

Chapter 7

Returning to the old environment for this youthful man was like placing something new into an old container. One could see the difference. With this enthusiast he began to apply for new positions outside the government and began to start working again with new eagerness with the hope that his job wouldn't last much longer. He again had ideas about everything including his job, the Parks Department, and the government, itself. He wrote reports, submitted proposals, made suggestions to his supervisor. He told me that his activity had a dual purpose: The changes were interesting, important, and in some cases, necessary. Plus, he thought he could get some recognition and get transferred.

He even undertook a couple of the Civil Service

promotional exams. In each one, he told me later that he had been distracted by a high pitched sound in the undertone and couldn't concentrate during certain sections of the test. And in fact, his scores indicated, which he predicted, very high marks on certain sections and unusually low on others.

My question now: was this just another government experiment with human guinea pigs? Maybe testing and passing only those who couldn't be affected by the sound. Was this a product of the fear of other foreign countries using this distraction? Or hiring those who would eventually be controlled, unconsciously, by it? At the time, I just thought maybe the government is just testing to determine the ability to concentrate with distractions, and our hero student failed another one. I was amused at the thought but did not communicate it to Thesus.

(Now, I can idealistically see the possibility of the government passing those who it wanted to pass and failing who they considered a security risk.)

After another month, he fell back into his old syndrome. I again encouraged him to move, but he didn't relate the events. I informed him that the container eventually forms the contents; I implored him to leave before he slowly and almost imperceptibly became stupefied. He was deep into it again before I even saw it. He slept a great deal, but still went to work tired, came home watched TV, fixed dinner, watched the late show, and slept, waking exhausted.

For almost a month our victim quit mentioning his physical ailments, and I had assumed that his problem had straightened itself out. (In this revision I again replaced this horribly, cruel pun because I guess I just can't resist trying to be clever.) But one evening I was at his apartment fixing dinner for both of us. The first phenomenon I noticed was that the salt that I put into the boiling water for his vegetables began to float, then fell to the bottom in one big lump. We stopped the preparation and began our investigation by pouring some of the water and salt (?) into a glass. "I have never taken notice of the properties of salt before," he mumble quizzically, but, ..." he added with firmness, holding the glass up to the kitchen light, "should this film which looks like alcohol be floating on the water?"

"I don't know. Maybe your salt is old, but I have never seen it act like that before. Better buy some new."

"Forget it for now; eating a salt free meal will probably be better for us," he said with a smile.

But when I heated the oil to fry the fish, it began popping in the frying pan when I assumed it to be unused. I poured it down the sink and cleaned the pan and tried again. Again it popped. After my comment, he just said, "I thought that was a natural occurrence."

"NO!" I answered, "I am sure, it means that it is filled with impurities, although we can't see them."

"How is your health?"

"Horrible and getting worse, but I thought it was in my head."

"Another occurrence is that my coffee in the morning has an oil slick on it; I mean you can see a rainbow floating on the black liquid."

"You know, it is so obvious that maybe someone wants you to move. Does anyone have a key to this apartment? Have you changed locks since you moved in? Did your ex-girlfriend give you back her keys?" I was somewhat frightened and very enraged, so much so, my words popped like the oil from my mouth without thought.

"No, I didn't change the locks. No, she didn't give me her keys, but she doesn't hate me or anything like that so just get that out of your mind. No, I probably don't know all who have keys. The landlord and managers for sure; the janitor, maybe. Anyone who owned the apartment before could have access. But it is easier than that for anyone who wants to enter, all you need is a cardboard card in between the two patio windows to lift the latch and very little more to open the patio doors. And you know, I have noticed that people have been getting into the apartment, but I haven't worried about it because I don't have anything to steal and nothing is ever missing."

"But you have left yourself totally vulnerable. Look at what is happening. Are you physically ill? Are you still impotent? Do you still have your itchy butt, diarrhea?"

"Yes, as a matter of fact, and I seem to be growing breasts," his soft laughter was slightly sick. "I can see your point, but why would anyone want to do something like that to me?"

"Like I said, maybe someone wants you to move? Maybe someone wants you to be inactive, sexually, maybe mentally. I don't know. Many weird people are running around with terrifically weird ideas and imposing them upon others. Can you think of anyone who might have a grudge against you? But no matter what, you should get the hell out of here; you should protect yourself. Move! Throw out this food. Change your toilet paper.

"This all started while your girlfriend was still here," he winced and began to interrupt me, but I continued, "I don't mean it was she, but someone who wanted you two to separate. Maybe jealousy. Maybe to isolate you. God knows ...."

"You know, I have been feeling differently lately, more strange, all wound-up at nights, lying in bed grinding my teeth, almost hallucinating. I can't concentrate on anything during the day.

"But I am not involved with anyone: my three friends, of course including you and Margery, a supervisor who I have never physically met, and ..... nobody I can think of."

"Who knows; it sounds like drugs: speed, laxatives, salt peter or even worse. Who knows and who cares; you should just protect yourself."

"You know if this is all true, it is really a case of dirty dealing. It is depriving me of my self-determination. It is a violation of my being, and even worse a subtle form of rape. Of course, it is just a supposition right now, but hell, am I angry. Not even during the wars did anyone use germ or chemical warfare. (Naive, for sure.) I thought it was me. I thought that I was suppressing homosexuality. I thought it was psychosomatic illness. I thought I was innately lazy. Even for a while at nights, especially lately, I thought I was going crazy. No, I am going to

116

stay and find out who is getting in here and doing what." He paused and then a strange, unreal smile emerged from somewhere deep inside. "It does sound like someone is after my butt either literally or figuratively." Then he laughed as a new person. He seemed to be different, slightly mad.

When all this was disclosed to Margery, she was at first surprised, then in total disbelief, then shocked when I tried to confirm it; I really don't think she still believed it. Jacoby, on other hand, wanted to go and beat-up the "Queers." "It'll teach them a lesson."

"Who?" asked Thesus. He explained to Ike that to strike out would be wrong especially since we didn't know who was doing what or why, and that innocent people might get hurt, and it would just bring more strife.

"Why don't you get some surveillance equipment?"

Later when I again asked him, he thought he had found a way without it. It was too much money.

He continued to live in that apartment for another couple of months just eating canned goods, changing the salt and sugar regularly, not leaving anything in the ice box, hiding his toilet paper and placing traps all over the apartment. Jacoby suggested wiring the front door so that whoever opened it would get shocked. Of course, our hero rejected that idea, but nothing came from all his precautions. Too much time transpired during the day when he was gone. A couple of days he pretended to go to work but returned and waited but to no avail.

It was about at that time that he noticed one of

the two men in Apartment 1, the managers, was always sitting in the front window watching the street. He had "probably" seen them before but never paid attention. It was at this time he began to notice small flaky particles floating in the bottom of his booze bottles. They weren't there when he first bought them .... that was for sure.

He roomed with his sister for four days but felt he was fighting her also. She thought that it was he who was causing the chaos. And he knew if she didn't believe and guard against the maleficence, not only would it probably continue but she could be endangered also.

I know she didn't understand. She didn't know half of the incidents nor their severity. She was busy becoming a success, and if she could with her potential, he could with his (this was her thinking). All he had to do was straighten his mind and focus on the important matters, something he never seemed to be able to do. My point is that she was not to be blamed for not understanding his situation.

Anyway, he found a communal living situation, where his rent was almost nothing. He had a small room and shared the living, bathroom, and kitchen with five others.

His timing was good, not only from the viewpoint of his mental health but because he had also "resigned" from the Park Service. I placed "resign" in quotations because it was forced. Three months before his move, his name was involved in a scandal. In his period of activity right after our vacation, he had proposed a project which was funded but not completed. He had no notion that someone had used his idea, much less that it was funded. The government investigated the allocation but couldn't track the money - it was just lost. Suspicion rested upon our innocent because his name appeared on the proposal. No person approached him and asked him to resign, but he knew "this was the end," either he would be fired or demoted, or worst of all: "I will never get promoted, never change jobs, never get the hell out of here." He quit, cleaned his desk, and left before his supervisor ever received the resignation.

Both changes, moving and resigning, did alter his disposition. He felt refreshed because he left no tracks. He had some savings, not as much as he would have liked, but in his new place, no financial pressure existed. He was meeting new people and thought his problems had ended. It was good not to have to get up every morning and not to go to a job he hated. He began reading, talking, thinking, in short igniting his mind.

Yes, at the beginning his changed life seemed to have worked. He was anonymous. Even his roommates knew him only by his middle name. Neither the telephone nor the apartment was in his name. He didn't have to sign a lease.

But it didn't take long, not even a month, before ominous events began occurring. One morning he found his car vandalized. The front windshield was broken; the seats were cut, and the antenna broken. The weirdest thing: probably a hundred stables were shot into his tires. To put it mildly, where he was living was not a good section of town so he dismissed it. His tires were old and needed replaced, so no big deal. He bought a new windshield after getting a ticket. Two weeks later, the car's electrical system kept shorting. After replacing the battery, the alternator, and some other work, he discovered a cut wire under the body of his truck. "This was not squalor on Waller," (the street where he lived) "but unmentionable intentions." I think it was still humorous in his mind because he didn't quite believe it. But then when some man called and asked if Thesus used to live at his old address and when Thesus said yes, "the guy hung up," our hero's strange sense of humor ceased. He became serious.

Within two weeks of the call, Thesus called me and told me something was wrong; something was mentally wrong with him. He was seeing everything with a blurred, distorted picture. By the time I arrived at his room, he had hallucinated and was on the floor, crying, yelling he was crazy, that his sister was right, and all the pressure and paranoia had driven him mad.

My first reaction was to call a doctor, but he replied, "No, I won't go. Maybe someone wants me committed or in a hospital." At the time neither of us understood the full implications of his statement, but I obeyed his request.

"Come on; let's leave. Come to my place."

Without questioning and completely pliable, he began to take my instructions submissively. I told him what to wear, what to bring. While dressing, I realized for the first time how much weight he had lost. He was talking to himself and in a slight delirium. On the front steps as we were leaving, a man approached us, showed us some official government ID and asked if Thesus was home. Our hero stood silently, and I said, "No, he just left," and we walked past him.

Undoubtedly it was some type of drug; someone had "found" him again, and I told him just to be calm and patient; "If it is a drug, all you need to do is wait eight to ten hours and it should wear off." I made him eat and go for a walk with me along the ocean in front of Golden Gate Park.

We walked for over three hours. I questioned him about the people in his apartment, and within six more hours he was "down," but he remained somewhat paranoid, even to the extent that I thought that he thought that I might have had something to do with his problems. When he asked who wanted control over him, I think he was questioning me. He directly asked if I thought Ike had any reason to harass him. Rather than let him dwell on any of these questions, I again made him talk about the people in the house and kept him trying to recall what he had eaten.

"When I first moved into the apartment, we were all eating together. Everything was fine. A vacancy occurred in one of the rooms, and this guy came to the door, told me he was a friend of a person who lived there. I had never seen him before, but I hadn't rented the room long enough to know everyone and their friends. He came in to wait. I thought he seemed awfully confused, like he'd just gotten out of an institution, but he described the horrible place where he was living in the Tenderloin district. I felt sorry for him and told him about the room for rent. He immediately left to get his stuff.

"A couple of days later when I mentioned him to his said-friend, she said she thought he was my friend. I told her that I thought he was hers. She said she had met him before but couldn't remember where.

"After a couple of weeks, one by one people kept dropping out the eating group. Within two months, lodgers began to leave. After a while everyone was eating separately and buying their own food."

"Does he work? Where does he get his money?"

"I don't know. He is weird though. I don't understand him at all. I still feel sorry for him. But I can see your point. I have to protect myself better.

"I started getting these headaches, well not headaches but a pressure point, in the frontal lobe area, not like sinus or any others I have ever experienced, but sharp flashes. Very weird, if I didn't know better I would say I was enlightened; they are right there where the third eye should be."

"Maybe he is just on drugs and wants you to experience them. But then again maybe someone is paying him, ever who was giving you shit ,....."

"You mean the 'shits,'" he laughed. Not being able to help myself, I smiled also. I guess he was 'down.'

"......at your old apartment could be influencing him. I am sure, someone has created a very good story about you, and he thinks he is doing it for the good of mankind or something stupid like that."

"Maybe someone found me through my car, then got second thoughts, because I could have sold it, and called to check. But the overriding question is who or why would anyone want to 'get at me'?"

He spent two days with me and then went back to his rented room. He wanted to find out. He checked through the belongings of the "strange new tenant" but didn't discover anything. Everyone in the house was under suspicion; he never ate anything in that house again.

We didn't tell his sister about any of this; it would have worried her. Thesus said, "All she would say is to go to a doctor or the police. What could either do? After going to underground web sites, I am starting to believe them: I am convinced many people are either being unjustly arrested and banded, in mental wards or are ending in the hospital with quick operations. I am beginning to question our authorities. And if I said something like that to sis, we would just argue again."

But actually, it was his sister who indirectly recommended a solution: after seeing where he lived, she said, "I would rather live on the ranch in Colorado than here. Go home. Or why don't you move back in with me, or move in with Ike or John?"

Later he told me, it was then when he decided to go back to the ranch for a vacation. "I'm sure," he said, "that what is happening is explainable or a series of unrelated coincidences, and a little time and distance from here might give me a different perspective or some insights."

He called Colorado and told his father he wanted

to visit. His father sent him the money for a one-way plane or an Express Train ticket, saying that Thesus could buy the return if and when.

He decided to drive and realized his father would protest and send him more money to fly if he knew.

A couple of years earlier when Thesus told everyone he was driving his truck to San Francisco, his father had given him some advice, "The roads are not safe. Stay mobile. Don't get caught in some small town with your truck in need of repair. Some of them are traps. The worse scenario would be that your SUV breaks or blows a tire while you are driving, and you are injured or worse killed."

In spite of his father's advice and problems with the truck, he was willing to take that chance and use his excess money to pay some debts.

Our hero had planned to be on the ranch three hours before his father would have sent a ranch-hand to retrieve him from the airport. But, of course, his truck did have a minor breakdown in Nevada. It didn't seem bad, and as the events evolved, he was only two hours late, an hour before his plane.

Within fifteen minutes of his arrival, Thesus' younger sister, Jenny, called Margery, "Someone has poisoned the well. Father and mother are in the hospital. Father is critical. Get here, quickly."

I drove her to the airport and followed two days later. On the plane after a good stiff drink, a double, I thought about all that had happened. It seemed to me impossible that all these events could be a systematic single effort of one person or even one organization, but maybe Thesus was the type of person who attracted abuse. Always one or more persons would, out of jealousy or just sheer spite ..... would try to knock him off his "high" horse. Even some, I can believe, would say something like: "We'll give him something to think about for a while," or "He needs a little more challenge; he's too smart for his own good," and then deliberately try to knock Thesus off kilter. This is not all supposition because I remember a young lady in a party point to Thesus and say to one of her friends, "See that cocky son-of-a-bitch, I'm going to make him love me, make him crawl on his hands to me, then.... Well, we'll see." I only thought "wow" at the time, lucky man. We were all somewhat drunk, and I've pretty much forgotten about it until now.

Anyway, he attracted abuse and oppression not only because he expressed his intelligence too freely but because he was too lax in his attitude: his dress and tone of voice expressed it. Other people worked too hard for what they obtained, and they resented this youth's too easily-floating-through-every-situation attitude. He did not care about the possessions which others had sacrificed to acquire. He never seemed to struggle, but received at will all he wanted.

Also most people knew that Thesus wouldn't strike back. He was involved with himself and his ideas, not with what others said or did. In fact, I could see that people thought he didn't care about anything but himself. Most aren't on a philosophical level; it was only on this field of battle where our hero sought to win.

Not to be too redundant: it is true, he didn't care much about most things. He didn't worry about his image, and because he didn't care, he looked a little eccentric. And yes, every accomplishment came too easily for him. His flow of ideas intimidated many. The speed of problem solving at first astonished others then because he was so flippant, it made them mad. All of this caused him to attract abuse even from strangers. And I realize that probably many, many reasons are given to rationalize "their" actions.

People will find the damnedest reasons for hurting each other: I'm right and you're wrong; I am a true believer and you are a heretic; I am more important than you; I have greater cause. Ego and inflicting pain and suffering seem to go hand-and-hand.

But then again, maybe it's fate. Poison in the well? And he wasn't even home. Someone could have been expected him home, maybe, sooner than his arrival. No, too much has happened not to make the connection.

Manipulation and oppression seem to be his lot in life, his cross to bear. We each have our handicaps; none can escape them, and his is society's reaction to who he is. He's too smart and in my opinion, too physically beautiful, too good, too....... an extreme. The herd abolishes everything not in its image; it tries to destroy its extremes, its deformities.

Individuals still act on basic urges, a primal level. Then from his perspective, I'm sure he felt he was different, sensed something strange, intuitively had knowledge of people's reactions to him, but maybe not. It was something I thought I would ask him when I landed, but in the meanwhile I had another drink and relaxed for a while by sleeping.

Chapter 8

The situation at the ranch was terrible. Our hero's father was dead; his mother was recovering in the hospital. His youngest sister and her husband were trying to perform the duties on both ranches. Livestock was dead or sick for miles around. Thesus' mother thought that finally the animosity in the town had exploded. "I knew they would try to get even," she murmured, but as Thesus said, "Her thinking is not right. She is delirious."

The immediate response was that it was nature caused, that the underground flowing water had uncovered a pocket of poison. This hypothesis was dismissed when a derivative of arsenic, not found in nature, was discovered in a pump-fed pond near the house. Its potency was enough to kill cattle.

The first order of business was to draw the well and test for the poison until it was eliminated, then bury the dead livestock.

The father's funeral was the day I arrived. He was dead and nothing could be done about that. So what could be done, had to be done: rounding up livestock that was unaffected, reducing the herds. "Driving the best of the breeding stock" over to the sister's ranch occupied the morning before the service. Thesus and the rest of the family participated.

From what I gathered, it seems that the well was part of an underground river that was connected to many people's wells. Ranches as far away as fifteen, twenty miles were affected. Humans and livestock in the direct vicinity were suffering the most. Almost everyone was slightly sick: nauseous, like a stomach flu with headaches. Although nobody else died, everyone had a story to tell. Good drinking water had to be supplied by trucks.

All day people came and went in condolence, bringing food, whisky, and flowers. Many removed their "Sunday best" and helped with the chores. As many as thirty to forty people were at the ranch at a single time. The delayed wake in the late afternoon was filled with anger and speculation. In farming and ranching communities, water is sacred. Each person had a different idea and attitude about what had happened. The common consensus was that whoever did this horrible deed was either crazy or not a local person for "all the folks around here" knew about the underground river and the effects of poisoning it. It must have been someone from "The Captain's" past. Of course, everyone agreed that whoever it was had directed the poisoning at Thesus' father or at his property, but even the father's enemies thought this was "the doings" of the lowest of low. "He had to be sick in the head." Some speculated that the government had "screwed-up" again, as they had done in Nevada." I guess these people were referring to some secret experiments, where cattle and sheep had died. It was our hero who considered the possibility of it being a natural occurrence, a release of a pocket of natural poison which the underground river had worn away. But as mentioned, tests disproved this theory, for the poison was a non-natural arsenic: something new.

A kind of funny consequence, sometime a little later, I heard a private song, a folk song as was, from an ex-student which started: "It must have been an arse with a bottle of arsenic, of course, which made The Captain a corpse." I had returned as a friend of the family's but to others as a local, so I heard a great many stories which, I'm sure, Thesus didn't. Some of the students who I taught and who were still in the area were either running their own spreads or had been hired out as ranch hands. It was these ex-students who considered me a local.

Later one of the rumors, which to me seemed the most substantial and was never disproven, mentioned a salesman who checked into the motel in town but then never made any contacts. The sheriff checked all the rumors, and this one led to a dead end. It was a fictitious name and home address. This man had rented a car in Denver using the same name and had driven out one evening and returned the car a day later. A decent description was given by the clerk, which was in turn relayed to the surrounding authorities, but no responses. This theory and these facts confirmed suspicions about the "stranger from the outside world."

And for me an interesting phenomenon was that for the first time, these local folks discussed Thesus' family as if they were part of the community. Upon hearing this, I just thought, at what a price.

For a while, it was questionable whether his mother would survive. Both of his parents were in their late sixties, and the final effect on his mother was a borderline case of insanity and senility. Now, two members of the family needed special care: the mother and the youngest brother. Thesus' youngest brother was mentally retarded. He had improved over the years but still couldn't reason very well. He could and did manual labor when told exactly what to do, but that was pretty much it. He had been spared the poisoning by having been away for three days doing some work for a near-by rancher. He was, of course, home when I arrived but I think he couldn't fully grasp the situation.

He knew that his father was dead and his mother was in the hospital, but he couldn't comprehend that it was the evil doing of someone. Although he was considered strange and because of that a suspect....... maybe the word "strange" does not really reflect the locals' feelings about him, "unpredictable" is a better word because his behavior was erratic, and because of that, for a while suspicion rested on him. It was thought that he had unknowingly, accidently, dropped pesticide or insecticide in the well but since he didn't drive a car, and the distance to the ranch where he had spent the three days was too far to walk in eight hours, much less accounting for the return, nobody seriously retained this idea.

I, who had not had much contact with him, considered him basically a good person. The local community accepted him and even accommodated his educational needs. His parents had accomplished a great feat in rearing him in the way they had, but even at our first meeting, I detected his retarded intelligence. Because the family had never treated him as such, in fact never ever mentioned his condition, I think had a great deal to do with his abilities and self-concept. He knew he wasn't intelligent as most people but considered himself a farm hand and a good worker. I'm sure he thought other people considered him as he did himself.

Our hero's sister's husband took control of the ranch. It was he who directed Thesus's youngest brother in the duties of rounding up the cattle and other livestock, getting fresh water for them from a canal which ran through the county, building a pond for the water, irrigating the crops, etc. As I mentioned the drinking water had to be trucked in from town, and a storage tank for water had to be built and filled.

It was probably good that the family had to work so hard to keep the ranch running; it kept their minds from the disaster which had occurred, not only the death but the fear. The family, as a unit, adapted to the situation in the best possible manner. Only at the funeral did I see anyone cry or feel sorry for herself. But they all pitched in and helped each other. The tragedy had brought the family together: they worked as a unit, made decisions as a unit and maybe for the first time felt like a clan.

In this revision of this manuscript, my last statement stops me. It is not a true account nor is it false. The complexities of a family "unit" are so much more complicated than a single statement. Of course, the parents always felt the closeness to their children. But with the children's age differences, diversity of interests, and discrepancy of intelligence, they each did not share the same intensity of love from their parents. Thesus' reaction to the whole situation is noted in his statement after the funeral. His objective and philosophical statement even disquieted me. Suppressed sorrow?

"Tragedies such as these bring people together, not only because of sharing a common grief but because they make us aware of our common destinies. Reality awakens humans and humbles us. We again see our life with a perspective, a glimpse of the inevitable. We see ourselves as we are transient beings in a transient world: A realization that friends and enemies alike exist for a moment in the flux and then disappear into oblivion. A new feeling for humanity is sometimes awakened. Why shouldn't we help the passing stranger as we would help our brother? For with this direct confrontation with death, we all are brothers; we all see and know each other for an instant and then are gone; we all know and see each other and ourselves basically caught in the trap of mortality. But then how much does one think of matters like this-- a moment of silence at the cemetery after the last prayer and before departure? The instant of throwing a bit of dirt onto the coffin? If this perspective, an awareness of this knowledge, were constant in mankind, think of how human beings would be elevated in their direction, their purpose, and their actions. But life flows on, and human's awareness, and human's perspectives change. The actions in a day distract, ambitions take precedent, survival on the most mundane levels is sought and humans become pitiful and poor."

*   *   *   *

I have been negligent in telling of my story. I should have first told the reader about Thesus's family as background, and I can see the necessity of still relating this information, but I think I will wait until a more appropriate place and further the direction I have already taken, bringing the reader to the present situation of our hero: in other words, just tell the part of the story directly related to our hero and all the events which led up to how he became who he is.

Two weeks passed before normalcy returned. Margery had taken her vacation-time from work, felt she had contributed what she could, and did not want delve into her sick leave, so she prepared for her departure. Their mother had recovered sufficiently to come home. A retired nurse became a live-in house keeper, including watching Thesus' younger brother. Another person was hired to cook and help with the cleaning. Before the poisoning, the ranch had five permanent hands. After selling the herds only two employees were retained, the foreman and another. The youngest brother remained around the house and began working full time. The younger sister and her husband returned to their ranch with full intention to oversee the daily duties.

Our hero was, of course, not in a hurry to return, for no job awaited him, but his "mind was made up,"

133

he would eventually leave. He felt an obligation to stay, take care of his mother, and work the ranch, but yet a larger self-assigned commission loomed in his mind. When his mother was well enough to understand her son, he used to go to her room and undoubtedly try to explain the larger obligation. I am sure it had something to do with the harassment he had received in San Francisco. But when he could see that she couldn't understand with the limited information which he knew and which he could safely tell her without raising her fears, then he just explained that he had unfinished business to which he had to attend, that he really didn't know much about running the ranch, and if it couldn't be run correctly, maybe they should sell some of it, but he would leave that responsibility to his brother-in-law. His sister's and brother's-in-law ranch at one time was part of the father's spread: a wedding present. The father gave fifty percent for their ranch as did the father-in-law. Thesus knew that his brother-in-law would probably not sell but just incorporate more land into his own and maybe sell some of the outer reaches to the adjacent farms.

I know some business transaction transpired concerning The Captain's insurance business, but that was after I left. I am sure that our hero conducted the transfer of territory and/or sell-of-clients, but maybe as the reader can tell, I know very little to nothing of this.

After another week of discussions, I was told that Thesus had made a promise to his mother to return to the ranch when his "unfinished business was completed." The way he explained the unfinished business to me was that if he stayed on the farm the rest of his life, he would "never truly find out what was happening." He was needed to run the ranch, which frightened him because he couldn't see his life devoted to it. He lowered his voice when he said, "Maybe that is what some people want for me, to stay home, to isolate me, to make me give-up," and he wasn't "about to be pushed." His pursuit for some explanations was too important. If after college, he was without direction or focus, these incidents and unexplainables gave him a mission.

During my stay a very important incident occurred which changed Thesus' life. It was the return of Adrian, our hero's high school buddy. He arrived and explained, at once, that he had heard of our hero's father's death and came to pay his respects and give condolences. Adrian's return was about one week after the funeral, and I was preparing my return to San Francisco. Our hero and I were sitting on the steps of the front porch when we saw the rooster tail of dust on the county road cease and minutes later a brand new, fancy car cruised up the lane, and a young business man stepped from the Cadillac. Both Thesus and I thought it was a business associate of the father's. Our hero was the first to recognize him. I didn't fully until he began to speak.

He wasn't the weak emaciated boy I had once known, but was strong and healthy with a tanned face. It was obvious he participated in some sports and probably played two or three times a week. He was well dressed with a tailored suit, befitting-cut trench coat, and an attaché case. It was his mustache which hindered my immediate recognition. After the greetings, he went into the house with our hero to pay his respects to the mother. I sat on the porch until they returned; I thought one can't really predict another person's evolution, ... then I laughed, ...much less know how one's self will turn out.

By the time both of them resumed their conversation on the porch, they were relating to each other as if no time or distance had separated them. Our hero was verbalizing as they neared the front screen door, then as they walked onto the porch, he said, ".........yes, I have thought about those two, but when I think of our High School days, I remember those discussions about God. Since that time I have thought a great deal about you and those discussions mainly because my beliefs are still unresolved. I know there are forces greater than me and greater than all humans put together, but I don't know the role those forces play nor my own role. I found myself appealing to some greater force to secure justice as far as the tragedies that my family and I have endured, but I couldn't tell you what forces.

"Will your mother ever fully recover?" Adrian, asked.

"She is too old. Even if she hadn't drunk some of the water, just the death of my father would have been enough to cause deterioration.

"This whole matter has caused me to try again and grasp and solve those questions which we attempted when we were younger. I have come to the conclusion that all humans deal in abstracts, immortal substances, partly out of recognition and fear of our own mortality. Everyone wants to identify or even become immortal, and they think through creating abstracts that this is possible, creating something that will outlast them. My attempt was to create an answer. I can see it was wrong; for a creation isn't necessarily the truth, unless there is no truth. So I have continued to search."

"Remember us spending a couple of weeks discussing, or were we debating," he smiled at Thesus, then me, "whether God was rational? Did we ever resolve that."

"Yes, if God exists, is It rational: a very important question because if It is not rational, then none of this needs to make any sense at all."

Adrian laughed out loud, "Somewhere in college I decided to make money. I gave up those questions after leaving school and joined a brokerage firm." He named off a series of names which neither of us recognized but knowing him, I'll bet it was top ranked. He even handed us his card and asked our hero what he was going to do with his inheritance. Thesus told him that there was none, at least for him that everything reverted to his mother. It was her money in the first place which helped buy the ranch.

Adrian then, out of politeness, or so it seemed, asked our hero what he had been doing with his life. Our hero quickly traced his history in as few words as possible and finished by saying that he was unemployed and couldn't find a job.

"A liberal arts major. You wouldn't listen. I kept telling you, business or math. Even science would

137

have been better than liberal arts. Give me a year or two, and I'll be in the position to hire you."

Both of them smiled. We three sat: those two on the porch swing and I on the steps. The newly hired cook graciously supplied us with lemonade. A warm feeling of comradeship existed as we three began to discuss what happened to whom, who married whom and just the general gossip, not only local but national. We three had a good laugh about events.

After a couple of hours Adrian stood to leave; he was hesitant about something. We anticipated his departure so we both stood. He paused, about to say something, but then without a word, turned and walked toward his car. We followed, but before using the key, he stopped. Still facing the car he said, "There is a responsibility to friendship that is greater than ..... He paused again, then turned and faced us.

"Something.......I must tell you. About two weeks ago, a man approached me and showed me government credentials. I, of course before complying, checked them the best way I could, by calling a number he gave, and they seemed authentic. He asked me if I wanted to serve my country, and in the same breath alluded to the fact that I had not been in the services and that I still had a duty to fulfill.

"His credentials were either Army or Air Force; obviously it was a branch of military intelligence of some type: secret service, but to me, it was just an acronym. He was a field representative; Mark Alberston was his name; I can't even give you an official title ..... but anyway.... my "so-called duty"

138

was to check on you. I asked why. He told me that you were involved in questionable activities, and the government wanted more information: What you were doing; what you were going to do; who were your friends, and as strange as it seems, do you hold any grudges against the government; have you started any political groups and joined any. If you disclosed you were involved, I was expected to indicate an interest and get information about the groups.

"As you can tell, I took the job. I thought it was better me than someone else, and I did it because I wanted to see you again and find out for myself if any of this is true. Also it was a good excuse for me to come home.

"But I don't see it. It doesn't make any sense, are you subversive? From our discussions, it sounds as if you are a conservative; you defended our country beyond what I would have,".... After his pause he asked, "What do you make of this?"

"I have no political affiliations at all. The only time I was involved, in any way, was in college, but that seems like eons ago. I barely have any friends. As I told you, I was working for the Park Service; ever who this Alberston guy is, ... all he had to do was check with my supervisor." Our hero slowly shook his head negatively when he said, "Why should I hold a grudge against the government?"

"Maybe it was college. I realized early that the schools give a certificate of accomplishment for completion, but at the same time they communicate to the authorities who control some aspects of our lives....... But this may have been a foul-up."

Thesus responded, "I always thought, or thought I knew, that it is a matter of categorization. Job inquiries always ask for transcripts. But I always thought it was just a societial categorization, a determining who completed what, who worked hard and wanted............"

Adrian's interruption put an end to Thesus' verbal contemplation: "I don't know, but your opinion about the government was definitely one of the questions he asked me to ask.

"This is what I will say; I will tell them you have a healthy skepticism of the government, that you almost never give the country a thought unless it is facing some disaster and that you would volunteer to help. I couldn't really tell them you are a "right-wing" conservative, (he laughed and winked at me) because they might interpret my statement as you are a reactionary. I am going to put you in the middle so no more questions will be raised."

Our hero slowly nodded his head in affirmation, with a pensive, almost quizzical expression.

Adrian continued, "Telling you this has relieved me of a great deal of pressure. Then again, I really can't remember if he told me not to tell you." Again he smiled and winked at me. "He should have known that I would never evaluate someone and report it without telling that person my evaluation to see if he thought it is just. Am I being just?"

Thesus' nod gave Adrian reassurance that his evaluation was correct, and so Thesus said, "Isn't this weird? Even in college and more so now, I would have described myself as patriotic; I believe in our country and for what it stands. I believe, respect, and abide by The Declaration of Independence and The Constitution. If fact I am in awe of the Founding Fathers. I don't even think I have broken the laws of the land. Where would anyone get the idea that I was a subversive? The most I have ever done is to test my rights. I haven't ever even done that to the extreme."

"The trouble with you is that you still have your head in the clouds. You are still contemplating the existence of God, thinking about what you call abstract problems while the world is going on around you with different motives. There is a real world out there. You know which one I am talking about, don't you?" He gave our hero a little friendly push which was just enough to make our hero stumble backwards; then he smiled.

"I really wasn't shocked that someone approached me and asked me to do an investigation. I am sure this kind of thing happens all the time. I am sure they investigated me before approaching me. It was better that I investigated you than someone else. Right?"

"Right," answered our hero. "You know in my search for justice I have just finished reading the Old Testament, and I remember a place where it said that in the house of your best friend, you would get your worse scars. I am happy it was you. I am happy you told me, and I feel that you are a greater friend now than ever before." He gave Adrian a deepening glance and reached out and touched his shoulder.

"Then you will recover from the wound I have dealt you?"

"You have touched a deep part of my being." Thesus' hand was still on Adrian's shoulder.

"Truth and honesty were values we sought in our youth; our search then and still mine now.

"Back then," our hero turned to me, "all our abstract arguments never turned into Sophism. We always stuck looking for the truth. Our discussion rarely ever degenerated into arguments, just for the sake of arguing. We never tried to argue each other down. "

"Yes you are right," said Adrian. "I may not think about those thoughts, but I respected who I was when we contemplated so heavy a subjects; (he winked at me then turned to our hero) I respected you, maybe even too much, even though you used to throw me into a turmoil with your damned questions. I can still see those same qualities in you as I did back then: a lot of consistency in your pursuits. Though I don't walk the same path as you anymore, and don't want to walk it, I still believe in the path and can wish you well in your pursuits. God only knows if you will come up with anything....But don't give up. Keep up your struggle.

"I want to visit my family before going back to work. If you get into my neighborhood, look me up. You have my card. Nice seeing you again, Mr. Jacoby." We shook hands, and he smiled at our hero again, paused as if remembering something, then abruptly turned and briskly entered his car and drove off.

Our hero and I sat for a couple of hours discussing what it meant to be investigated. Why was he being investigated? It was then that I told him about his IQ and the note not to tell him or his family. I was surprised he hadn't guessed it, but he wasn't shocked or surprised. He just assimilated it and didn't say anything. We sat for fifteen or twenty minutes not saying a word. Then he broke the silence, "But why the services?"

"Why didn't you go in?"

"It may have been because my name never came around in the lottery again because so many others joined from this county or maybe it had something to do with my father. I really don't know. It could have been just fate. Why, do you think the two events are connected in some way?"

"I can't tell. Maybe I can do some checking. See if you can access your High School computer banks and see what's in there. Harvey might still be working in the files at school."

"I'll see if I can check my college files. But I have such a low security rating on The Net, I couldn't even get a decent paying job when I was in college"

"Or a job worth your while. Yes, you should have been establishing your security clearance so you could access The System; in the same way, you should have established financial credit with credit cards, so you could access the financial institutions."

"It's too bad I don't know any of my father's friends from the service well enough to approach them. I must have a file from working for the government and from being a dependent to service personnel. Maybe these files contain answers."

What were a series of seemingly disconnected

events now jelled into a maze of confusion in his mind. How could this happen? Why? Possibilities upon possibilities began to plague and enclose him. Was there a pattern behind these occurrences? Some of the occurrences? Which ones? Or was there a connection among all the events? His harassment and his father's death? How could that be? He began to see and understand the labyrinth which surrounded him. But what controlled his destiny? A Minotaur trying to trap and devour him? Or did the rulers and bureaucracies build a system which is now out of their control, why... to protect themselves? If it is an organization like the services, are his rights being violated? And in his mind on the abstract level with which he views his world: is it possible to control one's destiny, become the master of one's fate, obviously not, but to what degree do we and don't we? "To know this is to have our maximum freedom." Then he continued and said something which didn't make sense to me at the time. I dismissed it because I don't think I was supposed to hear it. And in fact, I don't think anyone, but he, was meant to hear it. "If someone is trying to manipulate my being, is it fate or destiny? Was my pray answered, and I am a servant of God? Maybe, I have been chosen as I expected when I was younger and this is the message ...... how God is speaking to me? If any of this is true, can I back out now or has my destiny been arranged?" A strange laughed erupted.

Undoubtedly some suppressed guilt erupted in my mind: I was angry and slightly frightened. Had I been an inadvertent Pawn? Was I still? I decided to venture from my fear and investigate. I went to the administration of Thesus' junior and senior high. Harvey wasn't there anymore, so I went to the principal to get approval. He was another man I didn't know. I explained that I had taught in this district and thought a mistake was present in the records concerning one of my former students, and I would like to check them. He said it was impossible, that as a teacher, I should be able to see that records should not and could not be available to the public without a court order.

"What type of mistake was it?"

"I may have incorrectly evaluated or stated something that could be misinterpreted."

I explained that the mistake, if it were a mistake, might have been created by me and wouldn't be corrected unless I did it. Also, maybe another teacher might have misevaluated Thesus, and Thesus should be able to challenge it. I was on my way back to San Francisco and didn't have time to run it through the courts.

"It isn't public domain. It belongs to the authorities."

"What if I send my ex-student to see ...."

"The new law requires him to get a court order also. Just understand my position: I don't have any control of the records; they belong to the authorities; we just keep them. Even if your student-friend gets an order, it may not do him any good."

"You're probably right. What would be in his records at this level?" But the principal's statement was more subtle and not understood until later.

Instead of pursuing this path, both our hero and I drove to Boulder to view those records. Seemingly there was no resistance.

"Fill these forms and return in three days."

Repeating the trip, we found nothing important in his files, not even a statement about his IQ, his arrest, his lack of cooperation in the psychology "tests," just school transcripts.

"My arrest should have been contained because it was a legal action; it appeared in the newspaper, and I had to go before the Dean of Students to plead my case. Maybe two different files exist: an academic which we've seen and a personal. How would we get the latter?"

"In those three days, someone could have pulled all information which would have incriminated both you and the institution."

"I suppose so. How could I find out though? Look ...... maybe my paranoia is affecting us both. Maybe we've seen my college records; maybe we should be searching the governments' records?"

"Wouldn't this happen....... O.K., maybe it is paranoia, but what would prevent the records from being changed once "they" knew you wanted them. If you were a big organization and petitioned, I'm sure the records could be frozen, but an individual, what chance does his petition have, or of him really seeing his records?"

"Isn't it called 'The Freedom of Information Act'? But before I do something premature or stupid, I am going to research it, find the correct manner to approach it, get the right legal documents, create some safe-guards against changing the records and make sure I see the ones I want, the ones which are affecting me in this adverse way.

"On the way back home, I will stop in the Salt Lake City library and anonymously begin."

"So you are definitely coming back to the Bay area? You would be safer here on the ranch. But I understand your need for action. Can you think of anything I can do to help?"

When he answered no, I mentioned I was impatient to return for many reasons. He not only offered to drive me to the airport near Denver, but would buy me a ticket with the ranch's corporate funds. I thought of objecting then thought it would be dumb. I don't have a job or any money either.

Two days later during the drive, I thanked him for the money; he even added some for drinks. He told me it was nothing but a written-off business expense, a drop in a bucket. He was momentarily silent and then he began again, "If someone in San Francisco is playing around with my food and is trying to control me in any way, it is sick to try. I wonder if what "they" have done would have a permanent effect.... or if it already has. What could be the motives? What organization has categorized me? And why? Death is a serious business. This isn't just hazing; it may be a life and death struggle, for what? About what?"

Since I had heard this so many times, I knew responding would add nothing. And in ten minutes, his thoughts verbalized again.

"So someone or some organization thinks I am

extremely intelligent and am a subversive. If so, how much hindrance can "they" legally exert without infringing upon my freedoms? How much control, knowledge, and power should, ... does, ... or can an agency have over an individual legally, morally, or ethically? How can I find out how much "they" have illegally accomplished? If ..... not if but when, I discover the illegality would a lawsuit do any good? Would it be possible?" His voice drifted off into a mumble. Then "Could my father's death be related to my problems?

"Why am I a threat? What do they think I can do......... will do?"

Chapter 9

The next time we met, three weeks later, at four in the morning, it was at the San Francisco bus depot. He had called me because he didn't have any money to take a taxi home. It was so early in the morning that it didn't occur to me to ask him how he got to the bus depot without his car. But when I picked him up he explained the whole mess.

"I was up early and had said my good-byes the night before. My truck was packed except for my overnight bag. Walking through the kitchen I found a loaf of home-made bread with a computer written note saying, 'Have a good trip.' I fixed my breakfast and left. I stopped on the top of Rabbit Ears Pass for lunch. The bread was great. It was more like cake, with dried fruit. I ate almost a third, then drove for what seemed like days until I saw a hitchhiker. The sun wasn't even beginning to set, and I was tired and sleepy so I stopped for him. Picking him up revived me; we talked and shared a joint, and I drove for a couple more hours; then I let him drive. We didn't stop for dinner. He had some food which he shared with me, and we ate the rest of the bread. I could not hold my head up and went to sleep in the back. At two in the morning, he drove off the road. I felt us go onto the soft shoulder as if in a dream but regrettably it wasn't a dream. I tried to lift my head and couldn't. I just relaxed back into my sleep, but at this time it wasn't sleep. When I came to, the car was upside down. A trucker who had seen my SUV jeep on its side had stopped. A Dodge van, which had stopped, was driving off. I felt terrible. Neither of us was hurt seriously. He had nothing wrong with him, not even a scratch. I only had a busted lip and a knock on the head. This was the hitchhiker's story. I couldn't tell you a thing about what happened. 'It was a miracle.' We had gone off the road at seventy or eighty miles an hour, rolled over at least once, if not twice. He said he couldn't keep awake but didn't want to stop. 'It came on so suddenly. I had no idea that the truck could go off the road. I felt the wheel jerk as we went off, I awakened and quickly tried getting us back on the road; that is when we flipped.' He said he was sorry about ten times, and I told him if he wanted to do me a favor he wouldn't say it again. I was so tired that I couldn't stand it. Not even the accident awakened me. Looking off the road into a severe darkness, I thought of my father. He had told me to buy a computerized

Road Tracer. Even for my old jeep, it would have only been one thousand five hundred, and we wouldn't or couldn't have gone off the road.

Another truck had stopped with two drivers. All four of them rocked the jeep until it was back on its wheels. My eyes kept closing; so tired, I couldn't even help put the truck back on its wheels. After it was on all fours, I crawled into the back window, which was knocked out and laying on the side of the road in one piece, and I went to sleep.

"The next morning, I had a terrible headache: the worst hangover I have ever had. A State Patrolman awakened both the hitchhiker and me. The hitchhiker was in a sleeping bag in the ditch. The patrolman asked if it were my truck. We discussed what had happened. He took both of us into a Nevada town to fill out a report. Afterwards I walked through the town which consisted of eight gas stations, two garages, two motels and two cafes. First I went back and forth between tow places and found the lowest price for getting it brought into town. After getting it towed which took most of the morning, I had three hours to sell it or pay for storage. What a rip-off! I almost had to sell because it would cost more than it was worth to tow it out of this town, and they said they couldn't fix it there. The tow place offered me the price of the tow. I wasn't going to let that happen so I walked up and down the town and told everyone I met that there was going to be an auction at three o'clock. Only four people showed up. The man who bought it was a patrolman from the weigh station in town. I swore I had seen that guy before but couldn't remember where. It was like the whole event was a dream. He bought it because I think he didn't think I had the money to get to San Francisco. He paid me the price of the tow and the price of the ticket to San Francisco. I went with him to get the money out of his Dodge Van. It was filled with all kinds of electrical equipment. He had the money in a safe welded to the floor. As I was walking away, I had another Deja Vu experience. When I told the hitchhiker, who had been with me this whole time, I had the money for a bus, he said he was going to hitch a ride out of town He shook my hand and then the hand of the man who bought my truck and left. I thanked the patrolman for buying it even though I thought he had gotten a too good a deal. The engine was still good; I had started it, only the front axle was busted.

"The whole incident could have been worse. I could have been badly hurt or killed. Nobody could have bought my truck, and I would have had to wire home for money; my mother would have found out and worried to death ..... maybe literally. All kinds of bad things could have happened.

"The only nasty thing is my back. I noticed a sharp pain sometimes when I sat a certain way in the bus. Now, it is just a dull pain, like an infection.

And of course, I don't have a vehicle to get around in anymore."

He went to sleep for about five hours, got up, and had me look at his back. I was a swollen dot the size of an aspirin. Yes, it was a slight infection, about four inches below his shoulder blades, on his spinal cord.

Maybe it was a spider bite. It didn't look that bad so I told him it would undoubtedly go away. A couple of days later, he decided he had better go to a doctor. He rode the trolley, and because of a lack of funds went to the University Medical Center. At the clinic a series of people who looked at his back had a conference, then told him nothing was wrong. He told them that he thought he could feel an object in the middle of his back, especially when he leaned back in a chair. "Why don't you take an X ray?"

"No need, we know it's all right."

After the frustration of this attempt, he decided to find a private doctor who would at least X ray it. He called a downtown Medical Building and asked for a referral. A switch board operator directed the call, and our hero explained his situation, and received an appointment.

The next morning he entered the building at ten o'clock and asked for the doctor to whom he was referred. He was kept waiting then told that the doctor would not be in and was directed to another. The information desk gave him directions to the thirteenth floor. As he was telling me the story later in the central park surrounded by large buildings, he said something strange; he said he checked the time entering, and compared it with time he came out. He must have suspected foul play..... I don't know.... maybe some type of hypnosis, or drugs, or something..... what?

After questioning Thesus, the doctor took a scalpel and ran it across our hero's back, Thesus said, "to see if any part of it was protruding."

"Does it hurt all the time?"

"No, just when I sit back on it the wrong way."

"It's sloppy .... I mean slightly infested. It's like a bad pimple. Here, some disinfectant and a bandage should do. I could make it better or worse, so I'm not going to touch it, and you had better not either.

"Can you take some advice." the doctor continued.

"Yes, sure."

"You are a leader. Don't ruin it. Keep your nose clean, stay out of places you don't belong. Just let things happen, and it will come to you. And for God's sake, don't do anything you will regret."

Our hero told me he kept his composure until he walked into the elevator. When more than the floor seemed to dropped from under him, he knew he turned ash white and almost fainted. He was nauseated and just about unconscious as he made his way to the lobby door. The fresh air rejuvenated him, and his mind began to race: thirteenth floor? the scalpel, was that a possible threat if he didn't cooperate? Then he remembered the women at the information desk who nodded to each other, almost in agreement, before recommending this doctor.

He briskly walked around the block and called me, asking me to meet him in Union Square Park. After relating this incident to me, his questions exploded, "Is this my fate? Ear marked, sitting outside, waiting for what, unable to either walk away or enter? Are the authorities afraid of me, or as the doctor implied, are they saving me for a certain job? Is it because I quit my park job without notice and now they need another way to track me? Still is this an individual, or individuals, or it is just some impersonal system, protecting itself, breeding its controllers, categorizing its members through tests, selecting what they consider the best? Conditioning the selected? Why me? Has some god determined that I get caught in this trap? Don't I, or anyone for that matter, have some say about who we are, what we want to become, or who we actually become?"

"Whoa Steamboat, slow down," I laughed. "Aren't you over reacting?"

He ignored me and my statement.

"Maybe the human made systems which were created to control life and nature, now control mankind. Yes, maybe at first the system was a tool in people's hands but now the human-made systems control. The fault lies in that a non-human element is controlling humans, for I can't imagine a human being playing the role of God. Yes, maybe there is a computer someplace and people just follow its instructions." He laughed. "That would make my situation and me a causality of a technocratic dictatorship, a product of faulty automation. I would rather believe this than someone is at the back of all this,............" he laughed, "on my back."

Maybe he has a concussion. I reached out and took his arm, but he pulled away.

"Maybe if I weren't dependent upon the system, the system wouldn't in turn affect me ... as much. But then again what aren't systems? We are; nature is; the Universe is. Our fate will always rest in the systems upon which we are dependent. But maybe

I could just break-out of the human-made ones: the bureaucracies, the corporations, the unions, the technocracies, the governments, all those systems which I question whether anyone really controls. I can imagine some of them have not only grown greater than the people who try to control them but have grown greater than the countries in which they exist. Maybe they grow organically and have become functioning entities in themselves. It may have been people's greed which has been the breeding ground for these monsters. Could it be that those corporations, governments, etc. have become the god of the individuals who work for those systems? The people working for the systems follow the instructions or follow what is best for those systems without concern for humanity."

"I may see what you are saying. You mean like lawyers and judges carrying out "the letter of the law" irrespective of justice?"

"Yes, something like that, but then even more, maybe those systems have an organic life of their own and the men working in those systems think they have control because they make money and gain power through them. The systems, may not consciously, oh no, but the systems raise those who are willing to keep the systems alive and functioning: that is how an organism works. If it needs an inhuman being to destroy a human element, it will raise that being to power for its own continuance ...."

"You mean 'reared'?"

He thought for a moment, "No, I mean 'raised,'" he said impatiently. "We have become so dependent on our technology that it controls us: the way we think and who we are, our self-identities.

"I had lost my train of thought. But yes even with the example that we become who we project over the Net. And yet, pigeon holing ourselves in a medium, limits us. We are more than who we project, but some people believe and want to believe these created images.

"No, I lost it; let me think." His voice faded off as he said, "We are so dependent on it to keep us all alive that we have ceased to live. We want to control and are controlled."

His conversation, as sometimes in his youth, ceased being any type of discussion where I could have said anything and just became a probing, monotone monologue, which revealed his thoughts just to himself. But this harangue was more disorganized repetitious, and somewhat frantic.

"I've accepted where I am and the progress I can make. I have strived to make it better. This is all any person can do..... Are we all trapped in some type of institution or other? Yes, for sure, and there are those who struggle to make it better, and there are those who accept it as it is. I see the need for systems, for they kept the multitudes alive, but wouldn't or don't many people accept any institution which feeds and clothes them? How much would they, and do they, sacrifice for this security? If any of my perceptions are true, should I just lay-low, try to forget it, or try to change it? Yes, change it for all those who are dependent upon it? Or I could just build my world within, a better world. I am sure this is possible for I have been living within my own world already."

I laughed, then he saw the humor in his statement, smiled, but continued in all seriousness.

"I am a small minority within the system. Should I endanger the majority's position to change to what I think is right? It seems to be true that institutions do not change as quickly as the need for them to change ..... but to disrupt an institution, other human's security, could it result in disaster? What I think I am saying is that I have accepted the need for the systems and institutions but yet, I see the need to create a world with freedom using those systems again, not being used by them.

"But maybe I am jumping to conclusions, and this isn't the problem, the main problem."

"Yes, exactly my feelings," I interrupted, but again he dismissed me.

"I am lost in the gray area between illusions, my own fears, and reality. I am earmarked, but for what reason? Where should I begin to find out? The FBI? The Freedom of Information Act? I am definitely, still going to do that. But it would still be another organization, maybe another thirteenth floor; this time maybe get scalped," he chuckled cynically; I didn't even smile, "lobotomies are in fashion this year. But really, who could I turn to discover what exactly is happening in this country? If only one fact could be confirmed or disproved, I would have some place to start."

My only reference to any of this reality was literature. I thought how inadequate and stupid I am not to be able to offer "real" facts and applicable advice. As we sat sadly silent, my mind raced. But then again, I thought in terms of myth, an innate quality in us individually and societally, a method by which we, humans, have attempted to understand the unknowable, the forces greater than us, and it was to this which he needed advice. So I spoke, reminding him of labyrinths which we all face, internally and externally. I suggested that the minotaur which controls is the Minotaur which controls us all; "I am again implying an all pervasive Destiny," I said, and then felt really trite.

"The Master of the maze..... or wait, I should become the destroyer of the Minotaur and the master of the maze? But then again, if it is a system or systems like the federal or local governments or even some organic system somewhere which controls, who is that Minotaur? Should we slay them and bring on chaos or tame them, take control of them again?

His voice began to fade as he said, "Yes, make the systems tools in human hands again, not individuals a tool in the system's hand. Make it again possible for humans to control our own destinies." (We both still may have been naïve.)

We sat for a long time without saying anything. The park had turned colder. Most of the strollers who had enjoyed the sun had left. Only an occasional passer-by was seen. Our hero sat on his hands with a blank stare on his face. "Here I am on life's park bench, permeating life's sorrows but becoming nothing. The confusion is so around me, and in me, I don't know where to begin. Could my problem be more than just a dehumanized system? Could someone be taking a direct interest in me? Could someone or something have judged me without trial and found me guilty, dangerous, mentally ill, or in some ways detrimental to society, the government, or what? Could some individual have that type of control?

"Or could this all be coincidence, a roll of the dice, fate, chance and the labyrinth is an infinite maze beyond my comprehension? Yes, could everything bad had just happened at the same time, and no connection between any two events exists: that everything that has happened and will happen, happens in an impersonal universe, without connection, without reason or purpose. Was there a just cause or even just a reason for my father's death and my mother's incapacity? Who is going to square the books, level the balance with the evil which has befallen my family?

"No, I can't just base my beliefs on hope in a God. I have to learn to protect myself against .... well, even against my own beliefs. I cannot rely on an innate Justice, for if there is, there is, but if there isn't then I must seek that justice for myself and for my family, maybe even create my own justice; ... I'm beginning to sound like Ike, or worse, a fanatic. But really, though I can't say there is no Justice, I can protect myself if there is none.

"Should humans or shouldn't humans seek justice? Maybe it is only a human created concept, and no Justice exists except for mankind. I have been reared to believe in turning the other cheek. So if there is no Justice with a capital "J," then no justice at all exists. And if I seek justice, what kind of justice could it be without an overview to deal equally," he paused and laughed cynically. "Who am I to seek and create Justice? I don't know the overall plan and purpose."

"You are right," I interjected before he laughed again. "It would take a 'leap of faith' not to seek it but to live believing in its existence. I almost interrupted you while you were talking to say you needed more church and fewer computers and games when you were younger. But I can see now, the question is deeper than that. Because many types of justice must exist: maybe even intrinsic types of Justice. In a subtle but real sense, reaping what you sow is a form of justice; types of Karma. By breaking nature's rules, or any perimeters natural or unnatural, sometimes can exact justice."

"But as I have said, I should protect myself if no ...... what? ...... a conscious Justice? .... maybe! ..... exists. I hope I find out one way or another if an innate justice exists, before I find the guilty person or organization because if I haven't by then, and I don't think justice has been or will be carried out, then I will have to make a decision. But for now, I must prepare myself for anything."

I sat and watched him for a couple of minutes. The expression on his face was not blank anymore but would change with each passing thought. He suddenly said, "No matter what is happening or where it is coming from, fate, a person, an organization, it seems the only thing I can control is me, my own being. I can take dominion of my actions and reactions. I can take charge of my beliefs and my own faith and trust in myself, and I can only but try to command what happens to me, my situation, and my future. But I must and can direct my direction, even if I can't control where it will lead me...... and if it doesn't go where I want, I can still discipline my reaction to the defeat. If I keep redirecting, I am not defeated. Even if someone or something destroys me, I am not defeated."

The lights of the city seemed to blink on one at a time. "The sun has set over the ocean," I said. He didn't acknowledge my statement. A cold breeze was blowing between the buildings, and so I crossed my arms for warmth. Couples on their way to dinners or parties began to appear walking arm and arm through the park. Our hero was oblivious to it all. My senses and feelings seemed to be at their acutest, and so must have Thesus' for in three or four minutes after his last comment, he slightly jumped and said, "You know, here's an example. With a belief in God, it becomes too easy not to accept the responsibilities, not to seek truth or justice. It is too easy not to find one's own happiness because Heaven rewards, because God knows and will render.

"If God exists and has a real, encompassing control,......

"Omniscient and Omnipotent," I interjected.

"It has control and ultimately there is nothing humankind can do. If It does not control and/or does not exist, and we act as though It does, there could be real trouble. But if mankind acts as though It does not exist, and It does then the only trouble lies where there would be a discrepancy between God's Laws and the individual's moral conduct. For I can't believe God is vain and wants or needs recognition. So if there is this discrepancy, then what will happen would depend on what kind of God controls. I believe it finally comes down to how I conduct my life, and it makes, or should make, no difference in my decisions whether I believe in God or not, or if God exists or doesn't. It comes back to my earlier statement that I should try to control my own being, and my destiny."

"'To thine own self be true'; trite but true. Is that what you are saying?" I asked.

Ignoring my statement, he continued, "But I can already see some fallacies in my statements....for one, I have not included the possibility of free will," but by this time he was mumbling to himself.

We left the park, went back to my place. He gathered his belonging, then at his request, I dropped him at his room. I mentioned that I would like a roommate, but he declined my offer by saying: "I am going to protect myself and those around me," which he did. He bought a lock for his door and stored all his food and cooking utensils in his room. He watched everyone in the apartment carefully.

His health seemed to improve. Most mornings he would rise early and leave his abode to job search. Up until a few months ago he was still doing that.

"As the situation wore on," (his words) he began to feel more and more trapped. Money began to limit his actions. His funds were desperately low. His only recourse, besides borrowing or going home, was "going on the governments' doles," unemployment insurances, food stamps .....another control of him?

162

.... another dependency, for sure....."they" would have him and his whereabouts on record. If he went home, he would be out of "harm's way," and he felt too great a pressure to do just that. As earlier with the pressure to join a service, he wouldn't budge. Also the thought that because of him his family might be endangered prevented him from further entertaining the idea of returning home.

His sister's apartment, for him, was out of the question. It would be too intense. Part of the reason was that because she didn't know the full story or because she just didn't believe or understand what was happening to him, he thought she would hinder his quest. He told me that he would take my offer over hers.

But he didn't make any of these choices. The pressure was on him: he was in a depleting system and knew it. He began to spend more and more time looking for work. Almost every position he sought, the interviewers were friendly and assured him employment, but in about a week and a half, he would receive a form letter stating something like, "It is not your qualifications which makes you ineligible. It is that so many better qualified persons, with more experience, education, and credentials applied for the position."

The unemployment rate was reported to be very high and so our hero could understand the rejections. But after one rejection notice, like the one above, he continued to see an advertisement in the paper for a couple of weeks. His suspicion began to grow, especially after he called for another interview under another name, and they gave him another interview. But what could he do?

Money and only being able to go as far as the mass transportation could take him seemed to have our hero trapped. At the beginning he felt that it was to his advantage because the mass transportation covered a very large area, but as he became poorer and poorer, it began to limit him further for it was so expensive. Finally the point came where he was eating only one meal a day and just traveling within the city limits to look for jobs. On a drug store door near where he lived, he found a sign advertising for a janitor, to which he applied and was accepted.

"Is this the final lure to a trap? Is this what is left of my choices? Is this my only alternative? Has this been my predestined fate?"

He worked at that job for two weeks until he realized that he wasn't going to get paid. The store was losing money and going out of business. He quit looking for work and just sat in his room for a few days, thinking. He only had a hundred dollars left and had to make a big decision.

When he emerged from his seclusion, this was six months ago, he was very active for days. First, he went to see his sister then came to see me.

"I have begun to change my name on all my identification. I met some people who can do it for me. I think I can again become mobile in the society by getting enough identification to get some kind of job. I am sure I can make money where a social security number isn't needed. Also I have been working on a way to get a new number with my new name. I am sure that I can completely change identities both physically and officially. The only problem remaining is my finger prints, and I am working on those," he laughed.

"I can see suppression and oppression all around me. I fear the government is taking direct control in and through population intervention, through propaganda assimilation, and through the control of the movement of peoples in the United States. I believe they now have control of the labor market in that they intentionally have created a depression to give employers the opportunity to be very selective and thereby starve the undesirables into submission. I have seen facts and figures concerning the increased rate of missing persons; and yet, the general population does nothing about it. It is only interested in themselves and in accumulating wealth. It doesn't care what is happening in the colleges and universities unless it is one of their children who is arrested or shot.

"The overreaction of the authorities is just another example of suppression. It will breed on itself. The governments can justify cutting back funds to education, 'to keep the rabble out.' The fewer people who are educated, the more powerful are the authorities, the less control they need to assert to maintain control of the uninformed. I can see the authorities play up these incidents of violence so that they can create fear, and people will give them more power and more control, but I can also see that if they frighten people too much that these people will start to react on their own, and a revolution, if it does come, will begin not from the suppressed, for they don't have any power, but from the frightened majority, the middle class, whose power is almost unlimited. This majority will think their security is threatened and will react.

"But right now, the government is forcing the population to relinquish power and control because it claims a strong subversive element exists and is growing, and this element is harming the country."

I thought where did he derive these conclusions? What has he been doing and reading? Obviously, he has hooked into The Underground Internet or some other media I haven't, but I did add, "Even I can see and hear the public political plea for 'Law and Order.'"

"'They, the powers that be, especially overtly and even covertly on T.V. and The Internet, demand a vote saying, 'Give me the power to stop the degeneration of our great country.'

"I can see all of this, but what I can't see is how much direct control they have placed on me. I have even considered that it is a completely economical system that is controlling, a monetary dictatorship that people, including myself, have been kept poor so that we could be worked by the system like asses at the discretion of the master or masters."

"I can't believe it could all be so well organized."

"It, for sure, could have an influence like that over a large number of certain categorized people through the Government Lawful Information Bureau (GLIB) which supplies, upon request, information as to the acceptability, or lack of the desirability, of individuals seeking employment. Remember my rejection letters mentioning 'credentials,' that's where they got them."

His voice was high pitched. He was so animate that he was almost not making sense. He obviously believed this was happening to him. "Are you sure about this?"

"Yes, what started out as 'credit checks and arrest queries,' now has turned into requests for certification credentials. Undoubtedly many agencies supply corporations and individual employers with information concerning a potential employee, and their numbers are growing. This system may be subsidized by the government and has become associated with a branch of the Social Security. I am now searching for that main computer which feeds all or most of agencies with information.

"Let's hope there still exists a balance of power within the governments to uncover what has happened and is happening. Constitutionally the words "privacy" and "invasion of privacy" need to be defined. Each agency needs to become more autonomous and competitive.

"You know what my worse fear is? The people not only do not govern and control the governments, but that the governments have become organic, living beings, so large and so powerful that they exert a power and will of their own. I have confirmed with various examples that the servants of the systems who conform the best reach the top positions, and in this process are conditioned to believe, think, and control with and by the policies of the system. They thereby have become tools in these organisms' clutches."

"Do you think something like that has control over you?"

"I still don't know what forces control me directly, but I know something does. Even in my reaction against being controlled, I am controlled; I have become more radical, more doubtful, more skeptical: yes Margery would say paranoid. This country is not what it is advertised itself to be.

"Yes, I will become the subversive which I have been labeled; that is, of course, if there is no other way for me to change it and seek justice.

"But now, whatever it is which is trying to control me, I have taken precautions. If that thing in my back is a honing device, a small type head band, which could be used to locate me as they do criminals, it is inoperative. As you can see, I have been doing my homework, teacher, he smiled cynically. "Today I am going to Los Angeles to live. Undoubtedly whoever it is has now realized that the beacon has been extinguished and will begin the search for me.

"My main problem is money. I need to borrow to leave town. I am going to hitch hike. If nobody gives me a ride, then I'll take a bus so I am not under the scrutiny of the authorities at the airport or train station. I will get away with it; I know I will.

"In fact, I am going to find which force or forces are suppressing me and disarm them. In my life, if it takes my whole life, I am going to find out."

He borrowed the money from his sister, and that was the last time I or anyone else has seen him. Two months have passed without a trace or word. Whatever he is doing, I can't help but hope him the

168

best. At the same time I feel angry and sorrowful that he feels the obligation or has been trapped into this pursuit. Even if he accomplishes his goals, his ideals, energies, trust, and maybe even hope, will have been dissipated. Youth should be a time to have those dreams, which later in life we rediscover and find the means by which to fulfill them. We are only young once with the time and energy to dream against the flood of reality. If we lose this dream-time, then when do we have the dreams which can change what exists?

Why couldn't a young man like that be furthering the good which exists rather than fighting it all? What has forced him into his negative stance? I am not questioning what he is doing; no, his purpose is clear. He is not wasting his being by doing it. My anger is that somebody's time must be used to seek what he seeks rather than, as I have said, improving and furthering the best. In my opinion, he has had to go after the worse in our society.

It is these types of distractions, as valid as they may be, which detain us from our self-appointed goals and sometimes from our self-completion. If our hero was working at a self-appointed goal joyfully, working at his top efficiency, think of the contribution he could be making. Think of how much this country, and in fact, the world, could effectuate if even fifty per cent were achieving what they wished, fulfilling their best talent, completing their destinies. It is an untapped resource. An innate resource of a democracy is the individuality which it breeds - individuals with different potentials, different methods and thoughts, different perspectives: Over

169

four hundred million ways to see the problems and that number of possible solutions. I just remembered a theory they were discussing in college which our hero related to me. In the same way nature fills out blank areas in a tree with new branches, why wouldn't nature be filling its needs with human beings? (I will have to get him to expound on this theory.)

Then earlier in eighth grade, our hero expressed a vision of everyone in the world having stocks, bonds, shares and interests in companies, corporations, countries and world organizations to the extent that nobody needed to work. The majority of jobs would be menial and would pay the highest salaries. They would be a lure to those who were not creative enough to effectively use their time; these jobs would be sought by those who wanted to work, needed big money, or as means to spend their time.

Combining his utopian dream with the possibility of each and every person doing what he or she wished, think of the world we could have: human resource centers where we could get the jobs of our choice, without or with pay. People would be working because they wanted, and think of the good job they would be doing.

I can see, we are both dreamers, but the difference is that he at one time thought it would be possible, and I know it won't. But then again, he has come a long way in seeing what is possible and what is not.

PART II

MARGARET

Chapter 1

The main reason why I am going to dwell on Margaret's story and no one else's in Thesus' family is because she has a great influence, not only on her brother but on Ike as well, another story which I plan to tell, and because she is another case of not being able to fulfill her abundant potential.

Her influence on her brother increased as their ages increased. Six years and another sister, Jenny, separated our hero from Margaret, but in San Francisco no one would have guessed any distance existed. Maybe at one time Jenny was closer to her older sister, or our hero was closer to Jenny but this ended, if it ever existed, when Jenny went to college. It wasn't the distance of the college, which was less than one hundred and fifty miles, but I think a more natural evolution: their intellectual and physical pursuits; both of them were becoming self-directed, choosing their individual paths. Also Margery was more her mother's child and Jenny her father's which helped manifest a division of the family, and our hero took a side also.

Jenny went to college to find a husband and bring him back to the ranch. It possibly could be that she followed a fellow off to college. This last statement is more an opinion of mine than a fact, but the fact does remain that she did go off to an agriculture college with the idea of returning and helping her father run the ranch, and she did marry Prath Saunders, the son of a local cattle rancher, in her third year. Both of them finished school with the help of their families. Thesus' father gave them a parcel of land on the far side of the ranch, and they received large amounts of money from both sides of their families for graduation and marriage, to purchase more land, build a house and buy cattle. Both of them are very hard working, stable, up-right people, and from what I know, are now doing quite well running both their spread and the father's.

Thesus' mother, from what I have gathered, lived exclusively for the family and before the well's poisoning was a very gregarious person. She hated moving to the ranch because she thought it would end a social life which she had procured. Even though her husband was only a Captain, her sentiments, (a fact I don't think she ever forgave him for and maybe another reason for him retiring early) she had her society groups in the service and loved the protocol and ceremony which were demanded. She, in her own mind, was from a more important stratum (her father was an ex-senator from southern California) than almost every one she encountered. Her social rank helped her to hobnob with persons who out-ranked her husband, and actually from what I have heard, she not only carried it off with grace and charm, but snobbery in many cases. In my mind, maybe a reason her husband never obtained a higher rank.

172

I guess when they were stationed in Denver, her husband secretly bought a ranch. She was shattered by his betrayal. It wasn't so much his independent action, which she was used to, but that he would subjugate her to "these conditions." She left him, took the children, and went home to California for two or three months, then discovered that she had no way, short of divorce, to obtain support. Even though most of their savings came to her by way of her inheritance, she hadn't bothered herself with money, didn't know the intricacies of his investments, and couldn't even lay hands on it. In short, he had control.

With much fanfare, she returned to "give it a chance." It took a while to adjust. At first she traveled into Denver daily; sometimes even staying for days at friends or in hotels, but gradually this wore thin, and she became active in local affairs, mainly for her children. I don't think she ever quit looking down her nose at the locals, but she participated never the less. At first it was just the PTA to see that her children obtained the proper education. It was her disapproval of the schools which was the main reason Margaret attended a private high school in Denver for two years but when Jenny refused to follow, the mother became active, became politically involved in this issue and that issue until she was enmeshed. Even though she wouldn't admit it, she eventually began to enjoy her new society because of the power she acquired. She ran the show, something she could never do before. In fact, for a while, she was thinking of running for representative or senator to either the state congress or federal, (an attempt to regain her family's status?)

The mother was the main force behind her children being reared the way they were. She pushed all of her children into private lessons, special schools, concerts, and other social affairs. She didn't want her children to become the "farmers" who surrounded them. She approved of me, at the time, because I didn't have a Western twang and was a good role model.

She used to confide in me because I was not a local, and she thought I had a common disregard for them. A very revealing statement I remember was, "If my children can pick up a good book and enjoy it, they will never be bored; if they can enjoy a good concert, they will be in good company and have something to do; if they can play bridge, they will never be without friends." As it was, this statement was my introduction to the family, for it was conveyed to me in my interview for the tutoring position.

Jenny placed a damper on the mother's hopes, and she quit pushing as hard when our hero came of age. Jenny, for years, fought her mother tooth and nail. She like square dancing, didn't play bridge, hated classical music, and refused to go away to school. ("Obviously, her father's child.")

The father really didn't participate in the family's happenings. All of his waking hours were spent on business of one type or another. He could be found in his den on the computer or phone, in his private study reading, out in the district drumming up insurance clients, or riding his ranch. In his youth he was raised on a dairy farm in Minnesota. At eighteen, he bolted and joined the Army. When he told his story to his children, he always emphasized that what he ran away from (his father's beautiful farm) was better than what he ran to; in other words, make sure where you're going to land before you jump. He met his wife while stationed in Montery, California at the Presido. He was twenty-one, already a First Lieutenant training for the MIA, with a bright future. Ten years later, Margery was born. Twenty-five years later, he bought the ranch and returned to the life he knew and loved.

It was probably his age which accounts for some of the distance and aloofness from his children, and that his wife divided the family. The only argument I ever heard, she, the mother, ended it by saying, "My mother warned me about you. She always said, 'Once a farm boy, always a farm boy.' I should have known we would end up like this, out in the middle of no-where." He was sitting at his desk, and after she had finished her tirade; he went back to his work without commenting. She at these moments she would gather the available children around her to console herself, especially the youngest son or Margery.

She never overtly recognized his success. Their extreme monetary security, she took as her given in her life. When they first moved onto the ranch, they moved into a small ranch house built in 1992, but after the money started rolling in, the father told his wife she could have any type of house she wanted. She took an architect to Los Angeles with the idea of showing him her family home and having him design one like it, but when she reviewed her old homestead, she was disappointed; her "tastes and ideals had matured." So she decided on a different home, one that she always wanted when she was young. It was a movie star's house. It took two years to build and must have cost millions. Most of the money to buy the ranch had been inheritance from her family, or so she thought. Nearer the reality, the father had invested it well and had refused to spend it. He had some inheritance from selling his portion in his family's farm. He had saved money before the marriage, which the mother didn't discover until she wanted a divorce. While still in the service, they spent everything he made and then some. My main point is that after paying for the ranch lands and building the house, they had very little left, and when he told his wife she could have the house of her dreams, they didn't really have the money to build what they built. But, not a word did he say. And in a couple years, they paid for it all.

It was a huge, three story Victorian white house, fluted with ornateness. An "L" shaped porch faced the west, for "the Captain's Million Dollar Sunsets." It swept around to the north, where the family ate breakfast and lunch during the summer. In the back was a swimming pool and bath house, and on north side, a big English-styled garden. On the second floor, besides the guest room where I spent several nights, each child had his or her own bedroom and bath of which each was totally responsible. In the finished basement a utility room, a work shop and recreation room with a standard sized pool table, and of course, a safe room in case of tornados. The third floor was the master bedroom. In a tower further up the stairway, "the Captain's Office," a locked computer room, surrounded by windows, and right at the pinnacle of the tower, it is rumored that there is a garret with a bed, a chair and a telescope.

Whereas the original small ranch house was near the road, this house was nearly a half a mile from the main highways down a paved road big enough for only one car with a white slab fence on both sides. (Yes, he had help stop the county from paving its road but paved his own.) It ended in a circle drive and a three car garage, which contained a family car, a child's car, and the Lincoln, bought by the mother with the intention of a ranch hand being a chauffeur.

The white three slab fence (the mother's idea) surrounded three sides of the property as seen from the county dirt road. The bottom rail close to the ground was to keep-out the varmints. To me, it appeared out of place and would have been better situated in some place like Kentucky. Just acquiring the water rights to keep everything alive must have been a fortune. They had two wells, the rights to irrigate from a canal and a stream which dried up in early summer.

Many discussions with the locals expressed their resentment of the ranch's need for water. Having a garden "like they do in this semi-arid climate, when farmers and ranchers need all the water they can get, is a disgrace. I don't care how much money they have; I don't care who they think they are." To my knowledge, a well supplied the main house and the original house, and the canal was only used for crops.

The 1992-farm-house near the road was used for the ranch workers. Most of the livestock when rounded-up was kept near there in a primitive coral or in their new fancy barn. As I eventually learned, the mother hated the smell of animals, and so her house couldn't be built near grazing cattle, or any type of barn. I have no idea how large the ranch was, but looking in any direction from her house, one could, only see growing crops: sometimes corn, soybeans, wheat, but mostly alfalfa. I know nothing about farming or ranching but the whole spread is considered a technological marvel. It was pretty much prairie before the ranch was build and land cultivated. The land on the east is still prairie but slowly but surely being turned.

A stable for the horses was half way between the old and new houses. Each child had his or her own horse, but only Jenny and Margaret ever cared or paid attention to theirs. Jenny's horse was an Indian pony and Margery's was a Thoroughbred. The youngest son eventually became attached to his Mustang, but only when he was older did he consistently take care of it. He seemed to always have pets, a baby lamb, chicks, a duck; their fate was unknown to me except that Jenny adopted some of them. Since no animal could come near the house, every day she had to walk to the stable and care for the many animals. She also had her own Brahman bull which she bred and a fancy, blue ribboned sheep. Not even the two dogs which ran freely ventured near the house.

Chapter 2

Margery, as I have said, is another case: unfulfilled, working below her capacity. She is beautiful and intelligent, and after an intense struggle, has become financially successful and yet too many of her conversations express discontent. "These twenty-three years have gone too rapidly. The only difference I've noticed is that the seasons pass more quickly, and my mental attitudes change more slowly. My person changes so slowly, at times almost imperceptibly. I've the feeling that I am still that young woman of twenty-three. I know that I have wasted a portion of my life. It has slipped away. I look at the mirror and know I have changed. I compare past pictures, when twenty-three was really my reality, and I can see that I have changed physically; age is beginning to show. My face is beginning to show the battle, but that person in me hasn't changed."

I personally don't see her that way, but her statement concerning the battle is true. It has been a battle of doing something she doesn't really want, doing something that doesn't challenge her, maybe being with people she doesn't want, going to parties she doesn't want to attend, dating men she doesn't want to date, in short playing her role, a role she doesn't want to play.

Our hero commented about her feeling of being unfulfilled and feeling twenty. At first he said she had a fixation then laughed. But he concluded by saying, "Really, maybe there was something at the age of twenty-three which she didn't complete and maybe she had a glimpse at it but didn't carry through. Perchance she reached out and touched happiness for a moment but didn't hold tightly enough, and it got lost somehow."

I interpret her statement about being twenty as her spirit is still young, her energy, hopes and dreams are still that of a twenty year old. For in my eyes she has gone through what she has with dignity, self-respect, and a will to carry on, to endure in the face of it all. She still carries her self well, poised, almost stately, and well mannered. One can see her respect, not only for herself, but her respect for mankind in general. She is neither condescending nor humble in front of any one and treats almost all people equally, until she gets to know them, then each to the amount of respect she thinks they deserve. But the world has not shown her the same.

"I have never completely fulfilled myself as an individual, a woman, a person, and a human being. For a while I just worked to exist, worked to maintain, but I have learned: I am working, investing, and saving. I am going to break-out of this trap which binds me. I can see now that I was just making myself comfortable, not trying to improve it. The trap is what life, society, and my own lack of sight forced me to become. I am almost financially successful, but I am not any closer to myself than when I was at twenty-three. My brother is right in a way; it is a fixation. That person of twenty-three has not developed. That was the only period in my life when I experienced a great deal of growth. When have I had the time to develop? To reach inside, find out who I am, and what I really want to become, to touch my true being.

"My time with myself was precious back then; I enjoyed life and I enjoyed myself, but now it goes so quickly and means so little. I took those first few years in San Francisco without questioning them, myself, or the reasons behind them. I knew what was expected of me and did it............ Then I came too far to turn back. I thought I saw a goal in the distance, but it was nothing .... an illusion. It was there for me to see. It is the goal of some who begin a career: money, security, independence, freedom from the eight-to-five grind. It is that I let myself be deceived, used and then lured to want more. The trap now is that I have almost reached what I set out to reach. I can almost touch it and will not give up the attempt even though the goal means little to nothing to me."

Of course, she couldn't control her circumstances, her situation: a woman, starting out in San Francisco and the high unemployment situation here, the way the society is set-up and her unsuccessful relationships with men, for instance her involvement with Ike Jacoby. But she is very intelligent and if anyone can get through the maze in which she placed herself, she can.

As the reader can imagine, I have, in the previous part of this book, over emphasized each of their roles as a devil's advocate, which both sister and brother have played, in order to show a second point of view. Although this role is real and active, it was and is not their predominate part in the other's life.

181

They were very close to each other, not only because they belong to one another as relatives but because their interests and intellect make them close. Intellectually they share common interests not only in their topical choices but in their abilities to perceive. They are both very intelligent. I don't know her IQ, but I can imagine it is close to his and maybe this was another reason each decided to keep the other in line; they have the ability. Both of them could see the other's faults and cared enough to help even if it has been through criticism.

This sister-brother team was close spiritually, mentally, and physically in San Francisco. Very close. I guess before that time either the lack of them being in each other's physical presence or that they were young and their established roles of siblings kept their closeness at a minimum. But in San Francisco the relationship bloomed. They were more than sister and brother, for those roles, even though active, had been superseded. They were co-fighters in the face of adversity, friends, father and mother to each other and yes, even lovers. They protected each other, defended each other, helped each other and comforted each other in every imaginable way. This role reached a peak and after their father's death .... subsided somewhat .... the main reason for our hero not moving in with his sister at that period of time.

I know very little about Margaret's and her brother's life before I began teachings in that rural district. I have seen photos of her and her brother from the family album. Both seemed healthy, normally developing children. One picture I remember in particular: Margaret is standing beside a horse, a beautifully constructed animal, on which her younger brother, Thesus, had been placed, much to his chagrin. He looks extremely unhappy and uncomfortably out of place for he is dressed in a thick wool, blue "Little Lord Fauntleroy" outfit: short pants, coat, bow tie and even a little blue hat. Margaret is wearing a riding habit: breeches, boots, tight fitting jacket, and velvet covered hard hat. She even has a riding crop in her hand. It appears as if she had been leading the horse and her six year old brother. She looks extremely proud of the display: her horse, English saddle and all.

I had almost become a close friend of the family's before I met her. The family began our friendship by inviting me to our hero's thirteenth birthday party. I came as a chaperone, but later that winter they invited me to Thanksgiving dinner. Much talk was concerning Margaret, but she hadn't come home. I went home to my family that first Christmas, or I would have met her then. The first time I saw her, I didn't even get to talk to her. She was home for spring vacation and had brought a girl friend with her. I was attracted right away and made it a point to stay around at the beginning of summer vacation. At neither meeting was she receptive to me. Her head was off in a cloud somewhere for she was preparing to go abroad for the summer, but as the reader will be able to see, I have been more than persistent.

The first time we really talked was her third year in school, and she had come home for Christmas. The vacation was two weeks underway before I even got a glimpse of her, but I hadn't been expecting any more than that. Her brother had told me she was home during the tutorages, but she was either taking a nap or riding her horse. The longer I went without meeting her, the more I wanted to. I began to build her in my mind so that after three weeks, I began to fantasize about her. Also I had lived in that small school district for almost two years without meeting a nice eligible woman my age. Most of the women were elsewhere. They were presumably at school or working in some big city. My only proof of these statements was that a few older women did come home to visit relatives during vacations, but to me they seemed beaten by what they had encountered in big cities. The two whom I met must have been used by each and every man they met; used, then dropped, then used again; each man or job, or whatever, taking from them what it wanted and leaving the "girls" a little less. "Jaded" is the word that comes to mind: transparently bitter and hardened. These were the ones who came home and were available; the rest undoubtedly found some type of success or marriage, or both.

Anyway, our first meeting, Margaret and me, was at Christmas dinner. Fifteen were attending. Everyone in the family had invited friends except for Margaret. The father had invited two business acquaintances who were in Denver, and another family of three, toddler included, who the Captain had known from the service and had just recently been stationed in Denver. Margaret's mother had invited a couple of widows from town; Adrian attended because his family was visiting relatives and he didn't want to go; Jenny had a friend from school, the man she eventually married. So I guess I was expected to be Margaret's guest because her mother had invited and seated me next to her. So great was she in my mind by that time, that I could be nothing but displeased. But I was even more than disappointed. As I have said, I had only glimpsed her from the summer before, and I had worked on that memory, which was: she was very good looking. In reality, she still had a beautiful face but was dumpy. She had gained weight and was on the plump side and somewhat slovenly in appearance with a non-caring attitude. One could tell that her respect for herself was at a low. Even when I overcame my initial chagrin and decided to get to know her, she was not receptive.

Just lately she told me that she had her mind set not to meet anyone at home and being pushed together made it worse. She knew I would probably be there and remembered me from the summer before but had no interest in meeting me, a seventh grade teacher, teaching in a town where she never wanted to live and would never live if she had her choice. She did invite me to go for a sleigh ride though, to show someone, ... anyone her horse.

When she told me this, I told her that it was on that sleigh ride when I quit thinking about her for she had grown ugly in my eyes. "Weren't you lucky, then," was her response. It wasn't until Colorado University where we really even engaged in any real conversations at all.

But going back even before our first meeting,

she has recently said in one of our lengthy discussions that when she first entered her "Eastern School," an old established top ranking girl's school, she experienced coldness from most of the women because they all had a "name and rank"; they all were from famous families or had a hell-of-a-lot of money, and she didn't. She had been accepted to the college because of her grades, and the school needed some qualified candidates from the West. At the beginning she didn't even realize that they looked down on her because she had not been raised with discrimination of that type or any kind for that matter. This was the father's doing, and in this issue he had secured his way over his wife's.

Margaret knew she was at a disadvantage. Her family was only wealthy as compared to rich. Her family was not a famous name, or her father's occupation was not acceptable in the group, so she set out to establish her own identity, her own "name and rank." Her popularity grew the longer she remained. She became a joiner, an achiever, and worked herself up to secretary of this club and vice-president of that club. She knew if she stayed long enough that she would become the president of her class.

All this joining and socializing only took place after her freshman year. Right from the beginning of her school career, she began to have trouble academically. Her previous schooling had not been enough to see her through the first year. She had to get tutors for a couple of classes, but in her second year, she began to adjust to the demands by a tremendous amount of studying. From what she told me she would either be studying or taking care of her social duties. She never left campus; although men were available, she never dated, never had any contact with the outside world. She found a challenge both academically and socially and threw herself completely into meeting them.

Her life had been more isolated from the outside world and from people, in general, than most young ladies. For most of her years had been spent on the farm, going to a private school in Denver, and then a predominately all girl's school.

Her college career, because of the challenges, did not open her life at all. In her third year, I think she came to realize her isolation because she decided not to return to school to graduate but transferred to Colorado. She told me that she was dissatisfied with perpetrating the role she had given herself. And she hated accepting the role which was given to her, the social-political worker. She wanted to become her own woman, someone of whom she could be proud and happy. She didn't know what, but she wanted to find out, and she would never have time to discover herself in that school. This was the main content of her argument to her father. She knew her mother wouldn't agree, so she didn't even discuss it with her. Her father agreed. Her mother wanted her to go back and meet some "established gentleman from the East" and just experience the niceties of life. The mother thought that this would happen if she stayed the final year and graduated.

"But in two and a half years I haven't meet anyone, and I really should prepare myself for getting out into the world. Anyhow, I don't want to be dependent on anyone.

"At school I am living a synthetic life in an unreal world. I don't know life and myself, and won't unless I get out into it, and respond to something real." Her father agreed and stated that it is probably a good idea for her to broaden herself and meet different "mixes of people; that the writing was on the wall," she was going to have to "get out into the world" because without marriage, a career was a necessity when she graduated. The mother finally backed down when Margaret agreed to go to Europe for a year with her school and join a sorority at CU when she returned. She would be protected and yet, the possibility of meeting a nice young man through the fraternities prevailed.

I must admit that I was looking forward to seeing her on campus, but she was not a reason for my attendance. I had studied at the Colorado University Extension Center in Denver and needed to be on the Boulder campus for the last so many hours to get my Master's degree. Originally, I was going to put it off for another year but decided if I didn't do it right away it would get harder. Teaching and tutoring preparatory courses in the SATs and ACTs almost guaranteed my doing well in the GREs, which I did. I felt fresh and knowledgeable.

We saw each other the summer before attending the University. I was teaching summer school as a last ditch effort to secure money before moving to Boulder. It was pretty much the same situation as the Christmas, but this time she seemed to enjoy my company more, and we did much more together such as frequenting concerts in Denver, taking long horseback rides into the country, playing bridge with her parents or Thesus and Adrian. I found her attractive, not so much physically but mentally. She still had her sophisticated airs and projected superiority, but she never thought of me as a suitor which probably helped her relax and be natural. She eventually didn't bother to impress me anymore and let loose. We began to enjoy ourselves. Yes, I was looking forward to seeing her on campus and continuing our relationship.

But then when we were on campus my expectations were shattered. No romance developed; just a deeper friendship. We spent time together but not as much as I wished. She felt she had been locked-away the first three years of school and now it was time to get out. "It is my time to have fun, meet people." She had dates almost every night with different "boys." The only time we were together was during the day. She wouldn't date me, didn't want that type of relationship. After staying up to three in the morning for over a week and getting up and attending most of her classes, one night when she stayed home just to gain her strength, I went to her house, and we sat on the porch of the sorority. We talked for about two or three hours when she wanted to go in and get some sleep. I must admit I was turned-on, horny, frustrated and a little in love with her, all of which I say as an excuse, because I wouldn't let her leave without kissing me good-night. We had never kissed before, and I wanted to change the relationship from one of friendship to one of involvement. She refused. I persisted and blocked the doorway until I could see she was getting angry and was beginning to hate me so I let her pass.

Throughout the year I made various attempts to change our relationship as I mentioned, but each time she foiled my attempt and explained that she valued our friendship too much to change it. Every boy she met wanted to get romantically involved and that she needed a friend, not another involvement. I respected her wish and believed it was true rather than believe that there was something unattractive about me. I also understood that she was without direction, not even looking for a husband, nor thinking in terms of an occupation. She did what she wished, studied what she wanted, and accomplished splendidly without effort. So I decided to bide my time and just wait for her to come around.

At first I couldn't understand her popularity, why she attracted so many men. But then I took another look at her and saw the change. She had begun to care for and improve her appearance. She dressed better and had lost weight. It must have started during the summer or in Europe, but I hadn't noticed. I, and most men, would have described her as voluptuous, falling out of her clothes in the right places, downright sexy. Many men pursued her, but after a too brief a time she or they lost interest. In my mind, either they were dumb or too young. But that didn't stop them from coming. To some, it just made a greater challenge. She, needless to say, didn't end up with any of them.

After three semesters of being on the Dean's list, she graduated then moved to San Francisco. I stayed on campus and began my Ph.D.

Not until six years later was my first opportunity to see her again. First of all, I didn't have the means to pursue her to San Francisco and on top of her rejection were all rejections at all the schools in the Bay area where I applied to teach. Also I was given a teaching assistantship at Colorado with a promise of a tenure track teaching position after two years. When this didn't transpire, but I did finish my degree, I didn't go to San Francisco because I knew she was involved. It was rumored that she would get married, and so to save myself, I didn't venture after her.

Later she explained to me in her first few months in San Francisco, she realized all of her education meant little or nothing, and yet, it had meant so much for so long. She had to take secretarial courses in order to support herself. She expressed that she had felt a great deal of guilt because she had received so much money from her father for school and then she still couldn't even support herself. In fact she had to take more money to go to secretarial school. But by the time I arrived, she had worked her way up to an administrative managerial position and was generating a decent salary. She was saving fifty per cent of her income and investing it in a small business venture which immediately began to show a profit. At first it was a ten to twenty thousand dollar investment in some friend's clothing business. For a couple of months she helped her friend manufacture women's wear which her friend had designed. The grand opening was a huge success and her sewing skills were no longer needed. Then it wasn't a matter of one investment but many. She saw "the need" for a franchise in S.F. of a food place she enjoyed in Denver then Boulder. She found a partner, another woman, and they were off-to-the-races. They have three franchises in the area surrounding San Francisco. Each time she saw a good investment, she either borrowed or reduced her holdings in a not-so-prosperous venture.

Right now, I should begin discussing Margery's relationship with Ike Jacoby, another story of unfulfillment, but I really don't know how to begin. Talking to both of them should help. They had separated twice in a five or six year period. I gleaned this from letters her brother had sent me. On their second separation, I was free: no involvements, no relationship, no job, no reason to be living where I was so I ventured to San Francisco.

On first glance I was again disappointed. She was not that young lady of the past. She was not Margaret. She was no longer that graceful, aristocratic, flowing being. She was thin, almost harried looking. She had tightened. She was no longer acceptingly open to everyone but skeptical, even with me, reserved, almost cautious. Her face still possessed the beauty, but now it was a more subtle beauty: the lines in her face strengthened, in general were more chiseled. Whereas her brother had kept his childish looks, no traces of childishness were left in her; her girlish looks had matured into a woman as she had, both mentally and physically. She handled herself extremely well, to the point that, to me, she had lost a certain enthusiasm, an energy. She was sophisticated, or maybe I should say "worldly" and self-contained. Ike had nicknamed her "Margery." When I first heard this name, I rejected it, but then again, she is not Margaret, so I've accepted it.

An immediate understanding why I was in San Francisco bloomed in the first few moments, an unspoken understanding. She received me cordially, without fanfare, but with great reservation. She was curious about who I had become, as I was with her, and at the same time, she made me feel welcome. Six years had been a long time, but after meeting her again, I decided to stay and look for a teaching job.

Chapter 3

I hesitate to begin this chapter about Jacoby and Margery because to me it is too sensitive a topic. For one, I am bias, and I have been bias. Margery and Ike had a relationship which I have always wanted with Margaret. He "took" her youth. He knew Margaret as I never have. And for the second reason, I can only state my speculations from what they both have told me. What they have mentioned has been limited, and what I can communicate is even more limited due to my respect for both of them and their privacy.

To me I can't see how their relationship ever commenced except that at the beginning, I guess both of them were seeking, ... looking pretty intensely for a close relationship; neither of them had any experience in either judging what they wanted or judging other people. They both threw themselves completely at the other person. Margery's inexperience may have had something to do with it. She was in a new place without any friends. He was undoubtedly the first interesting person she met in San Francisco and in her mind the first she ever met. In all actuality I am sure, if I was an example, Ike was her first real involvement: intimately and intellectually. Also I am sure, he being an artist had something to do with it. Why would anyone with any intelligence pursue, and continue to pursue, a non-monetary career in a society like ours, where money is the gauge of success? He was a mystery.

Maybe their attraction for each other and their involvement at the beginning of the relationship was more than anything I have mentioned and could possibly know. I am sure it was, for the relationship lasted from five to six years. But from all I know, I don't see how.

To me they are both so different that no common ground of agreement could have existed at all. He is so totally involved in his art that they couldn't have had anything to discuss. She is so involved with work and her associates from work ...... of course, this is not taking into account who they were when they first met, nor that their independent lives helped.

But for a fact, I know from the very beginning they had trouble. It was always a matter of "storm and stress" or "love in bloom." She met him a couple of weeks after arriving in S.F., fell madly in love and a short time later move in with him. Something happened and she moved out. After a period of separation, they got back together. Both probably knew marriage would not result from this second trial. But then again, I am sure both had hopes. When they split, he went someplace up north of here and stayed at his uncle's cabin. She went up there and brought him back. Thus began the second phase of their relationship. Both agreed that when they first met was the happiest period of their relationship. In this second period, a "new understanding" emerged. They knew each other in more realistic terms.

For as Margery describes moving back in as a period of being on more equal terms. They both found an apartment together, "their" place, paid half for everything, and shared equally in all responsibilities. They made a list of all labor needed for up-keep and each chose duties from the document to move their living situation forward: even cleaning windows was itemized. They shared shopping, cooking and doing dishes. Each did their own laundry.

This period of new understanding lasted approximately a year but somehow it didn't work; something happened right before I arrived because I had heard about the break-up through one of her brother's infrequent letters.

From Margery's point of view, his interests in art became so obsessive that he was intolerable. "Our goals, our plans, our hopes, never agreed. He was only willing to sacrifice to art. His art, that is all there

195

is. His Art! Finally I realized this was all there was, and would be. I knew that if I wanted my plans, hopes, dreams to come to fruition that I would have to do it myself. I still wanted children, a family, and my job security. I was beginning to see my way through to financial success, and I knew from the beginning that he wasn't interested in it, so I began to do it for both of us. If I could have swung it, we would have had the security, at least financially enough to have children. So I started fulfilling my dreams without his help. At first it flowed easily enough, but the more involved I became with trying to make money, the more it seemed as if it wasn't possible with him around. First, he was a financial drag. He didn't deplete my money except in that if I wanted to go do something he didn't want to pay for, because it wasn't in his budget, I would pay. And that would be almost every form of entertainment we did, including museums. Why was I in San Francisco if not to enjoy it?

"The main problem happened when I brought home business associates and even friends. Entertaining at the apartment became out of the question. Jacoby was not only jealous but was downright rude, insulting everyone, including me."

I knew she was into a rampage because her speech patterns somewhat shattered and quickened. Now she was almost rambling like her brother does, her voice high pitched like the little girl's as when I first met her. When she is serious, her voice is slow and deliberate. It is lower, more smooth, but filled with intensity, almost demanding to be heard, definitely aggressive. She is a less passive listener, interrupting, in fact asserting herself both verbally and with body motions.

For series of periods, she tried working from the apartment, but as she has mentioned, not particularly successfully because of Ike. I guess they rarely had mutual friends, not even artists.

"At first they found him interesting, but he thought he was superior. No.....no..... he thought that they were boring, wasting his time and energy, that he could be accomplishing more important things with his life than spending time with them. But I thought then and I think now, he is insecure because he couldn't relate to what was happening around him. He was jealous because he couldn't share what my business associates and I had in common. It even got to the point where I couldn't go out to dinner with my boss without repercussions from Jacoby. Finally I had to leave Jacoby behind; he became an unexplainable entity in my business world, and I had to be intimately involved with it in order to get what I thought we needed. I couldn't explain him because we weren't married nor could I go out with anyone else, and I refused to introduce him to anyone, especially after I dragged him to a couple of parties,

"Finally I had to admit to myself that we weren't living in the same world," she laughed, "Really we were just mismatched and no way existed for bringing the worlds back together. There was no way of me fulfilling myself with him around. I respected him and what he was doing but I couldn't live that type of life, and I couldn't build my own life with him around, so I finally had to end it." This particular discussion transpired soon after I arrived and was in response to a direct question about her feelings toward him.

"I loved him and still love him in a particular way, but I couldn't ever marry him, and I had to end it because I definitely want marriage, children, and a normal home. I want to have a successful career, and none of this will happen or can happen with him.

"He never set out to hinder me. He wanted me to fulfill myself and my dreams as I do for him. He generally encouraged everything I did, but it didn't work in spite of both of our wills. I want him to pursue his art. I believe in him and his art but our conflict is hurting him. So I got out, left him and our apartment and found this one. My brother's arrival helped me achieve my resolve to quit him. If Thesus hadn't entered the scene, I don't know, we might have slipped back into our old relationship against my will. Sleeping with someone; having someone around; comforting each other; being intimate; having someone when you need him for over five years, someone to share almost everything, and then trying to live without it would or might have been impossible. It is hard to break habits such as those especially when we wanted what we had. Love itself can be like a stimulant that one can't do without. If it weren't for my brother I don't know and don't want to think about what would have happened. I am glad and relieved.

"We have never stopped seeing each other, and I suppose as long as I am not married, we probably

198

will continue seeing each other. We will always be friends. I probably understand him better than anyone else in the world, but the arrival of my brother ended our relationship as lovers, pursuers of the long commitment. I was terribly hurt, and I am sure he was, but deep inside maybe both of us know."

Ike Jacoby took the break-up harder. Harder than either realized. He was more alone and had greater time to contemplate his loss. In his eyes it wasn't only a loss of love, but he had lost his life style, his way of living. His world shattered. He says he still loves her but with a new type of love, a love without expecting anything in return, a better, more pure type of love. But what had hurt him the most (this is what he brought up at our Big Sur trip) was the destruction of their future together. He had expected them to resolve their differences as they had in the past, come to some agreement about what they both wanted. In fact he says now that he is willing to compromise, for example to have one child.

When this topic arose with Margret and me, she said she appreciates his willingness of compromise but she doesn't believe, even with his best intentions, would it work. "If he gave up art for me, he would be giving up his meaning for life; it would destroy him." Yes, knowing the little I know, right now, she is right.

I can imagine, at that time, he threw himself deeper into his art, the only involvement he really has and into his own mind. If he did, and I am almost sure of it, it was an attempt to close off some of the pain he must have experienced. He continued to live in "their" apartment, something I can't understand, and to work on his art. He didn't make an attempt to get out of himself even physically; he never went out, no money.

This lasted until after my arrival; he would only venture out if asked or to see Margery. Sometimes he would occasionally wander around without talking to anyone then return to the apartment. Margery must have seen his wanderings and began to worry because she sent her brother to meet and check on him.

Right after her departure, while her brother was living with her, Jacoby couldn't understand Margery's desire to end it but abided by her wish not to see her for a while. It would be too painful for both of them. So right after the arrival of her brother, he quit pursuing her. He intellectually knew the relationship was over, but who can totally control ones emotions?

Chapter 4

I was present at his first visit after their break-up. He had called and announced he was arriving to discuss something. Margery filled with anxiety. She had me call her brother at his apartment to ask him to come over quickly. At home, with no job interview, he left immediately. It was a bit uncomfortable for me, but I stayed even after her brother arrived. I guess it was mainly curiosity. I wanted to meet him. Thesus arrived five or ten minutes before Ike which was a relief for both Margery and me.

He was about forty-seven, balding on top, but his hair on the side and back was long. He almost looked like Benjamin Franklin except for his thinness. His face showed the stresses and strains of his life though I knew he never had any except for Margery and the frustration of his art, but maybe that was more than enough. Before I got to know him better, I thought he was a character right out of Dostoevsky's novels, a starving artist type. The book *The Possessed* struck my mind, for he was possessed. His ideology was his art. It was his religion. This comparison may be unjust, and maybe his involvement is a quality of greatness which I will never know.

He walked into the room and without even an introduction, said in a slightly frantic and choppy voice: "I have started questioning my sanity again. I just need to talk to someone, and you are my best friend, ... my only friend."

She answered without hesitation but backed away as he entered the room. "You only need to get out of yourself again, quit being so wrapped up with your own thoughts.

"And yes, I consider you my closest friend also, besides by brother." She nodded to her brother, and Ike acknowledged him, but without stopping she stepped forward and inserted before he could begin again: "But isn't strange how friendship, or sex, or even love are not the only criteria for a good relationship and especially a marriage or what I know of marriage. If it were only those, I guess it would have worked. But it seems to take a want for the other person, a want for what the other person wants for

himself, and the will and determination to make it happen, and a hope and belief that it will. I don't believe we can help each other. I trust you, believe you and believe in you; I think what you are doing is important, but I can't help you. We need a common way of life, which we both want, and shared values."
I could tell she had thought about what she would say, maybe too much so, for it all came out slightly awkward in one lump sum, like an explosion from a cannon.

I could also tell this discussion had been repeated more than once; each knew the role to be played. This particular scene was just a nuance of previous scenes with different words.

"You named some important criteria," Jacoby continued with his rehearsed lines, 'for a good relationship' but when you said friendship, good sexual relations or even love are not enough, it is not that simple. Each is a separate entity; each can be enjoyed without the others, but then again each one magnifies the others' effects. When all these pieces are together, at the same time, one can experience fulfillment, the full intensity of the others.

"Damn it. I didn't come here to get into another debate with you, but to let you know I need you. I have come close to experiencing this full intensity with you and so much more, a completion, a fulfillment. It is even more complicated than that, more complicated than words........."

Ike's face lit up, and he looked intensely into Margery's face for a response to his amorous statement. Her rigid stance did not change

Because of the tone, intensity, and content of their conversation, I felt as if I were not meant to be included. It was all too personal. It was an exchange of feelings, deep, emotional, almost profound feelings. But maybe this is the reason I was present. Margery had wanted to stave off this scene. There was a moment of silence after his spew. Her brother almost said something then stopped himself, though a moment later said, "I think I had better fix us drinks. What would you like?" We all requested, and he walked to the kitchen.

After Margery sipped her gin and tonic and we received our drinks, she continued: "But trust, respect for each other and yourself or who the other person helps make you become; may not be the most important but are necessary. More necessary is that each person's want to continue the relationship .... That was awkward and maybe not understandable...."

"Not to say impersonal," Jacoby interjected.

Her hesitantly chosen words fell out of mouth like bricks falling off of a flatbed truck on a bumpy road. "Let me put it this way- A bit of anxiety which existed while I was with you, … existed, at least on my part, was because of who I was, … and who I was, was partly who you helped me to become, who I was as a reaction to you." Her words picked up speed and fluidity. "I am not saying that that was bad or wrong; you helped me to grow in many ways and continue to....but I finally couldn't accept your way of life; I accepted what you wanted and still want, … what you are sacrificing with your life. All this made me who I

203

really didn't want to be. I was forced to decide whether I wanted to change who I was, whether it was right and good to try to change all the ways I felt about you and your life. Was I just too involved with my self-interests? ... And not giving enough?"

She hit some more bumps in the road. "At the beginning I forced myself to accept your perspectives, your ... behavior, but later I couldn't and ultimately I didn't want to. You are right it is very complicated... Belief, acceptance and respect are very ..... In the beginning of the relationship, and even now, I accepted your beliefs for yourself, but I can't and don't want them for me. In the beginning, I was willing to change with you and for you. I was searching for reasons: who I was and even why I was with you. But at the end, now, I either had to accept them and try to figure out why I feel the way I do about you, or leave."

Thesus took Margery's empty glass and brought her another. She took it, had a gulp and continued, "But in the final weighing, except at the end, for me, it was worth it. The good outweighed the bad, for a while, to me .... our relationship was worth more than I gave at the time. But at the end, now, it is painful. I didn't give all and couldn't give all because as I have said, we are both hurting each other and each other's lives. I could trust your decision to do what you wanted for you but not for me. I respect what you are doing, for you, but not for me. Maybe it is my conditioning. But I don't want to change you or for you, not anymore, not now." Her voice drifted off, "I can't."

She looked down at her drink. I thought she

was going to cry, but I think Ike's statement prevented her. "Time and work have distanced me from what we had. I don't think I could have been here without that distance. The pain for me of our separation has been horrible. This distance has sheared all the superficialities from me, all those time consuming things which distracts one from one's goals."

Margery gave a hurt, quizzical look, so he continued, "You know the distractions which consume time and only time, without any other benefits or products."

"Yes, I can see the building intenseness of your involvement, again. I can see it in your gaunt look again," she gave a nervous laugh.

Even I could see without knowing him, his movements were slightly jerky, and he had a distracted, distant look on his face. It was probably this involvement which worried our hero also later at Big Sur. Maybe Margery had said something to Thesus about Ike's over involvement. Maybe he could just see it; I don't know.

"I am beginning to see," our hero said as he walked over to the window, stopped and looked out. He was speaking to no one in particular, "all those forces which condition us, make us who we are........ either positively or negatively. I have felt anxiety because of who I was, who I wanted to become, and who I have been conditioned to become either as a reaction to the conditioning or a conforming. All three me's have battled, but I think I can see the light.

"I have begun to understand how one gets conditioned, why it happens and now I watch for it, guard against it. A lot of it occurs through the media. It helps to form the images which we seek both in ourselves and in the world around us. It helps us form who we want to become, what we want. It dictates to us an accepted and an unaccepted life style. It buys and sells us through accepting and rejecting us," he laughed at his own statement. "We are part of the law of supply and demand. Yes, to a great degree it is a matter of acceptance and rejection. These are the tools in the media's hands as well as individuals'. They force us to change through rejection and force us to become more of something-or-other through acceptance. But who exactly controls the acceptable image? A general need of the systems? A few very powerful people at the head of each system? Or nobody and it is completely random, filled with stupid needless trends? And if it is controlled, how far has the system or individual gone to control what image will be accepted or rejected? The subliminal message stuck in our brains without our knowledge? Hypnosis, with its repeating monologues or slogans, slightly below listening level, making us strain to hear its message? Advertisements, unconsciously appealing to our most primitive instincts? It all has conditioned us. The system is destroying itself through conditioning its members, and for what? The almighty dollar, our god."

"Says the man who's never been without. What are you talking about and why?" his sister chirped in, happy to be off the other subject.

"What does this have to do with what we were discussing?" Ike said with some irritation.

Also relieved by the change in conversation, I encouraged him, "You sound as if you are a knight preparing his armor."

His sister picked up my thread, "Just let's hope you are getting the armor ready for protection and not just to encase yourself.

"Maybe a fish swimming up a stream," Jacoby added laughingly.

Turning to Ike, Thesus replied "I have liked you from the first because I think I understand you,"

I had no idea what those two meant. Jacoby raised and empty glass and in a grandiose manner said, "Let's drink to rebirth into new knowledge and truth and regeneration which this truth will bring; for it is only onward."

Margery smile at him and nodded as if to say, you will never change.

As we moved into the kitchen, our hero added, "Let's drink to betterment. Margery filled our glasses, and we toasted to both statements.

In one gulp, Jacoby finished his whole glass. "I guess I am a fish going with the stream, a floater. I just float along seeing what I see and commenting on it with my art. But I know better. I know I should learn through all means available, stand my ground so I don't get washed into the sea of chaos, take what I need and let the rest float by. But I just struggle to make decisions and then decide that the fight is not worth it. That is not my chosen purpose. I don't care what happens to me anymore. I am just going to record it as I see it, and if I float out to sea, then let it be. Let it be. I will at least float out to S-E-E," he laughed as he spelled it out.

"I wanted to function in the world with a purpose...... but without acceptance, my purpose as an artist becomes nothing. I used to work for monetary subsistence, but it wasn't worth it because I could obtain subsistence without working. I would love to flow in the change which is in the All, but those brief moments are too few and far between to justify the struggle to attain them. So, I just float along, hoping something will happen, something will turn up around the next bend."

He must have had some drinks before he arrived because his words were slurred. At the time I didn't blame him for building his courage with a couple, but later I could see it was more than that. He was maudlin and feeling sorrowful for his "lot in life" and drank as an escape from his chosen destiny.

Margery, who was angered by what he said and/or his manner, turned to him and yelled, "How can you possibly say what you have? The three choices you have named and their combinations are but a paltry sum, compared to the number which exists. You can do better than that."

Margery's statement made his face go blank, then red, but he regained his composure, "I would like to thank you all for the conversation; if it hasn't confirmed my sanity, it reassured me that either we are all crazy or you are very good friends. I enjoyed it." He placed his empty glass on the kitchen counter and walked to the door, turned and smiled at each one of us individually, (almost his first acknowledgment of my existence) then opened the door.

Margery quickly said, "See, just being me hurts you. I don't want you to become who I want but who you want. You are better off .... We are better off without each other." He shook his head and left without saying another word.

Margery said, "That is one of things I never could understand about him: his exits. He used to walkout all the time. Those damned departures, even in front of my friends."

"A theme of his life?" I questioned.

Chapter 5

As she said in the conversation, love wasn't her only criterion, and she lived and made it true. I thought at the time Ike couldn't accept her love because he couldn't or didn't love and respect himself. I had seen this syndrome before. He couldn't respect someone who respected him because he didn't respect himself. He could love someone who loved him but couldn't respect them for loving him. Another symptom of this syndrome is that the people he loves, don't love him, and he loves them because they don't love him. He respects them for not loving him.

Margery's and Jacoby's relationship since that conversation has become more distant both physically and mentally. The only time he has mentioned her since then was at Big Sur. I don't know whether it is because he does not dwell in the past or if it was out of respect for me. But his visits to her apartment have become less and less frequent. I don't think she has ever visited him in their old apartment.

Her brother, Ike, and I have become pretty good friends. It was definitely that trip to Big Sur which changed our relationships, and that was over two years ago.

Margery's and Jacoby's last meeting to date has been when he brought her back from the airport after her father's death. She related their conversation to me when she retrieved me from the airport after the funeral in Colorado which was a little over a year ago. From what she told me, she loved him more than ever. "It is easier to love him at a distance; we don't depend on each other for so much. We don't have to depend on each other for security, happiness, planning and creating a future together, nothing. We can accept each other, and appreciate each other for who the other person is. It was just the combination of us together that was a disaster."

Hurt by this revelation, I asked, "Do you think you could have an intimate relationship with him again?"

"I don't know. My feelings for him were.........and are real. If only in another world, at another time. Maybe if that financial-break ever occurs, and I am not dependent on him for that; if I could again get into his thoughts, his world ..... if he would let me in again; if I could again know him to the depths which I knew him and still respect him as I do now; if, if, if .....

"There are times I can't understand what he says; he is beyond me in some way, and silly as it is, a way I miss.   Those things that I can't fully understand are usually exciting; like he is into creating, creating almost everything, and I can see his excitement, but I can't share it anymore. His searches are usually exciting, and I used to share them with him, follow his developing, evolving thoughts. But now I don't truly … or completely, understand his statements. He is always at the brink- the forefront of conceptual thought.   He has stretched his thinking until he stands on the unknown, and unless one has been with him and followed his path, one can't really know where he is. Right now it is a little impractical to be with him as much as I need to to follow his thinking. I would be living in his world again. I can't or don't want to; I have to fulfill my goals."

After I asked and didn't get a reply to "Does he know he is on the edge?" I told her about her brother's concern and some of his statements at Big Sur, and we discussed that. Then she said, "Ike developed his being in a way that I haven't. I guess that is part of what he gave me and can still give me.

"But .... I don't question, ... he does,... whether he is correct in accounting for his life, whether he has justified his existence. He questions whether the balance of his justification will ever be obtained. He is caught in his own self-doubt. He wants too much to justify to himself his reasons for his existence, and at the same time afraid that he doesn't or hasn't. The stupid thing is that the bases of his fears rest in the lack of public acceptance. It is so stupid because I think it is his ego which prevents him from seeing that everyone is so wrapped up with their own lives that they don't care about him or art, and unless someone can use him to make money, they will just leave him alone. It is too bad he doesn't fully understand the motives behind his actions. He wrote a poem: "Existing in an abstract realm,/ Thought./ Aware of but one pain,/ Death drives the search." Can't you see; death drives the search because he tries to maintain the balance of justification of his existence. Yet, really it is his search which, to me, justifies him. His search for justification has become his god. But he thinks that art, maybe creating art for art sake could be his justification.

"Doubt always fluctuates in his mind. When he is without it he is a better person, but it does have its purpose. There are times when he thinks he is nothing, that he has done nothing, and he weighs himself in the negative. This would usually happen when he received a rejection notice but not always; sometimes for seemingly no reason," she paused, "but now as I look at it, those were times when he didn't work. There would be times when he was on top of the world, no matter what was happening around him, and he thought he was making a great contribution. It was at times like those that he would be working like crazy, believing in what he was doing, and in himself. If only the belief in himself and what he has done would be enough for him.

"Yes, he walks this thin edge. On one side is greatness; the other is nothing. This is of course in his mind. When his work is going well, and he feels he is accomplishing in his mind, and in his art, I think he really is a great artist. Then on the other side, he falls into these depressions, where nothing he has created has been worthwhile. If he obtained some type of societal and monetary success, maybe this would keep him on the positive side of the edge - but it hasn't and doesn't seem forthcoming.

"He is a wonderful artist but is pretty stupid about life or at least the business aspect of it. He keeps sending his manuscripts to publishers who don't want his type of material. Or when he breaks-through to something new, a new idea, concept, or system of belief, he sends the material that is new, and it is usually out of context or written in a language, which nobody wants to spend the time to understand because it is not polished, not finished, but crude. But this is his art, not the finished product, but the creations, the newness. Sometimes it is completely un-understandable without knowing him. But of course, his troubles are caused by more than this.

"The world of finance, agents, galleries, and publishers wants entertainment, commercial items which almost completely eliminate 'art.' Either they are after profit and are towing the government line, maintaining and furthering the status quo, its values of the good, right, and just of the powers that be, or they are struggling to survive and need sellable products."

"But if what you say is true, it is not his fault society is not set up to promote unknown artists. Individual people only buy art as an investment or because it is beautiful, pleasing or at least elicits some big emotion. And if they buy it as an investment then they buy known artists who will probably become more famous. If they buy it because it turns them on, then the artists are competing with movies, magazines, TV. Those are inexpensive media for the masses. So few people really know enough about art to promote art which furthers art and that is, from what I have gathered, Jacoby's main concern."

"Yes, more with the conceptual than perceptual." She didn't take these ideas further but continue with an earlier thought.

"The governments are subsidizing art not only because of what I have mentioned and not because they see it as a thermometer of culture or innovator of ideas, but because they want to pacify the artists and also because they need a spending policy, a way to get money into the system. They have built a huge bureaucracy, The Department of Art and Culture and that system feeds itself through giving moneys to organizations and artists who walk the straight and narrow policies. They further what they want to hear, not what is happening. If they furthered what was happening they would more truly know what is going on in this country. Suppression isn't going to keep it from happening, especially in the field of art."

"You are right," I added, "All are out to further themselves. Jacoby doesn't seem to be in this type of world. He doesn't know it exists or doesn't care."

At that point we had driven to my apartment and were stopped in front of it. "Do you want to come in?" I asked.

"No thanks. There is much to be done today."

Margaret has changed because of Ike. Even in the name he gave her "Margery" shows it. She is more

214

a "Margery" around me also and to me now, less formal. I wonder at work whether they address her formally? I wonder if she is Margery to them ..... any of them at her work.

Anyway, her relationship with Ike changed her, especially in its final throngs. In that she had to make a choice between love and her goals hardened her. And she identified with being harder. I tried to tell her there are many different types of love, that her love for him is but one type. It was good that she did not sacrifice her life and her goals for that type. She will love again, "maybe this time with a type that would be as strong and better for you."

With this statement she turned to me and said, "If my belief in him was great enough, maybe the sacrifice would have been enough."

"Maybe it is really a lack of belief in yourself. If you would have believed in yourself more fully, you could have believed that you would have ended up in a good place with or without him." This is a statement made by her brother after he got back from Colorado and his father's funeral.

"You may be right, but it is easier, and I am more sure of being in a good place without him."

Anyway, in a sense it is too bad it didn't work out between Ike and her. All their time invested. His influence on her has not been bad or harmful. He is neither bad nor harmful, but a good person. He has helped her grow in some beautiful ways. Her mind has been developed. He encouraged her to keep up her dancing and generally the aesthetic side of her character.

Even though Jacoby is a real loner, he had a reputation as an artist and just as a matter of frequency, they began to meet other artists. Of course, it was probably Margery's initiatives which lead to the introductions and I am sure, her attractiveness didn't hindered the process.

This generated an interest and depth to art which she had not known. They would go to openings of art exhibits, galleries, museums, lectures, concerts, and avant-garde movies. For a while they were in the mainstream of art in San Francisco

I think this is a part of what she misses from the breakups, not the visiting of cultural events for we do that but the identity of it all: of having a real stake in the art world. And for Ike it was falling back into the lack of involvement and the loss of her energy to initiate exploration and attend events that helped shatter his world. She was no longer around to push him out of himself. And in doing so she fulfilled a part of her own being which she hadn't needed to develop. I think the emotional break was intensified because it was a break of psychological dependency also.

They both needed each other to complete themselves. She needed him to develop the spiritual, intellectual, and cultural side of her being. He needed her to develop the realistic, practical, and social side of his being. But of course, as in most cases neither completely developed themselves but only came to depend on the other to give m these things. Consequently every time each left the other, they left huge gaps in their persons. In Jacoby's case it was a matter of him either not wanting to complete those parts of himself or an inability. With Margery, it was that she quit seeing life from a more complete perspective as she did with Ike. I think the need for.......... let's say the cultural .... was not really what she thought she wanted, but it had been drummed into her by her mother and her schooling. It is strange that this "created-need" was fulfilled by someone whom neither the school nor her mother would have approved.

Five years with each other, satisfying each other's needs, not just psychologically, but on a basic primal level kept them together. Their attempts to become complete people and to have more full type of lives helped keep them together. And for those years, it was the threat of losing what the other gave, made them hang on. It appears to me that the eventual realization that neither could really give what they both needed to move forward in their beings and in their lives eventually drove them apart.

Now, what I really don't understand is her renewed interest in him. It has almost been three years since their break-up. Her renewed love as expressed in the drive home from the airport couldn't still be the psychological dependency or even the need for sexual gratification, or the need and habit of other types of comfort which an intimate relationship gives, or even the guilt of quitting him and its effect. I am not, however, completely discounting the guilt of her giving up on love. She may want to return to her former being: that idealistic person who would sacrifice everything for love, but no I don't see her that way. She is too practical, and she knows herself well enough to know who she is. She wouldn't want something she isn't. I guess I still don't understand. It could be a bias which prevents me from seeing and understanding. Maybe it is not true at all, and Margery just tells me she is still in love to keep me in line, in this case to keep me at bay, or maybe she thinks she is and isn't. It is easier to look into the past, remember the good things, forget the bad and wish for those good old days. But the reality of the situation is different.

I have even encouraged their reunion, have told her to go back to him and again experience each other. It is my last defense against this burden in our relationship, but she refuses. It is impractical she says. It is almost as if she wants to live in a state of limbo, to hold fast to a perfectionistic past, to grasp something which is not manifest, not real, but which exists only in her mind. If it is true it could be a convenience, a crutch, to help support her against the real world she faces. The worlds in our minds can be so much more beautiful than the world to which we awaken every day. Maybe I have discovered a bad influence which Jacoby has exerted, to stay in the mind and not face the adventure of the real, either out of convenience or fear of being hurt.

But rather than take this chapter as an answer, I will plead ignorance, and say I don't understand her feelings of love, in fact, her feelings at all.

Chapter 6

When our hero first arrived in San Francisco, Margaret boarded him until he could find an apartment. He stayed only for a couple of weeks. I suppose in his mind it was too long because he didn't want to be controlled, under any obligation, or in any way dependent on his sister. He didn't need another mother as he put it. He had experienced a certain amount of freedom in college and didn't want to relinquish it. I am sure that Margaret gave him advice as to where to find an apartment, where to look for work and probably introduced him to some of her business acquaintances; in general, I am sure that she tried to establish him and set him on the right road.

From what they both have told me, when he first moved in with her, right after arriving in San Francisco, the intenseness of their relationship was explosive. Neither of them had met anyone like the other before, and the discovery caused an eruption of thoughts and feelings. They would get involved in conversations which would last most of the night. It was never that the conversations would finish, but exhaustion would overcome them.

They awakened themselves in the other person, their sameness, their heritage, their common backgrounds, interests, intelligence, and similar thoughts, thoughts which they felt no one but they had. This intensity grew and grew even after he left: At times it became almost violent. An extreme love that expressed itself in an over concern, an over involvement, to the point where when they disagreed, they would express it physically. Basic disagreements were unresolvable, but yet, totally disruptive to their core beings, virtually unacceptable. Once their core beings emerged, any deviation was like a puncture wound ripping the flesh. This is my theory as to why they almost bodily hurt each other.

They were naturally physical with each other. They were always jumping on each other, pretending to beat on each other, touching each other: she fixing his tie, him taking a piece of fluff out of her hair, and I've seen her tangibly try to shake some sense into him when he disagreed with her. He would push her to the ground and sit on her, trying to explain his point of view, generally in a deluge of laughing or crying, but all of it as an expression of love.

As I have said, he had been at college, away from his family and now didn't want to account for his actions to anyone. And in spite of their discoveries, he moved out post-haste, against his sister's advice: "Find a job first." His excuse to her was that he had found a perfect apartment, and this chance may not come again. She had to agree about the apartment because it was better than hers and less expensive.

For Margaret his stay was too short. She was in the process of breaking up with Jacoby. She had recently moved-out, this last time, after living with him for almost a year. Her brother's presence probably helped distract her from her problems, feelings, and even, in my opinion, insecurity.

Against intuitive thinking, Thesus' departure nurtured their relationship. He was no longer under her direct jurisdiction; although he felt obligations as they both did, the relationship became more of a give-and-take situation. She would invite him for dinner once a week. They would sit, drink wine, and discuss everything imaginable, and sometimes they would talk late into the night, and he would stay over.

They were good for each other; no doubt about that. They helped each other to be more objective about life's confrontations; they shared the most intimate doubts, fears, hopes, desires, ambitions. By knowing themselves, they basically knew each other's internal psyche, but not exactly. And what they didn't know, they opened each other with sincere questions as a psychiatrist would expose a patient. In the final analysis, as much as they disclosed to each other so were they that vulnerable. If love hadn't grown between them, but hate, they could have destroyed each other with the knowledge they had, especially of each other's weaknesses. The depth of knowledge they obtained was reflected in a short-hand type of communication. I've seen one make a statement producing an amazing effect in the other, either extremely positive or negative; whereas, I wouldn't even know what they were discussing.

Margaret could see some of the problems our hero was facing from the beginning. She anticipated many problems, especially dealing with finding a decent job, money, loneliness and others, which she experienced when first moving to San Francisco, and in spite of his statement that he didn't need another mother, Margaret was of great help, and she, in a way, did assumed the role. But she really didn't know the world well enough to prevent a great many misfortunes. She had lived a sheltered life in institutions of one kind or another and was still secure in a system. Still employed by the same company she had entered right after finishing secretarial school, she didn't know the problems her brother would have to face. She didn't really know the dangers of a uniquely and independently spirited person for she hadn't even rocked the boat muchless threatened it. She had walked the narrow path, knowing that is what it would take to get her where she wanted to go.

The entrance of our hero's girlfriend ended some of the intense involvement. Margaret's relationship with her brother became less physical, less personal, less involved. Mentally it continued to grow, the depth of understanding didn't cease, and a certain type closeness remained.

Margaret always considered her brother's girlfriend a "ding-bat." She couldn't fully understand his involvement, except from a sexual point of view. She, for sure, couldn't understand his belief in her or what they had in common. She never expected it to last and thought it was for the best when it didn't.

It wasn't until that departure when Thesus began to confide in Margaret again. I had since come on the scene and saw the difference that existed between brother and sister before and after Thesus' girlfriend. Thesus had had another place to direct his energy, his thoughts, his emotions but the absence of his lover caused him again to direct all of this to Margery.

Even though intellectually Thesus had

expected, well maybe not expected… but imagined his girlfriend leaving and thought it would be best for her because he had become a vegetable; he was hurt and shocked when she did. His mental loss was multiplied by the physical loss. Because it was his first love, first sex, first loss, he constantly wondered where she was, what she was doing, constantly talked about her. He was almost obsessed. In short, he experienced the pain of withdrawal and loss, and Margery comforted him.

This is how their intense relationship began again. Both were suffering from deep losses. Margery again became his chief confidante. Not holding anything back from her nor she from him, both obtained even more information about the other's past partners, daily life, working problems. And so, the periods of sexual impotency which our hero experienced during his relationship were known and were of great concern to her. It became almost a fixation with her. She would always question him about it in their personal code, and I am sure when they were alone they discussed it differently. Her obsession with it may have been her concern of carrying the family name, or a fulfillment of his being, something; for she didn't see any hope of her youngest brother having progeny.

Right now, I am torn or have been torn between disclosing an incident which has had a great effect not only on Margery's relationship with her brother but her relationship with me, or not mentioning it because of moral and ethical grounds. I have played ignorant earlier. Nobody knows I know, and it is something about which I would never directly confront either of them.

I have decided to describe the incident because I want her to know I know and that I don't condemn her or her actions on a moral or spiritual level, but that emotionally it will take many years to get over it. I also have an obligation to the reader. Unless I disclose the incident, I don't feel that anyone could fully understand all of our relationships. No one could fully understand why their and mine relationship changed. I guess I knew I was going to mention it because not to is not to see beneath the surface of Margery's image, the business facade which she has developed. It would be to see Margery as she presents herself, not as she is.

Before moving into the communal situation, our hero's concern about his impotency had peaked. He had failed to discover the cause. He was confused about all the events which had happened. Everything was unexplainable, dangling in his mind, suspended with no base. Nothing fit together; possibilities flooded his mind; he was out of control both mentally and in his situations. It was then he decided to move from his apartment. He conversed with his sister who immediately recommended moving in with her. They could control the environment (although, I don't think she fully realized what was happening or the significance of the situations, because she didn't fully believe his perspective: she thought he was paranoid).

He wouldn't need to pay rent or do too much house work and would have plenty of time to think (her promise).

After very little thought, this is exactly what he did. It was quite convenient for me; visiting my two favorite friends at the same time. About three days after he moved, I made such a visit. The only unusual circumstance was that I didn't approach her apartment from the front way but from the back. I had a job interview. It was close to her apartment so I decided to visit and ask what they were doing for dinner. I walked up the alley for expediency with the idea of short-cutting between the buildings and entering her apartment from the front door, the only entrance.

Directly behind her apartment was a large shed in which the garbage dumpsters were hidden. My immediate response was what a classy place, but upon examining the proximity more thoroughly, I realized I could probably look into her apartment by climbing it. Maybe I could even get in through a window, and if I could, so could a prowler. To test my theory and give a dramatic demonstration as to the dangers of the condition, the possibility of break-ins, I shinnied up the shed. But I was the person who was surprised.

He was lying on his back lengthwise on her bed. She was standing beside him wearing only bra and panties. It appeared as if she had just massaged him for a bottle of rubbing ointment was opened on the bedside table and his body glistened. But now she was touching him all over his body with one hand and gently rubbing his penis and pubic hair with the other. His eyes were closed, and he was stroking one of her legs with tenderness. Her eyes were also closed, and by the expressions on their faces they were not only enjoying this, but were experiencing a state of ecstasy.

His hand which was touching the outside of her leg slowly began to gently press her inner thigh, then rose and began caressing her between her legs, rubbing her gently. His fingers went under her panties, at first pulling on them then following the outline around her leg and then back to her crotch and began pressing with more energy.

My immediate reaction was to turn away and jump from the shed. But I watched; I couldn't help myself. I began to feel guilty because I was invading their privacy. I felt like a Peeping Tom. I turned my head, but turned back. I had always wanted a sexual relationship with her, had dreamed and fantasized about it, and now it happening before me. Thinking back now as I write, it must have been vicarious gratification; I couldn't pull away because of some pent-up desires were being fulfilled. I had to watch.

He pulled her black panties down to her knees and began to masturbate her clitoris. Holding his hand in place, she covered his body with hers, then removed her bra and crawled upward so that a breast was placed in his mouth. Both of her hands began to pull at his hair on the sides of his head. Her pelvic region was vibrating on top of his. The intense pleasure on her face abruptly changed to panic. He had stopped masturbating her and tried to move from under. His attempt was without success. She rolled from his body and stared at his penis. It was still limp. She threw herself on him and began sucking.

He stroked her head gently, no longer passionately but lovingly as if telling her it's all right; it doesn't matter; let's forget it. But she increased her tempo, pressed his testicles while orally trying to erect him. Then she tried licking, him on and around his groin. He raised his body and was sitting while she still pursued her course. He raised her head with his hands and kissed her on the forehead. She jumped up and began yelling at him, nothing coherent, just yelling, then began hitting him. She threw herself on him and kept hitting him on the chest, then the stomach. He jumped up. That didn't stop her, and she tried to grab his groin. He prevented this by holding her hands.

I hopped down and quickly ran to the lobby door. Someone was entering, and without a pause, I ran the small flight of stairs to her apartment. After ringing the bell, I began pounding on the door. The noise inside subsided, and she yelled, "Wait a minute." About five minutes later, he opened the door. He was dressed except for his shoes.

"The way you pounded on the door, I guess you heard our fighting."

She emerged from the bedroom completely dressed however hadn't bothered to replace her bra. He didn't look at her as she walked from the bed room nevertheless said he was leaving for the evening, and probably wouldn't return. She didn't reply but just stared at his face with a sorrow and longing, knowing that he was out of her reach, probably forever. I didn't see quilt on either face, just misery.

When he left, she began to sob. It was completely involuntary and almost exploded into a convulsive fit. She collapsed onto the floor. I really didn't know what to do. I raised her gently and coaxed her back into her bedroom, so she could lie down. I tried to comfort her, but my comforting turned sexual, and she quit sobbing and began to respond. My own excuse is that I was still confused. I, at the time, didn't know what I wanted. I was turned on, for sure, so was she, but I didn't know how I felt about what I saw. It all happened so quickly and was still happening too quickly. I touched her breasts because they seemed so available under the loose, silk blouse. Her nipples were still erect, and her breast were full, uplifted, seemingly young, untouched. I touched them without expecting any response, just to feel them because I wanted. When my touching became a caress, it was as if I had sprung an uncontrollable reaction. Her sobbing stopped, and she began to respond at first just by touching my hand which was gently squeezing her breast, then she reached up, cupped my face with both hands and brought it down to her lips.

Our kiss persisted without interruption, and I seemed, to fall deeper and deeper into it, deeper and deeper into her being. Her blouse seemed to fall away by itself, for I had made no conscious effort to unbutton it. Within a very short time we both were pass the point of controlling ourselves. Into complete abandonment of our passions, we plunged. She unfastened her skirt with one gesture and was completely nude. My clothing had never seemed to be such a nuisance to discard, but we succeeded in removing enough to make love. She climaxed; her whole vaginal area pulsated in spasms, like a milking action while I was still in her. Never before nor since, have I experienced such sensations.

After the passions had died, we were distant. She rolled over to the edge of the bed and pretended to sleep. I just then began to realize what had taken place and didn't know how to react. Making love to her had been my desire ever since the second time I had seen her, but now....... now that the relationship was finally changed, I regretted it. I regretted how it had happened. The purity of our relationship had ended. Lust had taken it. It wasn't the way it was supposed to happen nor what I wanted. At that moment, I couldn't understand my feelings about what I had seen with her brother. I had considered her completely pure before all this. I had never even imagined her making love to Jacoby, or to any of those boys in college. Of course, rationally I know. With Ike their relationship had lasted five to six years. But then confronted with real life, something I never ever imagined and with someone as close as her brother was to me, destroyed my image of her. What I felt wasn't really as clear cut as all this because my emotions and feelings and thoughts battled each other and left me tense and questioning. I decided to comfort her, not because I really wanted to or felt like it but because I didn't want her to become suspicious of my feelings and coldness. I moved over to her side of the bed and put her head on my shoulder. She began crying again. I understood that she wanted me to leave so she could be by herself, but I didn't. We just lay there for the whole night without sleep, without saying a word to each other and with very little movement.

This all took place what seems like many years

ago. As I say, I can now rationally accept, and maybe even understand it. I can even consider her actions not in the light of what had happened physically but her motives behind her actions. The attempted seduction wasn't necessarily lust on her part but an attempt to help her brother, an attempt which symbolized the culmination of their love for each other. I can really believe that. My seduction of her was our weakness together. Both of us are to blame for that. That is my only regret. There was a better time, place, and situation to change our relationship.

The giving-in to our lusts hurt our relationship. For a period of time, it was a barrier in our relationship: Emotionally. The whole experience dampened my …. wanting…. my desire for her. Likewise she became distant. Our friendship continued; we had dinners together, went to events. But emotionally it hurt. The writing of the event has been painful, but as I see it, necessary to overcome the barrier which has existed between us since then. The truth of my knowledge had to be spoken. Our respect for each other had diminished. We could not even look each other in the eyes for months afterwards. But it did not end our relationship by any means. We, four, Jacoby, Margery, Thesus and I, are too enmeshed with each other to be destroyed by a single event. Our lives have become interwoven. To break with one would be to break with all.

This event created a tension between our hero and his sister, as one can imagine. They continued to see each other, help each other, confide in each other, but they no longer were as close. They both became reserved in their actions and in their conversations. They didn't tell each other everything. They didn't physically play around with each other. Their confiding was serious, factual and, as I have said, reserved. But as I see it now, their relationship wasn't hurt as much as Margery's and mine.

Their father's death brought them together again, physically, mentally, and spiritually. They shared grief, fear, a shock to their faith, and they conjoined all the rest of the confusion which occurred. Their relationship was not like before, and probably will never be again, but they again came to terms with each other. During the funeral, Margery broke and our hero comforted her by placing his arm around her. Later before he disappeared, she kissed him on the forehead and whispered something to him. They both genuinely smiled at each other and hugged, without guilt or regrets. I envied both of them and their relationship for the first time. I wished it would be as easy for her and me: that understanding and forgiveness could and would grow, a reason I have written this.

When our hero returned to San Francisco after the funeral, he again began to have his weekly meals with his sister. Before this period of time, I don't think she could fully accept what was happening to him as being an outside force with intent. She had her interpretations of all the evil he was experiencing but thought that a great deal of what was happening was his own sexual frustrations and psychological problems built by the pressures of boredom from work, his unsuccessful relationship with his ex-girlfriend and then "living in that horrible place with those horrible people." It wasn't until he re-arrived in San Francisco and discussed his meeting with his childhood friend, Adrian, when she began to think that some greater evil force was at work. She had heard rumors about what was being inflicted on "others," mostly degenerates and parasites of the society, so when Thesus told his story she at least listened. Of course, to her it was a mistaken identity, a miss categorization. So she encouraged him to become anonymous and to move from his room. She would have preferred him to return home, to help his mother but could see his point of view, his conviction to discover the cause(s). It is now obvious why he didn't or even couldn't move in with her again.

When he left, disappeared, they were on good terms, as well as can be expected. If worse circumstances would have befallen him, I am sure that he would not have hesitated to contact her first and foremost and probably would have even considered living in with her again, but as I have said this would be if worse came to worse. They did acquire an understanding and acceptance.

Even though I don't know factually, I suspect that he contacts her without my knowledge. I know it is not by mail, nor phones, neither of which they can trust but by some other means, probably the Internet, using synchronized websites and fictional names. I am sure he is in transition, on the move all the time. He went down to Los Angeles, but I know for a fact that he has been to Syracuse since leaving. He hitched to Washington DC. He also has been back to Denver.

Chapter 7

Her name "Margery" is not just a case of being less formal, especially with me, but her sophistication ... sophistication? ... has been tarnished. Even her image of herself was changed to "a woman of the world." I suppose she would appreciate my title, but further, it is something deeper: She is less loving and lovable; there I said it; of course, these are my personal feelings. Am I saying it was easier to love a "young lady" than a woman, ... less threatening?

What I know is she is too conscious of time. The age thirty hit her like a bomb. It is this battle which, because of time, she feels she is losing. Whether she feels society has placed the identity of an "over thirty woman" as too old for a single woman to fulfill herself as a woman, or it is a battle within her own being, I don't know, but I can see it in her. Maybe she had expectations of who and where she would be at the age of thirty, ideas and ideals of marriage, children, career, and money. Yes, we all, at one time or another, awaken to what we, and our lives, have become as a result of earlier actions and decisions. But then again am I having regrets about my life and projecting them? And again, I sense she is resting too much hope in her brother to achieve, to get married, to have a family.

But it is even more than this; something ... more subtle. Her dignity has diminished. Not particularly in my eyes but hers because of too many compromises, too many times of letting herself down, letting down her standards, lessening and loosening her virtues and ethics. It is the subtle day-to-day wearing away of our self-conception, our self-ideals.

This erosion is so subtle and slow that we don't see our loss. Then for a moment when time slows we see the glimpses as a snapshot of who or what we are in the society and within our own lives, and sometimes we are shocked

It was this which was beginning to get to her when I arrived in S.F. She was starting to see mental snapshots, not so much in her appearance but in her manner, her attitude. She is not young anymore. She has the feeling of being forced into adulthood, from college to San Francisco in one big push. This was fine because it was expected. But then as time passed, her expectations were not fulfilled, not particularly of her slow movement up the corporate ladder, but of whom she became. The problem is the constant erosion of self in the day-to-day corporate world: the loss of idealisms: the negotiations, then the concessions; the reevaluation of goals to a lesser level: the need to be more pragmatic.

Maybe, I have hit it...... I just don't know. This whole discussion could be the result of a poem I read in a magazine written by Ike. The "we" in the poem could be Margery, Ike or me.

An Awakening

We are capable of change; can adapt, go with the flow
We can make decisions, meet challenges
We are able to face adversity and stand firm,
We rebound from our defeats.
We can recoup our energies and fight forward.

Our racing heart, our flushed cheeks,
Our mental adjustments to our new perspective;
Revelry in our victories:
Yes, these transform us,
Sometimes violently
But those don't completely make us who we are,
They become memories in the presence of present barrages.
Underlying is a stronger more subtle force at play.

In the daily viewing of ourselves
We rarely see the imperceptible change.
We awaken in the morning
Our room has not changed from the previous night,
We feel we have not changed,
We rarely remember our dreams
But change is constant......
Maybe what prevents us from seeing change is its
consistency.

We stand on a field of liquid corn starch
We jump, we stomp, we pound
Nothing gives.
But while we rest or pause
We sink.
We sink slowly, so slowly
We feel nothing, see nothing.

Occasionally something suddenly awakens us:

Gasping for breath because
Our mouth has become repressed,
Or less symbolically
A past remembrance
A past acquaintance
An old picture
A different outcome than we expect
Awakens us.

We look in a mirror
We have to squint to see through our own perception and
conception of ourselves
To see our yellowing teeth, our growing wrinkles, our
greying hair, our shrinking stature, our slightly glazed eyes
Yes, we can see a different perception than our present
youthful conception of our selves

So when did this happen?
How did we not see the change;
Not just the physical but the erosion of...........
On that which we based our decisions
About which we made our stands ,........
Our youthful conceptions, our ideals, our dreams, our
aspirations, our beliefs
Where is that person?

We feel loss.
Loss of what?
Youth?
Wasted potential?
Unfulfilled possibilities?
But do we truly know the tragedy of lost potential,
unfulfilled dreams?

Yes, when challenged, when pushed

236

We stand ridged, stop time.
When in opposition
Our conception of ourselves is firm and confirmed

.

But Time
The slow ticking awareness
The consistent reality
The constant flow of change
That is the threat.

As I would describe her now, I would say she is a matured woman, thin from activity but not harried. She has adjusted to her life, relaxed into it and yet, is mastering it. She is becoming successful in the business world whereas none of us, Thesus, Jacoby, nor I can be said to be even successfully supporting ourselves. But without her well placed official and unofficial vacations, she would begin to show the pace which she keeps. Most of the time she is in harmony with her environment, generally functionally well within it. She has her cycles as everyone does, but the worse of these, as mentioned, is the feeling of unfulfillment and her age, and that she too hasn't achieved her real potential, that she hasn't accomplished anything of value. Sometimes it is just a general despondency in the way she is living her life. But then the worst of these is like an Existential funk: the feeling of a meaningless life in a hopeless world, with no reason to do anything. I suppose she is internally cycling, and so I have not over responded to these depressions which I have only seen every now and then.

As a contrast to her despondency, I have seen her dance.

I have seen her dance on a beach with the ocean, with an abandonment to the sounds of chaotic waves breaking. Her movements were the waves, curves breaking into angularity then chaos, moving up the beach. Keeping harmony with the incoming waves, her feet never getting wet but yet every foot print always disappearing into the sea.

Other times I have seen her dance with sections of recordings which she feels, expressing an aspect of herself as one could only do with dance. She has been with herself so deeply that only dance could touch the chord of her being. I remember once when we had spent the morning sipping coffee and experiencing the radiant sea-coast sun, listening to a recording of a guitar playing a section of Manuel de Falla's _El Amor Brujo_, discussing nothing in particular on a Saturday or maybe Sunday. She was pacing the floor but stopped. I watched her face change from one of worry to a profundity; she seemed to be reaching inside and her face went blank. Knowing her as I do, she had found a feeling, touched a particular place in her being which needed to be expressed, and she began to dance. She danced not just to the music but to her internal emotions, freely. It began with a young girl hearing and seeing magic for the first time, then seeing the mystery of regeneration, renewal; it grew like vegetation. Flowing motions of upper torso placed her feet into movement: three or four steps forward as if they were forcing their way through thick medium of music, then her head dived as if responding to a blow in her stomach, tucking in all extremities, twisting, spinning on one foot, then, the other leg snapping into a large sweeping step in a different direction, breaking forth, breaking out, exploding into a fantastic suspended ballet leap, pointed toe touching floor first with a regained dignity strutting with head held high, toes still pointed until a slow series of jazz and ballet steps emerged which now expressed the beautifulness of her being.

In the twelve years since I have known her, I have only seen her prepare a dance twice. One time was for a class or recital that she presented to a small group of dancers, and once she danced for me to music we knew and liked, and she had rehearsed as my birthday gift. From that one dance for me, I could see, for the first time, how one medium could not only express another; dance expresses the music, but elevates it. The result was better than either of the medium separately. Times in that dance when she was the music, and times when the music seemed to be her; times when the music possessed her, but times when she was master of it, riding it, gracefully, boldly.

Once back on the ranch I saw her horseback ride in the arena, which both she and Jenny had prepared as a place to practice. After the hundredth time on this course, she had the same appearance. One could tell it had been practiced, but she was free in form because it was her dance, her creation. It was a set pattern, but her pattern; every move with horse and her was a prepared, a rehearsed dance move.

In her depressions she has referred to herself as a frustrated, undeveloped dancer but this is seldom now. She has realized the place of her dance in her life. But at one time, she moved from one dance class to another irrespective of the form. For a while she sought the instructor; for a while she sought the type of dance: Classical, modern; she even attempted India Indian and Asian, Balinese, I think. This was in San Francisco before I arrived. She would practice when and where she could. Jacoby encouraged her to take classes and to practice, because this was "her art form." Now, it has its place in her life, and it is one of the beautiful aspects about her being. It is one of the activities which keeps her beautiful in many ways.

In the last couple of years her despondencies have lessened. She is less anxious, less driven by fears. As I have said she is generally a happy, well-adjusted individual who, only in fear of conforming too little, conforms too much and is less interesting as the result. With her depth of knowledge about herself, she is extremely interesting, a little hard to understand, and at that time a little hard to identify and to identify with.

She is well on her way to becoming a successful business woman; she acts her role well: she dresses the part: suits, sports clothes, and at home, comfortable living wear. She is always well dressed, but looks natural, not immaculate or even over-dressed. She is comfortable in most situations that her daily life brings. But in the most extreme cases, or unusual circumstances, I have seen her become somewhat confused. In these cases, she simply withdraws, mentally, takes a step inside, much like her brother, mentally regroups, and then re-enters the arena and faces her confrontations.

Age has mellowed both of us. I'm thirty-eight, and she's thirty-three. We have matured; life has hardened us and either made us a little numb, or we have adjusted. Our aspirations for what life can be have changed. The man of her dreams and the woman of mine have turned back to reality and embraced each other. The world is not perfect. We are not perfect, and we would only be fooling ourselves if we thought someone else had to be perfect for us to want and love them. If only she could accept my faults, and I accept hers without losing our respect for each other, then our relationship will probably reach a type of fulfillment. But a great deal will have to evolve before we will even see. Isn't that the way it is for any two people? Two beings of almost infinite complexity meet and form a relationship. It is almost as if it is a mutual agreement which makes the relationship occur. Especially between a woman and a man, it is an implied or unstated contract to the type of relationship, its potentiality, which makes it what it is. But once the understanding is reached, it gives that relationship more meanings than the rest of our relations because of the spoken and unspoken vows. It is the commitments of two people to each other that create a significant difference from all of the other acquaintances in the infinite flux of our lives. The two people place meaning by deciding and keeping their devotion. Just in that act, their relationship becomes more than the rest of the chaotic chance happenings, in a sense more real. Two people have decided their attachment is to be a certain way, and they structure it that way in spite of life's fluxes, the society's chaos, individual tragedies, their own changing mortal, fragile beings; I believe it is possible to hold a commitment steadfast through two individual wills, and by holding it permanent, as I have implied, I feel that it can loom greater and have more meaning than the rest of reality. It does so because it is that upon which two people can depend. It is that which gives the two people faith in themselves and in each other. When all else changes, these bonds will not change because the two people will it so.

Until the moment of agreement, nobody but nobody could define the relationship because I don't think we could ever catch ourselves with an absolute knowledge of who we are. Even at that moment of self-recognition, we change: our new knowledge about ourselves changes us; plus, two people together don't add to change, it multiples change. So only through our spoken and unspoken pledges to each other do we define our relationship, ourselves, and even that aspect of reality.

No, even I, a long time ago, quit running after myself to discover who I am, and yet, moments of knowledge have manifested. But I know I can't, and don't want to define myself, for any length of time, and I am not even going to try to define Margery or our relationship. In fact, I am slowly realizing that any characterization in books could never really define a real human being. Only hints can be created as to whom the characters are, and the readers have to place the realism, through their experience and understanding of the world, into the characters. The readers give the characters life, not the writer, for no writer could write with enough detail, even about factual events, to really show a character's comprehensive actions, much less the range of reasons and motives behind those actions. Solely with the complexity of one's own experiences and empathy can the characters assume complexity and life. The reader is only awakened by the writer. The writer hints at real life and awakens similar experiences in the reader. Only life can really write a real story about a real person. Writers can only point at, edit, and create fiction.

Many readers right now are probably saying that I am a fool, and that the above is not the way it is at all. You are right, I am in way over my head, and so I am going to leave the philosophizing of art to Ike, and I am just going to report what has happened and let the reader decide how to interpret it.

In spite of Margery's and my relationship, as it is now, many times in the past I have been on the verge of leaving. Each time, I, of course, changed my mind and stayed. Two years of me looking for meaningful work has had its effect, and if it weren't for this writing, I would have very little to justify my existence. The necessity to justify me to myself is emerging as a predominate force because I have accomplished so little and at this moment my father is dying of cancer. It is a sorrowful state of events, but one where I've been told that I will inherit money. It is not the possibility of inheritance which only impels and assures this project but the retrospect of my father's life. He sacrificed for me. Put me through ten years of college. He lived for me, worked for me, and I am last of the line. His one brother was killed in a war, and his sister never married. Distant cousins may walk this earth, but I am not aware of them. So what am I doing with my life? Have I repaid anything?

This whole period in San Francisco has been stress-filled for me, and exasperating for Margery. For a while I resented coming here and staying. I resented Margery for "making me" make that decision. This period came right after I witnessed the attempted seduction......."seduction" is the wrong word. After checking my Thesaurus, the word "seduction" is not even close: it has the wrong connotations. The closest of the hundred or so words is "interest." "Arousal" or even "rejuvenate" seem to reflect more fully my interpretation of what happened. But I will restate it as "sexual encounter," and let the reader judge the incident.

After I witnessed the sexual encounter, I began to question her other relationships. How many other men has she known? It even evolved to the point where I hated her for deceiving me. Of course, it wasn't she who deceived me, but my own duplicity both consciously and unconsciously. Consciously I believed I knew who she was, especially earlier in our (my) relationship but really I made her who I wanted and then wanted her. 1 labeled her: said she was this and that; of course she wasn't. Unconsciously I placed all my idealisms on her and on the relationship I thought we could have and then expected her to live up to them and expected our relationship to become them. Minds are mysterious manipulators.

After witnessing the sexual encounter, I went through a period of disillusionment and didn't trust her. I was cold to her, but I never quit seeing her as a friend. The idea of marriage, which I have had since college, ceased. I more fully knew who she was and knew I couldn't trust her with my feelings and emotions. I wanted to believe that what she did with me, that is have sex, was all right, but because I couldn't basically even fool myself, I couldn't trust her. If she made love to me in that moment of emotion, I was sure she would or has with others. If she would have told me of the whole encounter, I probably would have trusted her more. But she didn't. As I have said, I have realized that this was my deception of myself. I had placed a morality on her and expected her to uphold it. She never said her morality was such-and-such. It was my expectations, a main cause for sorrow in relationships, and my idealisms, not hers.

I can see this now, not then. I believe in her as a person and as a friend. For a while, I expected her to make amends to me for a sin against which I thought she had transgressed. Of course, our friendship did not hinge on her making the compensation, and I didn't expect it to happen in such a way that my attitude would change, but it has, even though my ego and trust have not been assuaged.

Almost as a contradiction, a gradual merging of our beings has transpired. Before the window incident, I had begun to pressure her into marriage. I can now see that I was beginning to make demands of her, again expecting her to respond in a certain way, as if we were together forever. I guess I was trying to form her into the role that I wanted her to play. In my own mind she wanted it also. Her lack of response as I wanted was explained to myself as she gave as much as she could give.

But after the incident and after I became cold to her, I discovered she didn't need me. She didn't want to play my assigned role and didn't want to depend on me for emotional stability. She didn't want to need anyone. She knew what she wanted, and she knew could achieve completeness within herself. I have grown to respect her strength and independence, and because of those qualities, her loving me means more. I am not what she is stuck with, as it could have been if I had had it my way; I am her choice. When my respect for her remained intact and my understanding of the meaning of her love enforced itself into my consciousness, I again began to love her in a different and more profound way.

Her love for me may have been because I let loose of my attempt to create her in my own image. It may have been because of the partial loss of her brother and father. It may have been because I was around, helpful, without demands or expectations. Whatever the cause, her love for me has grown.

I have always wanted her love and was happy when she gave, even the littlest amount. But as I have said it was self-deception which lead me to think that that was the only type of love she could ..... should? ... give me. At first when she began to become affectionate, concerned, respectful, giving to a degree which I had never known, I didn't know how to react.

In fact, I thought it might have been guilt. But as I have said, I have always wanted an emotional attachment, and slowly but surely, have come to accept and believe in her. I have begun to accept her love, which has melted my doubt. Through her giving, I have begun to believe she is over generous, too good, too kind, too giving, too concerned.

Dwelling any time on those still vivid images reawakens the emotionality of the incident, but rationally, I believe in her and respect her. The only place where my trust in her remains shattered is our different moral standards. Of course, she will not and does not abide to what I consider right and proper but what she considers right. We have never verbalized an agreement. We have never stated what we both want or what we want individually. I trust who she is but still have to guard against emotionally being hurt because of her actions. Her actions may be completely right in her mind and yet, rock my emotional stability. I believe she would never intentionally maltreat me, but in doing what she wants may cause me some grief.

A week ago she came by to see me after work. After a couple of drinks, she happily announced that she had finally completed one of her goals. Her investments were giving her enough returns to live, or at least exist without working. She was not, she felt, financially independent because the interest on her money was not enough to accomplish sufficient growth. It was still a depleting system because of inflation.

"Step one is accomplished. Now it is a matter

of time rather than a matter of hope. I have the principle from which to get interest to pay for my assurance as far as future money is concerned, but now I need to secure enough to guarantee that my system will increase by itself."

"How long will that be?"' I asked.

"Well I am working in an arithmetical progressive system and maybe if I double the amount that I have now, I will have created a system that will not only be progressive by itself but will give me adequate insurance on the system itself and on the way I want to live. That day will be my Freedom Day.

"Tonight I would like to make a toast." This was our third or maybe fourth drink. "Lights have been dimmed.........misdirected. In my case, there is a part of me that I have wanted to develop which has been led astray through habit, monotony, and conditioning. It has been manifest in a concern for things valueless to life and to my life, particularly, and to the lives of those I love. It has been wasted time and energy."

She took hold of my hand and pressed the back of it. "But my case," she continued, "is minor and exists mainly because of my own faults. We know of far worse cases and think of all the cases we don't know. I can see my freedom from working the eight hour day, five days a week, fifty weeks a year. I still question whether I have spent too much to achieve it, but when that day comes, then I will join my brothers in their fight, against the darkening of the light."

"All right!" I resounded, "To our rage against the dimming and destruction of the light, against the powers which deplete our sacred human rights, may we not slip into this plight without a sincere and noble fight." Of course, I was drunk, but we both smiled then laughed as we clicked glasses, warm within each other's eyes.

I felt Jacoby's effect, almost presence, and her laugh told me she did also ... then I didn't even smile.

BOOK II

Part I

Chapter 1

Ike Jacoby's body was found, a bullet through the head. He had made a movie of his suicide. Thesus told me about the movie but was very vague as to its whereabouts. For some reason, to be absolutely truthful, I am not surprised. I wasn't even shocked as was everyone else when I first heard either about his suicide or the movie. I must admit I hadn't expected it, at least consciously expected it. He had been suffering from a depression off-and-on for the last three years, almost a manic depression. Since the reader may not be aware of my feelings for Ike, I must say, I am sorry it happened. I regret that he reached such a low that he felt that it was his only alternative. I guess I should feel partially responsible for his death. I could have helped him more in spite of our competition for Margery, and it was probably my insecurity which prevented me.

It seems inconceivable that his suicide could have been completely caused by their break-up, for that happened over three years ago, but maybe just the mentioning of it shows some of my guilt, since I feel I helped finalized the break. But as I have said, that couldn't be the total reason.

I know for a fact that his depressions were intensified by his desperateness for recognition, not especially from Margery but as an artist and a person. But no recognition was ever forth coming. Since I have known him, he used to sit in crowds at parks or bars, anyplace wanting to meet people but never created a lasting relationship, to my knowledge. He was too distant from everyone to converse, except anything but passing comments. He was too wrapped up with himself to communicate. Yet, I know that is what he wanted. I saw him time and time again sitting in a cafe in North Beach watching and wanting, but nothing ever happened. The first time I saw him, I faded back into the crowds so he wouldn't see me, but later upon seeing him again, I approached and befriended him.

Our only mutual interests, at first, were Margery and her brother, and our common name. He pronounced his name "Jak o be," and our family pronounced it "Ja co be." After much tracing our family trees, just what we knew first hand, we still didn't find a common ancestor. After a while we found a mutual interest in writing and literature; however, as strange as it may seem, I never asked to see his work. He, of course, always indirectly or even directly discussed it as I would try to discuss literature. But I never encouraged him to show it to me. I decided that he was an artist, and I didn't want to be in a position where I would have to judge him and his works. I thought that would probably end our relationship. I am too critical and besides that, I am sure I was prejudice against him, in spite of myself, at least at the beginning.

In fact at first, I didn't want his friendship, but it was my curiosity that attracted me: What could Margery have seen in him? Also, I felt sorry for him. I am sure those weren't the only reasons, but whatever they were, I came to find out that he was a damned interesting and intelligent fellow and a true artist. A true artist, not in the products produced, for as I have said I never read any of them, but in his pursuit and involvement. He lived art. Verbally he was always exploring his media, concepts, and new ways of expressing. Maybe his involvement was a quality of greatness I will never know and the products of his involvement nobody will ever know for almost none can be found. A great many of his manuscripts were found burnt beyond salvaging in a hole he dug in front of his dead body.

But then again I could believe that he never produced anything of importance. He just mouthed his achievements. I can believe that he never submitted any of his manuscripts because he knew they wouldn't be published. He couldn't have faced the rejection, the reality that he had wasted his time and his life. Margery said that he used to send his manuscripts out by the dozen but eventually gave up because nothing major was ever accepted. From what I have been told by him, he had a couple of poems published in obscure small presses. His deception wasn't malicious or even with intent, and he was no more deceptive to others than to himself. He believed in his accomplishments. He wanted to believe and had to believe. He had a child's mind so much so that he could have convinced himself that he was accomplished and had something he never had.

His involvement was so intense, people didn't want to be in his presence. His conversations were bordering on the obscure and were always so egotistical that most of the time they were offensive. No matter what the discussions he would always bring it around to something he wrote or himself. I guess this wasn't always true, but close. When Margery first met him, she said he was sociable and less egotistical. But the more he was rejected as an artist, the harder he tried, and the more time he would spend on his art until he was nothing but his art. Once, he defended his egotism as Artist's Conceit. "You have to believe you can do something great or you wouldn't try." But I believe he was nothing more than his creation. He was desperate to break out of his own mind and be more than his creation. He wanted something more, needed it. He wanted so desperately to communicate and be recognized for his communications. He needed for his life to have meaning. And I'll give him credit, he never referred to himself as wretched. He, for sure, thought of himself as a frustrated artist, unable to communicate what he had found. In fact I remember a poem he recited a couple of times to me.

> My creation is not a wall,
> A word, or a tree,
> But thoughts that live as seeds
> Carried by high flying birds
> From an isolated island.
> Will the seeds ever fall on fertile ground and
> grow?"

He used to recite poems often, most often his, but not always. He would get a very intense expression on his face, and it was obvious, here comes one of his. Seriousness filled the air and the presentation would be expressed very formally. The words would flow as if they were not his. In fact, in the recitation of the above poem he was feeling sorry for himself and slightly drunk, "really down on the world," but he recited with no pity, no emotion at all, only a concentrated effort to enunciate and beat out the rhythm. As the reader can see there is very little rhythm to mention, but that didn't bother him; he beat it out anyway.

From what he told me, his writing gave him everything he needed. He felt his dedication gave him his meaning and that he experienced freedom within his media, no matter what they were. Completion of works were his success, and "Nobody or nothing can take away who I have created of myself by creating my art objects. When I say, I have written a manuscript and finished it, I know I have accomplished something, I have grown, I have become, and I don't need society's categorization of success to feel good. I don't need society's money as a badge to let me know I have done something."

But deception was not a stranger to him. Oh, he may have been free in his fantasy, but he couldn't totally live in it. He had to contend with the day to day existence, and he couldn't cope. That is another reason why I think he killed himself. The twenty-four hours in the day killed him. Too much time in the day when he couldn't be involved with his writing. Where else could he go? What else could he do? Yes, the surplus time broke into his world of writing, into his fanciful world, and eventually deteriorated it to the point where he could see that it was hopeless, fruitless to continue. This surplus of time cracked his unreal reality, broke-in and destroyed him. Maybe in a moment of enlightenment, he saw the stupidity of his dedication: that he wasn't the artist he thought, that his works weren't as great as he had thought, that he was wasting his time and had wasted his life; and now what? Forty-some years old, too old to start anew. Oh, if he could have only held onto Margery, onto the one person who could give him love and belief in himself. Yes, now without anything or anybody, no reason to go on, empty and with nothing, hopelessness sets in. So why not end it?

Money had undoubtedly also helped to break him. He was in debt to everyone, Thesus, Margery, relatives, banks, loan companies, credit unions, Berkeley, the government in the form of the dreaded student loans, (a method to keep track of people, to say the least) and he owed me. I don't think he cared about any of the loans except for the personal ones. He had no way to pay any of them and knew it. Owing his best friends must have been onerous. It must have been hard to face us.

The funeral took place today. He must have been dead for days because the body was partially decayed and so they had to have a quick funeral. Only four of us attended the pallor, and only we three, Margery, Thesus and I, went to the crematorium. His uncle didn't follow the car procession across town.

Even our friend's death didn't have an effect on the weather. It was hot and dry for this time of year. The fog had burned off in the morning, and in the afternoon it was a beautiful clear day.

His uncle had arranged the cremation and after the service had gone out and gotten drunk rather than follow through with "the whole mess."

Later when we three, accidentally met his uncle at a bar, one of Jacoby's favorite, his uncle seemed to take the death as a vexation and nothing more. By the time we arrived, he was pretty far gone.

When we saw him, we quickly and quietly sat at another table away from his view. He must have seen us enter, for he came over and forced himself upon us. He began rambling about his nephew, the failure, who could never make his way for himself, who never could maintain self-support without his help. He and his wife were originally from the Mid-West, and his speech still contained a slight twang

"Time and time again, I supported the oaf. I lent him money. For years he stayed in my beach house until I had to kick him out. He never offered to pay rent or even help pay utilities. He even lived with us for six months until my wife and I almost went nuts. He was damned inconvenient. He always wanted and needed something."

At Margery's wince then stare, the uncle pushed forward, "I kicked him out. Of course, I ousted him, and I would do it again. What he needed was a good taste of the real world, ... work. He didn't know the meaning of the word.

"I tried; the Lord knows I tried. But that boy was thick. I even threw him into a mental institution a couple of times to straighten him out. But it didn't help. Those electric shock treatments only seemed to make him dumber, thicker in the head. Nothing could shake him out of his world of imagination." Margery who was sitting right next to me recoiled at these words.

He took another big swig of his drink. "What a damned failure, a disgrace to my wife and me. I would have kept him in that nut-house where he belonged but my wife made me get him out. Legally, he wasn't insane because he wasn't dangerous to himself or to others, but I told them. I warned them something like this would happen!"

At this point he broke down and cried.

By this time, Margery was visibly shaking and an ash gray. We had had a couple before the funeral, but that speech even shook me. Her eyes had become swollen; she too was on the verge of tears, but pulled herself together enough to say in an angry voice, "When did you put him in an institution?"

"A couple of times in college. Before college I had hoped for a recovery. But in college, he got more out of hand and being his legal guardian, I saw I had no other choice. Also I had to get him in there before he was twenty-one, or it would have been more difficult. I thought his marriage would straighten him out, but it seemed to make it worse.

It was for his own good. I swear it was."

Margery stood up with her fists clenched and yelled, "Get out of my sight. If you don't leave, I will..."

Ike's uncle pulled himself together very quickly but just stared at her. She walked over and took a swing at him. It struck him in the face but glanced off. Nobody stopped her. Nobody really expected her to do it. This frightened him; he quickly stood. He may have returned the blow if Thesus and I hadn't stood. He just backed away and retreated to his table, retrieved his coat and departed.

She knew about Ike's incarceration but not who was responsible. She told me later she thought that internment was one of the most detrimental events in his life. "Because of that he always questioned his sanity. He also thought the treatments had destroyed his abilities. He thought he was handicapped and could never recover. It gave him an identity from which he never escaped."

Margery has taken the death of Jacoby in a strange way. She is shocked, but seems not to feel guilt as her brother or I do. She isn't hurt or even sorry, or at least she doesn't show it. I would say she is curious. She questioned her brother about the movie.

257

She moved into a period of introspection, of wanting to be by herself. The funeral was her first appearance for me. I was worried about her and before the service tried to make her discuss her reasons for this response. She discussed his strength, beliefs, his art; facts which she said, "You would never be able to understand or accept."

I could understand at that point in our conversation that she was distraught with me because I wasn't discussing Jacoby in a positive light, but "speaking ill of him." Looking back on today, I think it was more, more than she would or will admit. She may not have wanted to see his desperateness, his defeat, his unhappiness because she doesn't want to take the responsibility for what has happened. I didn't press or even propose my opinions but ceased the conversation.

Jacoby's death has had quite a different effect on our hero. Thesus knew Ike as I knew him, through his association with Margery. He knew Jacoby around two more years than I. He had met him without Margery's knowledge and in fact tried to reunite them. Jacoby came to confide in our hero, cried on his shoulder, as it was.

Thesus thinks he knows why Jacoby killed himself but was surprised that he did "carried his ideas to their final conclusion. I could have and should have talked him out of it, showed him the fallacy in his thinking. But I didn't think he would do it." Yes, the guilt which I thought Margery would carry was felt by her brother.

It may be true that Thesus knows Jacoby's
258

reasons. Jacoby and Thesus had a very intense relationship; their discoveries were profound, "Sometimes more real than anyone would have ever expected," our hero mumbled almost to himself. "His conversations stimulated my thought. He gave me his ideas, and they would set off a thousand ideas of my own. But I should have listened more to what he said, instead to the thoughts he generated."

We three used to drink wine and talk for hours and hours until the wine or the late hour would finally do us in. I would always be the first to fade. I remember one conversation that I would like to insert here because it shows the relationship of our hero and Jacoby, and because it also reminds me of the conversation which I overheard and recorded earlier. It shows the evolution of our hero's thought and Ike's belief not too long before his death.

As you can see our hero's statement to Jacoby is almost an evolving restatement of earlier thought, when he was a youth. It must have been a response to something Ike said or said he did. "If God exists and is controlling then I will just live the illusion of self-control. But if It doesn't exist or isn't controlling, and I leave my responsibilities to It, thinking It can control, I will be in trouble. Yes, God's existence almost becomes an irrelevant question as far as how I should conduct my life. It is more pragmatic not to believe It exists than to live as if It does."

Jacoby interrupted Thesus and said, "I say a prayer to the greater forces which exist and which have control. Sometimes I have my doubts whether any are conscious and have a conscious control but if there aren't, may God help us," and he began to laugh. He always thought that his jokes were funnier than anyone else did. Then his face blanked and he stared at the ceiling and muttered, "I have experienced…

Thesus without cracking a smile interrupted, "If God exists; It exists and if It doesn't, It doesn't. It is how I conduct my life that is important. I must be responsible for my actions and if It exists, It will see my attempt and if It doesn't, still I try to live my life the best way possible without any dependence."

This conversation took place the last time we three met in a bar before going to Big Sur. In fact we met to make the final arrangements. In spite of the earliness in the evening, we were all pretty high and feeling fine.

As I have said, Ike's death torments our hero. I hope it isn't the proverbial straw. It was he who found the body at the beach house, or should I say in front of the house. Thesus had journeyed up there in his usual reappearing act. He needed rest, time to write some letters, and discuss with Ike "facts" that he had discovered. From our hero's observation, the body had been lifeless for a day or two. Ike had shot himself while sitting in front of a fire. When Thesus found the body it was being washed back and forth with the waves. It is Thesus' contention that it might have been Ike's idea to get washed into the sea and not burden anyone. This could be a reason for the camera, to let everyone know he just wasn't missing. I guess the camera was pointed at the ocean, below the tide level, where Ike must have been sitting when he shot himself. I am sure this story will advance when I acquire the recording. I am not even positive that the movie is of his death, but I have more than a suspicion, unless he fouled up this also.

He must have gotten the facts about high tide wrong, for he didn't get swept out to sea. Not even the hole that contained the fire and his burnt manuscripts had water. It definitely sounds as if didn't account for seasonal low tides.

Writings are surfacing in spite of Ike's attempt to destroy them. That he tried to burn any of them is a surprise to me. I would have thought he was too egotistical to eradicate anything he wrote. My new theory about his death is he wanted to die and sought a way, a cause, a spectacular method to demonstrate his plight. He at the most might have used his death to protest the condition of artists in America. This is somewhat what Thesus thinks. He wanted to give his death a significance. When Thesus implied this I added, even if he couldn't give his life significance. But if this is so, it seems he searched awfully hard to find a cause for which to die. As I mentioned, in that he wasn't washed into the sea shows another failing attempt, but I am speculating and maybe this wasn't his intent. I guess I am going to quit hypothesizing, until I see and listen to the movie and really discuss the matter with Thesus.

Chapter 2

I really don't know much about Jacoby before our arrivals in San Francisco. From what I have gathered, mainly from implication and second-hand stories, he had a very tragic childhood. His parents died in a car crash when he was very young. Both of them were returning from a party intoxicated, missed the exit from the freeway, and hit a concrete embankment. Both immediately died from the impact.

Jacoby was raised (sic) by his uncle and aunt. By raised I mean, sent off to military schools, summer camps and the like until he attended Berkeley. Something snapped when his parents died, and he closed himself into his own world. His only friend was his aunt to whom he really wasn't related, (his uncle was his mother's brother), and he only saw her irregularly. She, in her way, understood Jacoby, or at least this is what he implied. She was the only person after the death of his parents he allowed into his world. It was she who went in and retrieved him, brought him back into this world at the age of fifteen.

His uncle, as you can tell, was unsympathetic, intolerant, and un-understanding. He never wanted children, though his wife did, and when his sister's child was forced upon him, he reacted and sent him off as quickly as possible because (my guess) his wife began to show affection.

Jacoby spent the rest of his life looking for a home, a mother, and his lost childhood. He married at the age of eighteen to an older woman. His uncle because he thought he had rid himself of his nephew, more than encouraged the marriage and offered to pay for his college education which (my guess again) induced the older woman into marriage. Her thinking

262

was undoubtedly that the uncle would be a large source of financial security.

Only money for tuition, books, clothing, and if fought for, rent was forthcoming, and Jacoby's wife had to go to work if she wanted anything else. After three years she began to fully understand the relationship between her husband and his uncle and decided it wasn't as she had planned. Berkeley is "too wide open a town," too progressive, not to have other involvements. Her associations drew her away, and it didn't take long until she divorced her husband so that she could pursue her own life. To our knowledge, she didn't leave Jacoby for any person in particular, but because she wanted her freedom. She didn't want the responsibility of being his mother. She was tired of his childishness, his irresponsibility, his dependency on her for his emotional security, growth, personal esteem, even his school work. All this surfaced in an interview with her just recently in Berkeley. I decided to find her and let her know about Jacoby's death. Yes, she had heard about his suicide and was curious about the movie.

In spite of his wife's help, he did poorly in school with every subject except his major, sculpture, art in general, and English, writing. She left him in his second year which completely destroyed him. It was fortunate he was in school when she left and his uncle was still supporting him because he became more irresponsible, lost and confused. The shelter which school offered him let him indulge in self-pity. It must have been some time during this period when his uncle threw him into the institution, but he told me that he spent the complete two or three years drunk, never attended classes except when he wanted and only worked on art and writing. He frantically searched for someone to take the place of his departed wife but was completely unsuccessful, "meeting only girls" with whom he had affairs. Again and again, he threw himself at these "girls" only to be disappointed or rejected. This seems to be a manifestation of the syndrome I described from my first impression of him. The more he was rejected, the more he pursued them until they bluntly told him "to bug-off" or worse. These unsuccessful relationships helped to destroy his self-image, and the fact that he never felt he achieved anything worthwhile furthered the failure image of himself.

Just by the shear amount of time he stayed around Berkeley, his intelligence, and I am sure, with the good will of his instructors, the momentum in his art courses, he graduated. He lingered around Berkeley after graduation, began to work in sculpture as an occupation. Of course, his uncle wasn't happy with his choice, but just so Jacoby "stayed out of his hair," almost anything was fine. In fact his uncle supported Jacoby's first large sculpture project which was two female figures.

Jacoby created a morning bedroom scene complete with bed, dresser, chair and two life size female (epoxy?) figures. The first body is lying on the bed with her arms behind her head. She is completely nude and is staring at the second figure who has on a see-through night gown and is standing at the bed in an early morning stretch: one arm upward and the other covering her mouth. Their torsos are very realistic and sensual. The faces are more impressionistic, with no details; one can imagine a nose, mouth, eyes but nothing more. When I saw the scene, I didn't stand where the viewer was intended to stand, viewing the scene through a window frame. I refused to be manipulated by Jacoby. I ventured onto the set and ran my hand over the woman's body on the bed. In spite of the coldness of the plastic, it was a very sensual experience. The area between the hips and the stomach was one of the most sensual sensations I have yet experienced with something not alive. Then I noticed two larger black and white oil paintings on the wall. Both had figures in them. One was a bedroom scene with a window and moving objects in that window. The other had an elevator which seem to continuously move upward. I thought how did he create the illusions of movement? I would have stayed and explored the scene but a guard forced me from the set.

When Jacoby first created this scene, sculptures and paintings, he had placed it outside in the back yard of his apartment house and had a show with engraved invitations, alcohol, finger-food: the works. It must have cost a fortune, but nothing developed from his efforts; for besides the invitations, he didn't advertise, didn't try to sell it, didn't think to get any publicity, and therefore his only write-up was in the local underground newspaper. When he moved to San Francisco he abandoned it. There was no place to store anything of that size without money. The University must have claimed it, maybe for his debts, because it now rests in the University Museum. He tried to get the museum to buy it, but they wouldn't. He still didn't know what to do with it, didn't have the money for a legal battle, so he just left it.

Margery saw it while he was alive. He personally took her to the museum, I think as a means to court her. I've seen it just lately.

Another sculpture which he created at this time was a death mask which is now on his grave. It is amazing. It isn't what he looked like at his death, but maybe when he was younger. It is a bronze face with platinum eye brows, eye lashes, and hair. The effect is a handsome, pre-maturely gray, young man. An inscription under the mask is "Life,/Death,/ Before my time." As I have said, it surely didn't look like him at his death; he was a beaten man in his late forties who looked a very old sixty, lines prematurely etched in his brown cheeks and around his eyes. His long hair on the sides and back of his head was salt and pepper, not completely gray.

It must have been his uncle who put the mask on Jacoby's tomb. I think it is in poor taste because it doesn't represent Jacoby at all, and his uncle is making Jacoby something he wasn't. It could be that the uncle trying to create a celebrity because he has possession of Ike's art and would like it to sell.

At the age of twenty-four Jacoby discovered that he had an inheritance. It had been due since his twenty-first birthday, then another year passed before he could collect. By that time not a great proportion of the legacy was left. Ike forcing his uncle pay made the uncle angry. In fact, the uncle took executor fees, even for that year he fought against giving his nephew the money. The uncle subtracted every payment he had made to his nephew since receiving him. He deducted their wedding gift of his education, the funding of the sculptures, and the divorce costs.

Jacoby must have figured enough inheritance was left to survive, or he just didn't feel like going to court again and facing his uncle, because he finally let it ride. From what I gathered he started another sculpture which he never finished because of finances. It was a sculpture of Justice. She was sitting with a sword in her right hand and the scales in the other. She was not blind folded but was staring directly at the unbalanced scales. I heard from many different sources that she was magnificent. She was life-size and had a very desirous body. He told me that he wanted people "to covet her, in more ways than one." It also had the inscription "All persons shall be equal in the eyes of the law/ Equality in Justice." I have only seen the remains which are a head and a much deteriorated torso. The head is great. It is an idealistic, Greek style, symmetrical, serious, stately face; it is not, however, still connected to the body. The torso is only the stomach and the breasts.

Yes, from what is left, it was sexy. Both pieces are still in the original clay which he spent six to ten months working into form. At first, when he didn't have the money to bronze it, he was going to encase the whole thing in plastic, like a paper-weight. Nothing that size had or has ever since been encased. He ran into too many problems with money, a location where it could be poured. He personally had the money, but it was a gamble whether the sculpture would sustain the casting. I guess the temperature from a pouring could range into the thousand degree level. The whole thing could have exploded from the heat building on the inside, so he decided to make a casting, a mold to preserve what he could. If he ever raised enough money, he could cast it into bronze. Instead of doing that he commenced applying to different people and organizations for the money which was never forthcoming. He applied to the government which was a joke, to his uncle, another joke and to various people who he knew were wealthy, of course, nothing developed from any of his appeals. When he had to move, he left it and it fell into pieces. He knew it would - with no way to fire the clay to make it strong enough to endure the move.

It was a year after receiving a check for the inheritance that he decided he not only couldn't finish the sculpture but couldn't undertake any other sculptures. At the rate he was spending, it wasn't going to last. He had been writing all this time and threw himself into that completely, with the idea of going back to sculpture after making some money through writing or at least after establishing himself so he could get grants and awards.

I gathered from what he told me that the shock of his depleting resources made him desperate, and he tried to make a fast buck in the stock market. As stupid as he was about life, he was more stupid about business and people in general. His broker took him up that old road and back again. Rather than buy stocks, Jacoby was sold stocks. His broker explained that a holding company was "letting loose" of five hundred thousand shares of paper producing stock because the holding company needed equity. The paper mills had a monopoly in some of the southern states. The price of the stock would go down for a while until the quantity was absorbed by the market then it would rebound and probably go higher. What he didn't tell Jacoby was that his brokerage firm was the holding company; it did need equity, but it was also ridding itself of its losers, and of course, the broker was making extra commission by selling it. The brokerage firm thought that it was a "long term dog" because a nationally known company was building a factory in the South and was going to run competition. When the stock plunged almost as expected, Jacoby bought. The stock went down again as reports of the competition began to materialize, but not staying informed, he bought again and then a third time, before Jacoby asked another brokerage firm about the stock then went to the library and confirmed "the truth." His money was reduced. He began seeking employment.

With his art degree from Berkeley, right away he found a job decorating front store windows for a small store, then he joined a union and got regular jobs. Although he was a success, it didn't last long because he began rejecting jobs, either because he didn't like the people with whom he was working or later because he didn't feel he needed the money. He was happy living from hand to mouth. The union quit calling as much and then they quit calling altogether. But he didn't care; it would be more time for him to work on his writing. He would get something published; with the "big hit" he would get a studio and return to sculpture. With this kind of thinking, of course he fell into the starving artist syndrome; working cheap-paying, manual-labor jobs which didn't get him anyplace or anything except enough money to buy time to work on art. This period of his life lasted up until he met Margery.

It was during this syndrome that the number of girls he pursued was reduced, the few number of friends he still knew diminished, and he was on "his way to being a recluse." Money began to limit his activities, and as I can imagine him, he just let himself drift into this situation.

In a bar one night, he told me a drunken interpretation of this period of his life. I can imagine him wandering the San Francisco streets, dressed slightly eccentrically, in a slight daze, but maybe I am putting the forty-some year old mind on a young body: shades of the sculpture. A disclaimer: Yes, this whole period in time is one of speculation for me, a collection of bits of information picked up here and there. So some projection is inevitable, not only who I thought he was but who I am, filled with biases which can't be avoided.

Chapter 3

When he met Margery, his life was revitalized. He again began to look for a job. He tried back at the union, but only received few calls. It was his reputation. He advertised and found jobs as an independent decorator. He took an interest in people, especially Margery's friends. His own description of himself was that he entered "another real world." His involvement in the day-to-day life situations became so time consuming, he had to force himself to write at night, then he gave up writing anything but poetry and that only when inspired.

I guess, at first, they were in love, and their love generated energy beyond energy, hope beyond hope, aspirations beyond aspirations. Jacoby believed that he wanted marriage, a family, a home, an occupation, and at the time, he thought he could have it all because, as he later explained to me (in another night in another bar) at that time he realized that the sacrifice to art which he had made of himself wasn't worth what he had sacrificed: "A person's life is greater than the art which the life could create; the effect of life is greater or could be greater than the effect of the art objects."

At first he began to work on his writing when time permitted. He decided to accept art on life's basis, not life on art's basis. It finally became, "a hobby," but he had an extreme reaction to this stance. Looking back he admitted he became (more) obnoxious, physically distraught, and that he regressed to the defiant behaviors of a teen-ager.

By this time in our conversation, he was slopping in his sit, slurring his words, and holding an empty glass, which I didn't suggest filling. In my slightly inebriated state, I realized a reason I found him interesting: He had a perspective about himself;

he knew himself.   He was not the typical self-centered, egotistic artist.   He was into controlling himself and thereby had to know who he was. He was into knowing and controlling his thoughts, so he analyzed what popped into his mind and tried to figure out why. Then he would "reset" his thoughts.

In this case he did so by coming up with what he considered a better philosophical position. "If he created of himself a superior being and a superior artist, every object he created would be an exceptional work of art, irrespective of the technique or style. Then he decided he didn't need to create art objects at all because he was creating of himself. He did not do art, for he was still forming an artist who will create.

It is this type of reasoning which I found not just entertaining but interesting. Could someone take control like that? Should someone? And what would be the result? Well we found out!

Some of this belief was still maintained at the end of his life, but he later felt he was only an artist when he was working in art.

Through a synthesis of what I have gathered, during this period he had "run through" various jobs. Most of them were part time or temporary: tutoring creative writing or art, store decorating, being a guard at night in some large building, but what he was still seeking was a permanent job that would enable him to accumulate enough money and security to propose marriage to Margery, to begin to create his family life. Margery knew of his intentions and believed in him.

In a way I can believe she was beguiled by his sculptures. They were the best aspect of him and on a very impressive display. I am sure that involvement on her part was impossible without her belief in his art, but who knows. In the fields of art and literature, she was no one's fool. His works must have produced some belief.

Even though Margery wasn't quite ready for marriage, they both discussed it and moved in together to see if they were compatible. He, after a year of job hunting, found that permanent position. It was in one of those department stores where he was decorating windows, when he met someone who hired him to work in sales with almost an immediate raise to department manager. Margery encouraged the job. She was still "on the dole" from her father to go to secretarial school, and they had figured they would begin to save money. But rather than save for their marriage, they spent every bit on restaurants, shows, traveling, buying furniture, etc.

He worked for six months as a floor salesman then was given the raise when the manager of his department was transferred. He was still looking forward to the slowly evolving raise, but he eventually discovered he was still just a floor salesperson with a different title and a little more responsibility. They would also call him to window and floor displays. Those he still enjoyed but felt used, exploited. He calculated that he was making less money per hour than when he just did the windows.

It was boredom of standing behind the counter, straightening the merchandise on the displays, in short looking busy, which weighed heavy on his active mind. The most interesting aspect of the job was talking with the female buyer of his department.

He kept telling Margery he was wasting his time. When he eventually discovered that the raise didn't change very much, both of them were disappointed. He again began to complain about wasting his time and his life. The money wasn't worth what he was doing to get it. His thoughts again turned to his art, but rather than move in that direction, he decided to look for another situation. He investigated and examined without results. He began to think of himself as trapped on the third floor of life, with no way up and no way even to get back to earth.

This is when they began to save. Margery had begun some type of job and even though their combined incomes decreased, (Margery's father's support stopped when she told him she was living with someone.) they began accumulating. Jacoby had some of his inheritance left, but saving didn't help his attitude. They had a start, but he couldn't see his way out because their savings weren't increasing rapidly enough for them to undertake buying a house and having a family anytime soon. He had the down payment and then some, but they felt it was not enough. They would need a car, appliances, furnishings, etc. and what if she got sick and couldn't work?

He could see himself working indefinitely at something he hated, the permanent third floor trap. All this began to gnaw at his mind. One Wednesday he was standing behind the counter and began to cry. "It was the boredom, the futility, the hopelessness, and I finally admitted, the defeat." He said he couldn't help himself; he just broke down. The next day with Margery's knowledge and somewhat with her approval, he quit.

He told me if he would have stayed one more day until Friday, he would have had a two day paid vacation, but he couldn't handle it. "I couldn't take even one more day."

A decision was made to change directions again, go back into art, writing mainly. They could live on his interest and her salary until a break-through occurred, and then he would begin to financially support with his share from art. I don't know Margery's reaction, but it was something: an agreement, compromise, sacrifice, or what? Just plain hope? I can't tell you.

His only interruptions were Margery and the everyday necessities. He was happy for the first time since they met. He was doing what he wanted, and she had made it possible, at least this is what he thought. He began to revere her. She was the only person for whom he had time. He felt both of them were on a pedestal and growing. The only things worth his while were art and his shared presence with her. He thought his thoughts were on a very high plane of existence, but he could "see" he could be distracted, pulled down by the mundane people and events. His life and thoughts were pure; he felt he was fulfilling himself the best way possible. His self-image was running down a road at a comfortable pace, happy, going as fast as he could and as fast as he wanted to, with the excitement of new scenery, change, and yet not tiring: "a completeness growing."

In fact it was this period of time he thanked Margery for when I first met him.

Margery, of course, didn't see him as he saw himself. She thought that he was somewhat distant. He had become too engrossed in himself. He was soaring inward, and I think she began to feel insecure about him and their relationship. She had never met anyone who could achieve this depth of involvement. She began to suspect that he was out of control, that his bazaar thoughts had control.

While he was with her and writing, he tried to control his dreams. He hypnotized himself into turning his vivid dreams, which he had off and on since childhood, into lucid dreams where he was controlling them. He thought he could change the outflow of his thinking during the day and his perspective of life by doing so. He was shaping his reality as he was shaping his books, but he couldn't handle it, because knowing him as I did, he couldn't separate his book from the world around him. He thought of himself as an explorer of the unknown: the uncommon, the unseen. He thought of himself as on the crest of conceptual thought, a supersurfer riding the biggest, newest wave, first on the beach of the unknown, going the fastest and furthermost. He declared his freedom to search and threw himself completely into it. My interpretation: he was free to explore his own insanity. This may have been true, because he felt he had complete control to relinquish control of his thinking, to let his thoughts fly.

He did write, I guess, wrote every day from what Margery said: up in the morning, read a little, then started writing. At first he could only produce three or four pages a day, however that grew. He worked from morning to late at night. Margery would come home and make dinner. They would sit at the table; he would talk at her, explaining the progress of his the novel and other writings, get inspired, leave the table, and return to his desk. Margery couldn't really tell me which novel or what he was creating. None of his stories seem to connect. He prevented her from seeing any manuscript. He wanted to impress her when it was finished and published, and thought that any previous glance would prejudice her because of the faults he knew existed. In the evenings when he didn't work or they didn't seek entertainment, he would draw and even began a painting or two.

This lasted for six months. When he finally let her read it, the results were disappointing. "His book justified being created, a very interesting exploration, but it was not the type of manuscript to get published." His thoughts were "far out," and maybe too personal. Not enough people would understand what he was trying to say. It was OK, maybe even "good" in places, maybe even important but boring from entertainment point of view, not commercial; for sure, it didn't achieve this goal. Of course, she told me that at the time, she didn't say a word to him. He, still in a positive state of being, sent it to a series of publishers, but nothing transpired. (An example of his writing is in the appendix, if the reader is interested.)

Margery convinced him to find an employment while waiting to be published. So he again went into "the world" to procure job. His mental state was good, positive, but gradually this faded when he ended up in some suburb south of San Francisco. Margery received a call: he was crying. He wanted to quit right then because he didn't want to face his supervisor at the afternoon meeting. He just couldn't do it (couldn't take it) and he wanted her permission to quit. He was selling encyclopedia software and other software for which he had needed a car to commute, insurance, car tags, etc. New clothes were a necessity. Some of this was undoubtedly Margery's doings. She probably assumed the role of the mother. I can see traces of it yet. But the point is, that with the huge chunk which was depleted from his investments, they could no longer live on her salary. The commitment was made; he had to follow through.

Of course, he couldn't peddle door to door. He was as outgoing as a clam, as forceful as a falling leaf on a calm day. The only way he "made a sell" was to cover so large an area that someone in that tract really wanted to buy. And of course this didn't work because most people who let him talk were people who were just lonely and bored and any break in the day was eventful. His time was ill spent.

Margery even laughed when she told this story. Both of them were so naive, so in love, that they couldn't see anything but each other. "If I would have only known what I know now, that whole waste of money, time and energy wouldn't have happened."

During the six months he tried to sell, they never did regain their investment and could just barely live on what both of them were making.

Over two years had passed since moving in

278

together, and they weren't any closer to obtaining financial stability or their goals then they were at the beginning. Margery still had hope in spite that their personal lives had deteriorated.

Some manuscripts had been submitted by this time, so he had hope. But their real worlds over powered their hopes. Both were so unhappy with the way their lives were going that they began to fight. They expressed their displeasure, disappointment, dissatisfaction in different ways. They lost respect for each other and themselves. They belittled each other to the point where they were hurting each other mentally. They knew each other so well that no matter what defenses the other would use, in a matter of seconds, fortifications would be destroyed and one or the other would be crying. They were hurting each other, and they knew it. They would "put each other down" in front of their friends, guests, and her business acquaintances. They were constantly on "each other's cases," deriding the other for the slightest faults, the most minuscule mistakes. It got so bad that they spent all their time and energy fighting. Jacoby would intentionally embarrass her, and she would react by calling him a failure in front of friends

Jacoby decided to move out and leave town. He went to his uncle's beach house up north of here. She was relieved when he went. This was the first time she began questioning whether or not she could be happy with him. Before this time she never ever considered living her life without him.

Chapter 4

It has been a busy year since I have last written. This whole Ike Jacoby thing has been blown out of proportion. I still haven't seen the movie but have read reviews and commentary about it. It has been running for over a month in a local movie theater, interestingly enough after a main feature, so its patrons don't have to view it. I have finished reading the manuscript (see appendix) which Jacoby gave to Thesus, and I discussed it with Margery. She directed me to research any and all writings of his: published or unpublished. But Thesus believes that all of the important manuscripts have been destroyed. He has begun a search for any of Jacoby's other works. Thesus and Ike's uncle have run ads in most of the large newspapers and art journals in this country offering to buy his art but with only minor success.

Over a thousand pages were destroyed at the time of his suicide, but I still can't help questioning whether his death was a performance, another creation, maybe in his mind his greatest creation, creating death whereas he never could succeed in creating his life. I just can't see him destroying any manuscripts. They were too important to him. Maybe his death was his last performance, and the manuscript which I possess is a prime example of what he wrote. It is in the form of a diary, and to me without significance, because it is also "too personal a tale." However, his poetry is of interest.

In short I feel that his suicide was a final

attempt at stardom, his final attempt to be recognized as an artist, maybe even a final attempt to create a myth of himself. Did he intentionally close himself off to the rest of the world in an effort to create that myth? He had so little interaction with the world; he could have made each action add to a self-created myth, using the world's rejection to his advantage

This image of myth has entered my thinking because his death has cause quite a commotion. In the beginning the local newspaper did a feature story about him, then many nationally syndicated papers "picked it up." Other locals after reading about his death began to write personal articles about him or at least about meeting him and him giving them some advice that changed their lives. It's weird. Those encounters could have happened. He did wandered about San Francisco "slightly out of it," and could and would make the strangest comments. But these articles have created such an interest that groups of people have become interested in him. I have even had a couple of inquiries. The media are building him into something that I don't think he was. He is becoming a martyr to art. An editorial about him ran in today's paper which used him to show the "true deprivation of culture in the United States," that crowd pleasers, "Men and women who have ridden the crests of fads or publicity to recognition," are proclaimed artists and that the really "true" artists have still suffered "as they have done in the past" working and doing what they thought was art without any help, encouragement, or recognition. Few people really know what art is and "can't recognize an artist as a next door neighbor." None of this would have happened if "we weren't in a period of cultural depravation."

I am sure that the author of the editorial was a frustrated, second rate artist whose only recognition has been this article. But the fact remains, Jacoby is becoming a symbol, a martyr, a flag around which every "would-be artist," or suppressed or oppressed individual has begun to rally. A stampede has begun in the S. F. area to find his art, drawings, painting, sculptures, and writings. I even have a drawing he gave me. It took me three hours to find in a trunk; needless to say I am going to have it framed. Margery must have many of his works, and I know the uncle does also. I have a suspicion his uncle is prodding this publicity, if not as a motivating force.

Anyway after reading all this garbage about him, I have begun to question my opinion of him. I haven't thoroughly discussed Jacoby's growing fame with Thesus; he disappeared again right after the funeral. He knows about my writings when he gave me the manuscript. What would he say about Jacoby's martyrdom? Margery recently has been out of town, doing what? I don't know. We spent time together after the funeral, but at that time Jacoby's fame had not really begun, and we just talk briefly on the phone.

The logical progression of this writing would be to insert Ike Jacoby's manuscript right here: one, it fits in here; it was written during this period when he left Margery and went up north to the beach house. Two, I should let him speak for himself. But I have placed it in the appendix. It would be too much of a distraction here, too much of a diversion. If the editor recommends its placement here, then fine.

Yes, I have landed an assignment with a regional magazine to write an article about Ike Jacoby and have decided to include parts of my earlier writing. The remainder of his work, will hopefully get published posthumously, but I am gaining confidence of the publication of my developing book about him. A production editor told me that if I didn't write the article I would be refusing the world of knowledge about "a great artist." I almost smiled, but held myself in check, and I am glad I did because he continued, "Maybe other suicides as needless as this would be prevented." This type of talk has made me hesitate in completing the exposition until I talk to Margery and her brother and get their consent. As I have mentioned, I must admit I have been writing with the idea of publication but not in our time.

BOOK II

Part II
Preface

A doctor who attended my father's funeral strongly recommended a physical with special emphasis on checking for cancer. With no money and no insurance, I put it off until my father's estate was settled, and then with so much happening, I put it off again. It was the pain which sent me in for a check-up. Yes, a malignancy grows inside me, and now two doctors told me that if I don't do something about it, I have less than a year.

I want to finish this manuscript and finish Jacoby's before I die. He was not only my friend but a great influence on Margery, Thesus and me, and another story of unfulfilled potential, but Thesus' story is of the utmost importance to me.

If readers have forced their way through Jacoby's "masterpiece," I'm sure they saw parts of that manuscript which seem to confirm Jacoby's doubts about himself. (I have affectionately titled it "Diary of a Madman.") Margery has edited what I have written concerning Jacoby with the idea of publication in the magazine. Her only stipulation was that I change all the names, except for Jacoby's; and make as few referrals to all of us as possible; I have done so. She feels that it all works together; that I tell a side to Jacoby which his manuscript doesn't. It looks as if the

Sunday supplement of the local newspaper is interested in a full length feature. It could be a series.

She did, however, criticize my bias. She has surmised jealousy from my description of Jacoby and some form of deep resentment, a profound secret dislike, which she edited. If it still exists, it is unconscious, for consciously I deny it. I must admit that I thought him a bit eccentric, a bit extreme, too involved with himself and his art, but everyone thought so too. I know I didn't dislike him. She didn't know about the extent of our relationship. But then maybe jealous is closer than dislike. Jacoby's effect on Margery might have created an unconscious jealousy and definitely their time spent together. But can giving and receiving love either physically and/or mentally lessen the ability to love? I may have gained from their love of each other.

After Jacoby's article, I presented almost my compete document to Margery for more than one reason. I have been having doubts about writing this whole book, including the information about Margery and Thesus. As I mentioned, it was my plan to publish after our deaths. I have decided to stick to that. Obviously it is too intimate, too revealing. After my death is soon enough:

Since the manuscript *A Stay at the Ocean* is by rights Thesus', he computed his proportion of potential royalties and has taken his portion in advance. He has helped make revisions to help assure his anonymity.

Chapter 1

"The time is now," a publisher has told me "while interest is high." And indeed interest is still gaining. Jacoby has become the "Clara Maass" of the art world. But already other suicides have been contributed to Jacoby and his philosophy. Thesus has begun to write articles concerning Jacoby to stave-off any further incidents. This, of course, is under his new identity, but our hero not only feels responsible for Jacoby's death but the effects it is causing.

Everything is happening so quickly that each day brings a new development. When the movie was presented by Thesus, he kept the physical control of the original. Jacoby's uncle, of course, felt the movie was by rights his and began to sue. But an agreement was reached, and they have formed a corporation to promote all of Jacoby's art. Jacoby's uncle is only too happy to see his nephew's name shine brighter with fame and to receive some monetary compensation

The movie has been playing in an underground movie theater here for three months. Last weekend our hero began presenting a pre-picture lecture and discussion after the showings.

I even broke down and saw it. I was disgusted by it. People in the theater can watch it because it is just another person, a martyr, who is killing himself, but to me it is Jacoby. Death truly comes to all beings, but it shouldn't be displayed as it is, especially the slow motion scene. I don't know who made it into slow motion or why, but it terrorizes me. I must admit that the transition from life to death fascinated me. I watched carefully and painfully wanting to see when, exactly when death entered his body. Before the bullet? Did he feel the pain? I have my reasons for wanted to know, but Jacoby prevented me from seeing it. It was Jacoby who shot himself, not some person I could objectively view.

One reason for its popularity is not only its sensationalism, but it has become a challenge for people to see. Can you watch someone kill himself? This seems to be a progression, a logical conclusion, to our cultural heritage of violence. But what I can't understand is that other groups of people are trying to prevent the showing. It is only on the weekends and at midnight. It's not hurting anyone. One has to go out of one's way to see a movie at those times, but the theater is always filled to capacity

I guess my philosophical approach to his suicide is not much better: a curiosity as to why he did it. What surprises me, and no clear interpretation exists, are all of the opinions as to why he did it. Rather than dwell on them, I will let the readers decide; I had better watch my time because the serial is going to have deadlines.

*   *   *

After his stay at the beach, Jacoby came back to San Francisco, with a renewed enthusiasm because of new agreements with Margery concerning their lifestyle. He again became a social creature, as much as he could. This was not Margery's main concern. It was more or less a convenience having Jacoby handling their apartment.

She was totally entrenched in her work. She had begun to progress up the corporate ladder. Her boss had quit and wasn't replaced. At first her superiors placed ads for the position but after a couple of months and not finding "the perfect person," Margery was unofficially given the job. It took her two months before she realized she was running the works and would be. She applied for a raise, the title, a secretary and after a long fight, a compromise was reached.

Jacoby and she could live on her salary, re-invest the remainder of his inheritance and invest his salary. Her other investments would be untouched, so she felt good about her financial future. After three months of half-assly looking for work where he wouldn't be "wasting his time," she knew nothing was going to happen. They discussed the situation, and she told him quite frankly not to expect to get published. He promised he would find work to supplement their income if she wanted; all they had to do was to set a certain amount which they wanted or needed, and he would fulfill his part. Moreover, she had to see his point of view, "Why waste what I had already gained in my art?" Maybe she was right about not being published, but he was still making progress in his self-development as an artist. Where would he be or could he be in a couple of years: published, self-supporting?

At the time she could see the significance of his art to him. She rationalized that they could live on her salary, make some decent investments with the remains of his and so still make gains toward "their goal," of total financial independence. Her personal investments were still on track, so she didn't need him or more importantly he wasn't a drain on her future expectations.

Later she said that she had hoped he would become bored with writing or at least have periods where he couldn't or didn't want to write and would seek employment. However, those never happened.

After a year of living with this arrangement, Margery again became frustrated with him. Their investments with his money never materialized to her expectations. He rationalized: it was not his destiny to have money. She was still on her promotional schedule, her semi-yearly raises, but now they spent more as an escape to what seemed an inevitable fate. He relinquished the idea of having a family until he was published and could support his share. She thought this would never happen. She was almost thirty and didn't want to wait too much longer to begin a family. "Our goals, our plans, our hopes began to diverge, and we never agreed. He wasn't willing to sacrifice anything except to his art. We loved each other but couldn't get along because we couldn't agree ...... even on our goals. I could understand his art as an investment to him, that he had devoted so much of his life, his time, his energy, and if he gave it up, he would be giving up his investment; but as an investment in our future, it was even beyond speculation. It was a hundred to one chance at a dog track."

When she said that, I smiled to myself and thought: Yes, and on the outside lane.

She was frustrated with the idea that they were treading water; their future was what they had and no more. Her extracurricular investments stagnated. She lost some of her hope. She began to see him as a threat to her future, her security, and she, in turn, turned her fear on him. She even calculated the amount of money she could have saved and invested if she wasn't supporting both of them. Then the idea struck her that he was preventing her from meeting someone she would marry. She was wasting her time. This revelation, at first, just caused discontentment, but then it began to frighten her and finally made her angry.

He, during this period, was more than accommodating in everything he did, wanted, or even wished for. He had taken on the role of housekeeper, cook, and general manager of domestic affairs. She was provider and general anger of business affairs. These were his categories. They functioned well together; both were more free because they each had more time for their concerns, but Margery was discontent.

Socially they had switch roles and though Margery could accept it and could see the necessity for it, she began to demean him. She wanted to fulfill their (really her) financial goals and her personal goals.

She confessed to me that in a raging argument she actually said, "Why don't you go out into the world and become a man. You know, the first man I meet, I am going to throw you over and go with him."

"If I am not a man, you I better hope you don't

meet one. You cannot even handle me and yourself around me. You wouldn't know what to do with a real man."

But after that fight, he became more of what she hated. He began to intentionally act like an effeminate servant, at first just in front of her then in front of her friends. I guess her business associates reacted in extremes, either pro or con, acceptance or rejection. To her, adding this role to the rest of his eccentric characteristics, he became more than an unexplainable entity, and she didn't want him around at her functions.

He didn't care or didn't perceive it, and was more accommodating than ever. He gladly quit her parties and going other places with her. He really never wanted that world in the first place. He could see Margery's dissatisfaction and decided to alleviate some of the pressure by laying low.

Though knowing Jacoby, I can imagine that he really did react to all the projections by becoming more of what they projected. In almost all ways, but his art, he was a floater in life's currents. He was either oblivious to their images or didn't care. His act of the effeminate servant, which at first was game, later became a state of being. Of course, it was more complex than this and to give credit, he became a great cook, an advanced "gourmet chef." He made some outrageous clothes for himself and Margery. Of course, she wouldn't wear them, and often she was home late for dinner without warning him.

After a while Margery began to see that it was she, not particularly he, who was causing most of the trouble. It was her discontent, her fading respect. To her he was like an over dependent little puppy. But at the same time, she hated her feeling of entrapment, trapped in a type of guilt, and now his seeming compliance to her and their destiny. She hated that she was tearing at him, demeaning his labors, and that he would take it. He would take her unjust criticisms, like refusing to eat his elaborate dinners, and still try to fulfill her wants, making her late night snacks because he knew she was hungry and serving them to her in bed.

As we can see from the last recorded conversation, she hadn't destroyed him. He had held his self-respect by continuing his art. And in his mind, the rest was irrelevant.

Part of the problem must have been that he couldn't really have told anyone what was happening in their relationship. If he even ever looked at the problems, it was through an art medium, like the enclosed manuscript and drawings of Margery or self-portraits which she has shown me. Then to top that, I'm sure that without his knowledge and any sort of understanding, their relationship did affect him: her lack of respect caused an unconscious lack of respect, her feelings of entrapment made him feel entrapped, and finally her disbelief in a future helped him decide against an immediate family. A time came in the relationship where he did quit working on his art. He only did housework. Margery hated him and herself. It was her lack of respect, her hopelessness, her lack of faith which had made him become what she feared he would.

She decided she was doing more harm than good and moved out found her own place. Jacoby, who of course had no idea that their relationship had degenerated so far, took the break-up hard. Another rejection, another lost dream, and so he threw himself back into his writing. His life was stagnate, so he had nothing to say, but he needed to drowned his thoughts about Margery, what his life was and what his future could become. He began to reread and rework all of his previous writings. And of course, he began to deplete the remainder of inheritance. The principle had grown because of Margery's investments but now growth was finished. He undoubtedly could see his trap, but he didn't want any other route except through art. If that didn't work then let himself be trapped. What did he care? His art was his life, all he wanted to do, all that was worth his while. He was content with the potential outcome, though I'm sure he thought it would end differently.

I have an analogy with which to compare this period of Jacoby's life. The other day I was waiting for a bus and a black Labrador retriever would drop a ball indiscriminately in front of people waiting for the bus. I must admit I picked up the ball and threw it. It was great fun and what the dog wanted. It was a game to see if I could either fool the dog or make him do some special extra work to return the ball. But he brought it back every time, with no rests in-between. He had run himself ragged by doing this, but he continued. He was transfixed on that ball. He would place the ball in front of a person, stare at it until that person picked it up and again threw it. Panting, thin,

293

but without hesitation, without pause, or concern for the obstacles, or even his safety, he would return that ball.

After a while I could see what was happening and didn't throw the ball. Undaunted by my unwillingness, he found someone else. The next day when I saw the dog, still at the bus stop, still retrieving the ball, still panting, I wondered if it had a home. During the night had it returned home and eaten? I told my observations to the person throwing the ball. "The dog is doing what it wants. No animal would starve itself to death."

Immediately all those rats which Thesus had mentioned in all those experiments sprang to my mind: they kept pressing the levers to get their reinforcement to get their brains stimulated rather than even eat. Eventually they did starve to death. Could fate accidentally condition an animal, or worse a human being, to where he would starve himself? Could the pleasure of retrieving that ball or working on art become so great that .... Could one be conditioned to receiving pleasure from an activity? Because his art is hooked up with hope, respect, pride, purpose, accomplishment (real or otherwise), and probably much more, it is a pleasure to him, and in his life, his only pleasure. He could be conditioned not only by his environment but by himself, both consciously, and I'm afraid unconsciously.

Art wasn't an occupation; it was a drug, and obviously a drug not good for him. Maybe this is being unfair. I don't know. Maybe in his own mind he wasn't trapped in his own maze. Way over forty, without an occupation which could support him, much less get him where he needed to go: stagnating in a drying pool. The question is whether he was justifying his life to himself.

Of course, all of this is my opinion, (after rereading all of this so far, an evolving opinion) and my own conclusions, something maybe I shouldn't be stating. I should let the story speak for itself.

When Thesus first arrived in San Francisco, Margery persuaded him to check on Jacoby for her. They began to spend time together. Ike took Thesus to all the tourist places then to his own private stomping grounds. One of those places was the Coffee Gallery in North Beach. At the time some of Jacoby's paintings were hanging on its walls, and he was reading his poetry on Wednesday nights.

Coming from college, I think our hero was impressed: a possible reason, he suggested an attempt at reconciliation.

Even with the mere suggestion, Jacoby's hopes soared. He had always known they would get back together. But as it came closer to the time of Thesus talking to Margery, Jacoby withdrew a little. He didn't want to see her unless she had changed her mind about him and their relationship.

Margery reported back that nothing had changed. Because both had built their protective shells, neither was hurt that much by the incident. But Jacoby again fell back into his cycle of drinking and writing.

Our hero could do nothing. I think that Thesus had an inkling that Jacoby was possessed by his self-created philosophy: trapped, as were. These confines were too much for Thesus to observe. But as mentioned in the Big Sur vacation, every attempt our hero made to break through his philosophy failed.

I believe Ike had been building it for so long that it had dry-hardened as his plastic sculptures. The main problem was that we, all, thought that it was obvious, clear, see-through. And to take this interpretation one step further, he would always, I thought, take the easy way out: a philosophy based on the "easy slide through."

I think both Margery and Ike were looking for perfections in their relationship: the right time, the right situation, making the right amount of money, no sweat, no challenge, easy and rewarding, and, of course, the right type of love.

Much later in Jacoby's and my relationship, I can remember almost his exact words concerning their association .... Isn't it funny, I can't remember how the conversation started or even where, but I'm sure it was in one of our bar scenes late one night. A definite example of selective memory, remembering what's important to oneself.... "Besides," he said, "I can't see working just for money for myself. I could have done it for Margery, our family, but I wouldn't do it for myself. There is no sense in me striving for something which I don't really think is important. Margery ,............ I do want, but in my trying to make money in hopes that it works out and we get back together, I was becoming someone neither of us wanted. My time is too precious to strive for something which only exists as a possibility. By doing my art, I am accomplishing something immediately, determining myself and my future by present action; not living for a future which may never come."

Chapter 2

Our hero looked on Margery's and Jacoby's break-up as regrettable and unfortunate. He didn't blame either more than the other. He took Margery's dissatisfaction as "a want of self-reliance," an "infirmity of will." Her lack of acceptance of Jacoby was a lack within herself. She couldn't fulfill herself, and she wanted and expected Jacoby to do it. When he didn't, completely, she blamed him and not herself. She could have, if she would have had the strength, had children, a family, the life she wanted with him, "in spite of him." "They would have eventually come to some agreements, some compromises." This is the type of argument Thesus must have presented when he encouraged their reunion. At the same time, Thesus also began to think that Jacoby gave up too easily. He was too wishy-washy, and that at this time if Jacoby really wanted it he would have been more aware of what was happening and prevented it the best way he could. But it was only after Ike thought he was going to lose her that he became aggressive and assertive and proposed. By then Margery had more than reservations.

Thesus also thought they wanted too much, "the right time, situation, and everything. In waiting and wanting, they lost it. Their timing was off. If Margery had wanted marriage, a family, the works, when Jacoby did or vice-a-versa, they would have had it. In accepting both for who they were, one can't blame either." It was at this time in the sequence of events, right after the final break-up that our hero in one of his letters mentioned their break-up.

Both Jacoby and our hero were tough on other people because they disclosed what nobody wants to hear or see. They both sought the truth, and continually questioned, probing themselves and others for insights. It was always too intense and not many people want that intensity without at least some comic relief every now and then. With each other they were almost brutal, challenging each other, trying to tear down the other's beliefs, but they respected each other for it. It, of course, was more one-sided than this because Jacoby was more egotistical than our hero; he was more concerned and committed to his own beliefs, his life, his art.

However, when our hero asked Jacoby for help, Jacoby was able to come out of himself; he rose to the occasion and placed himself in our hero's position, through understanding, acceptance, or even empathy. As with the rest of us, Jacoby really didn't know enough about life to be of much help. He didn't know anything about politics, the workings of society, the government. His knowledge was limited to people, through knowing himself, and something about women, but very little about anything else except art, creating, and the philosophy of art.

Both Thesus and I accepted Jacoby's egotism,

his commitment, his involvement with himself as integral and necessary. For him to do what he was doing and to be who he was, it was necessary. That isn't to say we weren't overtly critical of him, especially our hero, but that some place inside ourselves we accepted him, and that seems to be a firm basis of friendship, acceptance: knowing who that person is and accepting his faults. We trusted him because we knew what to expect, of what he was capable, what he was not. I'm sure this was a reason Margery was not destroyed by him or his actions. She knew him, loved him, but protected herself against the harm he could have racked on her.

And yes, both Thesus and I could depend on Ike Jacoby, or so we thought.

Chapter 3

When I first arrived in SF, I was both cautious and curious about Jacoby. My curiosity was prompted because I questioned the type of person Margery chose. I was cautious because I feared him. I didn't know if I would elicit hate, jealousy, or what...... maybe even revenge. If it worked out between Margery and me, I could see where he would blame me for finalizing the break-up. But as the reader can see, it was not the case.

After the Big Sur trip, I thought I understood him well enough not to be cautious. I thought I knew what motivated him. I also knew his commitment to art bordered on insanity, an obsession. He was too quick in his answers, too determined to show what he meant, too ready to argue his point.

I have met people who were falsely committed, and when I began to question them about their beliefs, it always broke at the point where they couldn't talk about it anymore; they would fall back on a statement like, "Well, that is what I believe, that is what I feel, and I can't explain it," which to me shows undeveloped thought or beliefs.

These types of statements were hardly ever forthcoming from Ike. He may have contradicted himself, but one could tell he was seeking. Just in the fact that he would let himself be interrogated by our hero showed that he really wasn't afraid of what he would find. In that he sought our hero, one could see that he was seeking the truth.

As eluded to, our friendship developed in bars. It was neutral territory; one we both enjoyed, and after a couple of drinks, we could discuss anything. At first we met accidentally in a bar near the Marina facing the Golden Gate Bridge.

I was facing the bartender, watching her work, when I heard a voice I thought was directed at me. Thinking I was obviously wrong, I didn't turn around. But the utterances continued. I glanced around with almost fear of what I would find. It was Ike Jacoby in the middle of a conversation with me. I know the drink in his hand wasn't his first for the day from his alcoholic breath. I backed my face away from his and focused on what he was saying, "I can understand that you must think I am slightly insane, from talking to

Margery and Thesus. But if I had to choose between being insane and creating, I would choose creating. If in creating uniqueness, one has to be unique, and therefore off the normal curve, I would chose insanity. My individuality may be a slightly distorted view, but the world does not condemn other artists for this, even when it is displayed as blatantly as in Van Gogh. In that I am trying to express and explore, I gain my unique perspective, and I become who I am. When I express through art, I express my unique quality, my style."

I thought you are not Van Gogh, but said, "Only, we all are unique. Have you been talking to Thesus about psychology?"

"Yes." He looked as if he had been on an all-night adventure. His clothes were wrinkled, his hair uncombed; he needed a shave, and his eyes were puffy and bloodshot.

This was only the first time we accidentally met in the bars. These accidents occurred again and again. This is, of course, after being introduced at Margery's apartment and after I didn't let him see me a couple of times. I saw him on the street and ducked into a store. Another time his image flashed through a window as I was entering a bar, so I abruptly turned around.

Another time, I was standing in the Urba Yerba bar unaware of his presence when he started talking to me again. He talking to me like this entered my dream state. I can't now tell the difference between our real encounters and my dreams. But I began to listen whether I saw him or not. This time, we had a couple of drinks together, I bought, and then he left.

I had some dreams about him and decided that it was my destiny to see him, so I quit evading him. Later we would set definite times to meet. Our discussions were always about art, his life, my life, or Thesus, but as I have said after a couple we could discuss almost anything without restraints. We had some amazing discussions, or so they seemed at the time, but I'll be damned if I can remember what seemed so important at that moment.

One Friday night, I knew I would see him in North Beach. And yes we almost collided on the main street walking in opposite directions. We both had already been to a bar or two, and he decided he wanted to show me the city from a lounge at the top of the highest building in San Francisco. By the time we disembarked from the elevator, the fog was so thick, we didn't see anything, and after three or four more drinks, we couldn't even see the fog.

Upon leaving the establishment and after a hundred mile an hour fall, for seventy or more floors, I abruptly became sick. It was a question as to whether I would make the street before I puked. He was laughing all the way. We decided I should walk for a while, and we ended up walking until two in the morning when the bars closed. The more I walked, the more sober I became and the drunker he got. We walked from one bar to the next. He seemed to know every one of them intimately, their locations and the bartenders. I don't think we missed one from downtown area all the way to the Twin Peaks area. He could hold it; I'll say that for him. He sang and danced to jukeboxes in the bars and to his own singing in the streets; he recited his and other people's poetry, told some great stories and had at least one drink in every bar. I started drinking club soda, then <u>soda</u> pops, then tomato juice. He would say that he had to stop here at this bar because he knew the owner, or a friend, who would be there who he wanted me to meet, and it would be unkind to pass him by without checking in. Most of the times, he really did know the owner or a patron well enough to say hello, and sometimes he would get a free drink.

When we finally reached the trolley tunnel at the end of Market Street, I decided to catch the next trolley and go home. He knew of another bar just down the street on Castro which would probably open for him because he knew everyone. I was sober and hung-over which he could see. He almost convinced me a drink, a Bloody Mary, would do me some good, ease the pain. "Put a little juice in your juice that you're drinking." My only resolve which kept me from that fate was I had an appointment for a job interview the next morning. He waited with me for about fifteen minutes but decided if he didn't leave right then and get to "his bar" he wouldn't get that last drink. Somewhere between my throw-up and Castro Street, he made the statement, "If I had to choose between being insane and creating or going to a shrink and becoming normal..." Yes, I remember now, even more, he said, "Because if I were normal, I probably would not want to work in art and change things. I would see everything normally as everyone else does. I would let myself and my life conform as everyone

303

does. I would let the systems control, and I would not have the will or strength to push back. When I am weak, tired or foolish, I just step aside. Otherwise I push back with my individuality and insanity, my art." He laughed loudly.

Yes, now, I can see why he drank so much: his personality changed. He became more of whom he wanted.

As much confusion as exists in that statement, I think I can still rebut it. He didn't realize we all have that uniqueness which we would necessarily express in our art. We would all have that individual style because we exist in a distinctive place, at a particular time with our individual subjective and objective experiences and thoughts. He must have been reading something about insanity to think that insanity was an extreme variation from the norm, rather than what he thought at the beach.

Three days later on a Sunday morning he called and said that he was about to take a boat to Sausalito, and thought I would be interested in joining him. He was right but not on a Sunday morning at seven o'clock. I, however, dragged myself from my bed and met him down at Fisherman's Wharf. We both had breakfast on the boat which consisted of coffee and a packaged sweet roll.

He looked as if he had had another all-night adventure. His clothes were wrinkled, his hair uncombed, he needed a shave and his eyes were puffy and blood shot, or maybe this was the same binge. The main reason for him taking the cruise: he thought the salt air would do him some good. The main motives for me getting up were I really wanted to go to Sausalito, and by this time in our relationship, I enjoyed his company and knew we would have an interesting adventure. I would see and experience things only a native would.

In spite of his appearance, as the boat pulled out, his mind became clear and energetic. He pointed out places along the way, told stories about different historical events: the man who swam for hours to escape from Alcatraz Island, American Indians who had claimed it, and then stories about Angel Island. He was fun.

Chapter 4

All of the statements concerning Jacoby's philosophy should have been placed right here rather than scattered throughout the book, but I didn't know I would deal with Jacoby to this extent.

From the statement in *A Stay at the Ocean* to our discussion at Big Sur, one can see a shift in philosophy, ... or if not a shift, at least different aspects of the same philosophy and its development. In *A Stay at the Ocean* he seems to have discovered(?), experienced something beyond himself and his mortal being. At Big Sur he seems to have directed himself to that which was beyond himself, but more than that, that which was beyond even nature. He thought that mankind ..... or he, could reach beyond even nature. I say this because of his statements about reality, "What in the hell is reality?

... Maybe reality doesn't exist but is only a word in man's vocabulary to keep him seeking something, he knows not what, or a word that makes man feel secure in knowing or thinking he knows what exists." And also his direct statement about being beyond nature, "I see mankind as a creature who has the power to create a new world whether he wants to or not, a world excluding nature. ... Mankind already creates an order, meaning, and gives himself a significance which does not necessarily exist in nature, and he has had to do this by stepping away from nature. ... With knowledge and acceptance of what we control, what we create, we will have a greater, a better, control."

It seems Ike had put humans in the place of angels, third-person angels at that, beyond nature. In rereading that conversation at Big Sur, our hero's warning that one cannot "wantonly violate reality and nature" stands out. One should not transgress upon that which he is dependent.

My interpretation of Jacoby's philosophy doesn't quite fit together in my mind. Something is slightly off, but it the best I can do at this time.

Underneath his artist facade, the image building, to me, now, his death seems to be a fall: the only way out of a trap. But was it to him? Could he have been sacrificing himself to a greater being, that which is beyond, or to art itself? Or was it in his mind a fight: fighting his fate, something beyond himself for a place in the sun. Then again, the forces beyond himself may have become devils. What was happening in his mind at his death only he knew. I thought I knew him fairly well until he killed himself.

We seemed, as you can tell from our Big Sur conversation, to have discussions in depth with no holding back, but I didn't know he was capable of killing himself. And during the funeral I felt as if I hadn't known him at all. I wonder if his suicide shattered our friends' concepts also?

I hadn't seen him for a week before his death, and our last meeting was brief. I will disclose this last meeting, but first I would like to describe the last meeting we four were together, Margery, Jacoby, our hero and me. Only once were we four together between my father's death and Ike's death. I don't know if our hero and Jacoby ever saw each other again.

After that, it was only Jacoby and I. I showed Jacoby the beginnings of this book and all he said was, "Do it. Get it finished before you quit, then show it to me." Now I question whether he knew if he would ever read it, and this statement was a means of revenge for me never asking to see his work.

Anyway, I arrived back from my father's funeral late at night. Margery collected me and my things from the airport and drove to my apartment. During the drive we were almost completely silent, but I could feel the empathy she felt concerning my father's death. She not only knew what it felt to lose a father, but she let herself feel the remorse again to share it with me, to know my grief. He was my last relative, and though she wasn't empathic to that fact, she understood it. This feeling and understanding existed without words. We both knew, and no words need be spoken.

Both Jacoby and our hero were at my apartment waiting in condolence. They had a drink prepared, a willingness to let me express my grief then a distraction from my emotion. Our hero began this distraction by leading the conversation from my father's death to the relationship we four shared, what we meant to each other and what we now mean to each other. He described the value of our friendship in terms of an anchor, a permanence upon which we four could depend.

Jacoby related to our hero's statement and then started rambling about what the relationship meant to him. It seemed so forced at the time that I thought both of them had planned it. Margery who hadn't said a thing all evening excused herself and went home. She did, indeed, looked tired.

We remaining three stayed on, had another couple of drinks which helped loosen Jacoby's thoughts to the point where they began to be expressed. Jacoby's love for our hero became manifested for the first time, that I saw, in his concern for our hero's predicament. I don't think Jacoby could see the real threat hovering about our hero, but it surprised me that he saw the threat all. I had thought Jacoby was too enclosed in his own thoughts to be able to see anything. I was in the kitchen fixing another drink for all three of us, both of them were silent in the living room. When I came back in, Jacoby was staring from the window into the night lights of San Francisco; our hero was reading an article in *Time* magazine. For some reason I couldn't see disturbing either one of them, so I just placed both of their drinks

308

on the coffee table and sat down to think about the change which had occurred in my life, when all of a sudden Jacoby, without turning around, addressed us, "We are but transient shadows on a transient globe, not even being able to see the substance from which we are created, not even being able to see the part of us which casts the shadow and yet that vital substance is only temporary and will eventually metamorphorize into another substance that may be shadowless and translucent even to the eternal light which shines through us.

"Time is so short and goals so far away." He turned to our hero and said the following which makes me think that they had discussed Thesus' problems before I entered the room. "Don't get trapped in the mazes that sidetrack you from your true person. Don't let those temporary pit-falls hold your being from yourself. See yourself as you really are and want to be and complete that being."

"What are those pit-falls and what is my true being?" our hero asked laughingly, knowing that any of his answers to the questions would be absurd.

"The pitfalls are those mundane attempts of the institutions to hold you fast. They are the glitter that the societies place in front of all people so that they run, according to their rules after their goals, rather than pursuing your own being. The pitfalls are the categories and projections placed on you to keep you in your place so they can identify you. They are the envies and jealousies thrown at you in the forms of temptations and threats so that you know nothing but want or constant fear, and it is this fear which may hold you fast and may kept you from your objectives, which is ultimately to transcend all this and become the perfection which resides in each of us, the true essence and constancy which exists in all of us. It is the inception which created us which we must know, develop and attempt to transcend."

To put it mildly I was astonished. But our hero response seemed to just get more angry as he spoke. "You are in a completely different place than I. But then again you are partially right yet wrong. That which is used against me could be used against anyone. My individual freedoms have been violated, and you are indicating to forget it. You've got to come to the party before it is over. What if every person forgot his responsibilities to himself and his society? Nobody would be able to sit and dream his idealistic dreams as you do but would be forced to work in the mines in Alaska? True, forces exist beyond us, but not all of them are this essence about which you speak. Some of them are powers usurped by individuals and systems from individuals in an attempt to gain more power. Either the government or individuals in the government have over extended their powers and not only threaten my rights but my existence as well."

Our hero rose from the couch and walked over to Jacoby. I couldn't see his face but I imagined he was smiling because he said, "I don't even know how or why you can talk of transcendence. You sound like a religious fanatic, another person pushing his trip on poor unsuspecting victims, like me." He slapped Jacoby on the back and laughed, "We are all, already

310

sheep in the hands of a few who control us more than they should. When they open the slaughter houses and tell us to walk-in whether for a war or another noble cause, we will without protest, in the name of patriotism because we are afraid to move against it. We believe what they are telling and selling us without questioning it."

"But it is all so mundane, our individual beings, the society in which we live, even the world. All of it holds us back from obtaining our true goals. It is all so here-to-day, gone-tomorrow. I am talking about the eternal, if you could only see that, all this would mean nothing; you would be able to soar above and beyond it."

Thesus' frustration in the form of anger was building, "For me that would be running away. It would be a sin to let what is continuing. I won't ignore the crime just to preserve my faith. I would be a guilty victim, as guilty as the ...., and who is to say I am not doing God's work."

"Even Buddha rejoined humanity after being enlightened," I inserted, but I just thought: Who's the fanatic?

"The path back to the Garden awaits: all one has to do is see it. It is within us to reach and once in the Garden, we will again see clearly and always with an ever fresh vision without hindrance from within or without," Ike's voice had become like a child's which disarmed Thesus, and I could tell his anger was reflected from Jacoby to his own situation.

Because in a deliberate calmed tone he answered, "You are beautiful, but I am afraid too fragile ..... and yet you should exist. By rights, you should exist. You have your purpose and directive, and by rights you should express your vision and your being. If it wasn't for myself that I seek this enemy, it would be for you. I seek the common enemy which tries to consume us all, that enslaves you without your knowledge and prevents you from taking the path which you have chosen. My directive and purpose stands stronger because in you, I can see the possibilities of what we all can become and each should have that right to become."

"God's light, that Eternal Beam can't be diminished by man. When all of mankind is but an extinct race of dinosaurs, God will yet remain in All that exists. If each man could govern himself and could accurately judge himself and his actions, there would be no need for a government, and we could get on with what we are designed to be doing."

"But humans don't ... and obviously we need a government so let's talk about what we can do in the here-and-now. I want to believe in God and in a Supreme Justice, and maybe there is, but maybe also we are too distant from Its Will, and in this distance we obtain freewill and control over our destiny if not just individually then as a whole community of human beings. God in a case like this could be compared with a man standing over an ant hill. It is true there are many forces over which we have no control, but there are forces over which we can and must control to continue our existence both individually and as a whole so we don't become extinct."

Jacoby was absorbed in all that was said, and

I'm sure he was thinking of a rebuttal or another way to make his point when our hero said, "Let's try another bar. I think this one has closed down." He was right; the bar was closed down, three or four drinks, after not sleeping well since my father's death, totally consumed me. I was sitting in a stupor, just being a sponge, absorbing and feeling the changes in my being. I wasn't as drunk as they thought because when they asked if I wanted help getting up, cleaning up, and getting to bed, I stood, with some effort, and walked them to the door. Obviously I wasn't that far gone, because I have remembered this conversation.

In every meeting of Jacoby after this time, he began to talk more and more about art and religion. In fact near the end those were all we discussed, never Margery, Thesus, or the weather. Most of the time after a couple of drinks, I thought he really was becoming a fanatic. But then when he wasn't drunk, he would spew, it didn't seem to make a difference. The alcohol didn't seem to have an effect, but he drank out of habit. His only activity was writing. He was working on three or four papers at a time but as far as I know never finished them. In one he was trying to re-define art and another writing a history of art, of course his definition, his interpretation of the history, not an academic one; in one, defining aesthetics; in one trying to define poetry, but he said his thoughts went faster than he could record, that what he stated at the beginning of the paper was obsolete half way through. Then he said he didn't need to finish the papers because the ideas were completely developed in his mind.

I realized that nobody but me was sharing his art with him, and I was not taking what he said, his writing, or even him personally, as a serious thinker. Isn't it funny, strange, only by seeing him with my perspective now do I hear his ideas and take them thoughtfully. It is not only that I am putting together his philosophy for the first time in my mind, but the everyday seeing and hearing him made him almost a nuisance, and I didn't want to listen, much less understand. Anyway, by this time, he did his art for himself alone, only for his own development. He was no longer expressing to share it with anyone but only expressing to see his concepts more clearly; once he saw their development, he didn't feel the obligation to record them. I was there only as a backboard off which to bounce his ideas, so he could hear himself. Sometimes his concepts didn't make sense to me, and he would laugh because he saw they didn't, but they must have to him because he maintained his self-assurance........ Then again, maybe he was laughing at me because he thought I was so stupid.

But it's too bad I couldn't follow his thinking. It's too bad we can't even follow his confused thoughts as they must have been expressed in his writings. I can't and probably will never understand how he could have destroyed almost everything he wrote. He thought highly of his works; they were a part of him more than if he and Margery would have had children; they were a constant aspect of his being. They were a navigational tool in deep space, a directional finder, to say where he had been, his distance from another landmark, and a pointer to his future. He reread and reworked them constantly. His art did advance with the evolution of his being. It was his means of development, his means to transcend, to become. But at the end, that is all he had, the being he composed of himself. But I wonder if anyone really ever has more. No, I can't and won't say that or else I wouldn't be thinking of marriage with Margery. We wouldn't be trying to have children.

And maybe all those burnt papers in the hole in his movie were his attempts to express what he had discovered about art and religion, and he knew they didn't succeed. Then again, whether he succeeded in his mind or not, whether his manuscripts were understand or not, we'll never know.

Our last meeting was very strange indeed. It was raining like hell, and it had been raining off and on all day when the phone rang. It was Jacoby. He told me he had seen the light. He had seen the truth. He had found the Universal language which is locked in our language. I thought to myself, sarcastically, so what else is new, but didn't say anything. He told me to come over immediately; which I did, but he didn't answer the door to his apartment building. I waited, thinking he had gone to the store for a bottle of wine, but thirty minutes elapsed and he didn't show. It was still raining in sheets. I rang the bell but wasn't even buzzed in, then waited in my car around the corner because I couldn't find a parking space nearer. I had rung the bell three times in the thirty minutes and was pretty wet so I went home.

While in the shower the phone rang again. It was Jacoby. "It has come out perfectly." I had to come over and see it. He had heard his apartment bell ring, but he was so involved in writing it down, capturing the moment, recording his thoughts that he couldn't come to the door. He wanted me to come over again, and promised, "No matter what," he would open the door. I said ok, but under my breath cursed. He sounded frantic and ill. I finished my shower, changed clothes, but as I was walking to my car in the rain, I thought to myself that I must be a masochist to have a friend like him.

He kept his word and was standing by the door in the vestibule, looking into the street through a side window. He opened the door before I even rang the bell. He was very glad to see me, shook my hand again and again, thanking me for being such a good friend. He had coffee perking and made me Irish Coffee. While walking around the apartment picking up dirty clothes, he said he had been fasting for four days. While putting encrusted, food laden dishes in the sink, he began telling me of the last two days of his fast, and how he had seen the light.

With his sallow and slightly yellow face, he seemed little unruly in his behavior. He was cranked-up: his actions were more rapid and jerky than usual, up one and half times normal. After making me the drink, he fetched three large pieces of cardboard.

"I only had three pieces, and I only needed three. It all came out so perfectly. It was ordained." He read it while I drank the coffee. Initially, I couldn't understand him. He broke some of the words such as the word "a-tone-ment." At first, I thought something was wrong; he wasn't able to read what he had written, but then I realized that he was reading it as if he were reading one of his poems: slowly, deliberately:

"Our consciousness is the ness of con-science and has con(ned) our science.   It is only our unconsciousness which is the ness of uncon-science and will uncon-science and reveal truth. We need to flow in the thought and know.

"Human relay-tion-ships, trans-fer of en-er-gy, a re-lease of energy which we all only lease, our effect, the effect, the effect of throwing a pebble on to a pond, an ex-plo-sion of energy, just the func-tion-ing of our be-ings, the final thrust for life, of life, the trans-fer of en-er-gy, l-ov-e, Chinese infinity e, creat-ting a new u-ni-ty, 0; man unit-y, O; woom-man unit-y, O; come to-get-her to cre- ate, pro--cre--ate, to cre-ate an eight on its side, their in-finity, their e-ffect, their trans-fer of en-er-gy, their ∞." He traced the infinity sign with his finger..

"For I truly believe," he said in a slightly fast, sing-song, high pitched voice, "there are concepts in conception. Four exist in conception, the I--- the perceiver who is conscious of pre-cieving and trans-mit-ting, and still receiving his own trans-mission; the you--- the other, the outside; and the unity, the God --- the force which keeps it going, the truth behind the Darwinian theory, the drive, the l-ov-e. There are so many different kinds of love. In the plan-et there is the unite-ty, the larger plan, and one can find It if one looks."

I know this is accurate because these last three paragraphs were repeated in his movie. The viewer in the theater could see he was trying to remember

317

something and then he recited those three paragraphs in a rote manner with a stolid faced.

But the scene in his apartment that day was animated, emphatically emphasizing words. His cheeks glowed red at the moment he read.

A long minute of silence passed. His radiance lessened. I had guessed he was finished and was waiting for a response, but what could I say? That I didn't understand it or the part that I did I thought obvious. Or maybe I didn't understand the full implications of his statements.

"Let me try reading it for myself."

"You didn't understand it."

"At the end I sort of did but ....."

"Let me read it again because I don't think you could read it correctly, and the way it is read is important." He started out again, "The Way, say, play, mayday, foreplay,..."

But I couldn't understand it, and therefore couldn't follow and report it correctly. The second reading didn't seem to shed any new light about the three pieces of cardboard or what he was trying to communicate.

I could see his enthusiasm that he thought he had broken through to the universal language, but I'll be damned, he didn't break through to me. Maybe someone else would have understood him. I probably haven't even done justice to impart what I did record.

"Well what do you think?" he asked with pride and satisfaction.

"Can I just look at it?" He handed it to me. I studied sections which I thought I understood, and it still didn't make that much sense, but there were more symbols than he could pronounce such as in the part of four concepts in conception, there was Unity - 0, man unity 0; woman unity 0 then man and woman ∞ unity on their side, and God's creation ∞."

It may be too personal, too vague," I said after looking at it. "Maybe it is me. Maybe someone else would understand it better, and I am just not receptive at the moment. O.K. if I fix another Irish Coffee?" Without a reply, I left for the kitchen.

"It is as simple as existence and continuance, God's plan which has been kept in the Universal symbols of all languages," he yelled from the living room, "but," he laughed hysterically, "it is not that simple or easy."

Not to put him off, not to say that I had understood that and only that, but I personally couldn't break the key which he seemed to use to unlock the door. I decided to ask him a question not exactly dealing with what he was writing but yet not that far off. I asked him, not because I thought he would give me an answer but to see if he was thinking and making sense and for the stupidest reason of all, I really wanted to know.

"But what about after-life?"

"We continue to exist in our creations: our children, our effect. A bell cannot be un-rung."

"What if all humans were destroyed tomorrow? Where is our infinite effect?"

As I reentered the room, his words were rapid, almost firing at me, but it was as if it were all too tedious for him to say. "In God's imagination and the

319

next time He creates something, and I am sure it will be better than this creation; we will still be here; we are God's children, and we can create and create with knowledge and direction, and our creations can create.

The Creator
Created creators
Who could create creators
Who could create...
Without end

He recited this last ditty with impatience and tedium in his voice, but regained his seriousness and said, "As you imply, not only material children could be destroyed tomorrow but energy, consciousness. But energy is never really destroyed but only changes form. We continue as God's concepts; we continue as our energy both in the energy given off in our lives but also given off in our deaths. We continue in God's consciousness. The unique energy, which we are, exists in everything and everybody, e -very body, (he smiled) is the constant quality which exists continuously. We are both giving and taking this energy. It makes us continue in the form we are now, but more than that, it is everywhere and all pervasive, and makes everything continue in the form it is.

"Why didn't you say that?? Why don't you write it down just as you explained it rather than your jumbled words which only have meaning to you?"

It's there and more. It's in the basic symbols of our language and all other languages as well. Think of some of the root words to mother, zero, empty or void, the number one, love, and the amazing thing, is that this answer has been hidden in language from the beginning of time. If I could say what I want to say in other words or another medium, I would." Then he said, "Maybe I should make the final inclusive statement, the encompassing statement, a statement which will make all my other writing obsolete, a statement bringing together all of my knowledge."

Rather than giving any significance to what he just said, I answered, "No wonder you have never had anything published. It may all fit together, but only you can understand it."

"Oh, I'll bet there are people who could understand it, if in no other way but that it resonates in their beings because it resonates in mine. What I need now is a statement all people will understand, a Universal symbol."

Being the professional teacher that I am, I said, "I think you may have something in your beliefs which (maybe) should be communicated; you are right, you must find a way to express it, as clearly and simply as possible so that more people can understand it. Go back to college; study ancient languages, study semantics, study ancient world concepts through their different languages, then rewrite this."

He laughed at me. "What if," he continued with eyes widening, "each person's effect, energy and all, could be absolute love, uninhibited love, we would create a paradise here on earth." He touched my hand; it was as cold as the rainy outdoors. I looked into his face. His eyes were glassy, his lips parted, cracked;

dry foam formed on the corners of his mouth, with strange smile. At that moment he frightened me for he reached for my hand and began stroking it. Now I see it as a frantic state of ecstasy.

"Why don't I fix you something to eat?" I suggested. "All your ideas will mean nothing to anyone if you don't take care of yourself, keep your health so you can express them.

"I have eaten only the purest of substances for four days. I have purged my body of all impurities by this process. I have drunk the essence of being and nothing more. It is with you I want to share my being. It is you from whom I wish to continue to drink the essence of being, if only you wish to share it with me."

His manner had quickened, his movements were even more jerky as he continued to stroke my hand. To put it mildly, because I thought he was temporarily out of his mind and I couldn't understand him, I was frightened to hell-and-back. I felt flushed, then dizzy and didn't know how to react or what to say. I thought he needed help but didn't know what to do. I decided I had to leave, get out, that I couldn't think in this environment, and I had to think about what I could do for him.

I stood up and announced I had to go to a job interview. "Get some food and you will feel better. You do have something to eat don't you?" I briskly moved into the kitchen and checked his icebox: ... moldy cheese, bread, milk, rotting fruit and vegetables. I wondered about that coffee. "Want me to help you fix something to eat?"

"No," he said in a disappointing and frustrated

voice. "If you want something to eat, fix it. Won't you be late for you interview?" He had followed me into the kitchen. "Oh, yes, the interview. "I looked at my watch. "I must be going. Promise me you will eat something, or I won't leave."

Huh? O.K., I promise."

I left with the idea of finding Margery. She might be able to come back and take care of him or if not, at least know what to do. I searched for her two hours. She wasn't at her office nor home. She was probably at a brokerage firm watching the quotes, as she had been doing for the last three days, which firm I didn't know. I left messages everywhere and went home to wait for her. But it wasn't she who called first; it was Jacoby. He apologized for scaring me, said he had eaten something, that he felt well and not to worry. His voice was reassuring, so my anxiety relaxed some.

By the time Margery called, the whole incident seemed like a nightmare from which I had awakened. I told her that Jacoby seemed to be driven by unknown forces, and she should go over and see him to make sure he's all right.

"Can't you? I have a dinner appointment with two associates and won't be able to break away."

I told her about his conversation, that he had fasted, and what he looked like. "He has been carried away many times before, so involved with himself and his thoughts that nothing else existed. It will pass. It always has."

I told her some more about what happened, and she said, "The earliest I can get over there will probably be 11:00 o'clock tonight or after work tomorrow. You did say he called and ate something? .... That's good; the tides are ebbing. See if you can get back there and check on him. I'll look in on him when I can get away."

I left my apartment wanting to get the episode out of my mind but went to his apartment again. Either he wasn't home or didn't answer the door. I immediately found the nearest bar, half expecting to find him there, but when he wasn't, I ordered another Irish Coffee.

Chapter 5

A doctor who attended my father's funeral strongly recommended a physical with special emphasis on checking for cancer. With no money and no insurance, I put it off until my father's estate was settled, and then with so much happening, I put it off again. It was the pain which sent me in for a check-up. Yes, a malignancy grows inside me, and now two doctors told me that if I don't do something about it, I have less than a year.

I want to finish this manuscript and finish Jacoby's before I die. He was not only my friend but a great influence on Margery, Thesus, and me, and another story of unfulfilled potential. So onward:

Jacoby's movie has been playing ever since it was released, as I described, but now it is as a short to another movie which has been released nationally. Our hero would only release it when it was appendicized by an epilogue with one of his lectures. Both Jacoby's death and our hero's address are making the rounds in the underground circuits, not only in this country, but in Europe, mainly Germany. The original movie was released by his uncle and our hero, as a committee of two, who decreed that besides their salary, the money from the movie would go into a foundation for starving artists. "Something that Jacoby would have wanted." Although that statement was Jacoby's uncle's, it was our hero who created the foundation, I think as a tax deduction, but the money is rolling in.

Even though the uncle legally owned the movie, Jacoby died intestate and his uncle and aunt were his only relatives, Thesus had possession of the movie and not "wanting the uncle to abuse it," our hero viewed, copied, developed it and confronted the uncle with segments of a copy. His approach was what if there existed a last movie of Jacoby's suicide. That conversation, which continued off and on for over a week, resulted in the agreement: if our hero edited the film into a commercially presentable show and found a theater to show it, their contract would read 50-50. Neither of them could have anticipated the results. Both of them might have thought some money could be generated, but never to the extent of what has happened. It was the publicity which set the ball rolling, enabling our hero and the uncle to enforce the demands set by the committee to procure the just royalties from movie theaters and to regain control of the sculptures which the museum in Berkeley possesses. The foundation has a horde of lawyers.

Yes, the money is rolling into both the foundation and our hero in the form of contributions to the nonprofit organization established to help struggling artists, in the form of royalties, sales of art work, sale of articles, personal lectures, and I don't know what else. He has invested both his surplus capital and the foundation's in the company in which Margery is almost a charter member and on the board through early investment, and when it goes public next year, she will be a major stock holder and chair of the board of directors. The foundation's and Thesus' "inside stock" will give her the majority of votes she needs. This is not, however, the company for which she has been working for the last ten to twenty years.

The foundation, itself, of which Thesus is president and the uncle vice-president, is collecting moneys from other organizations and from personal donations in order to buy land with the prospect of creating an artists' colony. They are requesting contributions of both money and equipment: kilns, printing presses, photo equipment, pottery wheels, etc.

It kind of angers me that Jacoby's uncle is sharing the proceeds from all of this, he who charged Ike even for a wedding gift. But then again, isn't it strange that because of Jacoby's efforts which led nowhere have opened a path for our hero and me. Jacoby has helped set our hero free in a way where Jacoby never was. In fact, he who never received any recognition for his efforts in art has begun a new powerful art movement in this country that has had far reaching political effects in not just a new movement for freedom of expression but.................. He has stimulated the field of art beyond his wildest dreams. Underground organizations have been conceived in the name of art. It has even been suggested that a movement be started to create minimum standard income so that people who want to become artists can without fear of starvation. The idealisms which these movements have spawned seem monumental.

Our hero has become known in the Bay Area under his pseudonym. He has let his hair grow long then had it dyed by a professional; he grew a Vandyke beard and is wearing wire rim glasses. He puts gray in his hair and beard and has gained a heavy set appearance by lifting weights. Only those who knew him before and saw the transformation know him now. We have told him this, but he still worries about people from his past.

He has indicated that he thinks he knows the name of the person responsible for harassing him, but he still doesn't know why or to what degree that person is responsible for the rest of his problems. I guess before he changed his identity, he laid a trap for that person, and it was successful. He is investigating the situation. The harassment has ceased. And he feels it's a game of cat and mouse as to whether the person will discover his disguise

Both the money and the anonymity have increased his freedom. Today it was announced that Jacoby's uncle is now the president of the foundation, and Thesus is a non-acting VP. Thesus resigned his position to develop his latest theme: to become active in different groups to instigate change, but never to become the most important person in the organization, always just influencing, just adding a piece of information, an idea, letting others think the new concept was theirs and letting them take the credit. He is only hired on a temporary basis and wants it that way. He is looking for something, a bit of information, or for someone who knows what he needs to know. He is afraid that he will find a group, a braintrust, alien to his thinking, and it will try to slow or stop him.

Chapter 6

It has occurred to me that not everyone reading this manuscript has experienced the movie or will want to. I will describe it with my interpretation. Our hero has had copies of the dramatization since its earliest discovery and has encouraged us to see it if we wanted. Finally, we three viewed it at Margery's one Saturday night about twelve. Thesus had told us what to expect, and I proceeded to get roaring drunk on purpose. I knew I didn't want to view in any other condition. Margery screamed when the shot rang out then started crying. She shouldn't have seen it. She was at the point of exhaustion, was nervous about something, and although she hadn't had as many drinks as I was well on her way.

On the second viewing of it that evening, I wanted to see it to answer a question. Thesus thinks Jacoby quit mumbling and died even before the impact of the bullet. He didn't even think it was out of fear that Jacoby died but life left his body voluntarily. When he told me this, I thought that he was seeing what he wanted to see. My interpretation is different as I will describe. I called Thesus idealistic when he told me his interpretation. But the questions remain: When does or did life leave the body? Before impact, out of fear, during impact or when the vital functions have been destroyed? Did Ike feel pain?

The movie opens with Jacoby walking onto the scene with a red, five gallon plastic Jerry can of gasoline and a shovel. In the upper part of the screen is the ocean. The lower part of the screen is debris of all sorts scattered about him in dry sand. It is obvious that he is on the beach at a low tide, for a wavy line of debris separates the white sands from the cleaner, darker cakey sand. For almost one-half an hour he digs a hole just below the wavy line in the slightly wet sand. He places in driftwood which he had already gathered on the side the pit. He works almost unaware of his actions, but energetically, precisely; his face - a blank. Right before he lights the fire, anxiety seems to shake his body. With trembling hands, he finds and with a lighter ignites a piece of paper and throws it into the opening. Except for his shaking hands, all of his actions take place in one continuous movement as if he had practiced it, but it is not Jacoby, it seems to be a robot. The hole flashes into flames, unexpectedly, almost exploding. As he watches the blaze from a distance, he begins to relax; the expression on his face lifts and his purpose becomes clear; movements and attention are directed but yet his senses seem to awaken. He is observant of everything and when he finishes putting more driftwood on the fire, he makes a turning glance as a seagull flies, seemingly within reach, up the coast, then he immediately walks from the scene.

The blueness of the ocean and the sky make a stark contrast with the whiteness of the sands and the intermittent tongue of flames. The colors in the final version are so vivid, they seem unreal. The only manifestation which keeps the scene from becoming an over-colored postcard is the perpetually moving surf and its changing colors, the sound of the wind; the consistent building of waves and their crashing, breaking the sound of the wind, and then Jacoby's reentrance.

On the sand, he sets a large card board box and examines the contents intently. The fire is somewhat retorted by this time because he used his remaining kindling, and it burned much too quickly. Absent-mindedly, looking at the cardboard box, he rips off the flaps and throws them in. Placing the cardboard box a couple of feet beyond the hole, between the fire and ocean, he leaves the scene, checks the camera because it is moved downward and zooms in on the box. "Are you recording? Yes, the sound is recording." And again back at the box, he picks it up. He sits cross-legged where it was; faces the camera; touches his pocket, looks around and nods his head. Yes, everything is in order and ready.

He glances at his watch, quickly pulls the box over to him, reaches in and grabs a folder, saying, "Too much time has been spent in preparation. What you are seeing is my final art object. It may or may not be taken as a protest. I don't care." He takes a manuscript from the box and adds in a solemn voice, "Ah, yes a collection of poems which I have written and have been editing for years, entitled 'Inquiries.'" He gently tosses the loose papers from the folder into the fire. "Ah yes, more poetry, another manuscript, "Searching After God' which could have been 'Searching .... After-God' another one not understood. Oh, well! 'They are interesting but are they poetry?' everyone said. Now they will be ashes. Who cares what they were?" He laughs. "How many are here? Six, seven, eight, nine, manuscripts." He tosses them in. "They got me where I am today."

When these catch and the fire is high, he flings in another jacket of works. It bounces off the hole's wall and disappears. While observing the folder's flight, his hand reaches for another something else from the box and says as a matter of fact, "I'm no longer of use to myself or anyone else. I don't believe in being a drain on the system upon which I depend. I don't want to spread any more bad karma by depleting the system ..... taking more than I can return. I feel I have done the best I could with my life, and now I again feel I am doing the best I can. The fear of death doesn't bother me. I have known timeless moments, and in these moments have touched eternity. I have opened that door, peered in, then it closed on me. This time, it will open and I shall walk through. I've served my purposes, both to myself and the rest." No emotion is exhibited, neither in his manner nor voice.

331

I recognize one of his three pieces of cardboard. He smiles when he sees it, and begins to read from it. The wind seems to rip it from his hands and it goes into the hole. He laughs and feels in the box for another piece of cardboard, finds it and reads again as if it was a continuation from the first. Part of his reading of this second one was blurred because of a wave. He flips it into the fire. It spins downward out of sight.

He opens another folder, looks at its contents, seems to mumble something, peers back into the box while releasing it. It falls on the edge and flips into the hole. The fire subsides for moment because of the coverage. Noticing the change of intensity, he laughs again and says, "I don't even know what I've destroyed .... but it doesn't matter." I have heard some of the audience laugh at this point. Then reaching in, he gets a bound manuscript, "Oh yes, a novel," and throws it with force into the pit. Swiftly another manuscript is in his hands, "Ahhh......my definition of art;.........something no one has understood." He laughs, "Anyway, this movie will make it obsolete ..... Now, will anyone understand?" Shaking his head with a doubtful smile, he grabs a handful of loose papers from the box and almost unconsciously throws them. The bulk hit the hole but papers fly with the wind. "I guess I should explain the best I can, at least to my friends 'why?' I have reached a peak; there is no place to go from here; it couldn't get better, only worse. I know my ability to communicate is waning. My abilities in so many ways are ebbing. My need for knowledge continues to swell. My ideas are beyond what I can communicate already. They float in an absolute medium, freed from any restrictions but with no way to measure development, for they aren't mirrored anymore .... So this movie is an attempt to implant a seed, my final message home." For a moment he stares at the flames. I have questioned whether he is hypnotized, but I don't think so.

"Whatever's trying to hold me, it is not going to. I am breaking through. There is no sense in getting entangled in traps and mazes when there are many ways through .... maybe an infinite number," he laughs at his own declaration. "As a writer and sculptor, I have not found the way, but as an artist I have. This movie will testify to my success." He pauses a moment without a change of expression and then says, "Even if the film is not victorious or even destroyed in some way, it doesn't matter. My art object will prevail." He draws his stare away from the fire, throws some more papers in, and pulls the large box over to him, tilts it towards him, and looks in, takes two handfuls and says in a mumble, "notes, notes, and more notes, character sketches, ideas, poems, unfinished papers," the box tips and almost falls into the hole as he throws the handfuls in, but quickly catches it. More papers fly down the beach. He doesn't take notice and looks into the box again saying, "Oh, yes, another one of my novels," and throws an 8' by 10' box into the fire. It bounces off the far side of the pit; the top pops open before tumbling down. "Maybe it is not only the need to make a final statement, to communicate, because fate .... humanity .... America's art world.........whatever..... has driven me to this end, but…" The fire is raging and puffs of sparks rise with the heavy missive. "As an artist, I may be only successful to myself. I have created of my self, and I will create my finality to demonstrate my maximum ability to control this medium. I am mastering the medium of my own being. This is my supreme creation. I am not withdrawing myself from nature but am going back into it. I am spiritually transcending. I am, however, withdrawing from the world of the senses. I no longer want my unfulfillable desires, wants, and needs. I don't want any attachments; they just bring me back from the person I have created and am creating. It is a gamble whether anything will be preserved in the timelessness which I seek, but in the day-to-day world I know it won't." He throws another folder filled with two hundred or so pages, a book of some kind into the fire, and while waiting until the flames reach another peak, he pokes at the remaining papers in the box.

"Obsolete, all of it obsolete." He laughs, "My body is obsolete. As these papers can smother the fire, my life can and will smother me as an artist.

"How can I describe this state of being which I have reached? I have obtained a freedom, not only in my ideas and thoughts, not only in being beyond all this and even myself, but where I know, to live or die is the same thing, where there is no being and nothingness which exists as opposites. There where no concepts exist at all. I know I can go into a greatness beyond me ..... beyond me .... into this greatness......" For a moment he begins mumbling but

334

catches himself, looks at his watch. "It is about time for this movie to end." A blankness overtakes his face. His eyes seem to glaze over as he glares at nothing. He begins to mumble to himself, inaudible phrases. It seems like a chant of some type, maybe a prayer, and his face blanks into a deep mediation. It could very well be a religious offering. The chanting never ceases as he leans to one side, pulls the huge pistol from the box. Recognizing what it is is a shock. The first time I saw this my, heart seemed to stop. Where he get that? Every time since, my adrenaline rushes. The pistol is enormous, and he points it under his chin. The mumbling stops for a second. He breaths in deeply and exhales slowly. I think the chant begins again before the explosion, but our hero doesn't agree. Looking intently, as the picture slows, one can see the impact of the bullet exiting out of the top part of his skull. The expression on his face never seems to change for the preparation of impact nor after the actual impact. For a moment, his head appears to leave his neck as it jerks blurrily upward in spite of the slower moving picture. The body jumps from the ground so abruptly, his body is propelled upward and backwards with such force that when it crashes, his head bounces back from the sand, and it looks as if he tries to sit up again but falls to side. With the film continuously slowing, so slowly now, one can see the shoulder of his right arm grind into the sand. The collision of the dead weight with the sand made it bounce slightly again. All of a sudden one realizes that life has left his body before the recoil ceases, and he falls from shoulder to chest onto the sand. His face is turned sideward and stares under the camera. Blood is not pumping from the exposed side of his head but spreads under his face in the sand, outward, surrealistically.

In the original edit, (Thesus' version) the film stops. I guess the unedited version went on for hours until the batteries ran out. The ocean never rose to take Ike away, but Thesus told me after two hours two seagulls landed, one on Jacoby's head. The other landed in front of his face. It hopped around to the back and both began to peck, presumingly at his exposed brains and then both flew away.

In the final, in the movie theaters' version, from the moment he pulls the pistol out from his pocket, to when his face bounces on the sand, slow motion progresses until time seems to stop. The camera zooms back from the victim and sweeps to a wave about to crash onto the beach. Half of the scene is the beach and half is the frozen wave. An object organically emerges from far down the beach; when it is distinguishable, it says, "The End."

Chapter 7

After about a fifteen seconds of darkness, our hero appears on the screen with his new identity. His presentation is that of a college professor or an older intellectual, wearing a sweater vest, a tie and wool coat with patches on the elbows. All he needs is a pipe, but he decided that was a bit too much. He sits behind a nondescript, light wood, professional's desk, but stands as he begins, "This need not have happened." He walks around and sits on a corner. He expresses his assumptions concerning the art world in the United States: its present state of deprivation, its lack of freedom and how it is being used by the powers-that-be as a tool of propaganda; that this state of affairs will continue if the majority of American citizens interpret art as a sport for rich people, or worse useless. "We cannot let the people in power and/or governments determine the definition of art through its subsidies, because the definition of art is the products produced by artists, by the people for the people. The real, true artists are starving because they are not singing the right tune; they are expressing new ideas, new ways of looking at life. They are exploring, conceptualizing, and yes, even expressing their visions of the present state of affairs, their understanding of truth, and projections of future possibilities. Unless art becomes adopted by more people, supported by the average citizen, artists will continue to be suppressed, and valuable resource to understand ourselves and our world plus to create a better, more true world will be lost.

"Ike Jacoby, on the other hand, if he would have known his end result, mainly on those who have killed themselves, would not have killed himself, for he would not have wanted all human beings to act the way he did. He believed in existence and the potentiality of people. He tested himself again and again to find his true potential. It was a part of his search to know himself.

"Some of you may be thinking that death was

part of his search also. His search, and not death, was his motivating force, what he made his life's work. He was but a human and had his weaknesses. It can be said that he gave into his weaknesses and maybe took the easy way out.

"But in his own mind he was an artist. He explored his chosen way with control, then recorded his exploration. This film is his last art object, his last record, and death does seem to be his goal, but this is a goal we all necessarily reach. True, he set out to prove that this goal can be reached with control, but then again, he would have conceded: control could have deterred death. The exploration of death as a goal does not need to be sought, for it comes to us all. The exploration of life is the challenge. The control of the here-and-now.

"One of his main mistakes is that he didn't know his weight in our society. He didn't see that the impact of his death would reverberate and resonate in the lives of so many others. Also as part owner of this film, it is my responsibility to try to control its effect.

"And who knows what positive consequences he could have permeated through living, or how great an artist he could have become if he would have continue his life. As great an artist as he was, he could have had a better influence on mankind; he believed that 'effect' is a criterion for great art."

The camera pans away from Thesus' presentation and rests on the green blackboard where the credits (almost all pseudonyms) begin unscrolling.

Jacoby would have been pleased, if not elated, with the movie and its outcome. To be recognized as an artist and to revitalize art in this country was beyond his wildest imagination. And I am sure he would have wanted to help Margery, Thesus and me which he has.

My main question about his suicide, and a sign it was insanity, was that he wasn't consistent. How could he have found a reason to live while in his uncle's beach house (his diary) and later kill himself, unless either what he wrote or what he did was fiction? Was his sacrifice his life and not his death? To me, we have to live for what we absolutely know and should not make sacrifices to what we really don't know. Our hero put it better when he said, "The 'me' is more concrete, more real than a belief."

Yes, if he was such a great artist, why couldn't create of himself a being who could create a livable reality? Why couldn't he create of himself a person who would have wanted to live? Ike was trapped by the path he had chosen, and he knew it.

I have decided to add another conversation, mainly because it was in this conversation that Jacoby attempted to define himself and what he was thought he was accomplishing. It shows the turmoil of his mind. I can't put it in context because I don't remember the circumstances in which it occurred. It may have been at Big Sur Inn; we three sitting around the fireplace after dinning, having drinks; nevertheless, I am not sure; ... it doesn't quite fit. I know it existed, for I can almost hear Jacoby's voice.

Our hero commented about art being a thermometer of culture and then Jacoby referred to the Ancient Greeks at their zenith and how strong their beliefs must have been from the art they created. "It must have been a grand time for them (the Greeks) and art. If we would or could only achieve a culture, beliefs, a fulfillment of man's potential, both individually and collectively as I think they must have had."

"For sure, they were (probably) simple in contrast to us and our society, if only in dealing with the number of concepts and individuals." After this statement, our hero thought for a moment and in anticipation of our response: "Do you think humans are innately good, and if they are, should they become the complete person, not suppress any aspects of being? We are taught evil by both other beings and our societal environment; that is my belief. Those ancient Greeks could have been closer to their beings, their real, natural beings.

"Yes, I govern my life by the natural. Nature is free of morality. Good and evil do not exist in nature. Therefore, I let each part of my being play as much a role as I feel is natural, good, right, and just. My mediations help me decide whether what is motivating me is natural or induced."

"So, you believe that there is a division from which you must choose: to be a good person as dictated by the society, which is trying to condition us to serve it, or to create your own moral values, or to be a complete person as determined by your natural potential?" I asked.

"It is just not that simple," Jacoby jumped in, "I believe I have the potentiality to become a great artist although I was not born with any special talents for being an artist, but I believe each man is more than just an animal in his ability to create, in his ability to improve upon nature, his ability to express himself and to improve himself. In this ability to create something greater than himself, something that will outlast himself, something abstract, maybe something immortal, each man can extend his effect further than he personally can, than his physical being."

I chirped in, "This is one of the main reasons why we have a civilization: our capability to pass on knowledge and experience to the next generation."

"But should a man sacrifice himself," Ike continued, "for something greater?"

"You mean for art, itself? People do devote their lives to it." Our hero interjected.

"A couple of years ago, it never ever occurred to me. I thought I was an important artist and that was my contribution. But now I know there is more."

Our hero didn't give Jacoby a second before he answered, "You make it sound as if it is your egotism which holds you back; isn't it egotism which makes you contemplate any sacrifice to anything greater than you? Why would our insignificant beings be wanted as a sacrifice? Do monks think they are sacrificing their lives to God? Or are they just staying pure or redeeming themselves?

"If we each are immortal through our effect, at least as long as mankind is continuous, wouldn't any unnatural way to create an effect be negative. A positive, natural effect might be better for all concerned, using both your intellect and emotion to determine a sure, good way to create it. The slow but sure way: create it, test it; create it, test it. A smaller but better effect.

"And time tests truth. Any fake effect will deteriorate through time. If it is real and natural it will last."

For the first time that I have ever known Jacoby, he was shaken by our hero's probes, not visibly, not greatly but subtlety and it only could be detected in the quickness of his answer and in the desperateness of his voice which was too strained and squeaky.

"I believe in myself enough to believe in my judgment of my effect. I believe that art is greater than man, that if all the art in the world was in one room and someone, or even many people, wanted to destroy the room, I would kill them all to prevent it from happening. I believe that one person can create an object, a work of art that is the best part of himself, a condensation of his being, leaving out the superficial part, the stupid part, the mundane, the boring. In that an artist can become something greater than himself for a moment, as maybe in the form of inspiration or identification, and because that momentary being is expressed, the art object can itself be greater than the human life. Maybe in that it (the art object) is more than the sum of its parts, maybe that an artist can express knowledge beyond his own understanding, or that art pieces are additive to the concepts and world of ideas then art objects can be greater than any single individual human life."

"Of course, I don't agree," interjected our hero.

"Neither do I," I added, "All the great art

objects in the world, given enough time could be created again."

"Yes, John is right; you are forgetting the almost infinite potential of each human being. When you said that the artist can express something beyond his own understanding, you expressed the potential. It is that that we need to unlock."

"If some cataclysm event happened and destroyed all art and most of humanity, the remaining human beings would recreate art."

"No, you are wrong. Art maybe created, but not the same art with the same significance, with the same effect."

"Yes, you are right, because as we have expressed, art objects are manifestations of time, place, and individuality of the artists."

Something interrupted our conversation because this ends my recollection. I hope I have recorded it correctly and will let our hero read it to test my memory.

I have received a strange letter in the mail. A note attached asks me to include this manuscript in my "biography," my series in the newspaper about Ike Jacoby. "This manuscript" is in Jacoby's handwriting, or at least seems to be. The note was signed by a reporter from same local paper. Of course, he does not want me to disclose his name and so I won't.

The manuscript is a letter to a famous Chinese artist. The artist is in exile, self-imposed, as opposed to being in prison. He opted to leave China for he had a series of prizes awaiting him, not to mention the money from royalties. It seems that Jacoby has sent this letter directly to the artist but received no reply, so he resorted to offering it to an editor of a newspaper. Of course, the editor did not publish it.

Jacoby would have had a better chance of publication if he would have presented it to an underground newspaper or published it himself on the Internet in a news group. But he tried another grand-stand-play and sent it to one of the largest papers in the country. This stupid attempt to get published seems typical of Jacoby, as does the paranoia displayed in the letter, but discounting the mysterious source, I never knew Jacoby thought he was suppressed. To me he never thought in those terms; true, he may have used those terms, but too loosely, not knowing the full implications.

The exact date of this manuscript is questionable, but I would assume it was within a few years after he graduated college. The note mentioned that when Jacoby presented the manuscript, he went into a long story about being drugged by a college organization. It could be true. Many radical pro-government organizations exist. It has just occurred to me why anybody, much less an organization, would be interested in Jacoby. Then again it could have been those sculptures. And you know, thinking back, it does sounds like what happened to our hero in college

"All Persons Shall be Equal in the Eyes of the Law" was the inscription on his sculpture of Justice, so it may be true. The stupid fool even applied to different branches of the government for grants to turn his clay figure into bronze.

I can believe that this governmental system

could focus upon an artist, which the system wishes to make inoperative and in fact do it to him. People in power must have known his location from his student loans. But I don't think Jacoby even knew he had been financially trapped by those loans much less marked as a subversive. (There is a great deal of evidence that the government gave loans to students, knowing full well, that the students would not be able to get jobs to repay them, for the government could also insured that.)

Also about this same time, I know for a fact that an unknown person discredited Jacoby to his uncle by telling him that Jacoby was taking drugs, that he was gay, and that he was a sexual pervert. Of course, his uncle believed this unknown source; especially since undoubtedly he questioned Jacoby and found his mind a little more deranged than usual. These revelations helped explain some of the uncle's actions: the institution, encouraging Ike's marriage, etc. This distance between these two was never breached, even after death.

And Ike Jacoby is right, it is very easy to distract, discredit, distort, or even destroy an artist because she/he must be on the fringe. That's what Jacoby thought about his situation, but he thought it was the government. In my mind, that whole idea was an ego trip of Jacoby's. He was unknown. Why would anyone, much less a group, be interested in him? But then again ……..

I present this document - with the supposition that it is a document - a manuscript which may represent the truth even though the truth is not directly presented by the manuscript. It is written to a famous Chinese artist in hiding.

As one artist to another, I ask which system is worse for artists? Which system is more oppressive? Which system can suppress art more effectively?

In this country we also have governmental acceptance and rejection of art· Grants are given to the acceptable and not to the unacceptable· This is natural· The government furthers that which is in its best interests· But there exists a more subtle type of suppression in this system: economic sanctions·

Art by its very nature is a newness, and unless a well-known artist creates it, it is this newness which can prevent the object from being accepted as art· The populace will not buy an object unless it is recognized as art and an artist cannot function as an artist unless objects are sold· So the artist is torn between "reproducing" objects sanctioned as art or creating unique, questionable objects· It is the first type which most people buy because Art is what is liked· The second reason art is brought in this country is because it may be an investment· It is bought by the law of supply and demand, the same law which determines the price of toilet paper, or maybe a better analogy, a futures contract of a commodity. It is expected to be a good investment because of the name of the artist.

I have presented this argument to different people and their reply is: "Don't be an artist." It is easy for them to say. And they are right in that one can choose to be or not to be. This choice exists in your country as well. Wherein is our freedom in this country which doesn't exist in your country? In your country, you know your opposition and can gain recognition by standing against it.

There are many different means of oppression. The less cruel is the most obvious; the most cruel, the least obvious. There are many means of suppression. From first-hand experience, I can tell you that economic suppression in a land of plenty, which values money as power and success above human concerns, creates an invisible prison, a subtle but real type of exile. The suppressed are cast from society, set afloat on a boat of 'Have Nots.' It is like dying of thirst, floating in the middle of a lake. Surrounding you is more than you or anyone could possibly drink and yet, you are dying of thirst. Artists, as a general category in this country, live on the boat of 'Have Nots' because they are not valued by this society. They do not carry the torch of culture. The culture is created by the media, social

347

fads, and money. It is either sellable or it doesn't exist.

Artists are stifled because they do not even realize what is suppressing them. We do not have something tangible to fight, only some vague idea that we *can* create something that sells, that hits upon an idea, a style, a technique which will 'make it in the art world.' When our art does not peddle, or we are forced to sell it at a ridiculously low prices or not at all, we feel that it is our inability to express, our inability to create, that we are not dedicated enough; we have not sacrificed enough. Because of this, artists in this country are more likely to cease, to sell out, to quit the fight because they feel the enemy is within.

Knowing your enemy, you can remain a hero to yourself and your people. Your government can destroy you but not defeat you. It can physically suppress you to the point of succumbing, but if you are strong, it can never defeat you.

In this country we do not know our enemy. In many cases it *is* ourselves, our desires, our wants, our needs to be successful, to be accepted, to have the "necessities" of life. And we can truly defeat ourselves.

Where are artists more productive, more useful, more significant, more needed???

348

Chapter 8

As mentioned in the description of Jacoby's death, some papers didn't fall into the fire. I noticed them during the movie but really didn't give them a second thought. Since viewing the film a third and fourth time, I asked Thesus about them. When he removed the camera, he had found some and picked them up, more as one picks up litter. Undoubtedly the wind must have taken some, which have not been found. One of the two which were recovered was burned so badly that only a complete paragraph remained. I recognized it and restored it as you will see. The second page was partially in the hole and partially covered by sand. It is written by Jacoby whereas the first one wasn't. A third piece of paper was recovered by an unknown person, who had kept it because of its interest, but realized its significance when she assumed it was written by Ike Jacoby. I assume it was a next door neighbor of the Ike's uncle. She gave it to Thesus after a show when he was still personally appearing. Then demanded it returned after another show. Thesus kept a copy of it. Our hero never mentioned it because of the negative effects of its contents, but he has consented to place it in this manuscript for the sake of truth, to present a full, complete story as we know it, and I agreed.

The more material and knowledge I have about Ike Jacoby, the more unsure I am of conferring any truth or justice in regards to him. Logic would seem upside down with that statement. So I am soliciting the help of Margery, Thesus and Jacoby, through his own work to present the complete story because I admit I still don't have a full understanding concerning his death. His reasons for killing himself are confusing, contradictory, and, still to me, unjustified. Multiple reasons are emerging as possibilities. The more I write, the more uncertain I am that I even knew him; therefore I am presenting more and more of his own work, so the reader can attempt an understanding.

The first of the three papers which wasn't completely destroyed by the fire wasn't even something he wrote, but an excerpt from _Demian_, a novel by Herman Hesse. As I said I recognized it and restored as much as I thought is relevant

It is s story which Frau Eva told to Demian about a youth who had fallen in love with a star. "He stood by the sea, stretched out his arms and prayed to the star, dreamed of it, and directed all his thoughts to it. But he knew, or felt he knew, that a star cannot be embraced by a human being. He considered it to be his fate to love a heavenly body without any hope of fulfillment(,) and out of this insight he constructed an entire philosophy of renunciation and silent, faithful suffering that would improve and purify him. Yet all his dreams reached the star. Once he stood again on the high cliff at night by the sea and gazed at the planet (star) and burned with love for it. And at the height of his longing he leaped into the emptiness toward the planet but at the instant of leaping 'It's impossible' flashed once more through his mind. There he lay on the shore, scattered. He had not understood how to love. If at the instant of leaping had he had the strength of faith in the fulfillment of his love he would have soared into the heights and been united with the star." (If these next sentences weren't in his notes, they should have been.)

"Love must not entreat," she added, "or demand. Love must have the strength to become certain with itself. Then it ceases merely to be attracted and begins to attract..."

The second page which was found by the hole is a completely personal statement of Jacoby about himself. He probably wrote it after The Big Sur trip.

"I can see an existing duality in my being. The duality exists between seeking reality and creating reality. For everyone there seems to be a part of reality which each individual and mankind in general create and control through creating. One place where that reality exists is in the value system in which humans participate. It exists in the individual's interpretations of the world, his individual reality, in the beliefs which we hold, and besides these abstract creations, there are concrete ones: the physical world which we arrange and re-arrange, our environment, and that which we give birth to children.

"But generally, the physical world makes up a part of reality which man can't control through addition or arrangement. It, for the time being, is man's situation whether we look at it as our physical make-up, the natural surroundings, or the universal structure. We take mind enhancing drugs; we build buildings, dams, cars, but have we really changed anything ultimately? We haven't complete control over the systems in which we exist nor do we even know the set-up of the systems upon which we depend.

"Maybe God's Laws are the one and only Reality, and our reality is but a game. What effect do my creations have on the Real Reality? Where is that which there is no more, where there is no beyond, and where is my reality? How much fiction is in my thought, word and deed? How much Reality do I know and can I know and how much is just my reality?

"Oh, to be in the flow, to know, to be attuned with the All, The Thought, The Word, The Deed. To be able to even just be launched in the right direction, so that someday, ah, yes, some day, this vessel............."

Our hero suggested that I preface this last paper with: "May the Last Direction the Helmsman Sets, be the Truest."

This next paper was given to Thesus. Neither our hero nor I really approved of putting this into the manuscript because of its content and source, (it is also muddled) but we do so for the sake of truth and honesty, to present the fullest possible picture of Jacoby. It may be questionable, but it is more than relevant. The mid-section of this doesn't make sense to me. He may have written it, drunk, stoned, or something and not proofread it afterwards, but I am submitting it as is. After reading and rereading it, I think it is notes for the beginning for one of his novels. I am sure it sets off as a dialogue but then turns into an exploration of his ideas, almost a debate.

"WARNING: When death takes on the meaning that life should have, does one lose control of his life?

"'But what comes after?'

"'Nothing!'

"'Doesn't that scare you?'

"'No, it is the best, or is it the worst? All my experiences, all my thoughts, all my energy will be gone. There will be no 'me' to be afraid. Humans are frightened of change, something that is all around them.'

"In this half century for the first time, generations seem to be so aware of empty death that complete philosophies are built around it: Nihilism, The Nada.

"Because we can help create our beings, it may be possible that we could reach this point before death and slide backwards into a lesser state, one where we can't maintain as much control or maintain the being which we have created. Also it is possible that two or more routes are available for the person. I should take the longer one that would get me not only to my greatest point, but that there should be the minimum of (this is the section which is blurred and confused, notice the shift to third person) that he will slide back to a lesser state that he should build a foundation that would be a less slideback as possible. The possibility of attaining this state to religion or thru religious experiences is not impossible, but I question probability. Using an analogy, of traveling from one area to the next, it would seem that instead of flying from the first area to the second, which might cause a great deal of slideback, one should walk and know the area covered so that he will know the territory to which he will slideback. By knowing the territory he will know where to take refuge. The state of walking in the analogy can only be known by control, knowing there is a greater state and how to obtain it (The above, to me, seems to be reasoning against suicide, then what follows seems to be reasoning for.)

"Maybe all living is a preparation or choosing a way to die. Maybe all living is a method for positive suicide? and all suicide is a way to seek out the best life. Artists create their meanings in life. This meaning should not be created today so that it disappears tomorrow. The created meaning makes a foundation on which man can create more meaning. Could there exist a demon which could destroy the created reason for a man's existence? If a man fought against this demon by living or by dying, he will have won. He will have struggled to keep his life meaningful. Because an individual creates his own meaning for his actions, we can be artists of our own beings, there may come a time at which any new action would take away meaning from previous acts and give him no new meaning. Rather than live a meaningless life, one may create meaning through death. This is not to say that one should kill himself because of an inability to create meaning, nor is it to say that one should kill oneself because he is disillusioned, but that one may kill himself to create more meaning to previous acts. (This sounds like a reaction, or response, to one of Thesus' discussions.) Death comes to all, so why couldn't an individual use death to create the maximum amount of meaning to one's life? Why couldn't a person regain control in his life through his own death?

"Maybe all of one's life is a preparation for death. And all the choices we make either directly or indirectly determine our death. If in choosing one's life we are choosing our way of death, then all life is a form of suicide. With this knowledge we could create the best possible life through directing ourselves to a positive suicide.

"Forms of positive suicide: One could believe in something so firmly that one's life becomes no sacrifice for the belief.

"Let's say, the only meaning which exists is the meaning which is created. This meaning should not be vaporous gas, existing today and disappearing tomorrow, but be created with the idea that it is the foundation upon which our lives are built. But it could happen that our life's meaning could be destroyed by an outside force and by fighting this force we lose our lives. I would rather create a meaningful death than live or have lived a meaningless life. If we create our own meaning, there could come a time that any new action could destroy the meaning of all previous actions, death at this point would be an alternative. (The redundancy seems to be a reinforcement of [what he wants to believe?] Why? Or as Margery suggests, a clearer way of saying the same thing. Through working he refined his thought.)

Chapter 9

In finishing the story of Jacoby, I have made two interviews to get direct and final comments from both Margery and Thesus. In fact, four days ago, I went to Margery's house to question her about Jacoby. She didn't want an interview but to record her statements and then have them transcribed. She said that she accepted my photographic memory concerning the conversations which I have quoted in the book and laughed, "Of course, but for the record, let's record this one." So the following is transcribed from the recording directly, leaving out the first part which to me wasn't important and a little too stiff and lengthy.

"To me he was leaving. We weren't sharing, because I didn't want, an extreme existence. By him pursuing art to the degree he did, I told him he was leaving me. Yet, he continued his pursuit, but this was only the final event. The relationship was turbulent all the way through. It was only good at the beginning when we could both form each other through our love, when we balanced each other, when we could over look or even love each other's differences, when we respected each other and the other's pursuits. But as it became more serious, as we started talking marriage, family, future we realized differences which we couldn't resolve. As the relationship went from his goals and my goals to our goals, conflict would emerge and with conflict doubt arose, maybe doubt about ourselves, but definitely doubt about the relationship, and doubt whether we could resolve the conflict and maintain our beings, and because of conflict and doubt, he withdrew. We became distant and with our distance, more differences arose, 'irreconcilable differences,' especially the ones, which to quote Ike, we 'couldn't control, couldn't resolve'; the ones which caused more serious conflict, strife in our daily life. More doubt arose, doubt and fear about hurting and being hurt by each other, then more distancing and............then he went to his uncle's cabin.

We got back together and were happy for a while, then he started off on one of his extreme thought tangents again. I respected him for his search, but living with him was too intense: asking questions which can never be resolved, asking questions which were too weird to even want to resolve. But I would get dragged into his involvements, and we would spend hours, days, debating points of view. When this happened, it was like falling into an endless pit: no way out. It encompassed our whole world. But yet these intense deliberations had no relevance to our lives or to our relationship.

Later after our final breakup when he used to visit, it was something else. He would leave; I would have time to think and resolve. I would be able to escape the questions and distance myself from them. But when he was with me, he would push, push, until it turned into a personal argument. It almost drove me nuts.

"After our first break up, when I moved out, he used to visit every day. I could almost handle that but

.... maybe that was the reason we got back together.

I guess in seeking what would make me happy, made him unhappy and visa-versa. But do you know what I now resent? That I didn't have his baby. I would have liked that. His existence should have been continued in that way also. If I would have only known ...." One can hear a short sob but it stops, and in a moment she continues again, "He had grown more distant than I realized. I didn't even realize that he didn't confide in me anymore. I can't but doubt, was his death necessary? If it would have only worked out for us. Maybe I was too selfish and wanted too much as my brother indicated. If I could have only loved him more."

"You are who you are and can only love as you do," I state on the recording.

"In going the way he went, he made his choice, and I think he was fully conscious of his choice. He intentionally withdrew from me and the world. But maybe I can't judge his intent or even his actions for I would not have predicted his death. I underestimated him."

"I think we all did .... Would it be impossible for you to judge him sane or insane? My main question since I had begun to write his story."

"Do you mean legally insane; harmful to himself or others? I wouldn't have before his suicide, not even in his fear of insanity because I think that was a game he unintentionally played and could have resolved it. And even it were not a game to him but a real fear, ... that didn't make him insane. But overall, I would say he was mastering his insanity if it existed

358

at all, but legally, after-the-fact, it would be hard to prove him sane. Also if we define insanity as not being able to adjust to the world or not wanting to adjust, we would definitely have to declare him insane. But I agree with him, if we were all sane, normal, conforming, the human race would lose its interest, its variability,, ... if not its potentiality.

"Wherein lays the thin line between genius and insanity? The difference may only exist in contributing something to the world or to the society, but then again who is to judge the positive effect from the negative and to say this person's life is justified and this person's is not. No, I am not going to judge him sane or insane. I'm not going to judge his worth, his art, his being, or his sacrifice. He showed me that art can express a more innate knowledge, a knowledge of the sublime. I thought that art for him was like running down a corridor of life. For him, his life and everyones' lives were like paintings on his corridor wall, four dimensional paintings but still paintings hung on a wall that his being passed while running. Either individually or as a whole, they were separate; hanging there disconnected from each other. Only at a fast passing speed did they appear to be closer together, and he so he ran as fast as he could, but as he got further down the corridor he saw the illusion.

"Even in the face of disillusionment he continued to run. Even when he discovered that the corridor, his art, was his destiny, his fate, he continued to run as fast as he could. He couldn't keep up with himself and at those times he showed me a knowledge of the sublime, an innate knowledge. Sometimes it was as if he were communicating wisdom which exceeded his knowledge."

When I asked Thesus about Margery's statement he said, "I must admit that Jacoby didn't see his own truth. He was trying to sell something about which he didn't see the true value. He didn't see his full potentiality. He had lost hope, a cardinal virtue. His vision was protected in part by his world, his created world of words. His mind was thoughts, ideas, words, abstractions; not existence, not the physical, material world, not the life and death struggle, not the work-a-day world. No, he didn't conceive himself in the physical realm in which the rest of us conceive ourselves. But I question whether Art is an appropriate romanticism or even worse, a religion. I think he based too many decisions on the belief it was and not on the here-and-now. Whether romanticizing himself into believing something that, in my opinion, was 90% belief and then committing himself to this belief, his religion, is right or ever could be right, I can't judge. Maybe he realized something I will never realize. Maybe his star was reached. Maybe he is the flow where he wanted to be. Who knows the validity of any individual's beliefs or reality. But we can hope for him.

"I can see through my last couple of statements. My hope for him may contain some of the guilt I feel. It is not a real hope, for I really don't believe he could or did obtain what he was after or maybe if he obtained it, he doesn't know he has. That would be ironic. But who knows what awaits us here, much less after this, when this ends?'

"Why do you feel guilt?"

"Maybe my questioning him drove him to his extreme stances. We both know that my questioning drove him into contradictions. Maybe I asked him questions which he really couldn't answer, although he had the appearance of answering. I should have seen the possibility of his suicide. I, above all, should have seen the conclusion which he was reaching and prevented it. But I was too concern in preventing myself from being squashed by social forces which have tried to control me. I was too wrapped up with my problems and was too willingly placing myself in the role of mentor for all suppressed people.

"If I would have helped him to find reasons to live and fulfill himself through his life rather than his death, if he could have found his meaning through life and communicating, if...... if.......if. In trying to change the world, I let my effect on a single human being diminish and maybe, just maybe, I could have had a more positive effect in this world by just helping Jacoby, by developing our friendship more fully, by listening to him, by reading the manuscript he gave me, by being a better friend. But I was out trying to change the world, hell, save the world, save myself in the world.

"Getting black to your original question, which of us know the true value of our life or our death? Which of us know the true value of Life or Death? I pray for greater Judges then us poor stupid, blind beings. We can only try to conceive the world as it is and make choices from our conceptions then hope and pray that our choices will have the best effect. But if we don't, may the knowledge we gain be greater than the cost of our mistakes; may we learn from them; for we never will completely fail if we learn.

"Jacoby was a man who was trying to create and live a valid reality. Don't we all? He was just an extreme example. Who among us can say 'I live in the real reality without illusion'? He was trying to have control over himself and his destiny. If commitment alone determines success, he succeeded; in as much as we can create our own realities he succeeded, but I feel, he lost hope in his ability to obtain this control through his life. He lost hope in the future which none of us can predict. Who knows, he may just have achieved the greatness and control through living rather than through death. But then again like I have said, how much of our personal realities are Real? If we each create our own realities and to some degree they exist after we have created them, he is living with the stars ...... or does it matter how much are real?"

I recorded our hero's statement and transcribed it word-for-word, not so much for what he said about Ike Jacoby but his statement that "Ike...a true form of him, is proof that too much thinking will just get you back to where you started, standing in the mysterious present, looking out into a dark unknown future and feeling the loss of the past."

The reader obviously has realized that in all honesty, I don't understand the reason for Jacoby's death and therefore in a profound way I don't understand Jacoby. I would like to hope that his death was not a cry-for-freedom as some indicate, and even he stated out-and-out that he didn't belong to the school of thought that freedom was the only ideal worth obtaining. In fact he stated that "freedom without control is chaos." And "we have to place on the harness and pull the plow, so we can reap what we sow."

But I think that he had a bad case of excelsior, too much ambition seeking too fast with too little control, and one aspect of his being where he had too little control were his thoughts. He thought they were too important. Yes, he ran too fast but not after freedom; it was truth and reality. In his egotism he thought that he had found something, that his thoughts were right and worth dying for, that his definition of art was right and worth dying for.

To end this section on Jacoby, I am going to quote our hero who at some time before the last interview said: "Life, sacred life. Our planet must shine like a gem in the Universe, but it is so fragile. Life is so precious and scarce. Our beings can truly be Temples, for they can hold that which is even more than sacred. Jacoby was an individual running in his self-chosen direction, veering not from his course, exploring the unknown and creating a temple of his mind: a reason? a justification? just a belief? but always wondering when and if both temples could become one, or is it only a temple within a Temple. Maybe Jacoby finally lived and died in that One Temple. Or maybe by killing himself he ostracized himself from the Temple and only dwells within his own created temple, if one exists at all."

Book III

Part 1

Current Events

Preface

Jacoby's Diary was printed in a series in the Sunday supplement in the local newspaper. It also has been accepted by a national woman's magazine, if a couple of legal matters can straightened out. The publisher mentioned he thinks a book should follow directly while the interest is peaking. I sent him the copy that I had written about Ike and a note to look for another author concerning a book. I can't do it nor do I want to ... not now.

The cancer in my body is taking its toll. "If you don't do something about it, you have less than a year to live," stated a noted authority. Yes, there is a greater chance that after a series of treatments, we can put this into remission, but I don't know. I want to finish this biography which I began before Jacoby's death.

With confidence that what I am writing is going to be published, I'm in the process of dictating Jacoby's story to fit this manuscript. Even Thesus has had "premonitions pertaining to a predestined doom, concerning publication."

Also knowing what I do now and in hopes that

this manuscript will be read at a future date, I must present my interpretation of the circumstances. In that so many facts and so much information has been suppressed today has awaken me to the possibility that a future generation may not realize the full situation in the United States while I write.

How much of the information which Thesus has provided is speculation and how much fact remains to be seen. Margery is helping me to compile this "information," but the reader must understand that I am only a lay person in politics, and so much has been suppressed that some of the following is conjecture, speculation, which may or may not be true, and even if true, may or may not be confirmed in the future because history is being created daily, fictionally and non-fictionally, and so much of this is so shocking that I don't really believe it, or don't want to believe it.

Chapter 1

Back-tracking to Jacoby's funeral: Thesus emerged from another of his anonymous pursuits when he read about Jacoby's funeral in the newspapers. The day of the burial was Thesus' grand appearance, but nobody including Margery recognized him. He approached us after Jacoby's casket mechanically rolled into the crematorium. Margery and I were walking slowly toward her car when he approached us. Only within feet of Margery did she recognize him, and only after he spoke did I.

He had let his hair grow and sported a Vandyke beard both of which he had had a Hollywood hairdresser shape and dye to a gray salt-and-pepper. He wore wire rim glasses and by lifting weights, had gained body size.

He stayed with me more than a week, and many of those nights were sleepless for him and some of those for me. Yet each morning he had risen before me and didn't return until late at night. He was driving himself to exhaustion. For him the nights without sleep were worth it because he felt he "had to tell someone just in case something happened," so his search "would not have been in vain." He explained what he had discovered about his circumstances, about the political situation in the United States, and about his "tormentors." This is the information which I must convey.

Within two weeks of Thesus' first disappearing act, that is after he discovered the honing devise and after he began to change his identity, mazes upon mazes confronted him: not only the mazes of the society, the government systems and organizations, but the maze of his own mind and in general natural mazes. The crux of the confusion was to demystify which maze was which; which were natural, which were only in his head, and which were the ones created by the government and society in general, and possibly which, if any, were created by individuals. He knew that by differentiating among the mazes, he might begin to discover those which ones he couldn't change, those which he could, those to which he wanted to devote his efforts, and to which ones he didn't. Then he would have to decide how he was to change those he wanted: thus place signs on them to disclose them and maybe a sign as to how to avoid them, or was he to destroy them, kill the minotaur(s) or even dismantle the labyrinth. His mind somewhat rambled as he discussed the above hypotheses because he was just beginning to realize what confronted him and didn't have it organized in his own head. Of course, I was his blackboard, where he could precipitate, analyze, and organize his thoughts.

So this story is more structured then when presented: Yes, it was that trip back to San Francisco and the placing of the honing device in his back which convinced him which side "they" thought he had joined. Now, in a way he has, just to protect himself, but then again, in his mind, he still doesn't consider himself a subversive. He is "just going to set things rights." He did not enlist into the underground, help raise an army, and strike out against the enemy. Oh, he knows his enemies, and it will not be easy: "Rarely does one directly confront an enemy more powerful than oneself and defeat it.

"There are dictators which control large aspects of this country; they control human destiny, human lives, and no one any longer controls them. They manipulate men and women. They place men and women in power when it will further their beings. They breed off of nonhuman people who let themselves be used so they can gain power, money, and prestige. Can't you see the different dictators? It is a bureaucratic dictator, where the system itself controls, and no one controls it. People struggle for position: power and prestige, and become that which is using them. It is a capitalistic dictator where money rules our lives. Money can make men and women act inhuman, and these inhuman beings gain money and become more powerful. It is a technocratic dictatorship, where our own machines which we created, now partially control. We are becoming more and more machine-like. The machines are playing a greater and greater role in our lives. Machines are ubiquitous, and they are always on: the computers, TVs, radios, cars, household appliances, business machines. With so much contact, we become more like them. We become robots to them. If we don't respond in a certain way, think in a certain way, they will not work; so we conform.

"They make us less human, and the less human we become, the more the different dictators can control our lives. The inhuman systems breed inhumanity, and inhumanity breeds more powerful inhuman systems.

"Then there are those who believe and support these dictators which make them more powerful; and in turn these individuals rule the rest of us for it is their right to rule; they feel superior; they gladly relinquish their humanity for their place on the top. They know what is right and wrong for the masses. The masses must be controlled, and it is their right and even obligation to do so.

"To me, it seems as if any type of extreme enthusiasm will help breed inhuman attitudes and traits. These extreme feelings of superiority, needing to control (for the sake of the populace), of needing power, money, prestige make us lose our perspective. And if we forget ourselves and who we really are, forget our place within our own lives, and forget that death will foreclose, we become the puppets of our own desires and in turn of those dictators. And again, if we don't further humanity, we are not furthering ourselves."

Because of the late hours, my mind had been saturated twenty minutes before these last statements, and so stupidly I responded to what he had said earlier: "Yes, money can make us play the fool, only sometimes we don't see it."

So used to people not being able to maintain concentration during one of his harangues, he commented: "And it's our own mortality, as viewed in the destruction and disintegration around us that can put everything back into perspective."

"But all of your conclusions are too vague, too generalize. What are you going to do to change it, reprogram all of us? Change our values?"

"You are right. This is but a condensation of my research and experiences in the last year. As for solutions, I am working on them."

Later and in a different conversation that week, after some hesitancy, he updated the events of his search. As he explained he thought that the specifics could put me in danger, but after more extensive thought I should know, so he spelled it out.

Shortly after both his sister and I had lent him money to leave town, his first, real, lucky-break occurred which is helping him unravel the mess of mazes. He went to Los Angeles, where he changed his name and identification, and was in the process of changing his appearance.

We have reiterated that only those who knew him intimately before and have seen the change could recognize him, but he still worries about a direct encounter with someone from his past, or someone who is somehow following him. This explains his hesitancy.

Thesus had found a cheap hotel in an area close to downtown LA, sent a change of address to the post office in San Francisco, and just waited for whomever to follow. Actually Thesus was very active making contacts while "he waited." As predicted, after collecting his mail from the box, he was followed. He recognized the person but couldn't remember from where

"It was a good idea to style and dye my hair because the person who relocated me had to take a second, closer look to make sure it was me. It was at that moment when our eyes met that a double recognition took place. As he was following me, I doubled-back on him. When he thought he had lost me, he went to his car. I copied his license and sent it to Margaret."

When relating this story, he explained the reason for his abrupt departure from town as: "I figured it wasn't any family or close friends, even though at the time, I suspected it; I apologize for my lack of belief, but I was disoriented by what had happened and was totally paranoid about everything and everybody. Later when a pattern emerged, I realized it wasn't you or anyone close to me because when I changed my address, they found me, but a lapse of time occurred, and it wouldn't have if ......

"Remember that call when I moved in with all those people? Anyway, the symptoms of what was plaguing me would stop for a while right after I moved, but would always begin again. That could be why they needed to put the honing device in me. But thanks to Ike, it was removed. Ike had done it with a biology-class scapula he found in a second hand store, and it was easier than I ever imagined.

"I was also having re-occurring dreams. Sometimes it was one person in a car, sometimes two, but each time I had those dreams, it was the same car trying to run me down. I didn't recognize the car or the people in it. Then after I went to LA, I finally recognized the person in the passenger seat: it was the person who followed me from the Post office. Was it that I saw the person first, then dreamed him? Or was it that I saw him in the dream first? No, it must have been. I have seen him following me and unconsciously it registered, then dreamt him."

Margery devised a method to disclose the man's identity without drawing attention. She called the police with the pretense of filing a complaint against the driver and gave them the license number. Contrary to her expectations, she didn't need to probe; the police voluntarily revealed the driver's name. The officer with the information asked if Margery wanted to file a complaint. She answered that she would investigate first because in the excitement, she may have misperceived the number.

Neither Thesus nor Margery recognized the

name. Thesus returned to San Francisco and furthered his search. "I even tried to break the code of a computer in which I assume the government has records of all of us. It's called the G.I.A. I have never heard of it before either. I was informed that it exists from "the gentleman" who gave me my fake driver's license in L.A. Theoretically anyone with a small pocket computer, which I bought from the gentleman, with a set-evolving-signal can unlock it, by calling a certain telephone number. It is the main government computer to which all officials have access. But the pocket computer and the mainframe must be synchronized, and it seems that the evolving signal changes speed, pitch, and codes every thirty minutes as determined by the time of day, day of month, month of year and by some other variable which I can't solve. One needs a certain type of preprogrammed computer to program the pocket computer and access the main frame.

"If I could only......," his voice faded into almost a silence, "If I could only ...." then it resumed at full intensity, "I would know about everyone .... and who knows what.

"I have called again and again; it has been a game as to all the different phones I have used, but the end result so far has been, I recorded the signal and tried to anticipate the changes. I know I had the right pocket computer, but I just couldn't get the program speed and some other ingredient.

"At the same time, I also went looking for my records in as many places as I could think. In most places, including the G.I.A. (Government Intelligent

Agency), FBI, and U.C.C., that was another one I have never heard of: it's the Unified Central Control, I called and inquired as to the possibility of one seeing one's records. In each inquiry I referred to the Freedom of Information Act. One the G.I.A. and U.C.C. are pretty much inaccessible because of the classification of material: Secured by Executive Order in the interest of National Defense. But I am still checking these while trying to remain anonymous.

"The FBI actually encouraged me, but I couldn't get information on anyone but myself because it would be an invasion of privacy. I'm sure if I would have pursued it, I would have targeted myself. I would have been investigated because I wanted information.

"Do you know what I did?" he smiled, "I gained a fake identification on the man who followed me and submitted a request. God, what a run-around! The report I received was so deleted, had so many black-outs, I couldn't make head or tails of it. It was stamped with statements like: Deleted: Confidential Source; Deleted: This Information may Endanger Law Enforcement Personnel; and Deleted: Investigation Incomplete. I am sure my request prompted the last rubber stamp. I only uncovered what I already knew. I couldn't even tell if this person worked for a government.

"In short, I haven't pressed these routes, for I didn't want it known that I was after records. If the records contain any revealing information, either something would happen to them, remember how our school searches ended, ...or to me. I am going to work this path but try not to expose myself.

"My brother-in-law sold some of our land and sent my share to Los Angeles, so I flew home, checked on my mother, resolved some financial decisions, and checked in on my sister's family. Rummaging through some of my father's memorabilia in the attic, looking for documents, I discovered his uniforms. A few of them looked like they would actually fit. At the time, I didn't know completely why, but I brought them with me. Then I realized that unconsciously I must have seen service personnel wearing these same style uniforms, and I began to devise a plan.

While I was still working for Parks Service, I had inadvertently discovered that one building in the Presidio in San Francisco was still under army jurisdiction after wandering into it and being stopped. I presented my Parks identification, and it was explained that the building was an Army local access to government computers. It was still fairly wide-open because I had entered without having any ID checked.

I ventured down to Presidio of Monterey to discover what type of access I had to that base with or without a uniform. Security ID was needed. While I was there, I took pictures of officers who were the same rank as my father, then I dressed accordingly and entered the San Francisco Presidio Army building.

"I had obtained a driver's license with a captain's rank but no military ID. I spent a series of days wondering the base and particularly the building containing the computers. After tracking the activity of personnel in the office, I uncovered the name of a first lieutenant who was running the main computer and made an appointment with him. It was Friday afternoon, and only he was present with a secretary. She was in an outer office. Once in his inner sanctum, I asked to see my father's record because I had served under him and was told that he had been 'Killed in Action.' I wanted a verification and his address so I could give my condolences to the family.

"It seems that the benign request and the captain's uniform were enough for he didn't ask for any identification but took me directly into the mainframe room. While waiting for the printout, I causally mentioned that I was doing undercover work-in San Francisco, but that I was stationed in Langley, that he was so efficient that I would probably seek his help again.

"I waited a couple of weeks, and approached his office again with a request for a verification of information. I gave him the name of the man who followed me from the post office.

He answered, 'Oh, yes, Captain so-and-so, I remember you, I can handle this,' and we strolled into the computer room. Five pages popped from the printer. The lieutenant glanced at them and said, "A bad back?" My mind flashed on the man's face, and for a second, I knew where I had seen him. But as the officer handed me the five pages, I became flustered and lost my remembrance. It took me a moment to regain my composure while I stared at the sheets. "Well, this may be of some use," I pronounced with

375

as much authority as I could. He had not been drafted because of a disintegrating vertebra.

"Next, would you run this name?" I handed him my name, social security number, address of my room. He said, 'Okay, but....' My face felt flush from his pause. 'Look at this, another person ran a check on him, just ... two days ago. It was on a priority level, much more extensive.'

"Oh really, what level was that?"

"Security Clearance 674."

"How interesting. Do you remember the man's name? Maybe it was my ranking officer?"

"I can't give you that. Major Smith did the computer run, and he has that information. I could get it if you ...."

"Doesn't matter ..... he probably will just check to see if my information is accurate."

"Here, I'll give you the same run," and he pressed a duplicate recall number after imputing my social security number. When the first five pages spewed from the printer, I thought what the hell? When the second five spewed, and was still running, stacking on the first, I swear my mouth must have fallen.

His comment was, "This guy must be quite a character."

I laughed. The computer and printer finished at eighteen pages. I had a big urge to reach over and rip the pages free, for the lieutenant was gazing at his watch when it finished.

"No wonder, I'm hungry. It's fifteen minutes into my lunch break." He handed me the stack of paper. I thought to ask him if I could take them, but instead asked if I could join him for the repast. I glanced at the section which was meant to contain my address. It stated: 'Whereabouts Unknown.'

"Sure, on base or off?"

"I know a good place in the Marina."

"Okay, I'll drive."

"What shall we do with these?" I handed him the stack.

"'They'll be safe in my desk,' and he carried them from the computer room.

"'Great!'" I responded.

"He turned out to be a very nice person who had studied Philosophy in school and had taken a couple of logic courses, so we discussed the function and uses of logic itself. It was a non-business lunch and only during the drive back to the base did I again imply-that I was with military intelligence and was engaged in undercover work in San Francisco.

"He reminded me of myself when I began with the Park Service: idealistic and with great faith in the government and in his place and possibilities in the service. He admitted that he had just been transferred from another post a month earlier and was still learning. He had been trained for a 'more important' position and would soon be transferred. Internally I smiled and thought, if my experience has been real and pertinent, don't hold your breath. He inquired if I knew anything about his new post. Since I had done a great deal of homework about all of the military agencies, I did tell him what I knew. He seemed to loosen towards me a little more. I think he thought I could and would be of help to him. I wouldn't say I lied, but I did lead him.

"Anyhow, when we arrived back in his office, I looked at my watch and said, 'I'll probably get back with you at the end of next week. I have to go.' We both stood silently for an awkward minute before he said, 'Oh yes, the reports.' He reached into his desk and produced the stack. 'Thanks,' I responded and rushed from his office.

"It wasn't until I was off the base and stopped at a light that I was relaxed enough to peek at the papers on the seat next to me. When I started driving again, I focused on the face of the man who followed me, but it was his bent back and slight limp that helped me to recognize him He was my ex-landlord's maintenance man! The landlord had asked me to help him paint the apartments because his maintenance man had a 'bad back.'

"In the last week, I have had the greatest urge to return and input my ex-landlord's name, but I am going to give it another week. At the time I didn't even question why the landlord hired me and paid me so much and me without any experience. My unexpressed reason was he was attracted to me, but now I believe it was something quite different.

"I have some other places to check. How much influence could he be having on me and why?

"My record was fascinating. It contained every encounter. It had information from my high school like not only my grades, IQ, but personal comments from the teachers. One in particular was from my seventh grade teacher who titled me an 'Under achiever.'" He laughed when he said this.

I didn't say a thing, but I'll be damned, I couldn't remember writing it but I guess I did, because looking back I think that was an accurate description.

"You weren't the only one with that category. But it is even more absurd that, it seems I still owe a library fine to the school. The report has comments from the principal about my response to the Army Recruiting Officer, my paper on Democracy. It had a list of my friends including Adrian, and that girl.... or I should say, my mother's ex-girlfriend for me.

"Most of this information was compiled before I was hired for the Park Service. That position required security clearance." He laughed again, "You figure that out!"

I just shook my head in disbelief. He continued, "The records are even more extensive for college, even that psychology experiment that I failed. It had a list of all of the groups, associations, meetings that I had attended in college. How .... and why they acquired that information is beyond me, except to determine my loyalty, my compliance, my reaction to authority ....all this because I have a very high IQ? .... it doesn't make sense.

"My dossier is filled with codes that I have no idea what they mean, so I arranged a 'spontaneous' meeting with my first lieutenant friend in the Officer's Club, and after buying a series of drinks, we discussed codes. He had no concept of an overview of why people were categorized, but he knew codes, especially codes.

"And my records were revealing to say the

least. From what I can figure, from high school on, I was given a questionable rating as far as controllability, but yet I had a very high rating as far as potentiality. In college, I was rated as a suspected subversive with questionable patriotism. It listed all of the groups with which I was affiliated and the ones I 'joined.' Of course, I really never joined any organizations; I may have attended a few meetings to see what was going on, but I never joined.

"Luckily, I was 'potentially re-educable' and didn't have any higher ratings than I did. I could have become a candidate for a mental institution or the prison system. What they are doing with 'those types,' the lieutenant stated, is 'run them' into the Army or some type of government job and recondition them, reeducate them, 'straighten out their thinking.'

"Upon graduating from college, it had to decide what to do. I guess from the government's point of view, it would have been so easy to 'educate' me, if I would have attended a government controlled college. But they had such a heavy track on me that they knew I would leave the country if I were drafted."

"This is very hard for me to believe," I said giving him a breather from his story, "that the government would want to have this much control over individuals and all this is possible without public knowledge and protest."

"I guess I was a chosen few," he laughed, "but I don't understand either how this has happened. Now, ... in thinking back, I remember some of the warnings at some of those meetings in college that I didn't take very seriously. Every now and then my mind flashes on incidents I read in the paper: political statements, statistics of missing persons, unpublicized laws which were passed. I guess I just wasn't paying attention.

"Anyway, I was placed in the Parks Service to further their study of me and determine what they should do. I was so naive, so stupid as to what was happening, that the authorities didn't find me threatening. I cannot be sure, but I think that they tried to make me pliable with drugs and with subliminal messages on my computer screen at work. The scary thing is that I was two steps away from my mind and/or body being obliterated, (I smiled and said, "pooh," thinking his sister is right, illusions of grandeur. But he didn't hear me, which was good because my doubt just indicated my ignorance.) and it was only my naiveté which kept it from happening. If I would have had any idea of what was going on, I would have rebelled, and far worse would have happened. They thought that they would eventually control me. They must have done various experiments on me when I was in the Park Service.

"They contemplated firing me, knowing full well that I would have to come back to some government employment, willingly. Between recommendations, social security clearance and my own self-concept, no jobs existed on the level where I would have applied. They knew jobs would be available but none at the level where both they and I had placed me. I had categorized myself as well. And when I returned I would be more willing to accept and do what I was told.

"It was close, too close, but I am almost untouchable now. Nobody knows who I am, where I am, and that I am gaining power and prestige. I am starting to effect change."

His monologue continued another twenty minutes, but it didn't totally make sense to me, and what I did understand may be too revealing to present at this time.

No, he does not label himself a subversive; he is just doing what his rights and obligations demand, and when life-threatening, what he needs to survive. His method is a little extreme, but so is his case. He cannot battle his enemy face to face and expect to survive, and he knows it. It is I and the system who label him a subversive because we know that in order to make things "right," he will have to change that which exists.

He has a plan and has said it is not by violent means, and he believes no one will know from where the ideas originated. No, he will not stick his head in a noose, nor the sand, but will subtlety make the changes. Some of his ideas are in the air, as the expression goes. "It will take time to turn the public on to what is happening," and to initiate the changes necessary to turn the tide and for the people to regain control of their government. Thesus knows that "the public is going to have to be re-educated for the responsibility" which he will attempt.

He, in his own mind, has accounted for all contingencies and has set the wheels in motion. I am not going to venture any further statements until he gives me the O.K. Events are happening so rapidly because of him and to him that it is hard to keep up with the latest, but I have a firm belief that every action has a directed purpose and an immediate meaning.

It was after these revelations that I decided to use my education and begin to research the political situation in the United States. I half-way don't believe, or don't want to believe what Thesus has said. This search will be not only for me and this manuscript, but to help Thesus so he can place his circumstances in perspective.

Chapter 2

One night during his stay with me, I was at Margery's sitting in Thesus' place at the dinner table and in a sense taking his space at their weekly scheduled dinner, when he opened the apartment door with his key. He began his monologue the moment he unlocked Margery's door. As I have realized, it can be just a verbalization of his flow of thoughts: "Sometimes, it's impossible to control forces greater than you. At times one can barely keep progress occurring, and at other times one can barely protect oneself from being forced backwards. Like right now, there are only aspects over which I can control, for example my questioning attitude, my hope in the form of maintaining a favorable outlook and more; we all face adversity, but it's how we respond and our attitude which determine who we are. It's control over my own being, not my destiny, but more in the form of the immediate state of my own being: a hope and trust in myself, my immediate conscious effort not to betray that belief in myself. I know that if I don't let myself down, don't deceive my promises to myself, I can be my best friend, but the moment when I let go and let myself down, lie to myself, I become my worst enemy. In this subtle but real sense, only I can defeat myself. This society, these governments' systems, organizations, and individuals can destroy me, but only I can defeat myself."

His sister laughed, "Are you talking to yourself again? If so it sounds like you are finally growing up, but what did you say? Do you really think someone or something is trying to destroy you?"

I jumped in because I thought his response to her would distract him, so I asked, "Would you further explain that 'subtle but real sense' you mentioned?"

"I was talking to John. Someplace in that book you are writing about us, you mentioned how I became aware of conditioning, how my being was conditioned to the point where I questioned my freedom. In what ways, if any, am I free? It is true I did question it, but now I have resolved this conflict about psychology and conditioning. In your terminology I have passed through one of the mazes and by figuring it out; I am free of it."

"You do have a firm belief in yourself, that's for sure," his sister said laughingly.

He glanced quickly at her but continued, "Psychology at its best, especially when dealing with the minds of human beings, is an art, but in trying to make it a science, the psychologists have not perfected it as an art. Thinking that they have a complete or even a teachable knowledge of human beings' mental facilities is a gross misconception. Some psychologists only breed confusion, and at the same time limit who we are and what we can become by categorizing us. They teach only half truths for they cannot know the whole because it is greater than the sum of its parts. I guess I am a Gestaltist. Because to me, each of us are greater than the parts that make us. Can any part really comprehend the whole of which it is only a part especially when the system is so complex? And yet they taught these half-truths which had me confused for a long time, but now......."

"Please get to the point!" Margery's voice was on edge with irritation because of her impatience. What were we doing that she considered her brother an interruption? Or was she tired of his free thought?

"Uh, ok, I am free in that I am more than the sum of the parts which made me what I am. We all can be more than just our conditioning: the environment and heredity. Therefore we all can't be completely categorized and controlled by forces outside of us. We can be directed by more than just positive reinforcement as the behaviorists say. I am not saying that reinforcement does not control us to some degree because we would be foolish if we did not move in a positive direction through want and will. We seek reinforcement as a tool to continue, so positive reinforcement would naturally affect us to some degree. But experience isn't just the total of sensations nor is it the total plus one, as a concerto isn't the total of the notes plus the rhythm. And even if it is not just the musician and her or his mood, it's also the observers of the experience. They add their own states or interject their own individualities into the experience which make the experience different than the sum of the sensations. The observer interjects his present feelings or knowledge, his past experience and his future expectations into each and every experience he receives. The observer adds the subconscious and unconscious. Before you ask, John; the subconscious are the innate evolutionary needs to survive and the unconscious are the unremembered events.

This is not to say that positive reinforcement or other outside forces do not control us to some degree. But it is my attitude and self-identity which help direct me, not necessarily positive or negative reinforcement. For instance in a case when a self-appointed goal has been set; many reinforcements may be turned down and yet the reinforcements we decide upon will help us attain. So reinforcements may make us behave in a certain way, but they do not absolutely determine who we are.

"It is in this way I am free from this maze, the maze of conditioning. One, I am learning about it and therefore can control it better, and two, the main reasons for me to make my choices are, in most cases, not placed on me by the environment, including society dictates, but come from within myself. I, in most cases, have created my own goals. Some of them are spiritual which definitely have come from within; some of them are mental goals which I have decided upon through hours of meditation. Mainly my preoccupation for the past couple of weeks has been to strip away the conditioned beings of myself and find my subconscious wants and needs. I meditate to seek within my own mind a greater knowledge than I consciously have. I know that my innate will to survive will bring me through these mazes; whereas my tainted taught knowledge sometimes just entangles me farther. This innate knowledge has kept generation upon generations alive since the beginning of time. Whereas the systems have taught me false knowledge, knowledge designed only to perpetuate itself.

"My conscious, external being has been confused by all of the different systems' conditioning, but my internal being couldn't, and hopefully can't be. I have found a truer me, the more subconscious me in my meditations, dreams, and thoughts which surface. It was hard at first to decide which were true because I was so filled with hatred, fear, wants, and desires which were projected into my dreams, thoughts, and meditations. In short, I have come to know and develop my deep being, my spiritual, mental and physical beings which have existed through time. I have come to know my innate goals as determined by these beings.

"It has even gotten to the point that for some reason my thoughts, dreams, and meditations have become an early warning system to me. I don't know if my mind unconsciously plays out my thoughts and the events of the day to a logical conclusion or what, but sometimes my dreams and surfaced thoughts foretell the future. For instance, sometime awhile

387

back, I had a dream. There were these two men in white. They had lightning bolts in their hands. They zapped me and the bolts broke into little sparks which charged through my body.

"Now, later, I found out that I have pinworms, a strange new hybrid. Am I a guinea pig? I can't be sure when I was beset, but if it happened at that time, it could have been those doctors at the Public clinic."

When Thesus discovered that his ex-girlfriend was fooling around, he went to a clinic to check for AIDS or any other possibilities. Two doctors were present when they asked him to bend over a table and inserted a cotton-tipped swab. He thought they were checking his excrement for something. If this were the case, then the worms were caused by a two men hired by a government institution, or at least under its jurisdiction. It could have not just been an AIDS clinic in the Dept. of Public Health, but some type of population control station, for pinworms not only induced fears but disturbed the lymphatic glands, "especially this new kind." So maybe it was another government experiment, another government grant, "for society's betterment."

But as I have mentioned, and the reader knows, Thesus' "conversation" didn't hesitate for a second, but he continued with the intensity of The SuperTrain hurdling itself to its destination at two hundred and eighty miles an hour.

"But now thinking back, maybe the dream was a result of the incident, not a precursor, or maybe it was a coincident, that both happened at approximately the same time. I wish I could remember.

"Anyway, the point is that I am freed, ... although not completely, ... from conditioning by being internally directed, by letting a survival mode, a deeper level, organize, understand and dictate to me. This level of consciousness can know what I don't. It has not been fooled by hypnosis, by conditioning, by material being fed directly into my unconscious. I may be conditioned, but if I act more spontaneously, I am more prone to do things correctly. And now that I am not still being conditioned, I may be able to break away all together.

"Look at Ike: he was un-conditionable by society, his uncle, and even us because of his internal direction. He was rarely ever reinforced for his art and, yet, continued to do it. And now I can see a similarity with me. My goals are set and whether they are reinforced or not, I will achieve them. I am not playing the acceptance-rejection game, the money or no-money game, success or failure, the reward or punishment game, or any games with winners and losers. I am playing my own game and will determine my own success, knowing full well it is not a game."

"What is your identity, the one you seek?" I was surprised by the meekness in my voice.

"In the purpose and cause for all existence." He laughed. "In the unique qualities which make me who I am. My individual concept of everything...."

"Oh," I answered not knowing why he laughed and taking him perfectly seriously, "and in the combination of the forces which drive us." I thought I knew what I was saying back then, but now writing this, I'm not sure.

"Yes, you see! These 'forces' specifically come out of our own beings, if we let them."

"Our wills?" I asked with enthusiasm, "And the Will with a capital 'W'?"

"Yes, all of us are filters and at the same time, swim either with the forces which created and control us, or against them. Our wills and T-h-e W-i-l-l (he spelled it out.) as you put it, are the determinant, not conditioning. We must flow in the forces which we can't control, but that is not to say we can't use them. We can filter these forces ......

"But getting back to what we were talking about before (his sister laughed. At the time her laugh irritated me, but now I see, nobody was discussing anything, it was really just a re-enforced abstraction). It seems natural for other people to try to beat each other down. It is a form of survival either in a conscious or unconscious form. We continually step on each other in order to perpetrate our own success. But what we don't fully comprehend is that each man and woman will continue to exist only as long as humanity can fight its way up the streams of entropy, of the depleting systems. One, we can't destroy the stream upon which we are dependent, and two, we have to come to think less about our individual beings and more about the total of all living beings.

"Truth, even as we can know it, (and that ain't too well) expressed, the best way possible, will lead to better results than lies. Falsehoods can be human-made minotaurs. If only each person spoke the truth as he or she knew it, reality would be intensified, if only in the way of a greater real knowledge would be coommunicated. Each of us would be able to see ourselves better and in a more 'real' world. We would be able to make better choices, to improve ourselves more efficiently and correctly and solve more problems in the world.

"Before you ask the question, John (I wasn't going to ask anything.) the answer is that time tests the truth. Truth has a higher probability of repetition than falsehood, because truth is the real, the natural, that which occurs without deceptive change. Let me put it this way, humans have to go out of their way to deceive one another while the truth happens in the natural sequence of events. The extra energy put into lies does not occur naturally. This energy, and these lies, must be constantly maintained. In the long run, truth will be discovered, or if not found, will at least be corrected because the natural occurrence of events will be resumed.

"Even on a personal level this is actual. Think of how much energy a consistent liar uses in maintaining and perpetrating a lie. There are undoubtedly people who spend all of their energies lying, just to continue to live in their worlds of lies, and after so many lies they don't know the truth. Nervous breakdowns occur because of their inconsistency."

Thesus' sister who appeared bored by this disclosure of belief interjected, "Are you really even interested in what you are saying? Your statements and ideas are still too simplistic, not to say too idealistic." She began to continue, but I interrupted her.

"Go on,.... continue," I insisted, "I'm interested."

"I have come to understand that without this opposition they have imposed upon me....."

"The mysterious 'they' again," snapped his sister.

His only response to her was sticking out his tonguer. I felt like applauding but held myself in check, and he continued.

"I would not have been freed. That whoever or whatever has tried to control me and my being, and it was sick of them to try, has only made me define and free myself. It would seem that without opposites and opposing, conflicting forces, contrasting sides, a breaking of harmony, or disharmony, there would be no choices, and therefore no freedom; our freedom seems to lie in the resolution of the choices, not in the outcomes. The outcome cannot completely be controlled by our choices because fate and other forces play their parts.

"I am slowly coming to see that which I can control and that which I can't. Control of my own being is my starting point. Before, I felt like an incapable master in an uncopable stream, fighting forces unknown to me and doing a poor job at that. I still have a great many facts, events, situations to sort through before I can determine which is what."

"Have you been locked up by yourself, not talking to anyone, since you left here?" his sister laughingly asked.

"This is my release, my synthesis of understanding, and without this, how would I know what I know?

"Both of you have to forgive me for spewing as I have."

"Nothing needs to be forgiven. What I could follow and understand has been enlightening. Thank you for sharing with us."

"You are too nice to Thesus, but I do love you both."

He looked down at his hand. He was still holding his keys. "Thanks for listening. I have to go. See you both." He put the keys in his pocket, and used that hand to open the door.

"I hope he is ok," his sister said with some emotion after the door closed behind him. "People with strokes or heart attacks ramble as he does. "

"I am sure it is as he said, his 'release,' his method of getting it out and looking at it, of formulating not only who he is and his choices but who he wants to become, his way of creating his new identity." I felt like him saying those words.

Chapter 3

Even though so much of the information I am about to relate is speculation, rumor, and even fear, without delay I will continue and present my research because time is pressing me.

From what I can surmise, the oppression and suppression which exist in this country began increasing in magnitude approximately sixteen years ago. Dadalus was only the Vice-President then. At that time the government through its propaganda machines spread the alarm of a left wing radical uprisings. Nightly, and continually on the Internet, the media displayed protests both within this country and outside it. In my opinion, the left wing has never ..... or at least at that time in this country, ... never had the power and strength to cause such a consternation. Assassinations and other forms of violence, overt or covert, have occurred but who knows who really perpetrated them, with or without justification.

And of course, the history of the United States is peppered with petitions, strikes, demonstrations, and protests. In a general sense, fractions have been instilled in our American way of life because it is written into the Constitution, and it is part of our nature as human beings.

No, at that time and now, we are experiencing extreme inequality. Forty percent of the population could be considered in the poverty range. Although the government statistics says it just twenty percent. Now we have ten percent unemployment but everyone knows it is fifteen to twenty percent. The divergence between rich and poor has never been so vast. People "in the know' have invested well and the rich are growing richer, especially with their disproportionate percentage of low taxes they pay.

So of course there were protests. Of course there were underground militant groups. Even from my alternative sources, I was told about assassinations of supposedly "capitalistic pigs," who were exploiting the underprivileged. The raging poor have nothing to lose, and too much time on their hands.

But in my life time, I have never heard of

any attempts to "over-throw" the government. Certain groups, President Dadalus included, used the government machinery to instill a terror, to manipulate the fears of the American public, to imply or directly state the existence of a growing power of underground subversive groups intent on an uprising and unwanted revolution. Certain elements of the government concurred and successfully stirred the mass media into seeking out this subversive group or groups. Pro-government mass media participated with commentaries: "Radicals Want to Destabilize America," "Subversive Groups are Undermining America," and "Protests are hindering the Government's Ability to Govern." The national media churned American sentiment by focusing on the disturbances "the underground" was causing: Nightly News emphasized protests, strikes, espionage, assassinations, bombings of power facilities the failing economy and American prestige. Then the furor was whipped to a peak with subliminal messages sandwiched between blatant pro-government advertisements. In an ad to "Buy American Products" during the picture of a waving American flag in-between the patriotic music was "Have Faith in the Government." Another subliminal verbal message, in a "Join the Army" ad was "Be Patriotic." On an underground web site, I actually saw and heard these.

The to-be-elected President Dadalus was the first person to use a verbal subliminal message in his campaign. It was the seemingly benign statement: "Be a good American, Vote." But it was he and his

395

cronies who firmly established the use of subliminal messages as a propaganda device.

With the combination of the private and public messages, both in this country and abroad, to support this government, to "re-establish law and order" and "do not to be a pawn of the radicals," convinced many people that the government needed more power to control. Bills were purposed by participating congress people. When the time was ripe, Dadalus scheduled a TV appearance and finalized the furor by demanding that good citizens petition their congresspersons.

Yes, I am sure real incidents perpetrated fright, which the people in power used to convince the American public a threat existed. Yes, I am sure it was more than propaganda. I can even imagine some of those bombing and assassinations where initiated and carried out by people who "understood" or thought they understood the government's wishes and needs. Many extreme pro-government groups existed and continue to exist.

The apparent consensus of the term "American Public" in our democracy is that of the majority, but because of a general apathy, the majority didn't need to be convinced .... only those people with power and the will to control, those who thought they have something to lose. With the structure in place and the President's presentation, the power machine opened like a Chinese fan, with a spreading effect. Power knew power and begot power.

The power fan grew when selected messages were given to selected people. The hierarchy was created because he who gave power retained power, or because "I give you power, I have the right to control." And it was the President who opened this fan. It opened when the orders rang out by channels from the subliminal and hypnotic to the unsubtle and undeniable command. In one key instance, Dadalus commanded of America, "Give me the power to stop the ever growing plague in this country."

Now I question whether, or how much, the security agencies had control of Dadalus' mind. Once the bag of worms of subliminal messages was accepted as policy, I am sure that the agencies which were created to protect the President learned to control him, to change his mind, to make policy.

Yes, a dictum was sent from the President to all those on whom he (I feel like capitalizing the "H.") bestowed power. It was no longer a sentiment in America but a scream. Individuals within the systems heard the demands of the "American Public" and complied. Governments' agencies were in competition with each other to help. Pro-government groups with extreme ideologies gained members and power. But yet these groups vied for power among themselves. Power struggles were raging. Add to this all those individuals who did what they thought was good, right, and patriotic.

In my opinion, with all of the mental institutions filled with political undesirables, the majority of mentally ill were walking the streets, and in a large part it was they who were most directly affected by the subliminal messages ... and to cut this discourse in length, the President's prediction transpired.

The physical manifestation of conflicting human beings, set on certain goals, caused an unstoppable flash of anarchy, and Dadalus appeared, appealed and gained immediate power to suppress.

The cry of "law and order" became the demand of the upper-middle and upper classes. "We have not worked for what we have gotten just to have it taken away by the radicals who want to destroy this country," said a middle aged minority woman in a commentary during the nightly news.

The immediate results were that people lost their lives in demonstrations, even pro-government ones. People were imprisoned through an improved, more efficient legal system. The Right to Assemble was adulterated again with laws regulating unlawful demonstrations.

The F.B.I, NSA, and other newly created agencies had extensive information concerning any individuals or groups who could or would oppose "the regaining of America by Americans." This information was available to any and all who had access codes. And because of this and because it happened so quickly, the forces, which would have opposed, were suppressed or eliminated by appropriate means. The small forum which could and did arise within the government to oppose these occurrences was impotent. No government agent wanted to be labeled as "Unpatriotic."

An overall result was that the power structure tightened. It became smaller. The five thousand most powerful families became fifty. To them, they appointed Dadalus to his second term. These people thought they knew who was in power and that they had placed him there. And no matter what the party title, Democrat or Republican, they were united as a single power: pro-rightwing and nationalistic.

This united front was pro-business in a big way. They knew where and how to raise money. They knew how to control the economy. For a while earlier, international cartels dominated the U. S. economy, and the government officials at the top let it happen to personally gain power. In spite of inflation in this country, the dollar was stable against the international currency. Thesus tried to explain to me how this could happen. It was something about a "two-tier" currency, an internal value and worldly value, which remained steadfast. And they used the economy to control the masses. An artificial depression was precipitated. "Artificial," it seems, because the stock market was breaking new highs, and this was spurred by ever increasing corporate profits. Selected businessmen grew more and more wealthy, and seemingly selected "laborers" were fired. While massive unemployment not only created a cheap labor market but gave employers opportunities to rid the system of undesirables. Again, groups of unemployed gathered, gained some power, and protested. But now the system was in place to suppress. First the police were used and then the state militia. These "lower-class" protesters became the "undesirables."

Within ten years the government had adopted appropriate means by which to locate every citizen in the United States within twenty-four hours. This power was seized so that every subversive could be located and if need be arrested at any moment day or night.

In order to secure this, the majority of the masses had to be immobilized. The designated depression, the increased cost of transportation, and an extremely high tax on fuel helped. The fear to quit any type of job, no matter how underemployed, how low paying, helped. These reduced the numbers of travelers. Stateline checks supposedly to stop the spread of insects, diseases, drugs, and undesirables sprang up first in agricultural states then everywhere.

Identification was required to purchase an airline, train, and even bus ticket. This was instigated to cut-down on hijackings, terrorism, and any other illegal acts. Many people were arrested upon arriving from trips. From the time they had entered a mode of transportation to the end of the trip, they had been computer checked.

To compensate for the lost revenues in the transportation industry, subsidies were allocated. Cooperation for tracking and subduing undesirables paid well. And of course, the transportation industry became more dependent and under control of the government.

The new government agencies and their computers made locating and tracking possible. When Dadalus was Vice President, The Government Information Agency (GIA) was created. An irony is that its initial creation was for the protection of individual's privacy. The agency investigated which organizations and corporations had what information about whom. It gathered the information to investigate if rights were being violated, first from complaints by citizens, then as case studies. The G.I.A. would raid computer centers and absorb all information to determine if rights had been violated.

In Dadalus' first term as President, he created the U.C.C., Unified Central Control. It was created as a "mandate" from the public, but yet without general public knowledge. It has his Executive Order to classify all information as "Top Secret" in the interest of National Security. To my knowledge, Dadalus gave an indirect order to "legally" not process any F.O.I.A.s, Freedom of Information Act requests, which explains why our hero either didn't receive replies to his requests, or they were so blacked-out with statements like: "Intra-agency Memoranda," that no information could be extracted from it.

The U.C.C. superseded the FBI, CIA, NSA, and all military intelligence agencies, and of course, the G.I.A. The order was given that the U.C.C. absorb all information from the other agencies. The mainframe computer for the U.C.C. is believed to be four floors of one square block in some large city. The lack of public information concerning its creation, and continued existence, has created a myth. I have heard that the computer has creative intelligence. I have heard that it can decipher, deliberate, and determine who is a threat and then deliver a direct order to detain or even eliminate that person. So as it has evolved, Dadalus thought he was in control, the powerful families of this country thought they were in control, the secret service agencies thought they controlled, but it may be that some super computer controlled and is controlling it all.

Yes, I have started attending underground political meetings. But with the confirmed information I have, I can almost believe anything.

As I alluded to earlier, sometime in the past twenty years, the communications revolution ended and an intense propaganda blitz began, first by the government then other organizations. The grip tightened around the masses in a geometric progression because most were, to some degree, hypnotized by the media. Between always having the radio, TV or the Internet on to overt and subliminal messages, one-third of the populace could be told something in various programs, even in a very obvious manner, and they would believe it beyond a doubt. Another ten percent, mainly the power groups, were media-controlled directly by government agencies. This whole period of time and the societal environment reminds me of the 1990s alien invasion movies, where individuals couldn't tell the humans from the invaders, until finally so many beings walking around were aliens, a real human had no chance of survival. A lynch mob mentality existed against anyone not pro-government.

With the media always blaring their messages, how much was entering humans' psyches, although the persons were not paying attention? How much and what type of messages passed the conscious and went directly into the unconscious and even sub-conscious? When the effects of government control were obvious, industry took advantage, and then individual organizations. Individuals, either through corporations or their own initiatives, became so powerful that they could control huge masses of people. It was like discovering the "Key" to control.

One of the last strongholds against this seduction was the university and college campuses. The universities have always been a breeding ground for dissension and conflict, and in my opinion, as it should be. The youth with their ideals should practice democracy. In a general sense, protests were accepted and had evolved from earlier campus demonstrations. These groups were practicing their rights.

For years, campuses could maintain their resistance to indoctrination because students didn't generally watch TV. When they listened to the radio, most listened to campus broadcasts or underground stations. They bought black-market recordings. The Web sites which they accessed were controlled by nongovernmental organizations. They existed in a government free and/or anti-media oasis. Only certain smaller campuses were completely controlled.

The government, seeing this "weak link," began to cut back funds to education to keep the poor, "rabble radicals from using the system." Some schools were closed. But the young idealistic rich, who in some cases could see what was happening to their parents, their parents "in power," raised the figurative barricades against the indoctrination; but in my mind, they didn't know their true enemy or its weapons, and gradually all of them were subdued. While Thesus and I were attending, (This reminds me of a series of incidents concerning our hero which I will elaborate later.) the college atmosphere was not protests for the wrong doings of the government or for the rights of individuals but a battle ground of one faction against another. But now with my new perspective, I can see something was wrong, and yet this was the undertone of the nation. It was racial: black against white, Asia against Hispanic. At the time I thought it was the white supremacists' groups that were initiating the conflict, but now I don't. Because looking back it wasn't only racial but just one extreme group against the next: conservatives verses liberals in the form of sororities and fraternities verses independents, gay liberations verses straights, freaks verses establishment, haves verses have-nots. And the "powers that be," the establishment seemed to be against all of the above.

By identifying the "hot spots," the schools where the radicals congregated, the governments began pressuring them with their existing and future subsidies. The schools changed their enrollment policies and fired some instructors. And with further careful monitoring, government infiltration, these campuses, these institutions, began to conform to the system at large. In some of these colleges and universities, students were again being programmed, categorized even more than other institutions, as to how well they could be and had been programmed, graded as to their potential as a type of desired citizen and to the type of government worker they would become. They were told what to believe, then tested to confirm their indoctrination, and of course, graded and labeled. The machinery of the higher education was in place and well oiled. Graduates were placed into the society with identity papers and ready to fill their slots as good, hardworking, conforming, complacent, and complying citizens.

But this system didn't work completely. It broke under its own success. Nobody trusted another person, group, or organization to the point where even family members couldn't trust each other. Communication ceased among members, either because of distrust or because individuals were on different levels of indoctrination.

Small family owned businesses began failing in large numbers. The corporations gallantly took over the more profitable ones to strengthen the country. Multinational corporations with all of their subsidiaries began to monopolize production and the products by purchasing the nationally based companies.

As there is a myth about the U.C.C computer, there exists a myth about president Midas, the controller of the biggest corporation in the world. It was he who commanded Dadalus to build the political structure in the United States, for he is King of the World and controls.

But the last of "the old guards of America" saw that the system was too effective. America was becoming an international pawn, if not a pawn, a more powerful piece, but still a piece and not a player. Democracy was being replaced by Dadalus, the dictator, who it was thought, was in turned being controlled by forces outside the country, and the country no longer reared individuals who could and would lead. The "outside influence' should not be dismissed, because was the U.C.C. programmed to account for other nations and their power?

But as was, the system tended to reduce the potentiality of the wrong people, which was "good," but it also reduced the potential of the "right" people. The people who were running this country, and the people who were gaining power were also caught by the system and weren't capable of handling it. They had been molded too carefully to see the necessary discriminations to have a working perspective. Creativity had been programmed out. The ability to solve problems in a creative manner had been "accidentally" eliminated. Constructive imagination was rare. Also no one seemed to have an over-all perspective. No one had the vision to create the goals, an image of the future where it all worked, partially because no one knew the truth.

For a while, nobody was running the country, and in some ways this is true now. One, Dadalus is using all of his power, energy, and resources to end the two-term restriction under the Twenty-second Amendment. Does he really want this or do all the factions want this? Also The Computer has been given decision making abilities over different areas of the system which nobody wants to control or can control. ("I believe in the mainframe of the U.C.C. I believe in Its decisions, and I follow Its commands.") It seems as if the system is running in a preset direction, which no one knows or has influence over that course.

Some of the "sub-surfaced" old guard, understood the possibility of such an occurrence and shielded against it by not destroying the radicals with an above average IQ; ("destroying" [maybe] is too strong a word). They guarded against degeneration of the country by incapacitating the youth with potential, by making them immobile, impotent, but ready to reactivate. New technology was initiated to "re-educate the educable," and to continue to control the uneducable. The Park Service served many functions.

The Park Service became the holding-pens and the re-education centers. Neither Thesus nor I know in which stage, which sector, Thesus was placed, whether they were trying to re-educate him or just subdued him.

I have reason to suspect that The National Park Service throughout the country has taken a very active role in categorizing and eliminating undesirables. One of Thesus' ex-colleagues explained, "The parks are like fly traps. Originally lured by the scenery but later trapped by the inexpensive life style, the unemployed came to live in the parks." These park dwellers have to register to stay in the park more than three days, and they were unofficially labeled, "parasites," and placed in the computer as undesirables.

Now, I believe the worse. Hugh numbers of people are "traveling through" the park system, which has become a filter of subversives. I suspect that people are held in the parks against their wills. They have become permanent residents, caught in the created contradiction. Some areas of some parks retain their visitors; and my fears venture one step further in believing, some parks have even become elimination centers. The maximum permit is for three weeks and so these people, including whole families, have to move onward. Without jobs and no place to stay, they are forced into this life style. The parks keep track of them and ....

I am frightened by what I know, have discovered, and by what I don't know. I am way over my head and out of my field of expertise, but I swear I have seen or heard, either directly or indirectly, messages to "Go To the Nearest National Park: Enjoy Nature." Are my fears out of control? Has what I have learned made me 'paranoid'? But more and more numbers of people are disappearing. This we know is true. People are trapped against their wills in one system or another. I personally went to an interview which was more than suspect; therefore, I played dumb: I was an unemployed teacher lost in his own world of academia, "where all those radicals are breeding." I think my act saved me; for another professor I met at the second interview went the whole route of interviews, and his family found him in the state mental institution. The large and rising numbers of institutionalized cases are blamed on foreign powers' abilities to induce drugs into the American food chain due to cut-backs in FDA employment.

The small groups of people protesting the disappearances of relatives are receiving documentation that their loved ones cannot be found: Among the main suspects causing these disappearances are radicals, foreign agents, or minority elimination squads. The foreign agents have infiltrated the U.S. and seek revenge because of our armed forces and their action in South America. No reasons are given for the other two groups and their operations. And the government uses all of these cases as a plea: "Protect ourselves; protect our children. Give us more power so we can protect you."

And the legal system - which was created to save us – from legal aids to judges, including lawyers sought power and money through their interpretations of the law, lost justice, and then lost the respect of the people. The people, in turn, felt justified in transgressing the law, especially the "new laws." The law tightened its grip through force, and the violators went underground but violations spread widely: a type of anarchy, for sure.

And yet, I am sure more abuses exist. The ones I mentioned above were pieced together from various sources; some are just fears; some are common knowledge. I wonder if anyone really knows to what extent power has being usurped and individuals' rights have been subtly eliminated.

Synthesizing the information as I have, I am starting to believe Ike Jacoby's theory that dissatisfied individuals' wills can and, hopefully, will be the saviors of the society. Ike thought artists by being outside of the systems, by being the abnormal in our society, by creating alternative worlds and life-styles, by being able to project an ideal nation and living it, could and would change society, but I am more negative now: This group of people is generally impotent: no money and no power. Ike is an aberration, but a hope.

After all this research, added to my experience

with these systems, plus my knowledge of what has happened to Thesus, I believe change must happen, if not by addition then by destruction - a destruction of the systems which stand in our way from becoming full potential human beings.

In contrast to me, Thesus is a saint. Now as I mentioned I would, I recall one incident which happened to him, which at the time neither he nor I saw in the above context, but was obviously a method meant to gain control of him. A closed, secret society "rushed" our hero at the university.

It was in his first semester sophomore year, and saying it was one incident, is a misnomer; it lasted two weeks. As I remember it, a group of twenty to thirty masked students approached Thesus. They approached him with honor, gave him a book to read which described the ritual to which they would subjugate him. Part of the ritual was that two or more members were with him constantly for the two weeks: presumably to be his guide, arguing their presences and the reasons for it. They chauffeured him and attended classes with him.

The campus knew it was happening because of the masked "body guards." In their eyes, Thesus was being honored. But our hero didn't see the ritual in the same light. He felt these people were impinging upon his rights, invading his privacy. For a couple of hours, he evaded them, came to my apartment and called his father's lawyer to see if he could get an injunction against the group's presence. The lawyer advised him just to play along. Belonging to this organization would help his future.

But when the secret society held a public formal ceremony to accept Thesus, he, at first chance, stopped the meeting and said, "I don't even want to know your noble reasons for such actions. I don't believe in your philosophy, or your means to spread it. You have violated my rights by invading my privacy against my will." The next publication of the school newspaper contained an editorial laughing at our hero for shunning an honor and a tradition of the university. It stated that Thesus was immature for not accepting the initiation, ritual and society for its "true, deep meaning."

Rather than give the reader my interpretation, I will call Thesus at his new office and ask how he has come to view that event. I will transcribe his comments from a recording.

He laughed when I mentioned the society and said, "Thirty or more people know me much better than I would have liked, and I don't even know who most of them are still." Then I asked him why he thought they rushed him. "I am sure, it was a political organization which tried to indoctrinate me .... looking back, I would even say it was some type of Christian right wing organization with white supremacists overtones, but at the time, I couldn't tell you what they represented. They did change my views. Coming out of high school, I had no political opinions, was totally naïve to the political systems and so I was an easy target.

"Anyway, for two whole weeks, it was movies, recordings, documents, testimony from well-known persons; they were bombarding me with 'facts and information.' I would show up at my room and some media would be playing. I would go to eat at the Student Union and someone would sit with me playing his computer. They were trying to close a curtain on my view of this country and the world. Now, I would say it was like they were trying to convert me to a religion," he laughed again.

"But you know, my main objection to them was they wouldn't let me sleep. Oh they would say, go right ahead and sleep that they were not there to prevent it; but they would talk and talk, recordings would play as I was falling to sleep, saying things, that under any other circumstances, I would question and argue with. At first I did fall asleep in their presence, and I don't know and probably will never know what happened.

"That only happened once, every time I needed sleep, I would disappear. Once I went for a hike in the mountains when I was expected to go to class. When I couldn't lose them, I told the two characters with me I had to pee. I went up hill and once I was out of sight, I took off. I hid in the woods until it was getting cold and dark and then I came over to your place, remember?"

"Yes,"

"But they were effective. It was too much information, too many startling discoveries about what was happening in the U.S. I was saturated with their political views. I didn't want to believe, but I did, and they would have probably had me, if they hadn't used the force they did. As a response to all of this, I spent two to three years of college seeking other political view points, trying to disprove their viewpoint.

"Remember how the university created a different college of Ethnic and Minority Studies to preserve individual cultures. Within that college was: Woman's Studies, Hispanic, Asian, Third World Studies. If I understood this group's intentions, they had infiltrated the different minority subcultures with the idea of pitting one against the next, of causing incidents, strife, conflict, all in the name of Ethnic pride and even revenge for past deeds. Of course they didn't say this directly, and what I believe now is precipitated from all of my roaming from one affiliation to another, but I think their intent was to create bigotry, hatred, suspicion, and distrust. And they seemed successful; remember all of those race riots?

"They tried to prove that their society was being subsidized by the government, which may have been because all organizations over which the government wanted control were subsidized, but I am sure, this group had governments' sanctions. Much of the testimony, facts, and documents dealt with how some of the minority groups were un-American. The well versed young men stated they were reporting their data and what the findings represented not just to me, but to a government agency as well. At the time, I just thought they were trying to impress me.

"You know now, I believe the government itself had infiltrated these groups and were even leading them. It may have even used different techniques to control different subculture's thoughts

413

and turn them against each other. I hate to......

"Listen, let's discuss this later; I have a meeting in ten minutes for which I have to prepare. Talk to you later."

Chapter 4

I have reread what I've written. Much of my writing is awkward, hard to read, and that last chapter seems unorganized. I apologize to the reader; I am doing the best I can; everything is happening so quickly; my writing has not kept pace with the events. In the time it has taken me to research, write, edit, and rework, just the last chapter, so much has changed. Maybe I was too thorough with the last chapter, spending too much time running around gathering information; and just placing the words on these pages distorted the events, the truth, but the reader will have to bear with me and suspend belief just a little more.

Anyway ..... how to update without a great deal of detail. Ike's film is still a success as a midnight cult film, and not just here in San Francisco but across the country. It has started to represent an action with layer upon layer of meaning to different organizations.

In promoting the movie, establishing Ike as a significant artist, preparing a posthumous exhibit of his work, etc., Thesus had inadvertently created career contacts.   He also, I might add, made himself president of an organization which first arose with the profits from all of Ike's endeavors.

Then as a response to the most recent oil

catastrophe, the eruption of that off-shore drilling rig because of the *sumami*, Thesus decided to raise money to clean and protect the ocean's environment. He contacted all the artists with whom he has met because of Ike, plus contacted all those listed in Internet directories and then used both to meet the more famous. His idea was to have each artist create a work of art and donate it for an art show, and then sell them for "this worthy cause." The contacts of the Berkeley museum curator, where Jacoby went to school, and the San Francisco Civic Center museum, where Ike's retrospective exhibit was shown, were perfect for this charity raising exhibit. In both museums the exhibits were squeezed between two adjacent shortened shows. The fund-raising only lasted one week in each museum, but almost each and every work was sold.

In certain circles, these two openings became the social event of the month. The mayors, council members, social leaders, the Who's Who of the local art world were invited and appeared. Thesus, as president of the art foundation, chief organizer, and principal fund raiser splashed his way into the wealthiest and most prestigious circles of the Bay Area. "Art Aid for Marine Life."

His second successful fund raiser was a $150 a plate dinner banquet for artists' rights. Now it has become an annual event. It is a defense fund for artists, protecting them from censorship, civil and legal lawsuits, and guarantees a biannual competitive show. Also these two exhibits provide a "get together" where artists not only exchange ideas but where they have created a register, a check-in; if not present, a committee tracks them and determines their wellbeing. The result is that artists are again beginning to experience a freedom of expression, unafraid of the consequences of their efforts, or defiant while the focus is on them. A large and growing Neo-American Expressionists' Movement, equivalent to the German Expressionists between the world wars, is gaining strength and has shows in contemporary galleries. Before, all shows were underground in temporary galleries. Political art is on the rise. Political cartoonist have a more free hand again, and even they are exhibiting.

From these fund raisers, Thesus has not only reaped an income, fifteen percent on every dollar crossing his desk, but he has built quite a reputation for been associated with philanthropic organizations: his pseudonym goes before him as a calling card for initiative, new ideas, worthy causes, and big bucks.

As one can tell, both the money and the new identification have increased his freedom. His participation in these different groups, organizations, and committees effects the changes he wants, but he intentionally never becomes the most important person, never takes the lead, always just influences, just adds an idea, a piece of advice, and usually lets others take credit. His experience of being president of the art organization and being pushed out into the public frightened him when he realized its dangers. Obviously he does not want center-stage, in fact, does not want to be on stage at all, but wants to influence from behind the scenes.

His main fear is being recognized by any persons who could disclose his real identity, including his ex-landlord or the first lieutenant, so he keeps his face from being photographed and has quit appearing publicly.

Some months ago, as this new world of charity organizations opened to him, he volunteered his time to this committee and that; but now they seek him, and not just to volunteer but as a paid adviser. His sits on different committees, as an advisor, board member, hired organizer. He wants to be able to move freely among the organizations, just contributing, paid of course, his initial reactions, his spontaneous ideas, and then after a brief time, move to the next committee. At first he sold himself as an effective neophyte who loses his viability after once being acquainted with the ways of thinking that have already been adopted by the group. He was a new and different perspective. But as he became more renown, he didn't need to sell himself at all. He would only accept contracts on a temporary basis. Under these conditions he is able to resign from most of the committees, once they become boring to him, and yet retain his reputation. "Boring" is the wrong word; it is more like he has explored what the committees were, their power, their control and then want moved on. He is still searching.

With his first cash flow, from Ike's retrospective show, he leased an office with three rooms, and lived in one. Now he has a receptionist in one and a secretary in the other, with his over-flowing office the third. He resides in various hotels around town.

For a while it seemed as if he had ceased pursuing the cause of his harassment. He had stepped away from it, and now it no longer resides on the top of his priority list. Although I must awaken some of his past thoughts and feelings because the last time I was in his office reporting on my completion of a favor for him, his face became blank and then he said, "You know it was Adrian who unintentionally or intentionally pointed me in the right direction. Then that trip from Colorado to California, the accident, and the honing device ...... I knew I was in trouble. I knew I needed to find the questions I wasn't asking.

"I am just so lucky that they did not label me 'uneducable' or not worthwhile; I could have been run through the court system, labeled a criminal and required to wear The Ban. Those bans are now not only locating the 'evil elements' but because the bands are obviously around the head of the worst offenders, they label the criminals, brand them like in the 1700s. But what most people don't realize is that the bands can now transmit EEGs. Authorities are monitoring thoughts and are negatively reinforcing in the form of mild electric shocks for aggressive, violent, or even angry thoughts.

"Yes, no doubt in my mind, they would have destroyed me if I would have failed another one of their experiments, ... their tests, and had been declared a poor potential. In my investigations, I have found that they have subtle and less subtle ways of eliminating who they want by placing something into the circulatory system to over stimulate the heart."

I stopped him and interjected some of my

research, "The latest development on that front is that practice has stopped. After too many officials, representatives of power, have had too many heart attacks, a demand arose for a counteracting drug and a law that that particular stimulant and all of its derivatives be manufactured with a bad taste. Ironically, people in power were using it to eliminate competition." Both of us laughed mildly. "Now a dose large enough to make the normal person have an attack would be so vile that the person will throw-up first. I'm sure it is still used in milder forms and in conjunction with other methods like extreme stress.

"Also that honing device, which was removed, was the most benign. Another type which is used can be inserted under the skin in the back of the head and can confuse thinking, like The Band

"But what I want to know is have you made any progress with tracking your problems and/or discovering the connection with you ex-landlord?"

"Yes, I imputed his name into the Army computer, expecting very little. When his name ran, almost twenty pages emerged. This time the first lieutenant wasn't even taken back. When he saw that I was surprised, he said, 'Hello, I've seen fifty to hundred print-out on one person. But this guy must be someone.' For a moment we both stood silently still after the printer ceased. I finally broke the moment and ripped the last page from the computer. 'Maybe this is what I've been searching for; I had better take this to the office and get right on it. I'm sure it's going to answer some very important questions. Thanks and I'll see you later.' I carried the stack of pages in front of me as if I were taking an offering to the gods."

Thesus paused to gather his thoughts, "You know," he continued, "it was fate that brought me to him (his ex-landlord) in the first place. I could have found and rented any other apartment in San Francisco, and a high probability exists that none of this would have happened. I'm sure my landlord thought the same thing."

"Well, who in the hell is he?"

"When he was a private in the Army, he was a computer operator. He started as a word processor, but as his education and skills improved, so did his rank. Within five years, he was a Major and chief program officer at a top security installation. In spite that he signed-up after only two years of college, his rise in classification and authority seems remarkable. His career collapsed, however, when one of his subordinates filed sexual assault charges against him. Because it was a question of homosexuality and how he was abusing his power, a question arose of whose brain child he was and the authorities just discharged him the quickest way possible.

"I had no idea why this affected me, except now I understand more of the incidents which occurred while living in his apartment. I crosschecked his information with my father's records, and the only connection I could find was that they were stationed on the same base during this incident and his ultimate dismissal.

"But the connection was greater than this. Remember my girlfriend, Andrea? I noticed her name as my landlord's dependent. I thought, what a coincidence! They didn't have the same last name. But there was her name in his record. "Of course, when I first discovered this, I immediately called her to check. She said she always thought I knew. 'I know you knew!' she exclaimed. 'One of us or both are mistaken,' I answered slightly intimidated. 'No, he's my original father. My mother divorced him and remarried when I was young.

'What difference does it make, and why did you call me?'

"I didn't tell her that I suspected that he was the Minotaur of my maze, ... as you would put it." He laughed after the statement. I joined his laughter. "But it is probably true, half human, half computer."

For a moment we were both silent, then I broke it with, "But still, why?"

"I don't think she was intentionally harmful. We were both young and naive. But getting back to your image of a labyrinth; I was robbed of my will-power. I was in a stupor for ... maybe a year or more. Andrea could have mentioned her father, but I don't think so."

"But why?" I repeated.

"Well, let me finish my story....."

His, Thesus's, receptionist announced on the intercom, "Your ride is here for the board meeting."

"Damn," he looked at his watch. "It half slipped my mind. Where has the morning gone? Come on; you are not doing anything, are you? Grab that attaché case from the couch. Let's go. If need be, I'll pay for your return cab ride."

Downstairs a chauffeur opened the rear door to

a limousine. I hesitated and pulled back from Thesus' grip on my shoulder. "Come on, this is not mine, it is just to impress me," he quipped. "Besides, it's expedient. We'll finish our talk, and maybe if you ask nicely, the driver will give you a ride home. Let's go; times-a-wasting." He grabbed me again and pulled me into the back seat.

"Where was I.... oh yes;.... I asked Andrea if she had ever heard of Captain (Thesus' father).

'Yes, stupid, that's your dad.'

'Did your father ever mention my father?'

'For supposedly being so smart, you are so dumb about certain things. Your stupidity always irritated me; you could see the sun set and then twenty minutes later say, "Oh, it's dark." Do you still analyze your dreams? You were always wrapped up in your dreams and not in reality. You're not on this earth but in a fantasy land.'

'Did your father know my father?' I asked with persistence. You know, time hadn't tempered her. She was treating me exactly as she had the last week we were together. On one hand she was evasive, on the other she was picking on me, trying to get at me.

'He did question if you were the son of someone he knew in the service.'

'What did you answer?"

'I had no idea. My dad blames some people for getting him kicked out of the Army. Don't ask me how or who, but the only job he could get for years was a TV repairman, and he had to go back to school to refresh and learn that.'

"I thought, Oh really, that may explain some
422

things, but I said, 'I understand what you are saying. How is your new relationship going?'

'We're getting married.'

'I will send you a beautiful wedding present.'

'So are you checking on me, huh? Don't bother.'

"When I hung up, I thought, she must be confused or even had intentionally withheld that information from me, or was I more messed up than I realized? Also, how much influence could her father have had in my life?

"But now, when I look back maybe my father was protecting himself and the family. We always had expensive, well trained dogs roaming freely on our land, especially out near the entrance gate. When I asked sis, (Jenny) she said the dogs were to protect us from loonies and that to her knowledge my father didn't have any enemies. But if he were intentionally poisoned, obviously he did.

"It must have been his court-martial or trial, and a transcript is probably available. Is this revenge? Am I reaping the karma of my father? I can see my categorization by the government as one regrettable situation, the landlord as another, but are they connected?"

In what seemed like less than ten minutes the limousine had stopped, and the chauffeur was standing beside an opened door. I looked out to see where we were. It seemed like just three or four blocks away. I slid slightly preparing to depart, but Thesus said, "Hold it," and he yelled to the driver, "Are you in a rush?" When the response was that he understood he was to wait for Thesus, Thesus asked him to wait for both of us. We walked down the side walk, him holding my arm.

"I almost broke the G.I.A. code," he whispered. "Watching the Lieutenant run the MIA computer, I kind of saw how it was done. I needed the right speed of input, the date, hour, etc. so I had recorded the tones for one whole day, then extrapolated the speed. I was in for a moment; but then I must have made a mistake after inputting my land lord's social security number, date of birth, because something went wrong, for a human voice interrupted and said, 'Please state your code ID number and the fourth level of personal disclosement.'" He said when he hung up and threw that disposable cell phone into the Bay, he started giggling like a little child. "But you know, from your research I know I want to break the U.C.C. entry barriers, not the G.I.A. The creature has grown larger."

Without a pause in his discourse, we turned to return. "At the height of confusion in my mind, while still in that room on Waller street, I sought Justice, with a capital 'J..' I prayed; I read the Old Testament; and prayed. I prayed that Truth would remove the sheath from a sword, that God would give me the insight and strength to see the weakest part of my enemy and that with a godly force, I would be able to slash to the core, the cord that held my being and the truth from me.

"And now I am free. The center has been seen. And I flow in what seems to be an absolute medium, and motion is derived from my wish and will." Then he seemed to pray. He closed his eyes and folded his hands, "May God give me the insight to govern my own being so that I do not spread more evil but insure good. May I do Its Will in this matter. May I be a servant to Its Will.

"Only the truth need be revealed. I hope I am worthy and capable."

I just stood there and thought Good God, what has been wrought. We had returned to the limo. The door was opened. But before Thesus could ask, I told him I would rather walk; I had some thinking to do.

As I walked, I thought, now what is his concept of God. I smiled at Thesus. Extreme adversity can make catholics of all of us. Then I laughed out loud. It was Thesus' laugh. I laughed again, my normal one. I am going to have to ask him his concept.

Chapter 5

In the past two weeks of this last month, I have tried just appearing at Thesus' office to get information so I can further my writing. But the three times when I have, he has been busy. This last time, he was absolutely rude to me, telling me to get out of his office and talk to the receptionist. But as I was leaving the receptionist's area, he opened the door and yelled, "John, I'm sorry; I'm too pushed. I don't have time. Tanya, (his secretary) give John the information he needs."

He really didn't know what he was saying. Of course, I didn't ask his secretary about his ex-landlord. But I did ask her about our hero's latest ventures, and why he was so pressed for time.

An uninformed reader may ask why haven't I just called him at home or at work? I don't know which of the super-computers control wiretapping, but one or more do. The rumor is that over fifty percent of all telephones, faxes, computer conversations are tapped in this country at this time. Knowing that almost every telephone is being monitored for any reference to national security issues or illegal terminology, any informed person has created a language which eliminates all sensitive words, phrases, or sentences. So in the US, a very strange language, like a foreign one, has evolved. It's a nuance of computerise. Then on the other hand, some "honest citizens" who are knowledgeable and at the same time rebellious, are discussing the most mundane topics but inserting, words like: bombs, guns, money, overthrown, government, CIA, FBI, NSA, cops, etc., ...but this is a regression from the main story. Back to our hero.

From college until now, I have noticed a fading intelligence in our hero. I don't know exactly when it occurred, but I would guess when he was living with those people in the "horrible room." Or maybe at the Park Service. Some of those drugs which were given may have really changed him. He is less quick, slower in both action and thought. He forgets more easily, gets off on tangents, can't keep to the point and can't retain as much. For a while, I thought all of this was caused by fear, but now since the fear has subsided, I can see definite changes. I saw a similar change in my father after his first stroke, a heart arrest.

In Thesus it is not as pronounced as with my father, and only at certain times is it noticeable. Maybe it is not caused by the stress or induced drugs but by his intent dedication. He is more cautious, for sure. And so it may be the complexity of his world, now as compared with then; nobody could maintain control, complete control over all the different aspects of the world in which our hero exists. Maybe it is a combination of everything.

In spite of this, he still had ideas. One that seems reasonable, and I am sure he wouldn't mind me expressing it is his "Pooh Pooh" theory. This was created when he was living with his girlfriend and both of them were cooking. "All living beings filter to gain sustenance. "All living beings filter to gain sustenance. All beings excrete. Lately, the environment contains toxins which our bodies try to cope with. The environment contains elements which we and other beings can't use and are undoubtedly harmful. What we and other beings can and do is excrete this as waste. This excretion in plants and animals probably contains more toxins than the rest of the body. We and all living beings undoubtedly slough what is harmful and what we can't use. Those little dots on most fruits and vegetables opposite the stems, I would definitely not eat those. I think those are the slough. Undoubtedly, they contain herbicides and pesticides.

In a toxinless environment did our by-products supply fertilizers to plants and plants supply food and oxygen to us, a cycle which helped to create life as we know it? If so, we have broken this cycle and now should not eat the waste of plants or animals i.e. Fat would seem a quick means to discard excessive toxins. What are other methods we and other beings have to rid ourselves of harmful waste? Where is the excretion point on celery, strawberries, etc.; are they the most toxic because they don't have excretion points?"

Interesting ideas, huh? Anyway from the questions I asked his receptionist, then his secretary, then Margery, and then adding to what he has told me, I have some very basic facts concerning his ideas and movements which he is promoting. The office is officially the headquarters for the foundations which Thesus has organized, but unofficially it is the coordinating headquarters for every one of his projects.

He has organized a series of "blind companies," companies in other people's names and "silent partnerships," to manufacture some of his inventions. He found a new, cheaper way of breaking down water into hydrogen and oxygen, and he is having "some friends" explore more innovative, cheaper means. This company is already manufacturing hydrogen and oxygen more inexpensively than most of its competitors. It is not in the black because of its research, and it needs to raise money to manufacture liquid hydrogen and oxygen. The company's officials are considering taking it public.

Another company, "up and running," manufactures a new spark-gap apparatus which can be used rather than a pilot light on stoves, hot water heaters, and furnaces. Including the personnel to assemble the items, to sell it, and to install it, to retrofit it, employment is over seventy-five people and growing. The three administrators are pushing forward with the patent, pushing the paper work, and pushing the employees. One salesman is devoted full time to selling the item to a large corporation, an appliance manufacture. Every person in that company expects this to happen and to be "bought out" and retire within five years. They all have privately held stock.

One of his smallest ventures, three people, is a local garage which installs air filters, which Thesus invented, for cars. He had taken his van into a shop, when he had his van, and met a person who whispered to him to take it someplace else; he didn't and it cost him dearly. Three years later, he went back found the young man with the advice and set him in business in L.A. Thesus is supplying, free of charge, an air filter which filters all harmful, (his guarantee) pollution from the outside. The young man has been designing and installing the filters between the air duct and passengers' compartment. Thesus' hydrolysis company is experimenting, developing, and manufacturing the filters. If this becomes "the thing to do," the filters will need to be changed every six months to insure purity of air. Most of his clients are cab drivers, who own, not lease, their cars, limousine companies, and some expensive cars. But "it may catch on." They are in the process of signing-up truckers, but they need to enlarge the garage to install. So they now ask for a deposit before installation and rent a larger area for installation.

Another committee on which he serves creates and conserves energy. This committee gathers information and coordinates industries' efforts. It helps individual companies to initiate, regulate, and continue creations of conservation. He feels that this country will have another energy emergency, need energy desperately, then again do something foolish to obtain or create it.

While his secretary was thumbing through the paper work from this committee, I spotted a series of drawings of a solar collector which not only refocuses light rays by the means of a trough, but focus the rays through magnifying glasses onto the top of tubing on which the trough focused. The title of this: "Steam Heat via Solar Collectors." Another drawing was a chamber where photovoltaic solar cells are created. It is magnetized and rotates so that the strata of precipitated silicon atoms either create layers or a spiral design to trap the photons.

Speaking about his inventions and ideas, I remember at one of our weekly dinners, before Thesus appeared his sister told me, in a critical tone of voice, of some of his more "far out" inventions and committees. He is an active member of a group to prepare a self-sustaining, ecologically-sound space station. In case of nuclear war or some ecological disaster, natural or otherwise, space ships could be launched and could survive indefinitely either circling the earth or some other heavenly body. It would also have the capabilities to leave the solar system if the inhabitants so deemed. This "New Home for Humanity" would be launched in five or six different space ships but would meet in space and be reassembled by the people involved. One of the main features of this station is its ability to convert raw materials into usable products so that the station can continually grow. In conjunction with this, he has created a vacuum cleaner to pick-up space debris and rocks.

In conjunction with that project, he has commissioned a plastics manufacturing firm to produce printable tissue-thin plastic sheets and then print books like the Bible, encyclopedias, and important social documents, like the Constitution. These plastic books will carry forth human knowledge by placing them in the spaceships and by burying them on earth. Supposedly these can be produced right now and can withstand extreme heat and cold or any type of "holocaust" humans or nature could create.

One of the main ideas he is pushing is to make American more democratic. For instance, when the time to vote on an issue which arises in either the House or the Senate, all voting citizens in this country can either dial an 800 number and insert their specially programmed, magnetized computer cards, or can use the card to Fax or E-Mail to a special computer mail box of their representatives and let their preference be known. Each person would use his or her social security number to vote by having it programmed onto the card. These computerized votes will go directly to the floor of the House or Senate and directly to their representatives. The representatives, knowing their constituents and the reliability of the voting systems can decide which way to vote. The payment of these calls will be a reverse charge paid by the government on a sliding scale of income. Our hero feels that this will preserve a representative type of government, but "the people" will have more control, and they will be able to see their congresspersons in action, and thereby determine more fully if they are indeed being represented.

Thesus feels that by giving more people more control through participation, they will be less apt to strike, riot, and cause general disorder and ultimately prevent what seems to be the inevitable revolution. He has a company working on a fingerprint scanner which will be connected with the voting cards so that only a single person can vote at a single time.

Privately he told me one evening at Margery's apartment, "One can see the full implications of this idea: it is giving the country back to the people. It is putting power back into the voters' hands, creating a more pure democracy. Of course, our educational system will have to be improved. We all will need to be re-educated to the policies of the government especially, to what is happening in this country and in the world, to discriminate politically involved representatives from actors and actresses .... and other subtle American intricacies."

"Our society, our democracy, and even our world, all on which we are dependent, will only continue if we continue to pass on knowledge so that the next generation, or even the next person facing dilemmas, the possible causes for our destruction, will not have to go through what we have. Uninformed or misinformed people in democracies cannot exist, for how can its citizens correctly vote. All of this lack of knowledge or incorrect knowledge on the simplest level wastes time and energy. For example, if our society breeds unjustified hope, each new generation will face disillusionment. On the worst level, misinformation creates misunderstandings, distrust, miscommunications, etc. Wars have begun for less reasons than this.

"Aren't you exaggerating the effect of letting the populace be represented?" I responded, "Not that much would change."

"No, you don't see the potential. Once the people are used to their power, why will it need to be a representative government? Why can't the people completely rule as they see fit? Remember, it worked in Athens. The congress people will only propose bills which can be printed on each home computer or mailed upon request. The computers could access government information centers and get transcripts of debates and bills with their dates of vote. The congress-people will be totally devoted to researching and debating on the floors and in subcommittees, then writing the bills proposed for a vote. That main frame computer could easily handle that load.

"I predict that when this occurs the United States will become a multi-party nation. Representatives will run because they will want to introduce change by researching and getting support at the local level and then presenting bills to a larger populace."

When he discussed this movement with us, Margery cynically said that I haven't heard the half of it. "Even though he has become very religious, he is pushing to get the statement, 'One Nation under God,' omitted from the Pledge of Allegiance, for he believes that it is discriminating against atheists and that prayer maybe one reason for our recent and past troubles in the United States. God's wrath has been upon us because we, both 'the people' and persons in charge, may not be conforming to God's Will and Laws. 'Either we take the statement out, or we had better learn to be less hypocritical.' Go on deny it," she goaded. "Thesus, you are too far out for future control." He just laughed, not cynically, but happily. She has made this statement again and again, and only by writing it do I see its full implications.

Anyway, in my attempt to play diplomat, I tried to dull the edge of her statement and asked, "What's the chance of initiating any type of change like your vision?"

"Oh, there are pockets of freedom left in the US. Even in the House and Senate, there are congress-persons who represent, or want to represent, the people. But I must admit the majority in both is "The Machine," and it is The Machine which generally decides what is happening in this country and what is not happening. These individuals represent money, power, the government, and not the people. Even though I say government, I mean the giant organic beast which is not controlled by individuals but which controls them. But those aren't the worst types in the system. The worse are the ones who represent self-interest or small powerful groups.

"It's the underground which is trying to reach

into both, the government and these influential powerful groups, but its main push is to provoke the public to the point that we can force it (the Democratization of America, which is also the name of one of his committees) to become an issue in the next election, or maybe the one after that."

Margery inserted with irritation in her voice, "If any of this abstract discussion materializes, you will be a threat, and the machine will turn on you and grind you into little pieces."

"I am maintaining a very low profile, but we, ... three, ... know that this country is not what it is advertised to be. The frightening part is that this generation and each generation after this will accept what is going on as the norm. They will quit questioning. We were awakened because we know how it should be. We were raised with the notion that it was as we thought it was. And now, we must awaken future generations to the possibilities of what it really could be. We must re-educate them to their freedom and rights and show them that what is happening is wrong: that we have the right to assemble; we have the right to protest; we have the right to change things when they no longer represent us. We should, of course, have the right to see our records, no matter who holds them, and be able to file a contest if we feel the records are not the truth.

"In general what I am talking about is a greater diversity of power. The greater the diversity of power, the greater chance that what has happened in this country won't happen again. Give the strength and power back to the legislative and judicial branches. If individual's powers are strengthened and other powers such as the mass media could each unite their industry and demand their rights, then this mess could be set right. But right now, the individual has no rights, and both business and the mass media gain too much from the government to stand against it."

"And have too much to lose by standing against it," I inserted. He nodded.

"So, the change is going to have to take place within the government itself, hopefully by getting the congressional proceedings again to be publicly broadcasted daily, and on an easily accessible public channel, and recorded, if need be, at the government's expense."

"Uh, oh," laughed Margery, "I said the wrong thing and unlocked ….

"If the people of the United States start demanding to vote on all issues, the politicians, no matter how corrupt they are or their precinct is or the voting booths are, they will have to compromise because, the fact remains, nothing can stop an overwhelming vote and they are still elected. Also, there are many powerful people who don't agree with recent, current events, and it will be those who will push the rest into a compromise. Hopefully, these will be correcting factors, and the house of face-cards will fall; power will again be diversified..

"I can envision a government that is so open and so efficient that private industry and individuals use it as a resource. It could be pliable, ready to adapt to the needs of its citizens. For instance, an industry could petition the government to coordinate research in that industry. And each time an individual or company uses the government for communications, coordination, or information, it will pay a 'users fee.' The government doesn't need to be such a money losing proposition."

Margery laughed again. This time, I smiled.

"A nuance of this is that prisoners should not only pay their room and board through working, and thereby not be a liability, but they should pay off the guilt and sin which they caused in the form of retribution. If a person takes another person's life, then let that person work for the rest of his life and use that salary to pay the family, person, and/or state, whoever was harmed. If one does harm against the nation or state or corporation or company, then that person should pay the entity.

"What I am proposing is that instead of giving the criminals 'time up the river,' fine them and make them pay their fines by working in a prison system. Contract different industries to build factory-prisons to employ the prisoners and give them a standard wage. Let them pay off their fines, and at the same time save-up some money, give them a skill, then release them into society.

"Of course, prisoners could elect to do nothing and not get paid, but then again they could work over time, work efficiently, get promoted, and pay-off their fine early and be released. (The capitalistic way, for sure.) For those who refuse to work put them in prisons already established. To really make this self-sustaining, the working prisoners could be taxed to pay for those who don't work.

"The greater the variety of industries, the greater the choices the prisoners would have about what field they want to pursue. Also the greater the number of industries involved, the greater number of companies who would hire the ex-prisoners. Imagine prison farms in the South growing enough food to supply the rest of the system; prison ranches raising enough cattle, sheep, pigs, then processing prisons to package and ship to the other prisons. School prisons teaching construction, agriculture, maintenance, etc. It could be begun by contracting the different fields of the construction industry to train prisoners to build the different types of factories, mines, and other facilities necessary to secure the prisoners. For instance, they could build a textile and clothing factory to supply all prisoners with their necessary clothing. One of the big names in the industry would finance and build this factory, and of course reap the profits. The salary of the prisoners would be divided into retribution, room and board, and savings. Let them work jobs which nobody else wants to do, like picking fruit and vegetables."

"Did you give up on your fruit picking machine?" He ignored me and pushed forward.

"Let the best be promoted to work national security jobs like manufacturing technical equipment and national defense supplies. Hell, the government is paying for this stuff already; it sure as hell can subsidize industries to provide itself with necessities to secure its own security. Why be dependent on other countries, especially for our prisons?"

"Easy steamboat," his sister inserted smiling.

"Yes, the whole system would not only pay for itself but would instill a work ethic, 'set them in the groove,' prepare them for release, show them that working pays, how to become successful, and train them with skills. Their savings could be released to them to help them get started.

"Isn't part of the problem: too many people in prison….. and for the wrong reasons? Wouldn't this just encourage …." My comment didn't slow him.

"Imagine a prisoner learning to weld, then being sent to a ship building prison factory where he makes over fifteen dollars an hour above minimum wage, then when he is close to parole being sent to work on a prison factory being built. In ten years, he could have paid the injured party $30,000 and saved the same amount and not cost the taxpayers anything.

"But my point is that the governments would have to work as one unit. The United States would have only one prison system, not city, county, state, and federal. Undoubtedly it would be just a federal prison system as decreed by the President. The President has usurped that type of power, he might as well use it constructively. By bringing the scattered systems under one authority, it could be made, not only more efficient but less expensive.

If Margery felt as I did, swamped in a tidal wave of his ideas, then we were just too overwhelmed to respond. So without a pause, for even a breath, he issued forth another proclamation. Neither of us smiled.

"Another totally inefficient and expensive government program is the welfare system. The paying out of funds should be handled automatically through the social security or the Internal Revenue offices in a regressive funding process which continually gives the recipients a progressive income .... so that it pays to work and get off the dole."

"The welfare department should only train and teach: for instance, teach child care so that some of the recipients can baby sit while others work; teach hygiene so that some of the recipients can in turn teach others; teach house cleaning, how to obtain a balance diet, shopping methods; in short teach the recipients to do the welfare work: Train them to follow through from their automatic dole and to assure that the money is used correctly, properly for beneficial purposes. Make sure the money recirculates a couple of times even before it leaves the welfare system. Of course, it would still be based on the few incapacitated, the few really indigent. But let those who are getting subsidized pay others who would be subsidized.

"Also if this subsidy program was automatically issued through one government agency, it would help lower the costs of issuing, and at the same time, help lower-income people without harming their dignity. It shouldn't pay for the father to disappear. It shouldn't pay not to work. Pay the father to be present; pay both parents to achieve.

"Imagine this: a family of four needs, let's us round figures and say, one thousand a month to survive. Give it to them; if the father is absent, give them only enough for three. Anyway, if one of the two goes to work and makes five hundred a month, then the subsidy should only be cut by two hundred and fifty, so their income increases by two hundred and fifty. The family is now receiving $1,250. If the working person receives a raise, to $600 a month, then their income should rise to let's say $1300, and so on until gradually this family doesn't need welfare at all. It should pay to work and stay together as a family."

Margery was the first to stop him. "Remind me to vote for you the next time you run for ...... what are you running for ....God? I don't know enough about what you are discussing, and I'm sure you don't either. It's sounds too simplistic, sophomoric."

"These are just ideas that I am going to present to a new committee, a political committee for government action, to research. Do you want to join?" Smiling, he first looked at Margery, who smiled and shook her head no, then at me.

For some reason, I was embarrassed and looked away. I thought of mentioning that he was, in my opinion, too involved with what he was doing to see objectively, and at the same time, too scattered in all his projects to focus his attention, but I didn't say anything. I do not believe in criticism, and who knows, he may accomplish what he wishes.

"More ways, many more ways exist where the government can be a resource and make a buck, become a tool in our hands again and not via versa. It could help create industries where industry cannot create itself. There are many ways to make the systems which already exist more efficient, more productive."

It sounded as if he was about to embark on another tangent so Margery again interrupted him,

"We need a drink," and she went to her wet-bar. "If these are such good ideas, why haven't they been tried? This world is filled with specialists who are paid to sit around all day and solve problems."

"You know, I've thought that also." He quickly responded, "Don't fix me one, I've got to get up at six tomorrow, and it's late. I've had these ideas for years now. When I was in high school or college, I sent them out to different people .... the President of the United States for one .... Department of Health, Education, and Welfare, but nothing happened, then I quit thinking about them."

"I rest my case," she said. "I think you are wasting your time and energy."

"Maybe," I timidly interjected, "it is a matter of undeveloped thought. If, over these years, you would have researched and developed them ...."

"We'll see. I have to go. You two take care of each other, bye," and he departed. As one can see, once he had found security and protection, his ideas have burst forth as a field of blooming flowers in spring, one may even say blooming flowers in a desert. He has ideas upon ideas which he is initiating into the system both for effect and profit. It was as if his suppressed psyche found fertile ground and could do nothing but bloom, flower, and seed. He believes in change and the effect he can create. And he knows, because of his money and power, that his ideas can be changed into products which produce change.

In a previous chapter I stated that he "is not going to join sides, help raise an army and strike out against an enemy," but he has made many contacts, especially through the underground movements, where he obtained his identification cards. The underground movements are very large, but to my knowledge they seem scattered both physically, spread all over the country, and in their goals. Each separate little group wants power and to become more powerful. These groups don't have a common goal or leader.

At first, Thesus didn't want to get involved. Although by getting his I.D.s and some pertinent information from them, at some financial cost, they considered him "one of them," and indeed he has maintained contact. He, without doubt, could bring them together into a single body, with a single goal, and create the means of communication. He knows this, but as he has said to me, "The temptation to join and attempt to lead, just because of my fear and hate, was great, but there was also a very high probability that this new organization could get out of control and just become another beastly system." I guess Adrian's questions of his affiliations loomed large in his mind. This is just another example of the system pushing him to become something it fears he will, and in a way he has.

Outside forces can determine us both in our compliance and reaction against them. Thesus is right; we more fully become who we want by being internally motivated.

Anonymously he is assimilating his own ideas into these groups and from what I have gathered this propaganda is fragmenting them even more.

Chapter 6

I knew he had discovered the information concerning his old problems. Had he resolved them? I didn't know the specifics. In a moment of inspiration, while writing that last chapter, I called his office and made an appointment. I knew he wouldn't deny me that. When I asked for two hours of his time, because I wanted to discuss his religious beliefs, his receptionist told me, she had to get back to me. She called had two hours two weeks away. I accepted.

When I arrived fifteen minutes early, Thesus said, "Great, you're not doing anything this afternoon and evening are you?" Without waiting for a response, he hurriedly said, "Come on. Tanya, do you have those tickets?" As she reached into her desk, he continued, "And the taxi?"

"It should be downstairs in ten minutes."

"Let's wait for it on the street. It may appear early. We're due at the airport in forty-five minutes. This is my, or I should say, the corporation's treat."

For some reason, Las Vegas or Reno sprang to mind, and I was excited about the prospect. I always carry extra cash so I do not need to use a credit card, and I will call Margery when we land. But on the freeway to the airport, I thought "corporation?" "Where are we going?"

"Sacramento."

"Sacramento? Why?"

"There's some land I need to see, a possible purchase for the foundation."

"Margery and I were kind of planning a movie."

"You can call her at her office. Our return tickets aren't until ten tonight. One reason I am taking out so much time for you is that I have read the beginning of your book. Margery gave me a copy, the part dealing with me."

I had given her a copy, but of course omitted the voyeur experience and other "too personal" statements.

"Just in seeing what you thought my beliefs were back then has helped me to clarify and develop my thoughts. Before this period in my life, I have always been hesitant in stating my beliefs, for I felt it would be limiting. I could get caught by my own words: that my words would become attachments placed on me by myself. I would title myself a Christian, Buddhist, Jew, Moslem, or even atheist and would assume that role either from other's reaction to me or my own reaction to myself; that I would be unable to break out of those bonds, the rules of the role. So before this, I have never sought to define and record my beliefs.

"But there has recently come a time when my beliefs have surfaced and are trying to define themselves; a need to express and develop them exists in me; words pop into my head which ......" He handed me a piece of scratch paper. "Here .... these do not represent my firm beliefs but are quickly passing recorded thoughts that I almost unconsciously scribbled while talking to a possible donor to the foundation."

I glanced at the piece of paper and upon exiting

the cab, absent mindedly placed into my pocket.

For money, humans multiplied; for money humans divided; now, for money humans diminish·

God's Way- a wide birth·

God sees through us, both to the quick and marrow, and to the universe, itself, through our senses·

God's sublime substances: The Purpose and The Cause·

May good beget good; may evil beget evil; may those who attempt to hold others, be held fast and forgotten·

"Now I wonder," he continued, "if I don't express and/or think through this, would I impede my development? Yes, it is possible that if I don't express my beliefs in one form or another, my knowledge may be lost to myself. And I just don't have the time anymore, so here I am making the time.

"Anyway, thinking about the piece of paper I gave you, years ago when I was reading religious books, The Old Testament, The Koran, about Tao, etc., a question popped into my mind. Why didn't God write Its own book explaining the Truth, The Way,

The Path which humans should travel. Why didn't It or doesn't It enlighten each person rather than have an intermediary, a writer of Its words, and then interpreters, who usually gain power and prestige from their interpretations, and subsequently conflict arises from those who oppose the interpretations or even their power and prestige. As soon as I asked, it came to me. It's the world, the universe: that is Its direct work. Ike was right; in part it can be found in God's Laws and nature's laws and in nature itself. It is in those that we may find Its Words, Its Truth, Its Way. And when I began reading Its works, I realized my limitations not just to see and understand, but to express what I've seen. Would or could any words or images communicate that which is behind the Words or physical Universe, that which is truly behind it All? My readings and my attempts to express have shown me that no religion nor writings have done this. Religion was and still remains a personal matter. In my case, my spiritual quest is an un-understandable knowledge, a feeling that I know … I know It is a power, a cause… but can't communicate It. Even if an attempt is made, like right now, once one's beliefs are put into words, they cannot but be less than the total belief ..... and beliefs, as everything, change. We change; we grow.

"You can remember when I rationally didn't believe in God,.... but you know, my feelings never left. I thought my feeling was an insecurity, that the need to believe existed because of my fear of change, my fear of the unknown, my fear of death, of the all-consuming; so I fought my feelings. I felt that the concept of God was a security blanket for the unknown, a warm, comfortable blanket, which I threw off because I wanted to face and feel the real.

"Yes, I am still set in finding and making right the unjustified forces which controlled and still control me, and............."

The taxi stopped in front of the airline departure door; the driver stated a price, but Thesus continued talking: "I still want to know the Real, especially that which controls me, but now I don't feel as frustrated about my beliefs. It is not confusing as it once was, no doubt remains, ... well, maybe that's not quite true,.... Let's say a healthy skepticism exists; I wouldn't be disappointed if I die and there is nothing ...." He began to laugh, "How much is it?" and reached for his wallet.

The driver pointed to the ticking price and his statement raised it by a couple of dollars, (I assumed to give himself a tip from this distracted person) and Thesus continued with wallet in his hand, "I believe, there is something beyond this human existence, and I hope and am testing to find out what. I am testing the existence of a greater justice, a justice for all that exists; a justice because it exists (I don't know how to punctuate his statements, whether to use a semicolon or a colon here and directly above or even to capitalize the 'its.'); a justice innate in all. Then it must exist in mankind, in all mankind, and in each and every human being; it must somehow be integrated with our self-wills, maybe more than I can understand." He paused then said, "Oh, I'm sorry, here," and handed a credit card to the driver. "Take twenty percent."

"I again believe in the justice, which I did when I was young, that there is a justice in human beings, where if one does a good deed then that person is rewarded within his or her own being, that the being is ennobled by the deed, and the persons doing the deed have created of themselves a better person to live with."

The driver returned the computer tab. Turned off the meter. Looking over at it, I saw that he had jacked the price another couple of dollars after taking his tip (in anticipation of sitting there for a while?). And without a pause and without verifying, Thesus talked, "For sure, this innate justice exists in that when we do the right, the just, and the good, we continue God's majesty. I feel that we help to continue the immortal goodness, righteousness, and justness which must exist because everything exists, ... because there is existence."

"Have a good trip," the cabby said while holding Thesus' receipt. Thesus took it, looked at his watch, and said, "We'd better hurry."

With no luggage, only his attaché case, Thesus walked to the front of a line, held the tickets face-first to an attendant who scanned it, then waited for a computer read-out, and said, "Which concourse?" The attendant muttered something. "Thanks," and turning to me said, "Come on; it's about to board. We had better run." Before even getting to the X-ray, his opened attaché case was in one hand and his lap-top computer in the other.

With two minutes to spare and in our First Class seats, I said, "How can you believe in justice when so much injustice has been perpetrated against you?"

"Great! Let's don't lose track," he answered. "Human beings, or should I say people, can, because of Free Will, pervert or even destroy Justice. Greed, power, or even just a narrow view of justice can distort this 'true justice,' which I feel exists. We do our injustices to each other; nature and God doesn't." While the flight attendant mouthed words of what to do in an emergency, Thesus lowered his voice to a whisper: "It seems we are not only rewarded but are punished by ourselves. When we lie to others so much that we cannot tell the truth from falsehood, we have betrayed our own beings. We have lost contact with who we really are. When we do what we consider wrong and evil, we suffer guilt either consciously or unconsciously, and we have to live in a worse world, one of our own creation."

"It kind of sounds like the karma."

"Yes, but more subtle, I think. Maybe Heaven and Hell are in part our attitudes, our way of perceiving what happens in our world and to ourselves: our optimism in the face of adversity as compared with our unnecessary fears, doubts, and worries." The attendant finished and walked the aisle to check seat belts; Thesus again raised his voice, but was still leaning in my direction: "If our attitude about ourselves and our lives is our justice then this knowledge keeps us from my concept of Heaven. Before you ask, it is a mental disposition that exists for animals, or at least my belief of some animals, that they have no attachments, no fear of the future, what is going to happen will happen: they are instinct, fight or flight, pure and simple, living in the vital immediate moment ….. and in heaven?"

"Yes, they were not ejected from the Garden of Eden."

"This kind of makes us on a lower scale of evolution...... Or in the example of Ike, if he saw clearly and had an understanding of his own mental dispositions, knowing why they were there, the purpose they served,...."

"You mean that you think he really was an artist and creator of his own being?" I interjected with surprise.

"Hopefully, but if not, then at least in full contact with himself, and maybe he was in Heaven in his mind, through his involvement. He may have been truly enlightened and had renounced all desire and choice. It was your view of his movie which interpreted his last moments of his life as being a religious offering. He may have truly been committed and commended himself to something to which he believed. If this is true, he could have obtained a freedom, because he lost the fear of pain in the hope of reward. In his mind, he could have thrown himself into the void with pure belief and pure submission."

"'In the perfect freedom of fervent love,'" I quoted, "but I know.... we both know that he was but a poor, fallible fool, and maybe his fallibleness lead him to his fall."

"Who is to say whether he reached his star or plummeted to earth in his own mind. Maybe he was holding tight, holding together that which is sacred or at least what he considered sacred and did not veer from his course. He could have reached the Cosmic flow."

"TV/Internet headsets?" a stewardess inquired.

"A scotch and soda, please." I responded.

"And you?"

"Nothing, thanks."

I continued, "You are saying one thing to me personally and another publicly. In that movie you stated Jacoby didn't need to kill himself to maintain control. But now you are saying, he needed to die for what he believed. But we both know, Jacoby did try to hang on to his meaning for life."

"Even though ultimately maybe no purpose to living and meaning to life may exist, we humans do create the meaning. And this meaning should not be transitory, no matter whether it is our revelation, our discovery of meaning, or our created meaning, because meaning makes a foundation on which we base our decisions and can create more meaning. Therefore, by choosing a way to live we may indeed directly or indirectly be choosing our way of death."

"Boy, do his ideas have you. …. From guilt, are you rationalizing his actions?"

"I don't think so ....for sure his life was slipping, ... but in his mind? Slipping in relation to society and to us, his friends? Both of us agree that he truly was an individual exploring human possibilities and the unknown.

"But to get back to my point, yes, maybe there is a Heaven. To get into a place in our minds where we can live a happy, complete life. To get to some place in society and in nature where we feel our life is worthwhile, and we would do it again: that we believe that our existence has not been futile ... a completion of being. So we can move on."

I glanced at him in his pause and saw an expression where I could tell he had lost himself in his own thought. I waited about ten minutes before saying, "Are you saying that Jacoby could have built a temple in his mind and entered it?"

"Maybe, a variation of perfecting an attitude, which I am trying to do, also..............

"The key theme with Ike was 'effect.' If we continue our individual existences through our effects, as he thought, we should have the most positive effect possible, especially if reincarnation exists, because we will come back and live in the mess which we helped create, and a positive suicide could be one way. Either rightly or wrongly he, in his mind, was walking the 'path of righteousness.' (I assume this is a quote from a definition of Dharma)"

"We will be landing in ten minutes; fasten your seat belts," announced the loudspeaker.

I didn't want to hear this redefinition of Jacoby so I asked him, "What is 'a complete life' for you?"

"The completion of inner necessities. The necessity to understand my potential, my fate, if one exists; hell it even may be the reason we are here in the first place, why we have come back. Those are speculations but what I can do is to define my beliefs. And with this, the opportunity to fulfill my created goals. And by doing this, to test my understanding. This takes place in the spiral of time." He laughed and said, "At the same place each night in bed but after a day of experiences.

"To experience that slightly heavy breathing moment, running comfortably at a pace where everything can be easily assimilated, comprehended, and yet productivity can take place, putting back into what makes it all possible........... as much or more than I take. But feeling that I am moving as fast as I can and yet, not destroying myself by over exertion."

"I've always wondered, what is fate? Is it what God controls? That piece of paper indicates that you believe....,"

"You know, you're not only my friend, you are my good companion, which is the reason I volunteered you for this trip: you ask good probing questions, and you really want to know. Anyway, as I mentioned, that piece of paper was but a moment of contemplation, not absolute or firm beliefs, not beliefs created from contemplation and decision.

"Before you ask, I don't know which are truer. There may be a God and then there may not be. We must prepare ourselves for any possibility; I am trying to cover the possibilities; I make decisions based on both. I have my eyes opened trying to read a possible Bible. I am listening for possible communications. The real question is: Would I know if I heard because I listen with limited perception and a certain amount of skepticism and always testing?"

"'Be ready for anything-that perhaps is wisdom,'" I inserted not remembering where I heard the quotation. My growing cancer passed through my mind, "'Give ourselves up to, according to the hour, to confidence, to skepticism, to optimism, to irony, and we may be sure that at certain moments at least we shall be with the truth. Good-humor is a philosophic state of mind; it seems to say to Nature that we take her no more seriously than she takes us.'"

"Yes!" he laughed and slapped my leg.

I could also quote and think at the same time, another asset of twelve years of college particularly useful during oral exams and attacks from unruly students. I really wanted to tell Ike that I thought he was a fool, more than a fool... more than crazy..... some thing more than dangerous..... but I couldn't think of what or how.

"Yes, good-humor is a great part of the temple, and as I said before that feeling, that innate feeling, has been with me. Even my testing has produced positive results. I am somewhat convinced that more than a possibility, but even a probability exists that there are supreme beings, and/or a Supreme Being. Evidence is mounting in my mind. The results may have been coincidence. The occurrences may have been coincidence, but I believe it was more than that. Of all the apartments in San Francisco which were available, why did I end up in that one?"

It was the best deal, but why? Popped into my head. Again, I was getting tired with the bombardment of his ideas and was slowing down in hearing and responding to his expose. So when I finally comprehended the content of his last statement, I snapped, "Gods?"

"Gods." At that moment the wheels touched ground, and we both held our breath, but even before

455

the second breaking, he continued, "There may be not only one God but many gods. There may be even a polytheistic progressive system working up to a monotheistic power. By gods, I mean beings, consciousness, and will power. They may help control what we consider fate or they could be just individual powers which try to control us. They may be able to communicate to us by different means, other than language. If they do exist, we should know them. If they exist, and if they could be detrimental to our existence, we should learn about them, and we should leave as few possibilities of other beings controlling us as possible.

"It is possible that there may be some type of demon, an opposite type of god to the gods which promote and secure life. If there is a god like that, it may be compared to the void, which tries to consume all. This type of god which, hopefully, has an endless task with purpose."

I thought, god, this guy has been more spooked by what has happened to him than I possibly thought, but I just confirmed by saying, "Literature is full of it."

"Maybe," and he raised his voice because the Captain began his thank-you-spiel, "The term gods is incorrect, and there are just different beings, spirits, forces, opposites, or what-have-you to existence and continuance. But then again, maybe my original conception is true and gods upon gods walk the heavens, a hierarchy of divine beings, working their way up to all that is, to The Great Almighty All." His voice contained mirth, but he added with a serious tone, "To know Its reason for existence, and our places within the scheme, would be to have the key ..... our destiny which needs to be fulfilled."

He stood and jousted passengers moving down the aisle, so my statement was lost, but I added, "Literature acknowledges Angels as part of the hierarchy."

We exited and found the rented car. While still sitting in the parking lot, Thesus said to himself, "Now where is that piece of.... Oh yes, where are we going?" He examined a computer generated map and found the entrance to the freeway and headed toward north. I was about to ask where we're going when he spoke:

"Perhaps a reason for life ..."

Anticipating a return to the conversation, I interjected in a whisper before he began, "Some would say it is 'love.'"

".... is that it is a progressive system. It expands beyond its own bounds. It multiplies, not just adds. It can and does through evolution - become more than it is. As the Universe expands, it fulfills Its potential.

"That could be one of human's purposes also, to expand the Universe, the number of possibilities, not only physically but mentally, spiritually, conceptionally, and in all the ways that humans can. We could even be a form of sense organ for God and/or the Universe, where God and/or the Universe can see through us, not only that It sees into our beings, but It sees itself through our perceptions and conceptions."

"That was on you doodle-sheet."

457

"So conceivably, the greater the diversity of man, woman, and child, the greater the potential of not only humanity, but, possibly, the Universe. If the extremes don't cause harm to the whole then uniqueness would seem to be a virtue.

"Even on a social level, the qualities which separate us into individuals are those qualities which give our society a potential... Wait a minute, there's the turn off now to the west."

The mountains were beautiful, I stayed silent so he could verify the route but after about ten minutes I asked, "So that is your concept of God?"

"As I alluded, It is beyond my powers of conception, but that does not completely answer your question nor my attempts to discover my conception. I guess I would say It is the Primal.

"Stupid and weak, huh? 'Primal' is the wrong word, with the wrong connotations," he added.
Maybe as close as we can get to the basic being, the evolving, yet constant being, within each of us and within what we can know of nature is as close as we can communicate with that Source. Yes, in that we are part of the Universe, we can seek the Universe, the Basic, the Real within ourselves. When I was praying for the wisdom to find my path through the labyrinths, I was examining my dreams, my intuitions, my surfacing subconscious and unconscious thoughts. I, without knowing it, was praying to the Basic within me, to some knowledge greater than my conscious being   Wait a minute!

"What did that sign say? The turn off must be up here about two miles. This is really great. Not too long a drive, yet enough to make sure one has to know the way. Yes, there it on the right. Now from what I was told, it is just a mile or so up this steep road."

The vegetation became more sparse as we seemingly climbed the mountain. Yes, buying a house up here would be isolation, for sure. But when we stopped, it was right in the middle of a ghost town, and it appeared as if nobody was within miles. I thought, what the Hell, and when Thesus asked,

"What were we discussing?"

I replied as I rolled down the window, "Trying to communicate with God or something." A fresh air smell rushed in, predominately pine.

"Communication? Hmmm? We might be able to think in some form of Universal language as you seem to indicate that Ike found. Yes, I can believe in that, our language evolved from the communication of our Basic being. If we found other worlds, other types of existence, other types of life, we would probably get closer to understanding that language. If we could communicate with other planets, other beings, other species even on this planet, we would probably get closer to knowing this language. And even conceivably other beings on this planet, if they exist and why shouldn't our planet have attracted and produced other types of life than we know, other life than built from DNA?"

I thought this whole situation is bizarre; he's talking about gods again, I felt high..... I started to laugh, I am high. Nothing seems quit real. We were sitting in a car in the middle of a ghost town, miles from nowhere talking about God, ghosts, and spirits.

"I need to get out of this car."

He came around the car while I was standing next to the door, talking: "When I was young, I believed in a naive way. You were right about that, and my beliefs were easily destroyed. Rather than just hold on less tightly to what I believed, as I do now, I let the destruction of my beliefs shock me, because I held so firmly. Part of that was ego, my pride. I then went to an opposite extreme with disillusionment. I got to the point where I didn't believe at all, in anything. It grew: I didn't believe in God, life, people and then myself.

"You know about all of this; you've seen it happen, but before you began to know me, I felt I was a chosen person; I didn't know why, but now it can be explained by different people's reaction to my tested intelligence," he began to talk more rapidly, and so I turned in the direction he was looking and saw an old man walking toward the car, "but then, to me and only to me, I felt I was chosen. To put it mildly, my feelings of being exceptional found a religious direction because I was searching in that direction. In a way, I was conditioned by circumstance because both happened at the same time.

"Thinking God had a purpose for me, I prayed and waited to be directed but nothing happened."

"Remember your poem?"

"Yes, ... I began searching into different religions, but it was of no use. I again prayed and waited, wanting to know which religion was truth, but again nothing happened, and then the pendulum began to swing, my beliefs faded."

The old man was standing beside the car; wearing work over-alls and a beaten up cowboy hat. Thesus introduced me, opened the door, and pulled out a miniature hand held recording device from his suit coat. Then threw his coat back into the car. "Do you want to go on our tour guide?" he asked me.

"No, I'm not feeling well." They walked off together, talking. I walked up a hill overlooking the town and car. Yes, it was a ghost town with about fifteen dilapidated buildings with two streets creating a "T," both ended in dead ends. This is the end of the road, for sure. It must have been a mining town because it was surrounded on three sides by mountains: mining tailings scarred the slopes of two adjacent hills. Big huge chunks of granite surfaced in contrast to the tailings. It was desolate, probably hot in the summer, and stark and cold in the winter. The trees must have been timbered for the mines. Why would Thesus want to live up here?

I felt a pain in my stomach. That's my problem. I haven't eaten all day. The flight was too short for food, and I only had coffee for breakfast, then that drink. Maybe I have a hang-over. Scanning the town, I found the least ramshackled building which looked like a saloon, and headed straight for it. Upon closer viewing, I realized this was the building from which the old man emerged. I knocked, feeling stupid, and entered. It was a bar, but nobody was there. I smelled food. He must live upstairs as caretaker. I called out. .... Nobody.

Outside again, I scanned the different buildings for life, then resigned myself to sitting on the hood of

461

the car. Thirty minutes later the old man and Thesus emerged from what looked like a theater. Still with the recording device in hand, Thesus was listening with his usual intenseness. Within speaking range he called to me, "Quite a place, isn't it?"

My response was sliding from the hood and opening the car door. The old man spoke slowly, "You boys want to come over to the saloon (he pronounced it with too many O's) and have a drink?"

"No," responded Thesus with a bit more Westernize in his words, "looks like my friend is ready to travel."

"I'd love a drink." Don't screw this up, Thesus. Damn, a beer would be good: soothe my pain and fill my stomach. The thoughts rode through my head with a Western twang also.

"O.K.." Thesus turned to the man as we three strolled back to the bar "Well, you will probably know in a month or so. If you want to stay on, I'm sure it can be arranged."

Thesus and I sat at the bar, and the man acted as bartender.

"It can be restored," Thesus assured all three of us, "not only the buildings but the landscaping as well. We can get some environmentally aware, historical group interested and raise some money. The erosion should and can be stopped.

"By the way, where do you get your water?"

"The misses and me have a well, but when this town was a booming, there's a lake up-a-ways with a stream coming out of it and the water was diverted. It was used for drinken and sloosen."

"Slousen?" I asked.

"Yelp, separating the ore from the sand, dirt, and rocks."

Oh, sluicing, I said to myself.

"We had better test the water, especially for radioactivity and heavy metals."

I tried to eliminate any condescending tone when I asked Thesus, "You buying a house up here?"

"Me, no, it's the foundation. The proposal is to create an artists' colony, to buy Granite, the whole town , lock, stock, and barrow."

"You want another?"

"Please," I answered.

"No thanks," Thesus responded then looked around, "Yeah, this saloon can be made into a print-making studio; the hotel can be individual artists' studios, the theater can be restored just as is ...."

"A grocery store?" I inserted.

The old man spoke while I was, "Too bad you gonna change this salooon; there's a lot of history connected with it," and he began a story about the first time he entered it.

After another beer, I was bombed and quit listening. The next thing I know we're walking to the car, and Thesus is saying, "I wanted you to drive, so I could get some work done, but it's o.k.; I'll do it on the plane. Four beers in less than an hour; aren't you ashamed of yourself?" He was miffed.

We started down the dirt road, and Thesus was still talking, "If the water is ok, my proposal will say 'grant it' to Granite," he laughed out loud. I lay my head back onto the seat and thought to say: well, I got

463

stoned in Granite and am still high, but thought better of it and went to sleep for a bit.

He awakened me at seven when we stopped in Sacramento for dinner. I had a slight headache and was embarrassed. We didn't talk for the first half of the meal, then he began his conversation with, "I not only need to do the paperwork for the foundation, but I have about three other hours of work. So as soon as we finish dinner, you drop me at the airport and return the car. I'll meet you in the terminal.

"You know, continuing our discussion of religion, I had a dream the other night: I don't know who they were but two women were always present when I knew I would encounter alien beings. In my vision of how I was going to meet beings from outer space, I was going to have a child in each arm and was going to walk up to the silver space ship. But how I met the being was different. It was raining. My intuition told me it was time. I ventured into the rain, and, of course, seeing those two women watching me confirmed what I knew. Today was the day. It was only misting as I walked through the park, just enough to keep others at home.

"On my right was this giant spider web, and all of a sudden out came this monster daddy-long legs. Its body was as large as my head, and I started to run in the direction from which I had come. It kept up with me on a parallel course, but it wasn't running on its eight legs; it was flying like a squid through water with its legs trailing. I thought, how the hell can this be happening. It had no mouth or eyes or any sense organs, I could see. After a moment, I realized this was the being I was expected to meet, and I stopped running and reached over and touched its head. It was just brains and legs and seemed to be a non-consuming being: without orifices. The skin was like snake skin but loose fitting; I awakened.

"You're good at dream interpretation; what do you think it meant?"

"The first part is easy. You thought you would be like the father of Adam and Eve, providing a new world with two humans. But what really happened, your destiny, is something you thought would be harmful but was actually .... what? Helpful, insightful? Also the alien beings were right here, and maybe have been here all along, only we haven't been aware of them."

"Could I have the bill?" he asked a passing waiter. "Yes, your background in interpreting Literature is good for this kind of thing, and I think it has something to do with that also. But maybe it is more about us not being superior, or the superior beings in this world. Now, if I think about it, if the children and I went to a new world, we would not be the superior beings; the sailors, the masters of the vessel, would. That is how I thought it would be, but when I met the being face to face, I thought it was superior for it didn't consume other beings, a reason I didn't need to fear it. It must have functioned like a plant. However, maybe we were equal and that is what I was expected to realize, that this world if filled with 'alien beings' on equal footing as we ..... or superior .... I don't know.

"How are you feeling?"

"Fine." His idea of gods, again?

"Let's go; you drop me. Here's the corporation's credit card for the car. Come on; let's hurry."

Later when I found Thesus, he was sitting in the airport facing the runway, dictating into his laptop computer. Plugged into its side was his recording device, and when he saw me, he pushed a button on the hologram key board and an inch round disk popped out of the other side.

When I sat, he didn't even acknowledge my presence. He quit speaking and began to type. It was about nine. I thought I saw an optical illusion. We were sitting in the concourse where we were to board. I assumed we were facing the plane we would fly. It looked exactly like the ones I always knew, but when a gas truck carrying compressed liquid hydrogen drove up beside it to fuel it, I could see the plane's fuselage seemed really small. Is that the size of the plane we arrived on? Is that our plane? I tried thinking back: I never saw our plane from the outside, but it only had two seats on each side of the cabinet and it seemed short probably forty seats total. I guess I hadn't paid attention.

When we heard the announcement to board, I was apprehensive. I thought my fear was because this was a really small plane. We were the last to board and sat in the front seats. Still first class; Thesus continued to work. I felt frightened as we accelerated down the runway and lifted. After the stewardess asked if we wanted a drink, (I foolishly declined because I was still embarrassed) two men walked to the front of the plane. One stood directly in front of me, and the other bashed the handle on the door of the cockpit with what looked like a metal fist and entered. The other pulled out what looked like a submachine gun from under his trench coat.

"Please be calm," he said. A gasp and moan drowned his next statement. A woman screamed. "Shut up," he yelled in a broken voice. Immediately silence filled the plane. Only the muffled engines roared. "This is a hijacking. Don't do anything foolish, and nobody will get hurt. My friend and I are from an organization, Peaceful Change through Terrorism. We mean no one harm." He pulled a piece of paper from his overcoat, and read, "All we want is the media to recognize our cause. There will be a slight delay in landing; all we want is media coverage, and our rights be heard. So while San Francisco Airport authorities are notified, the media are gathered, and an agreement is reached, this plane will be detoured out over the ocean."

He seemed as nervous as I. His speech was rehearsed and his voice cracked a couple of times in his presentation. I just thought for God's sake, nobody do anything. I looked over at Thesus. He seemed unconcerned. He was still typing. I felt like yelling obscenities at him, smacking him in the face, waking him up to the fact we were being kidnapped. Then I realized I should have gone to the bathroom in the restaurant. To aggravate this situation, I was physically shaking. The drinks in the mountains, the coffee at dinner were about to explode.

"I need to go to the bathroom," I whispered to Thesus.

"Tell them," suggested Thesus in a matter of fact tone and without looking at me. I raised my hand like a grammar school child.

"May I use the rest room?" He laughed nervously, releasing some of the tension.

"Sure."

His submachine gun was pointed at the ceiling, with his finger on the trigger. I carefully passed him. While peeing, which actually was hard to do, I thought if he accidentally pulls that trigger, puts some holes in the ceiling at 20,000 feet, over the ocean, the plane will rip in half.

Upon returning to my seat, I brushed against the gun: it was plastic! I almost laughed. It looked real enough. Then the realization: No, it was really real! No wonder the metal detector didn't stop them. No wonder they didn't hijack a plane coming from the S.F. Airport, with one of those more sophisticated detection devices. It must be one of those printer-machine-made guns. I wanted to tell Thesus my thoughts, but he was still working.

Why didn't we rent a car in San Francisco and drive up here? The cost of the cab to the airport was expensive and took ten minutes. The flight with take-off and landing was an hour and a half, and then back again, getting the rental….. it would have been less money and even less time, there and back, and we wouldn't be in this situation. I would have sat in the driver's seat; he could have worked, until the mountains, and he could have driven. Again I felt like yelling at Thesus: Why did you do this, why did you let this happen?

Later, when I could see that he really was not concerned about any of this, I turned to him and said, "Would you recommend seeking God through prayer?" The hijacker, in a very loud voice, yelled, "I want everyone to keep quiet."

Within minutes, our hero's computer was silently created a paper like substance from its back which read the following: "We each have to find our own paths. I hope and pray that others don't need to go through what I did to find it. When I pray, I would like to think that I am putting myself in the correct perspective, humbling myself to God, to that which created all that exists, the Purpose and the Cause."

I thought what the hell is this? He's responding as if I had asked an earlier question about his beliefs. Maybe he doesn't realize that we are being hijacked.

After three hours and on our approach to S.F. Airport, Thesus handed me another note. "Don't leave until after the press-interviews and at least over half the plane is empty. Don't let any newspaper people either take pictures or stop me. You walk out in front of me."

Without a hitch, we exited. In the taxi back into the city, I expected a huge explanation of his actions and what he knew. However, he only said he wasn't worried because he knew "those jokers," and knew what they were up to and what would happen when we entered the plane.

"That machine gun was real, right?"

"Yes, one of those computer fabricated ones; oh, they were ready to kill and be killed. They had those new bullets without gun powder, but they were harmless, and the best thing, I wasn't discovered. Everything went smoothly. I am sure they got what they wanted. The press met them and recorded their story. But I'll bet, the mass media won't mention them or the flight."

"What were you writing that was so important?

"I had to complete what was happening, then flash drive and erase what I was doing. Remember when you were living with me and decided to do research about the governments and I gave you a computer? I gave you one that I got in L.A. It was safe and you really could access the whole Internet."

"What are you saying?"

"Even when I was young, I realized that I didn't have complete freedom to browse what I wanted, at first because of my parents. Later I realized that many could take control of my computer, including the manufacturer, the software maker, in fact anyone who could place a cookie. Any of those could not only have access to it but could trace it, could limit internet searches, and could follow, if not influence, what I placed on it."

"Manufacturers and software makers?"

"Yes, even more subtlety, our searches are directed. The search engines direct us to what websites we visit, what news we see, almost what is available for us to search. It wasn't until I was in L.A. getting documents when I was taught to find websites beyond the endorsed, sanctioned, authorized. Anyone can create a website but making it public is more difficult.

Also I used to think that it was all controlled by

money, paying to get on the top of the list of a search engine, paying to get a computer which couldn't be controlled and monitored by every Tom, Dick and Henry, but it is more insidious than that. Government agencies have usurped this power. So be leery of any companies or corporations who are making excessive profits without producing; they could be government subsidized, and therefore controlled."

It wasn't until home and in bed that I thought: anything .... anything could have gone wrong, and we could be spread out over the ocean; he's nuts. He's...........gods, spirits that affect our lives ...... he's nuts. He must believe in God for sure, or have a total disregard for his own life. He must have believed in that cause also, and those men, or not cared, or....... What was that?

Chapter 7

A month ago, I was approached by another editor from a big publishing house who wants me to write Ike Jacoby's story. He asked if I had written before, and I presented him with sections of this manuscript. Surprisingly, he wants to see it all with the possibilities of publishing it. He called me into his office and explained that my manuscript was very similar to a contemporary Russian novelist. My first response was Impossible. But after thinking a second, I told him I had done my orals for my Master's Degree on Dostoyevsky and maybe that was the reason. He said he needed to investigate the situation first before he could produce a contract. I, shocked and flattered, said ok. Now, a week later, I am obsessed with the idea of a book out there, published, like this one. It still seems impossible.

I called and made an appointment with Thesus. We had lunch together, at his corporation's expense. My first question even before ordering: "How could your story be out there, in public?" He quit reading the menu then went back to it. After we ordered he said, "I may know.

"It was doing the period when I was researching and traveling the United States. I found an underground cell of Russians; some were Americans and some …. I don't know, but we were all in Syracuse, NY. I was directed to them to get identification. It was going to take a week but the result was great. I got a New York driver's license and a Syracuse University ID stating that I was a graduate student working on a Ph.D. For that week I lived with them in his huge Victorian House.

"They were partiers! Almost every night eight to ten of us would sit at a long dining room table with vodka filled shot glasses for everyone. Doing dinner we would have at least two or three toasts to different occasions per meal. The first evening I met a beautiful blond woman who was very interested in me. She said she was Russian and the sister of one of the men in the house. She came to the nightly dinners. …. I don't know. I didn't really question it at the time, for I didn't seem to have a reason to do so. But now….. she had blue eyes and was slim with an amazing figure.

"Anyway Thanksgiving was coming up and at a dinner she announced that I should cook the turkey because I was the only real American. Her words were 'To have an authentic American Thanksgiving.' Everybody applauded and said yes and so I said fine, if she helped. In fact, I would buy the turkey to return the favor of staying with them.

"She was a student and skipped classes two days before Thanksgiving. Very early in the morning we started shopping. We talked and shopped. I found the biggest fresh turkey I could find, twenty-six pounds. I bought two pies and she wanted to make one. I bought fresh cranberries to make a sauce, like my mother's, potatoes both white and yams, Brussels Sprouts, everything I could think of,..... even string beans to cream, bake, and put those canned onions on top. We went to a Russian bakery and got day-old bread for the stuffing.

"We cooked for two days. It was fun. She was interesting, majoring in Politicks (he laughed), politics and did I mention she was beautiful? Strange, but cooking and talking, we became intimate. For Thursday morning, I had bought six bottles of champagne and orange juice. She had come over and got me out of bed. I don't know the time, but rather than have coffee we had Mimosas. First thing out after stuffing it, I put the turkey in the oven with a top at on a low temperature.

'We worked all morning, cooking and talking and drinking. Everyone who wandered into the kitchen was treated to a Mimosa. By ten in the morning, I was bombed and exhausted. We went to my room and laid down for a nap. At noon, we were back cooking. I went to baste the turkey and found the oven was off. I turned it back on and thought nothing of it, for it was for a seven o'clock dinner.

"She and I worked the rest of the day; I with a slight hang-over. To make a long story short, in front of twelve people, I carved the turkey and it bled. Some of them insisted on eating it 'rare,' but not knowing the result of that, I quickly rushed it back into the stove.

"The first toast which someone made was to 'rare American turkeys'; then to a 'bloody American turkey' and there were many more after that. Even though I was in and out of the kitchen constantly, it seems as if I never missed a toast. Again, I was gone before nine. Consequently, I never did get a taste of that turkey.

"Do you think me standing in front of those people representing America with a bleeding turkey was symbolic?"

"Maybe on some level, but you are missing the most obvious symbolism. One, someone was playing around with your turkey and two, other people view us differently than we view ourselves."

He seemed to dismiss my statement. When he did this I never knew if it was because he thought what I saying was obvious or that he thought I didn't know what I was discussing.

"Anyway at nine, their party began and mine ended. After starting on the dishes my friend said, 'Let's get out of here.' I was in no shape to argue. We went to her place, and I stayed for two days."

"This explains why a story similar to yours is published?"

"Yes, we became intimate. I was ready to stay with her. I thought I was in love. She kept asking me questions about myself. Over that week, I must have told her my whole story, as much as I knew."

"Are you telling me, she recorded it or told it to someone else …."

"Or wrote it herself. She was brilliant."

"Why didn't you stay?"

"Sunday morning, she wasn't home. I had received a note saying my documentation was ready, so I wondered over to the house. I knew who was supplying it, and I went upstairs to find him. He had my new papers. I went to my room to find my hidden cash and as I passed a room, I looked in and saw her in bed with some guy. I stood there and stared. When I turned around, Pepper, her closest, best friend was standing behind me.

"I can imagine the expression on my face. Almost crying, she picked up my hand, shook it and said, "Good-bye."

"You know, you have never mentioned her name, right?"

"I call her my 'Golden Hair Surprise.'" He shook his head. "That was really too bad. But with my problems, I knew it was over. The irony is that since I started traveling, all my physical problems had stopped. I was and still am healthy. But still, I knew I could never compete, I didn't have the time, and trust was broken. With my situation, being able to trust someone was vital."

475

"Do you want dessert?" The waitress asked.

Our hero said, "No thank you. It's my life style, what I am trying to accomplish, how I am working it. I have seen this often. My ideas, theories, experiences, stories and the-such come back to me from seemingly different sometimes strange sources. I don't mind. Only once did I mind: it was a theory. One of my main purposes is to get the ideas into society, to create change, to make a difference. I expect, ... I hope to see results, for them to come back and now you should also.

"If any of this Syracuse trip is true, you have to decide how you want to handle it. It's up to you."

"I should probably encrypt it and copyright it, (I laughed) so if I want credit for what I have accomplished, I can get it."

"Sign the chit and bring me my credit card. I have to leave."

Two days later, I was called into the publisher's office. After discussing the similarities of Russian novelist and my book, and me explaining what I thought happened, he told me that ironically it would be easier to publish because the first book was published. "If it were his girlfriend, she has used a pseudonym. The author is male."

"I am ready to go to bat for you. But you have to make an immediate decision, right now!

His argument, "Because of that book, ours maybe overlooked as a novel, but we have the means to protect you and ourselves at this present moment. The authorities could, at some future date, confiscate, and even destroy it. If they come to know the content, they may be able to stop the publication and/or distribution through various legal means.

"Right now, we can take the market by surprise, gain a certain amount of publicity which we need to protect ourselves. Also we have a war chest, enough money to fight any legal battles that may occur. Now is the time. The future is unpredictable.

"I have a passport; I suggest you get one. The least of our problems is a plagiarism law suit. In fact that may help us on various levels."

After a moment of deliberation, I signed. He's right, but ....

So two days ago I made two more copies of the manuscript, up to the last page, and personally handed them to Margery and Thesus. I gave them the whole thing. For the first time, nothing was omitted! I stressed the importance of them reading it, so they could stop the publication if they want. I told them to take notes, make comments, and edit.

Then I made an official appointment to see both at the same time. While arranging a date and time, I explained the situation, the signed contract. Both were skeptical about my intention and ability to stop publication. Margery even mentioned that she was skeptical about me even rewriting, since the publisher has Book I and II. But I would break the contract, rewrite, or whatever is necessary not to hurt them, either of them. I can see how this could hurt them. I promised to transcribe their conversation directly, so again I carried my recorder.

Let me again emphasize that both had a chance to read all of the preceding material and knew about the recording, although at the beginning of the interview neither saw it.

We three met at Thesus' office at eight o'clock in the evening; in fact, we all arrived at the same time and rode the elevator together, not saying a thing. Entering the elevator, I asked them not to mention the book until I was ready. I could tell that both of them were upset, to say the least. Tension, especially from Margery, charged the small rising compartment. I broke as we were walking toward his office. "Hell, I'm, dying. I could care less if I break the contract. What will he do, sue me?"

Thesus said, "Forget it," as he opened his door, "We'll just do the best we can with the situation. I know your intentions are good." Margery's face redden, and she could barely contain her voice as she added, "'The road to Hell is paved with good intentions.'" Thesus opened the door for her, and she entered and walked quickly through the reception area and into Thesus' office. When he and I entered, she was sitting on his couch. I took a chair, and Thesus, undoubtedly out of habit, sat behind his desk.

I reached in my breast pocket and switched the on-button. I stated the date and then threw out the first question, "Well, what did you think about the manuscript?"

Margery shook her head as if to say, forget it. Thesus laughed, then spoke: "First of all, I want to thank you for sharing your perspective for it has helped me gain insights about myself and my situation. I, of course, don't agree with your interpretations of many of the events, not even that those events happened. Besides all the fallacious statements, misrepresentations, and just poor writing, my main objection is that obviously if anyone was giving me trouble before, because of your book, that person or persons may know what is going on, who I am, what I am doing, etc. They are going to know: I don't look like I did but they could discover me through my activities.

"Of course that is, if they bother to read the book, and if they can put two and two together. I realize that by just changing the names and some facts may not be enough.

"I feel, I've finally broken out of one prison, or should I say labyrinth," he laughed, "only to be possibly put back into another by a friend. I am again beginning to feel the pressure of being confined, suppressed, trapped ..... (he looked up from his desk and must have seen my hurt expression.),.... but that is only on one level. On another level, your writing has made me more rebellious, defiant as hell; it has put much into perspective."

Margery, I think, misinterpreted his statement, because she jumped up and started towards me, but stopped herself. "I could have almost punched you in the nose. When I read your manuscript I had fantasies of smacking you in the face with my horse crop."

Thesus stood, came around the desk, touched Margery on the shoulder and coaxed her to be seated. "But," he continued, "then on another level, I can still just laugh at it all and feel that it won't make any difference; I won't let it make any difference.

"Still, one thing that you don't understand: you

have helped create a myth, not portrayed reality; you have created characters - Thesus, Margery, Ike and even you, John. And I am afraid that if we don't carry the myth to its full logical conclusion, none of us will be able to live or even die in peace.

"If we don't complete your story, someone else will."

"I think it is more than that," Margery broke in, "You have betrayed our ... (she looked at Thesus)..... or I should say my trust in the intimacy of our relationship. As far as your writing about my personal life, I don't think you have been honest or fair to our relationship."

I surely could see her reasons for saying what she did, and the conflict must have shown on my face for she said, "You're right, Thesus, I have been and maybe am a little harsh," then turning back to me said, "There is so much fiction in your book that you should title it a novel, not a biography. Also I....... Let me put it another way," she quickly walked over to me and opened my coat and spoke into the recorder, "Let me put it another way, am I the person on whom you have based part of this manuscript, this fiction?"

When I later listened to the tape, I could definitely hear a meek, "Yes," between the words manuscript and fiction. "The reason," continuing her tirade, "I used the word 'based,' because we both know that some of it is real but then most of it isn't; especially your sensational sections build to create interest, therefore, to be truthful to your potential readers, as you seem to indicate that you want, you should title it a novel or at least eliminate the sections as I have indicated...... Here!" She dropped the manuscript on my lap. I stood, I guess because I was intimidated, and managed a "Thank you."

She continued, "However, I also think it should be published but without giving the reader false ideas about the realness of the events you've described. It should be published because certain ideas, facts, and qualities should be expressed; certain truths must be told, in order to end the plight which exists..........."

After her statement a long pause ensued, while I checked the list of questions I brought; when I was about to ask one, she said, "It should be published because this has been your only accomplishment in...... no, that came out wrong, your most important accomplishment to date."

Somewhat flustered from her comments, I lost my train of thought but directed the next question directly at Thesus. "You have regained your belief ..... No," finish your story ... Did you get the transcript from .... take it to its logical conclusion.......

"Did you get the transcript from your ex-landlord's trial? Did you discover the connection between your him and your father? What is happening now; did you discover the reasons for your entanglements?"

"Yes, I did get the transcript from the trial; that was easy. He, my father, functioned as an assistant to the prosecuting attorney. I had no idea he had anything to do with the military courts. In fact, from my research, I've discovered I knew nothing about him at all. He was MIA. Anyway, he did research for the prosecution, interviewed the main witness and the enlisted person who was allegedly violated by my ex-landlord. He was present at the interrogations of the landlord himself.

"Andrea's father was charged and found guilty of sexual harassment and sexual misconduct unbecoming of military personnel........; justly or unjustly, I don't know.

"But that wasn't the main breakthrough; I eventually realized that my ex-landlord's records stopped two years after his dismissal from the Army. At first I didn't think much about it, but in re-examining both, my father's and mine, I saw neither of ours stopped. Pages existed of my father's activities after the Army.

"I again sought a way to break into the U.C.C. computer, but I was even further from it than before. This time I couldn't even get the preliminary access codes correct. Returning to my first lieutenant friend, I showed him the records and how they stopped at a certain date. "Why wouldn't they continue to track him?" I asked. He thought it was strange also. I asked if this run had been with security clearance 674; he showed me the code on the transcript.

"'What about running it on level four?' I was probing.

"'Level four?'

"'Yes, in the U.C.C. records.'

"'So you know about the fourth level, do you? Three weeks ago, I didn't know we had access to the Unified Central Control computer. I am just now learning about the fourth level. The first person I saw with a synchronized access computer was

General____ I've saw him use it. Then Colonel (his senior officer) got one. I have seen him use it a couple of times.'

"'Remember the man who came in and checked on someone before I did, and therefore you had the access codes available?' I was winging it, 'He was not my boss checking on me; he was competition. I've discovered that we both were given the same assignments, and the success of completing this assignment will undoubtedly determine ..... or help to determine my promotion. I would very much like to have a one-upmanship on him.'

"'Well, obviously we could go through channels and possibly get an authorization. We would need a document stating that you had Security Clearance 17, and you would undoubtedly have to present your credentials to my Colonel with an official authorization from a senior officer.'

"'One, I'm sure I can't get Security Clearance 17 because that's part of the promotion. Two, if I go to my commanding officer, he will know how I got the information. I guess this is a dead-end. I stood. I am just a peon in this ......person's army.' He looked up at me from his desk and smiled, but didn't say a thing. I positioned myself prepared to leave for an uncomfortable minute, ignoring his smile, and waited for him to break his hesitancy, then because he didn't say anything, I interjected, 'Well, my competition seems to have the key. I wonder how he got it?'"

"'If anyone even knew what I am thinking,' he finally muttered, 'I would be drummed from the corps.' In a louder voice, directed at me, 'maybe I can help you. The Colonel only works a four day week; this week he will work the fifth day ..... But how can I be sure you won't betray me?'

"'We're both in this together. I know I should not have the admittance; my ass is on the line also. If anything goes wrong, I don't need to reveal my sources. In fact, the way I'll do it, I'll create another way of discovering the same information, once I know what I am looking for.'

"'O.K. I'll trust you,' he said hesitantly, but in a split second, he smiled and with excitement said, 'Come back Friday, in the afternoon. This will be interesting; I'm going to learn something, and it may be a real challenge. I feel like I did in High School when I hacked into that department store. I had clothes delivered to the next door neighbor who I hated.'"

"On Friday at two o'clock, I entered his office. Without saying a thing, he smiled and led me down a hall into a restricted area. Outside of one room, he placed a latex looking glove on his right hand, inserted an ID card into a slot, then placed his covered hand on a screen. 'I knew that would work!' The door clicked open. The room was completely bare except for a computer terminal with one chair. He sat and placed what looked like a beeper into a rectangular slot designed for it. We were into the U.C.C. computer. I gave him my landlord's social security number, date of birth, then name. This time the computer displayed the request: 'Please state your code ID number and the level of personal disclosure.'

"'His ID code is easy, for the Colonel has it on

his remote control access-palmtop so he won't forget it, but what is this personal disclosure level?'

'''Insert his code very slowly, and let's think. Let's assume we have done it backwards, that you were expected to input your code first then the level of disclosure from the U.C.C. files. That first number must be for access, then the second would be what you are accessing. We want to go to level four, so punch-in four.'

'''Error' flashed onto the screen. 'Try fourth,' I quickly added. 'Working,' printed along the bottom. Great! Then in the middle of the screen flashed, 'Authority number.'

'''What the hell is this?' I responded. He looked up at me as if I had said a curse word. 'You need security clearance 17.'

'''I'll try 17!' 'Error,' my breathing quickened. He typed, 'SC17': 'Cleared for Entrance.'

'''Now try his social security number.' The screen just held the number

'''When the Colonel did it, the second number had dashes and slashes ...... what's his date of birth again?' : 'Working,' then my landlord's name was printed on the top left of the screen.

'''Where can we print?' I asked.

'''We can't. We can't even transfer to an authorized cell phone. It's designed so only authorized personnel with a certain palmtop can walk from here with info. You sit here and find out what you need.'

"After about five minutes and my continuous pressing 'Page Down,' he said, 'I'll be back in my office, watching.' I flipped through the first thirty

485

pages before I noticed the cursor was under the page number at the bottom, so I typed in 40. Bang, I had it. The last page of the old document and the first U.C.C.

"He was an agent. He worked for the Unified Central Control. I kept reading. He became an investigator and gained access to the computer, then a field supervisor. Then he became a director, in short an inputter, or I should say, he could input into people's records. His code name is Real Estate Agent (REA). I had seen that on my files and had wondered what it meant. His files were filled with code names and numbers, undoubtedly cases. After his code name were little blanked squares. I knew those must be his access codes. I put the cursor under the first box, and pressed Enter. The screen went blank, then printed, 'Please state your code ID number and the level of personal disclosure.' I looked down at the beeper-looking box and thought about it. To get that information, I probably needed a level 3 or even 2. Dadalus must be level 1. Top aids and such must be 2. Generals must be 3. Now what? Time to leave, but I can't leave it like this. I pressed 'escape' and 'enter' at the same time. Nothing. I looked for an off-on switch, nothing. I pressed the reset button, and the screen went blank. I stood, and began walking from the room. It took almost every ounce of self-control to not run from the room.

"In my hurry, I bumped into a uniformed officer facing down the hall. Panic struck. I froze until he turned around. 'That didn't take long,' the lieutenant casually commented, 'I decided to just stand and watch. What did you find?'

"'The person I was investigating turned out to be my boss, using a civilian code name. So it has all been a big game, but I've found the answer. I owe you more than a drink for this one.'

"He smiled then we both laughed. 'We did it!' he said laughingly. When we reached his office we again laughed like truant teenager boys. 'I can't thank you enough, and if any repercussions arise from this, let me know. I will confess that I did it on my own, solely, not a word about your involvement.'

"'As to the reason why I've seen the Colonel input is that he has fouled it up so terribly that he needed my help, so I don't anticipate any problems. If you ever get into a position, don't forget this "peon in this person's army."'

"I went home and again checked the print-outs that I had from previous connections. Before I entered the Park Service, I had been investigated by Real Estate Agent (REA). From then forward through my records were his initials and a four digit code number in parenthesis. I have more than good reason to believe that my landlord was an inputter in the sense he could change the records, but he had to leave his name and a code number when he did. The code number was undoubtedly a referral to a case. That revelation and all the "REAs" sort of punched me in the stomach, especially the ones after incidents which I knew weren't quite true. One time in particular, I noticed it right after the incident involving my scandal when I quit the Parks Department. Did he mastermind the scandal, the allocation of money and did he abscond with the funds? I also checked my father's records. Right before his retirement was an incident which involved reprimanding a junior officer and then REA. Had my father known of the record, much less the incident?

"The man has manipulated my life ...... for revenge?....... power? ...... perversion?........."

"Think of where you might have been if you married Andrea?" his sister laughingly inserted.

"This is not funny; he may have been the reason or cause of our father's death; but you are right, who knows where I'd be?"

"So what are you going to do about this information?" I asked.

"If fate is God directed, then I was chosen. My moving into the landlord's building was meant to be. This coincidence set in motion all my discoveries. None of us would have realized the evil underpinning of this government and country. So in some strange sense, this was justified, and there are more important matters than just this human injustice. Maybe on this same level of thought, a certain type of justice has been achieved .... but then again, all of this may have been coincidence."

Jumping to conclusions, I animatedly questioned, "If you come to believe that it is God's fate, does that mean that your fight is over; you are turning the other cheek? Do you feel your case is settled that revenge is not an option?

"You're free and making money, but what about the many others who are being oppressed and suppressed?"

I thought he would have an animate reaction,

but this was another case of him ignoring me. Did I say something stupid? In that split second, I knew I would publish this, if for nothing else but to kick him in the rear-end, keep him on his toes and force him around the track. Of course, he can meet this challenge.

After what seemed like ten minutes, his response in an almost distant voice was "I still have my life work set out for me, but I don't want to, nor am I going to fight burning windmills. My time is too valuable to chase those fires. There will be too many false alarms and/or too much will have been burnt by the time I get there. The main idea is to prevent fires from starting, to prevent the damage before it begins. When evil is disclosed, I will try to combat it the best way possible, but unless it is immediate, I am going to devote my time to my other goals. If it is a matter of walking challenged or standing still, I will pursue the fires, but that is not the case at the present time. Maybe more fires can be stopped by prevention than put out."

Rhetoric? I thought. It makes no difference; I have what I came for. But in all fairness, I presented another question: "What are some the main ideas, events, etc., have I omitted from the manuscript? What would you have discussed?"

"The only thing I can think of at the moment is the other means by which the system may have implemented control: One of the main topics in L.A. was the killing of celebrities who were the wrong images, especially rock-and-roll stars. I think part of the reason they died is that they represented the wrong ideas, standards, values. Yes, I can believe some of them were even killed for money: they represented a non-capitalistic, non-material or whatever ...... life styles, which certain people felt the youth would emulate. I don't believe all of the rock stars in the past decade died from overdoses of drugs, at least self-induced overdoses. It seems that if you sing the wrong tune about God, mother, country, or money ....

"And some of them were wiped out by big business, competing recording companies ...... not necessarily government. You should emphasize that once the government has set precedence for invasion of privacy, violations of human rights, destruction of individual citizens and the rest, U.S. corporations followed, then international businesses, world conglomerates, and now even small business owners. It's total chaos with the destruction because people with personal reasons are killing each other and are getting away with it."

"Other countries, interested in the destruction of the United States, or the reduction of our influence in the world, have used the chaos created by our own system against us."

"Don't you think," Margery interrupted, "some of them could have feigned death, in order to live a normal life again? Isn't that possible?"

"You mean celebrities, well, maybe," our hero said. "You know another one of Ike's concepts (obviously changing the subject) which I think would be good to bring up again and develop is his concept of the frontiers yet to be discovered and defined, which deal with the boundary between human-made ideas, concepts, and those which are already in the system: for example Laws of God, Laws of Nature, including laws of science, and Human Laws."

"His sculpture of Freedom?" I inquired. Thesus had found a one foot bronze sculpture of Justice that Jacoby wanted to enlarge. It was a big, beautiful woman, holding three documents in her right hand: one inscribed with "God's Laws," another, "Nature's Laws," and the last one with "Human's Laws." Her open left hand was extended from her waist with palm upward. "On one hand freedom and the other its limitations."

Thesus nodded yes, "But the frontier is not only in discovering the laws of science but in creating and controlling the human-made concepts. Our system can create, revise, or eliminate laws, the obvious concepts, but what our society doesn't realize is the subtle but real possibility to do the same with concepts which exist only because we have created them and yet are in the undertone of society; for example, a social concept like bigotry would cease to exist if we, as a species, didn't believe it existed." He looked at his sister and said, "Simplistic, for sure, but in a subtle but real way we are what we think and conceive, Jacoby's idea for sure, for if no human thought or conceived of certain ideas, they would not exist because they don't exist in nature, or if the people who conceived the ideas didn't express them, the ideas would not exist, or would only be short lived in the mind. On a day-to-day level, I am talking about anything from passing on dirty jokes to downright offensive, racial jokes; from the conceptual cluttering like advertisements to new slogans perpetrated by evil people in the form of propaganda; even to a concrete carried-out action such as the unwarranted killings. Someone had to conceive these; someone had to pass these ideas on; and in some cases someone has to act on them. We not only create our material environment but our mental as well, for sure a challenge to our law makers, intellectuals, artists, and all concerned creators.

"And in your case," he turned to me, "in your writing, there is a thin line between revealing the evil that exists, or possibly could, and by writing it, making it exist."

"Yes," Margery interjected, "I don't think your book is moral."

My face reddened, and for some reason I stood. Once up, I decided I needed a glass of water and went over to his hidden bar, saw the liquor and asked if anyone besides me wanted a drink.

"Let's both hope," Thesus continued, "that your writing is creating more good than evil," I looked at Margery; she nodded. "But getting back to Jacoby," Thesus continued, "if he would have just extended his line of thought to the point that we create more than just abstract ideas, meanings, and purposes, or that through dedication to some abstract concept or cause we can find God or for whatever he was seeking; but that through the commitments to each other as human beings, husband-wife, man-woman, relative to relative, friend to friend, citizen to country, human being to humanity, individual to earth, etc., we give our lives their meanings and purposes. And our commitments are as real and vital as we make them."

I handed the drink to Margery, who seemed a little surprised at its presentation, "Yes," she said, "We give our lives purpose and meaning through our commitments to each other. He didn't consider the effect of his death on us, his responsibilities to us."

Thesus, in his manner, didn't even bother looking at his sister before beginning again. "Even though I had a bout with conditioning, and am now, in some ways, freed of it, I can still see that we are formed by our environment and by each other, and we have responsibilities to each other because of it. Look at what each one of us has become because of our commitments to each other and our abstract realities."

"What?" I asked. He didn't even turn in my direction but continued.

"I was always aware of this, but it became a stark reality this week-end when I went up to the Sierras. Our trip to the ghost town introduced me and whetted my appetite, so I drove up near Yosemite one late Friday night and tossed my sleeping bag out without really knowing what was surrounding me. In the late morning when I awoke, I found myself under a large tree. Even though it is not Fall, the tree was bare because it was dead or dying. Its branches were contorted and deformed. As I continued to lie in my sleeping bag with my hands behind my head, I thought there was a certain type of beauty in those twisted and gnarled limbs against the blue sky above, but then I thought of 'a beauty' as perceived by whom, an impersonal human being unaware of the causes of the twists and deformity? Then I looked at the other trees around it. None were as big, some were the same species, and they all had leaves. I looked back above: it was not only deformed but a heavy wind would probably uproot it for the lower trunk showed decay.

I got up and looked around. Whatever had caused the tree to form as it had was gone. The tree had survived the vegetation and boulders which had surrounded it and made it what it is. At one time each twist of its branches was made that way by the need and want to touch the sun; each gnarled limb was forged by the instinct to survive under the existing environment. The want-to-live made it what it was. In a perfect world, that tree wouldn't have an upper trunk too heavy and limbs at angles of destruction." He laughed at his-own statement.

Margery interjected, "Wasn't it enough that you saw the beauty and its significance?"

"I see your point," I objected. "But is there beauty in viewing twisted minds and gnarled bodies of humans? What being is perceiving that as beauty?" I thought of adding "one of your gods?" but didn't because it would probably derail the conversation.

"Not quite," he responded. "Let me finish. Then I realized that this is not a perfect world and can't be. It is the conflicting forces which make it exist. We do what we have to do in order to survive, as that tree did with its distorted trunk and branches. We become who we can and must under the circumstances, and yes there is a beauty in that. Yes, there is a beauty in enduring… and maybe purpose. We were created to survive. While making breakfast that morning in the mountains, I could see that I have been too hard on myself and other human beings in that we cannot completely determine who we will become. We can only do the best under the circumstances in which we find ourselves; Fate and other people's wills do partly control.

"It is about obtaining our full potential within our natural......... and even societal restrictions. If God is judging us, it must be in this manner. Because in this respect we are all equal.

"We are all dealt a hand of cards ...."

"Bridge?" I inquired, smiling.

Without responding, he continued, "with which we must play. The hands are different to each one of us, but we must play them the best possible way. Ironically some of the best looking hands lead to the most disastrous results, and some of the worse hands, if played to their maximum get great results. Life is learning to use what we have been dealt."

"Yes," Margery added, "sometimes those aces, kings, and queens mean nothing. It may be a lowly jack or even a two of clubs that wins the hand. Also, let's not forget that different perspectives exist; that others view our hands not as we view them, and yet," she turned to me, "they may act on their perceptions. They may judge us and how well we do according to their standards, rules, and understanding."

"For me, a painful lesson," our hero said, "but it is how we respond to adversity, to the conflicting forces;..... do we let them defeat us? It is our attitudes about ourselves, our circumstances, and about life. I still believe, we create our heaven and hell.

"You know your statement about me being 'less

quick' and having a 'fading intelligence,' it may be that I did, indeed, lose that battle in my apartment, and with permanent damage. But is it better for me to sit around and bereave my loss or to understand that I value a different type of intelligence which I am developing. On one level, I am getting hooked up with myself, in as many aspects as I can, thereby seeing a more complex world and taking a longer time to make decisions. Maybe I am using different aspects of my being to compensate. And on another level, both of us know that intelligence isn't completely what the IQ tests measure. But what is it really? An ability to cope? An ability to adapt? An ability to solve problems, that's the official word, but what types of problems: the problems which keep us from ourselves, from our own happinesses, from life, from knowledge, from truth? I feel these are all part of our 'full potential,' and if my full potential has been reduced because of battles ....well, that's not my fault, and I won't judge myself against what could have been, plus I will not let your concept slow or stop me.

"No, you go right ahead and publish your manuscript, and finish the one on Jacoby. They're important, and particularly to you ...... I believe Margery and I will cope, adjust, and thrive." He smiled at me.

I glanced at Margery. She was shaking her head as if to say, I don't know, but when she saw me peering at her, she stopped and smiled. "We've come too far to have you trap us, or should I say to let your book and conceptions of us trap us. Go on, we'll be fine." I know she meant all three of us, and I smiled.

Part II

Chapter 1

As you can see by the few number of pages left, the story is coming to an end. Both Margery and Thesus think that I should include something about myself. I talked to the publisher, and he thought it was a good idea also. Margery said it as a challenge: to see if my "honesty" would persist. Thesus suggested it because he said he saw a common plight among us four, and he thinks my writing has not demonstrated it clearly, so far. His passing mention is interpreted by me as my frustration of not being able to accomplish what I have wanted in life; that I was trained to teach, I enjoy it, but my teaching career only lasted a couple of years. And now my final frustration: my destiny is foreclosing. Before I expound on both of those, first I would like to record something that I should have at the time it happened. It was a dream I had right after Jacoby's movie was released. I didn't think it was important at the time, but after it has "stayed" with me and after an interpretation, I've decided it fits and foretold the future. It relates to the dream I communicated in the preface.

This time though, I was in a castle. I was not in armor, but many others were. They appeared as if they were of the same clan, or at least on the same side, because soon another group of armored men crashed into the chamber. A big fight ensued. Even though I was present, I knew it was not my battle. I was not a knight, as I wasn't in the other dream. Afraid that I would die by being in the middle of the fight, I pounded on a large wooden door. It opened, and I entered. A man in a peasant outfit said welcome as if I was joining a group or organization. He led me down the stairs into the basement under the castle. It was not apparent what was happening until I wandered among the people. Many, many individuals were working at different tables or on different projects. My guide mentioned there were over 30,000 of us. 'Everyone seemed to be working in productive harmony. It was quiet and peaceful, and my thoughts flashed to what must be happening above in the castle. I don't know the purposes or goals of these workers, but in the quietude was commitment and fortitude. One could feel the amount of energy being directed.

My interpretation of the dream: I was accepted into the underground, that the people in power were fighting among themselves, and that it was not my place, nor my fight. Maybe it was the same people as in my other dream who were at that time united. And now while writing this I have contemplated even a further interpretation: In the first dream, the knights joined because the masses were out of control. When the masses were subdued, the knights began to fight among themselves for power.

This makes sense when you consider what is happening in this country. Dadalus, who attempted to change the law so he could run for a third-term, failed. So at present, he doesn't feel obligated to reciprocate to those who placed him into power. In fact, he seems to be downright recalcitrant. He in the past and now is stepping on too many toes, and it is these people who are trying to tear him from his pedestal. For instance, he has reversed the inflation in the U.S., none exists, but on the international scene, the dollar has fallen to less than half of its last year's value. Here it is again, I really don't fully understand it, but the "two tier" dollar has little worth in the inter-national market. The dollar in this country is unaffected or even in a deflationary cycle because the number of exports is increasing. He is also trying to reduce the national debt by decree. He is about to sign a bill that will devalue Treasury Bonds and Treasury Bills. He is striking back at those who have become rich by the demise of this country, at those who had found a haven to gain wealth because interest rates sky rocketed to pay for the debt.

He is hurting the international cartels because when they reduced the power of this country, they stripped the power of the President in international politics. He in turn almost single handedly pushed through import duty bills. Yes, these must be the knights in my dreams. Symbolically, no, on an abstract level, they are trying to destroy each other.

It was these groups who were justly afraid of the President's present power and his gaining more power and so they stopped his third term. A movement has started to impeach him. Investigations have begun and so have proceedings. I am not a historian, but this happened before.

I doubt his opponents' success because Dadalus has too much power. I can't say what is happening on the national or international level but on the common citizen's level, I'm afraid more people will disappear. One of the main forces protecting his opposition is the press and the notoriety it creates for these missing people. The press saved a woman who was deeply involved in the power struggle. The two reporters assigned to write her story found her in a hospital in Denver. The newspaper article described saving her "in the nick of time." She was in a drugged stupor, had been given a different name, the name of a woman decreed legally insane, and was about to undergo a lobotomy.

Of course, my interpretation of my dreams may be wrong and undoubtedly the reader will give them different meanings. Both dreams were recorded in complete honesty and at the time of publication will have an historical presence. It's strange that something can be made more real by writing than the actual happening. Both dreams were but two dreams from two different nights. Both were a fleeting moment, but now by recording them, they became more permanent. They have become a reoccurring event in my life, every time I rework or reread this section. They are more than dreams now.

Maybe Ike's fanatical involvement with his art and ideas can be understood because of the same type of phenomenon. Many different ideas flash through our minds which only have a small effect on us. But by recording a selected number, we make those more predominate in our lives. Usually the washing tides of the day's events tear away yesterday's thoughts and dreams. But if we went home each night and reread the thoughts, we would be creating a reoccurring event, which is not necessarily wrong because it can be a type of progress: taking up from where we left off the day before. But Jacoby's mind closed upon his thoughts, dwelling excessively until these "passing thoughts" were his life, his reality. He read and reread everything he wrote. His mind was grooved by the repetition, and he was caught in the groove, unable to see anything else. His mind was closed; his life was closed, and he could only follow the path, the only one he knew, the one that he had created, to its end.

Maybe Ike's negative example is what kept our hero from wanting to define himself by defining his beliefs. But the difference is that our hero will not dwell on what he has expressed. He knows he has only clarified them for the moment, and they will change as he changes.

To get to my story: The preface and first chapter were devoted to why I was writing the book, and this chapter will be devoted to how it became possible for me to write it. This is not to say that the book would not have been written if the following hadn't transpired, but that it would have been more difficult to write because of time limitations, and the quality (what there is of it) would have been different.

The main reason I have had the time to write this is, especially at the beginning, is that I have not been able to secure decent employment. To me the full story can't just be government cut backs to education. When I was laid-off in New Orleans, the administration didn't give any reasons except allegedly the budget was reduced and enrollment had dropped. Maybe it was completely true, but when I've applied for different positions teaching, and even some outside the Bay Area, I have had no personal replies at all, no interviews, no statements that I am on a waiting list, nothing but, at the most, a form rejection letter. Times arose when I wanted to leave this area, mainly because of Margery, for she was the main reason for me being here in the first place. After that incident through the window, I began to apply outside of the state. Right before Jacoby's death, when I had it in my head that she would probably return to him, I began to apply, just in case, but as I've written, nothing came from any of it. I have driven up and down the California coast two hundred-and-fifty to three hundred miles applying at every four year college and even at all community colleges. On first appearance the reception was positive but later, nothing.

For years I believed that no jobs existed. Because among the decreased birth rate in the past twenty years (I don't know if this is due to the economy, not having enough money for kids, or government policy, or just a populace movement.) and the governmental intentional cut-backs in education to keep the rabble out, as I have mentioned, fewer and fewer persons are going to college, and no teaching jobs exist. For a while I believed professors are being hired, but only the ones selected, screened, and preaching the gospel according to powers that be. This is undoubtedly true, my conclusion, because I know for a fact people do die; professors are people; therefore, professors die. I ain't ignorant.

Most probably, all of the above is true. The statistics are verifiable. So the government is not only helping perpetrate the impossible situation, but it is destroying itself in the process by not educating its people correctly. Education should be one of the last cut-backs that a democracy should instigate.

I see Dadalus' and others' train of thought: by keeping the masses ignorant, working like ants, they will create a prosperous society. But the government doesn't see its loss of potential. By not fully educating only one person in the best manner possible, that person could become a liability to this country and, for sure, not a complete asset. We still have elections in this country; we still vote on issues, and it is very critical to educate all voters so they can not only make the best decisions for themselves but so they will know sham from ham. (Even if you swallow sham, it ain't gonna do you no good.) An idea repeated by our hero.

When I once mentioned all of this to Thesus at dinner, he thought about it from the beginning of a meal to its end, and while we were cleaning dishes, he proposed: "From what I know of your situation and the educational system in the United States, the Federal Government should give all school districts in the country, from elementary through college, a subsidy of one-third the salary of a full time teacher, for every additional instructors they add to their staff, providing the school district does not have a class larger than fifteen students. The state could provide another one-third of the salary and the school district another.

"The number of teachers in this country would double, and education would not only get better because each student would have more personal attention but education would become more diverse." Then he added, "Maybe no student would be allowed to have the same teacher more than one semester.

"Teachers' morale will grow, and workloads would lessen. They would better know their students' needs and customize their courses.

"The Federal Government and states would get most, if not all, of their money back in the form of taxes."

"Yes, of course, I haven't paid taxes since New Orleans."

"With a quarter million more full time teachers working in this society, think of the effects on the economy!"

"I would have bought a house, a car; computers, software, TVs, appliances, etc. Think of the city, state, federal taxes on those. No, it would probably be an economic plus, not a subsidy loss.

"Ike could have obtained a job teaching art. That thought makes me smile. He could have been a strange one."

"I will have to put the idea into the wind, mention it to different people and see if I can get some feedback and get it generating."

All I said was, "Do it. It is too late for me, but get it done."

Choices demonstrate our freedom; to know the choices is knowledge, and to know how to choose is wisdom. And again, I see their reasoning, if our schools either indoctrinate or leave ignorant our youth, then the politicians running this country can persuade, convince, convert, or just plain mesmerize with sophisticated rhetoric, media, or technology.

More and more actors and actresses are running and obtaining office, to me a scary trend. Dadalus is the worse. He sings and dances, and people believe him. He shows and tells his lies to the people, and they believe him. Academic journals and documents disprove Dadalus, but nobody reads. And I swear he has a whole department monitoring the Internet and reacting to anything which mentions him or his government. His popularity ratings are high; but more importantly his Internet and TV ratings are high, and people trust what they hear and see.

But now I personally believe that something happened in New Orleans of which I can't see the full implications. It must have been something I said to some other professor or something in class. Maybe it is my general philosophy of teaching or even life, but I know, sure-as-hell, I am on the wrong list somewhere.

This fear of being on someone's list is a very common symptom of the sick society in which we live. How many people in this country think they are on the wrong list to get this job or that job, and don't even apply because they don't want the attention? After the rumors and the disappearances, who would want to take a chance and apply for a government job or a government subsidized job in case they are accidentally on the wrong list? Only the young and/or naive. How many are on a list because the card in the

U.C.C has been punched in the wrong place, either accidentally or, as in our hero's case, intentionally? No, the smart people who don't know their records are staying out of interviews. And who can get hold of their records? What a waste of human beings. Many qualified persons in this country have no say, no influence, no money, and no way of procuring any of the above.

Ideas aren't being communicated because of fear. No one knows who's an agent, as in the case of Thesus' ex-landlord. Ideas aren't being communicated because of the feeling of impotence. The ideas will either be stolen or have no effect because individuals have no power to initiate ideas. Competent people are taking lesser jobs from a fear of being in a position of envy, of playing with the powerful and rich and not having enough of either to protect themselves. (Shades of my dreams.) People like our hero are afraid of banding together to gain power and have influence because of fear of infiltration or jealous informants reporting them.

Because of this fear, this country is in a real, downhill spiral. On one hand, groups of people are still interested in maintaining the status quo because they are gaining money or power. They have too much to lose by venturing. On the other hand, too few people are living the way they should. For this latter group, it is existence, survival, not living but just getting by. With such a stale-mate between power and people in this country, no progress is being accomplished. Neither the country nor the people have money. And maybe it will take the complete financial breakdown of the system in order to recover. The collapse is a personal prediction of mine as our hero's optimism is a personally created state of mind. I know I won't see the collapse, if it happens. It is not that close, but unless trust, honesty, and promotion on merit are again firmly established, it will happen. Humanness must be re-introduced into the system, human qualities which promote trust so that each being can be more adventurous to follow his or her own dreams and drives. Yes, it is the fear that a government, other people, or some nonhuman element will reach out, grab hold, take away, and destroy. These keep this country crippled.

As a consequence, how many people in this country are involved in something other than their chosen professions because of the state of this country? This is the reason I began this book: I had time. I began it with the idea that it would keep my mind active and productive. When my subjects were more thoroughly investigated, I realized it was a story which needed to be told. When I perceived the bag of worms which I was uncovering, I thought, well I will write it as a secret diary, give it to my chosen heirs and let them decide what to do with it. But life does not always evolve as we either conceive or wish. And as mentioned, I am expected to live only a couple more months; at least this is what the doctors have decreed, and the possibility of this truth has extinguished my fears. Also the publishing of it and seeing it in print are driving forces now. My life is short enough to believe that it has been in vain with nothing but unfulfilled goals and frustrations. I am pushing to get it published while I am still alive because without it, my life has been a wasted postage stamp.

I think I have mentioned, I am the last of my line: no known relatives. My sperm is in the bank. Margery and I are planning marriage, and she wants children. She wants to have my child, which makes me extremely happy. We have made attempts with questionable results. And as long as I am alive, we don't feel the need for her to go to the bank. When I died, I've left her two banking accounts, free of any obligations or responsibilities. If I had many more relatives, I personally don't think I would want children in this manner and under these circumstances because I won't be present to raise them. I question bringing them into this world, and into this world without a father ....Well, ... But then again, Margery will be the mother. She wants it.

Maybe the reader is thinking I am too dramatic and that since cures have been perfected and daily breakthroughs are occurring, hope should be perpetuated. I have researched the statistics. In the past ten years, everyone ...... or at least over 90 percent have not lived, more than four years with all available treatment.

Ten years is a very long time for the field of medicine. In the past five years, forty to fifty percent of the people with the whole gamut of treatments are still alive. These last two statements were repeated by various doctors. Do I want to suffer their treatments to continue my life for four years, at the maximum?

No. If I went into the treatment and let the

doctors mess around with me, I may not finish the book, something that is more important to me now than living a couple more years. I don't trust doctors or the field of medicine, not only because medicine is still in a primitive stage, but because I don't want to end up in a Denver hospital as a vegetable. In the worst cases, too many people have died unjustly in the past years, or have been kept alive maimed beyond repair, or have been committed to mental institutions and on being released, never heard of again. I'm sure I am not on that type of list, so I am not really fearing that. But then again, I don't know. The reasons for not getting a teaching job. My associations with our hero and Ike. Who knows!

I know that once in a hospital, control and self-determination are lost. I am sure it will be for the "right reasons," in the name of science, humanity or the Hippocratic Oath. But I don't want to be a human guinea pig; especially if they use my money to do it, and they will. So in the best case, I am sure from stupidity or for money or fame, some doctor has eliminated my chances of me maintaining control over the way I want to die. And I've removed the possibility of survival.

I have enough money from inheritance that they would and could keep me alive legally for a very long time. It's not that I need the money, nor that anyone I know needs it; I just don't want to give it to the hospitals and doctors. Let them rob other people for the sake of the sciences, medicine, research, their Hippocratic oath, or whatever else they are rationalizing what they are doing to human beings.

Not me! I am not going to get trapped, unable to control what is happening and what will happen to me once they start to feed me their drugs. No, for the pain I am just getting a prescription of something I know, and I am going to let it happen.

Life - death, what do they really mean? It is going to happen; and I would rather die as I was meant to die, at the time it is designed to happen. I hope I die naturally. I have never been a religious person, but I think medicine should allow us to come and go from this world as naturally as possible, or at least as we want, and I, at the moment, want it to be naturally. What if Thesus is right, and something like reincarnation really exists, then prolonging our lives unnaturally could miscarriage the natural sequence of events.

If some type of afterlife with consciousness exists and we release into it, our vision may become blurred by dying with drugs and/or machines. We may not know where we are, or where we're going, or how to get there. Maybe I am an old fashion reactionary, at least about medicine, but I ain't gonna let them touch me, if I can help it. I suppose if fewer doctors had other interests besides their patients' well beings, the problem would lessen, but things as they stand are now horrendous.

This chapter has become a too lengthy gripe session, too freely expressed. Of course, it is about me, as I said it would, because if for no other reason, it expresses where I am mentally, but it is still a gripe session, nonetheless. So The End. Onward.

Chapter 2

This book is ending - my life is ending. This morning, I gazed into the mirror: I appear old and fading. Without this writing and my friendship with Margery and Thesus, my life and impending death would be meaningless. It seems to me that everything would come to nothing. Without these, I would have lived a life without purpose, and my death would pass without significance or even observance.

A part of friendships truly is what everyone says it is: seeing and accepting the faults of our friends but still loving them; knowing them for who they are but still accepting them. Just think back at how much trouble each one of us has given the others; I mean, it wasn't two weeks ago that Margery and Thesus read the manuscript and were furious because too much was disclosed about them. Both of them know how much this writing means to me. They have forgiven me. It didn't put an end to our relationships.

I called them after our meeting and told them if they wanted me to, I would bury the manuscript as one of Thesus' plastic books or give it to one of them (my chosen heirs) so they could see that it wouldn't be published until it means nothing to all three of us. I would break the contract with the publisher. All three of us know it is going to make matters more difficult for both of them, but they said they are willing to accommodate with the difficulties for me. I almost cried when Margery reiterated Thesus' sentiment. They know that I really want to see my effect in this country before I die, and, for me, they are willing to sacrifice. They know I want to see my one and only achievement, my one and only contribution on the stands and people reading it.

"But couldn't I change some of the scenes?" Margery added.

"I examined your comments and did work on some of them."

"Thank you."

In spite of the difficulties we have presented in each other's lives, we have given love, a certain amount of understanding, and the main thing, we have cared about each other, and we still care. No, I am not a religious person, but I do believe in what we four have shared and have given each other. This means more than my book and my feelings of accomplishment. If I could accept Ike's concept of positive suicide, it would be to our friendship which I would lay down my life. An easy thing for me to say, huh?

Thesus has said that it is our commitments to each other which give our lives meaning. We make our relationships mean something or nothing. Margaret was right. We decide how much we are willing to sacrifice in order to promote these relationships. We make our marriage contracts mean something or nothing. We either commit ourselves and our lives to each other, or we decide we are more important than other people.

I feel that in this fluctuating world (even if our existences have no reasons), we create a little substance through our commitments to each other. We live for each other and thereby create meaning and purpose. We find each other and ourselves through our relationships, and sometimes we are called forth to die for each other.

It is so important to associate with people with whom you can be yourself; that you can express yourself fully without fear of being ignored, rejected, or attacked. They listen to you, believe you because they care. Without this unlimited expression, how could we possibly know our true self; for we would never express this self, then hear and see a reaction to it. We would never see and attempt to understand others' reactions to the expression of our beings, nor even see our own reaction to who we really are. Our deep beings would never manifest, never become objectified, but only exist as a hazy potential, an unfulfilled will waiting and wanting completion.

Where else would we be able to even try to fulfill our complete potentials? Where else would we dare try; where would we be secure enough to open our beings and let the vulnerable inner self be exposed? This is another argument against lying. Our friends' acceptance of us lets us fully be ourselves so we can know each other's inner beings, and because of that we will know each other in the future. Yes, I believe, true friends may be separated for years but yet know each other upon return, and their relationship will resume exactly where they left off. The intensity, the trust, the level of communication the feelings for each other, all will return with little or no effort. Whereas facades and superficialities wear thin with time; the true self changes little. My stay in New Orleans proved this to me. The return of Adrian was proof. No matter how much time had passed since our last communications, we still had the knowledge that this communication was possible because we had been honest in our expressions and in our search for the truth within.

This process is also a reinforcing cycle. We gain confidence and security knowing ourselves and each other. When the chord of communication is sounded again and again, even though the people involved seemed to have changed, we hear the sound of truth from each other, and we go forth with trust and belief. Thesus is right: this created reality may supersede the natural one because we construct it and make it real.

Through my relationship with Thesus and his sister, I have come to realize all this and so much more. I would do anything for them, and I only wish I could think of something worthwhile. I have even thought that I would just disappear when the time comes. I could jump into the ocean at high tide, so my body will be swept out to sea (to see what? Jacob's influence for sure). Seriously, it would save a great deal of trouble, sorrow, and expense. It sounds natural enough; in fact more natural than incarceration in a metal casket. I am quite positive that Ike wanted to be washed out to sea. It makes sense. Think of the millions upon millions of bodies entombed or cremated and are no longer returned to nature. It is like our last effort to deplete nature, by not returning what we borrowed.

Then again, maybe I'll ask them to commit my body to the sea because of the uncertainty that my disappearance would cause.

My impending death is affecting Margery the worst of us all: First her father, Jacoby, himself, now me. To quote Ike Jacoby,

The grim reaper reaps in packs
And leaves an anguished heart collapsed.

I was meeting her downtown for lunch two days ago and was late as usual. She was standing on the street corner. As I approached, her facial features were so pronounced from a distance that, for a moment, she looked like a caricature of herself. At a closer view, I could see deep thought and sorrow had taken her from herself. I felt great empathy for her and her thoughts. I hesitated and waited for the mood or thoughts to subside which they did when a passer-by jostled her. For a moment she was slightly shocked and embarrassed by her removed state. She quickly scanned her surroundings, saw me, and approached. Our eyes met. Immediately our bodies expressed the sorrow. It was in our eyes. We both observed and knew. It's hard, hard on both of us.

She is slowing her activity level and her work schedule. We are together almost every night now, and this alone is exhausting her. She isn't quitting work, however, and won't until she gets pregnant. She doesn't want to quit altogether and neither do I because it keeps her occupied, both physically and mentally. But in spite of her slowing pace, she looks more harried than usual.

I have begun to lose weight, and only this writing and wandering around when I am not writing keeps me from thinking too much. As of now, we have decided to hire a nurse when I am no longer mobile, so some of the strain on Margery will lessen. Dwelling on this subject is not helping my disposition, and will not help, so I am ceasing.

Margery in the last six months has made a killing on an over-the-counter stock. Her brother gave her a tip. After investigations, she bought several thousand dollars' worth. She bought again when the news was confirmed that the company had found a better way to manufacture its products. Both she and her brother agreed that the public did not understand the full implications of the invention. Actually that may have been true: it was undoubtedly the media which didn't understand the implications, for it wasn't publicized as it should. When projected facts and figures were released, the stock went crazy. Margery has been playing the market for years and considers herself an expert, so when she sold half her holdings at what she considered the peak and the stock still rose, she became angry. She had determined this peak by her calculated price-per-earnings share ratio with her calculations of the company's projected earnings over the next two years, plus what she calls 'the speculation' factor. Two days later, when the stock was still moving, she sold the remainder but the stock jumped again, so then she started selling short. It "spiked" another two and half dollars. She bought more shorts. Then within two weeks it fell fifteen dollars. When it was within five dollars of its original price, she took all of her profits and rebought. She hasn't mentioned the exact figures, but her profit must be in the tens of thousands. She had shared every step with me, and the night of her repurchase she took me to a fancy restaurant in an alleyway off the park from where Thesus and I sat that night seemingly so very long ago.

At dinner, our discussions were great, exciting. For those two weeks, we were engrossed in something other than ourselves. Her main problem now is having too much time. To anyone else she would appear busy, but she can feel the time. "Go back into dance," I've said. She kissed my forehead, "Our dance of love is enough for right now."

She is spending more time with her brother in his office. Because of that, them not needing to see each other, we three aren't together much in the evenings. It is mainly Margery and I. We attend a great many concerts, movies, plays, etc. Almost every night we eat dinner at different cuisines, and San Francisco is the place to do it. We are spending money, mainly my money. Twice in the past two months we have flown to Hawaii and stayed in the most expensive hotels we could find. I am paying all the bills, and she invests everything she makes. Even though we are planning marriage to sanctify our relationship and are working at the prospect of children, if neither happens, by me spending my money, fewer taxes will need be paid on inheritance. It is a strange type of logic, but both of us are happy with it. She is still achieving her goal of accumulating wealth, and I, who never had much money, am enjoying spending it. It is my treat to her and myself, (actually me).

An irony – and I have heard this from various people - as we get older, and in my case, need less money, it begins to roll in.

A strange phenomenon is that we are growing more distant emotionally. Of course, it is my fault as well as hers. I don't want pity. I don't want what we saw and felt the other day on the street corner. I don't want a constant reminder of fate foreclosing on my dwelling place. And then again, I can see her reason for it. It will save much of the pain when the end comes. I am sure it is not conscious on her part but an unconscious defense mechanism.

The strangest part is my evolving feelings. It is weird. I want more, …. more what? More life? More something, more than she can give, more than maybe anyone can give. Maybe I am seeking the idealistic love of my youth, the love I never experienced. I am torn between desire and fear. I lust...... no, that's the wrong word. I desire a deepness of passion, of intensity, of involvement ... yet to be fulfilled. I want a love that will put all previous loves to rest, a fulfillment that will end the wanting, the hungering, the searching; a love that will put an end to all the false memories of love, and yet it must be a mysterious love, which I will never fully grasp but pursue ..... endlessly.

Maybe it isn't a person I seek but life itself. Maybe it is a love for living, a love of God, the love of something beyond myself and this world. I don't know. Maybe it isn't even a love of something outside of me but the desire to search within my being, to find, to hold, if only for a brief moment. Maybe to find an essence, the permanence, if there is any, inside me and to hold that tightly.

Maybe, it is this ability to search which may be taken away, to search for more, more than I have, more than I am, and if I found that something beyond, wouldn't all-time seem brief, in comparison. But yet, the ten minutes of experiencing would be long enough to fulfill my life;

But now, there are times when my desire is out of control, and times when I battle it down with my fears that I may end with nothing; that by searching I may lose what I have; that no such love for anything or anybody exists, that all my searches will reveal nothing, that time will freeze and catch me before I find this lover or find it doesn't exist. Yes, I have a fear of being Don Quixote, in search of idealisms which don't nor may never exist. But no, not Don Quixote, for he never questioned his folly; he never faltered with doubt. In just doubting as I am now, I falter. Am I too wise to be foolish and too foolish to be wise; caught between desire and fear? And only a short time is left.

I appreciate, respect, admire, trust Margery and love, yes love her, and am afraid of losing her, but this want burns inside. She feels an obligation to me as a friend, a lover, and the mother of our possible children but where is that fulfilling lover?

As you know that besides my relationship in New Orleans, I have never wanted or sought another person. Has she changed so much? Have I changed so much? Where is what I sought in her? Where is Margaret and the completion of my dream? I should be happy. Why am I not? A fear of experiencing loss?

Maybe it is because she is still working and involved in things other than us. But I have a feeling that it is I, not she. She is she, and I should accept and love her as she is, but how can I when I am driven as I am? Besides this writing and spending evenings with her, I am out daily looking ,... searching ... for what? A person? An involvement? A belief? Something? ,... to love? ... no, not just love but to be in love, to be consumed by it, to be so engrossed to be unable to see the light of day nor the darkness of night.

But I guess I should know and accept that .... this world and my life may not give forth the love that I seek. I should quit lusting, ... there's that word again.... after something that may not exist and more fully appreciate that which does. I should seek to die in peace, not with desire in my soul ......

I'll be dammed if I do. I pray that I die with such desires in my soul that they bring me back, that whatever rages inside me will not rest but will seek completion even in death, that this desire is a light which burns in the darkness, that it will awaken me; I will follow it; or that remembering it, I will cling to its remains, letting it wrench me from my sleep.

This desire may be my means of completion. Yes, I should be happy that I can feel such a desire, the intensity of which could drag me from what must be a peaceful sleep, a dreamless sleep.

I pray that it does, that reincarnation is caused by desire. And with this wish, now I can hopefully control my drive and focus on more immediate goals. Margery needs me; my work needs completion, and what will happen will happen.......

Maybe it will build to the point where it explodes me through death's door and into another room .... of consciousness, of awareness, of life.

Chapter 3

It's my fault. He warned me, and himself, but it still happened. Thesus is dead. He was shot at Land's End yesterday by an unknown assailant. Margery and I are preparing to leave the country.

We didn't know whether to report it to the police or not, but decided it was for the best if we did. They are searching for the body, but I am sure they won't find it. He fell into the ocean. Some person was in the shrubbery and shot down at him, and the hit blew him off the cliff. There was only one shot. There only needed to be one shot. Hell. The shot wasn't loud. It sounded like a cracking branch, and neither Margery nor I realized what was happening until he fell into the turbulent ocean.

We were at Land's End because of another of his projects. It is a beautiful wild area on the northwest corner of the San Francisco peninsular. To my knowledge, it is government property belonging to the Golden Gate National Park. He realized the tract was unsafe, and yet was being used. The main problem with the area, and why it wasn't being improved, was that the land is sliding into the ocean. Our hero comprehended the possibility that the Veteran's

Hospital near the area would eventually slide into the ocean, and he figured a way to save both the area and the hospital. His idea was to pound two to three hundred foot "I" beams into the ground to prevent the land from sliding any further, and to construct paths, definite and well defined paths, so people could walk or ride a bicycle through the area without either endangering their lives or destroying the wild life refuge. He had started working on the problem when he was in the Park Service but couldn't think of a solution and forgot about it. Just recently he had wandered over there again on one of his long walks pass the museum and remembered the problem. Within three days he had plans drawn and was meeting people to fulfill them. He felt that it was one of his contributions, "positively paying recompense" to the city of San Francisco and the country. He was supposed to meet a specialist and discuss the feasibility of the final part of the project, the "I" beams.

It was Wednesday, and we three had taken a picnic. With knapsacks, we parked at the VA Hospital and ventured down onto a flat area which protruded into the ocean. Thesus had carefully walked to the edge of the cliff to get a better look at some seals swimming and honking below us. He was discussing the possibility of erecting a railing on the bluff when all of a sudden, the crack resounded. It sounded like the snapping of a small dry board. I glanced up the hill into a spread of low trees to find the origin of the noise. I didn't see anything and returned to the seals in time to see Thesus splash into a wave. My first response was to jump in after him, but I saw the hopelessness of that. It was hundreds of feet down with huge swells. Instead, I scrambled up the hill after the person who had fired the shot. Undoubtedly because of my hesitation, I never did see him or her.

On the move up the through the underbrush, I peered backwards and for a moment saw Margery, standing staring over into the rolling sea. It seems as if nobody else saw the havoc. People were visiting the area, but when I confronted them, they were surprised by my hysteria. Later back in the car, Margery confirmed my assumption. Only two of us saw it happen; I'll bet Thesus didn't know what hit him. One-half an hour passed before Margery and I found each other. It was back at the car. She was sobbing, asking what could we do, what could be done? I just sat in driver's seat in total shock. Too much time had passed. Even if the bullet hadn't killed him, the crashing waves against cliff-lined shore would have. In spite of how I felt, I told her to just wait; he may still be OK.

I started the car, but felt I couldn't drive for about fifteen minutes. I was very confused. While we sat there Margery assured me that reporting this to the police was for the best. We agreed it should be reported under his second name, because of a greater chance for immediate action. But what the hell, almost one hour had lapsed since the incident. Another half an hour had gone before the police, and I was back on the scene.

Margery stayed in the car while I walked the

shoreline, in case he was just wounded and swam one way or the other. It was more than a hundred yards in either direction before he could have found a place to crawl onto land.

We are now expecting, waiting for what ..... a miracle, a phone call, him walking through the door, anything.

*   *   *

By the time this is published, hopefully Margery and I will be out of the country. It is mostly for her that we are leaving. She doesn't want to raise a child here where either she or our child's life could be endangered. I really don't care where I die. But she thinks it might be possible to find a doctor we can trust. I don't believe I can be cured, but we can look. The thought of a false prognosis to get me into a hospital has occurred to me. To me, a better idea for her and our child would be to stay and change her name, turn all her assets into liquidity and end all of her dealings. She could just drop from sight. But she feels we all are in an immediate danger, so she is selling all she can't handle from another country. She is exploring all of the countries with the best medical facilities for cancer treatments.

The reader must understand that if this writing ends abruptly, we are on our way. I will, of course, take a copy with me, but what I hand to the publisher will be as far as I am going to take it.

I don't think we will ever know who shot him, whether it was an individual, a person representing the government or some other organization, or a person "inspired by God." I told Thesus; I warned him. What I am talking about! I am probably as responsible as the person who pulled the trigger. My only saving grace: the book hasn't been published, yet. If it were an act of revenge, the person researching Thesus could have discovered his appointment. The person who shot him was probably only a pawn in someone else's hands and did the killing for money, the country, the government, god or something. Or who knows, maybe he alone hated our hero and did it for himself. Another possibility, it could have been a random shooting: some weirdo out for target practice, getting kicks by killing. It is not unheard of, for sure.

It is, however, an impossible situation. I am sure if the investigation gets into any depth, it will come to the conclusion that no such person, Thesus, existed, and therefore no killing. Only Margery and I will know and, of course the person or persons responsible; so undoubtedly Margery is right: it is definitely time for us to disappear. With our money, I am sure it won't be too difficult. The identification forging industry is creating great works.

Damn it. It was such a beautiful day. Everything seemed fine. Thesus had called us while we were preparing breakfast, or I should say brunch. He was going to Land's End early to further conceptualize some of his ideas and then meet his appointment. He asked if we would like to join him. Margery proposed the picnic.

Thirty minutes later he arrived filled with energy and enthusiasm. One of reasons I assumed he was happy because when we discussed the intrinsic qualities of honorability and worth, he was very up-beat.

I reiterated Margery's and generally our previous views of the qualities of uniqueness and the potentiality therein derived. But Margery now stated that she disagreed with her previous view. This conversation, to me, has more relevance now than when she spoke it. It was almost a precursor. She believes that each human can be a god, but a god like Abaraxis, capable of good and evil as part of their natural beings. "Each individual has so much power. Each one of us can move faster and farther, not only than ever before but faster and farther than any other species on this planet. We can communicate at a greater distance and have a greater effect. In fact when I think about it, all of our senses can be magnified. Many of our abilities have been extended, strengthened, and because of this, our effects have a greater influence than ever before.

"But this gain in power which extends our senses, our abilities, and our beings has come so quickly that it has been out of control at times. Some individuals, I feel, have gone berserk. Some feel their powers in perverted ways. Some have exerted their wills over each other and other species in evil ways."

"Just to prove they can have an effect, an importance? That they too have power? That they are someone?" I inserted

"Yes, I believe people are capable of evil, with intention," Thesus said, "but I also believe all persons are capable of controlling the evil aspects of their beings. We can make a conscious choice to overcome the evil, even that which we are taught, if we see within ourselves.

"It was less than a year ago, I hated so much that if could, I would have dropped a bomb on San Francisco to rid the earth of some of its vermin.'"

"But you didn't strike out," I affirmed.

"And luckily because I had no idea what was happening. But to return to Margaret's statement: yes, each one of us does have more power, more potential for evil, but we should look at it from the positive side, also. We have greater access to knowledge, and even to wisdom. We probably know more about the 16th century than the people living at that time. We know more about their past then they. We have a larger view of their time, for instance, we know about the happenings in Europe, Africa, Americas, Asia, where as each of these civilizations had very little idea, if any, about each other. Likewise, we know the results of their actions.

"And the knowledge for our existence as a species is cumulative. We have access to knowledge and wisdom of all times. So true, more individuals are alive, and you're are right, we have power and are a greater threat to each other and ourselves, but we have at our disposal greater and more knowledge to control the technology and our beings. Through our personal computers, each one of us can enter any library in the world. Each one of us can communicate with almost every other person alive. Consequently, with the greater number of us, we have a greater number of perceptions. Also we can probe our inner beings and see what is driving us.

"Unlike the 16th century, we know what is happening on the other side of the globe, minutes from it happening. When our scientists see a mistake made by other scientists miles away, they can stop before making the same mistakes; think about that last nuclear reactor explosion."

"And also," I added, "You mentioned we can communicate with every living person, well the dead communicate with us through their artifacts, their writings, their music, their recordings."

"Just from sheer statistics, the number of people alive," our hero continued, "undoubtedly some of the most powerful and/or intelligent human beings are alive who have ever lived. Even more than that, some of the greatest human beings must be alive and the numbers of these must be the greatest.

"Ike was right in saying that the situation is more complex than it once was, but there must be a greater potential to handle this also. And it seems we're handling it. In spite of the set-backs, humanity seems to be moving along, ... to be progressing. This is, of course, unless my positive attitude is really a personal creation, a personal illusion," he laughed.

As you know both Margery and I were used to his tirades, neither of us said a word, and he did, as we expected, continue: "I can understand that someone in power could have the same hate I experienced, but to the point that that person could pull the plug and ..... either destroy on an individual level or create mass annihilation.

"Yes, I can imagine and have seen individuals

so dissatisfied ...... who can't procure justice any other way, strike out and destroy."

"A fear and a warning, huh?"

"Right, this is my point," Margery inserted, "We read about this every day in the newspapers: a man kills his past employer; a woman stalks and kills her rapist; a child shoots his abusive parent, a person blows up an airplane, a train, a building."

"Good versus evil: opposites destroying each other?" I question.

"No," insists Thesus, "more than that- individuals can use the non-human systems to multiply their powers: the obscene caller using the phone; the killer, a submachine gun; the terrorist, a bomb; the politician, the TV; the bureaucrat, the system to promote or suppress; and, of course as in my case, the computer.

"We, individually, socially, democratically, are holding a gun with a hair-line trigger, and it is up to us not to accidentally or unjustly discharge our power. We, as individuals and as a society, have the right and even the obligation to obtain our full potentials, to become complete beings, but as we grow so should our feelings, our sensitivities. An awareness of our responsibilities should expand as rapidly as our power, as should our control, especially our self-control: for the advancement of our society lies in the advancement and evolution of each individual. We have to evolve morally, intellectually, and spiritually, not just in our potentials to create change."

"You know you may be right," I added, "maybe, courses in philosophy, particularly ethics, should be taught in high schools. Give the students moral dilemmas which they may encounter in real life...... Applied Philosophy."

This time when I stopped talking, it took me a while to begin to follow his thought because I thought his thinking had jumped track. "You know, in spite of my new won freedom with money and my disguise, it has caused me a certain amount of confusion. The trouble is my created image. I have started to respond to how people are responding to me. Without notice, I have become my image because other people project who they think I am and I accept their response. I portray a single, older man who is successful, in fact, rich. I am constantly being dragged through too much because people think I am .... and the type of women I am attracting .... well. Between my created image and people's, I have lost touch of myself. Even in my dreams, I am more of an observer, not a participant. But this morning while waking, a thought, from where I do not know, popped into my mind: 'seek not the image but the being.' The image limits possibilities because in seeking it we fit ourselves into our own vision. Yes, we try to fit ourselves into our own view of who we have created, like those projected images on the internet, those social web sites, and we bias our perspectives by who we want to be, how we think things should be, therefore cut off possibilities beyond our limited visions. (Yes, Ike!) But by being the 'being,' we are opened to new possibilities, to unforeseen developments because we can't really completely know or categorize ourselves. This internal being is a culmination of all that goes to make us plus the qualities beyond our own definition and understanding. That being we can't completely know for we are only a part of the total which we try to view. We will always be elusive because we are one step beyond ourselves."

Whoa! You are beyond ...... Oh, "You mean, because when we know who we are we have changed and are changed by this knowledge?"

"Something like that, but let me complete my thought. The lack of development, my development in particular, did not only rest in the oppressive and suppressive society. This I discovered when I was free from it. It rested in me. It rests in us. I have limited my own being. Almost all the Minotaurs I've met were me. They were perceptions of my own limitations. The Minotaurs only limit, and the dictators only dictate to me when I exist in their realms. When I want something from them, money, power, success, acceptance, it is then I have to confront them.

"When I designate myself, let's say, a computer operator, I begin to think like a computer- I begin to act like a data inputter; in order to be successful, the machine forms my physical behavior and my patterns of thoughts. And in deed, after months and months of inputting, I am a computer operator. I introduce myself as one: I play society's role of one. I accept society's status of one; and I can respond even to my friends as one. This role really can become all-encompassing when as a prioritize self-identity, I first think of myself as a computer operator. And I have completely limited my being when I believe, accept, and determine this is what I want for myself, when I am functioning as a computer operator and not for any larger purpose."

I am sure that the other two thought again of Ike Jacoby, the artist, as I did in this moment of silence.

"But it is we who have limited ourselves. It is we who have limited our potentials. Remember when I trapped myself? I felt I was the suppressed, oppressed victim. At the same time I accidentally discovered an answer. When I no longer let the society wholly show me my limitations, I found a potential. By me controlling myself, I not only change myself but I have an effect, and I have changed my environment through my effect. In a subtle but very real sense, we change our society and the world, when we each change ourselves. This in turn, has changed my being.

"Freedom was gained by slaying a minotaur of my own mind and becoming more internally self-directed. I've set my own goals, my own identity, and in some sense, my idea of success.

"I'm sure self-perception is that which still keeps me from a more full potential. I am now making an effort to refocus my perception to a wider horizon. And I'm sure," and he laughed, "if my perception expands into the universe, I will no longer see my own limitations." He took on his far away stare, and said, "Can the finite part of our beings know or understand the infinite?"

I just thought, Oh Icarus don't fly too high. The higher you soar, the farther you fall. But I said instead,

"Who was it who said, 'we have one foot in the finite and one in the infinite'?" I interjected, but I thought: Has this been my effect on Thesus? A little too wrapped up in his self-created myth? Have I only encouraged this type of thinking?

Yes, I suffer in what I have wrought. Some of my projections have reflected back negatively... but then again who am I to judge that. I thought at that moment, he will read this, and I will be absolved because his knowledge will help set him free. Man, I don't like to suffer guilt, and so I shed it as quickly as possible. "Hell, where has the time gone. I'll do the dishes while you two get ready."

I stripped the table. Margery prepared our lunch. Why couldn't something have happened to prevent us from going? Where was the fate in which he believed? Where were his gods to intervene?

On the drive he explained what he wanted to accomplish with the park. He laughed when he said he was having more of an effect on the park service now than when employed by it.

Anything could have prevented us from going. This trip was not necessary. Could it have been a jealous god? An insane man shooting at people? Was it powers controlled by the systems, and their fear of Thesus? A paid assassin? Had our hero become that powerful .... possibly in someone else's mind.

To him he saw the flaw in his plan, which was me, and did it anyway. To me I didn't see the flaw in his plan, but did it anyway. But for sure, for the last five years, he had been an angel in flight; and in another way, it has just begun - for who knows where he is now, not only in the influence of his being but as a being.

Epilogue

If I die soon enough, I may be reincarnated as Margery's and my own child. A beautiful thought, for me.

Entry I - Appendix

The manuscript which follows was given to me directly after Ike Jacoby's funeral. Thesus wanted me to see if I could get it published as a remembrance to Jacoby, "for Ike's sake." We all assumed it's Ike's only remaining manuscript. Following the scene with Jacoby's uncle after the funeral, our hero remembered having been given this manuscript. Our hero's description of the presentation may be of some interest to the reader.

"We were drunk," these are Thesus' words, "He was drunk for sure. I had just quit my job with the Park Service and was "celebrating." We were at his place. He was rambling again, and had been all night. He said he wanted to give me a manuscript because it was about Margery and that he had shared so much of his past with me and maybe, only I could understand. He was going to give me a remembrance.

"'Yes, a piece of time. I hereby offer you a piece of my time for what it is worth,' Ike said. Then he began to explain its context but became distracted and went off on another tangent about something.

"Not wanting to hear another spiel about something or other, I made a big deal about his present. 'I accept this with the knowledge of your commitment and with the appreciation that you have taken the time to condense your experiences so that others may share and learn from them.' I don't think any of this would have happened unless we were both drunk. I put it away that night without reading it, and only now do I remember the conversation.

"He mentioned something about seeking truth through catharsis, and I replied, "I'm sure you have.'

"Then he went off again on one of his themes, 'If I could have only retained those states of being which I have experienced. If I could have only retained that level of existence. But life wore away the states. I feel that the gains I have made are lost. The feelings experienced were lost in the ebb and flow of my memory and now the feelings are only remembered by the rereading the frozen moments of experience. I continually fall back to a lesser level of existence, the only difference is that I am older and only have vague memories of my successes. Always at the same place again, older, in a too old body, and with my personal world waiting, wanting to begin anew. Hoping the door will open, I will enter, experience again, but this time retain and progress. In the repetition of attempting that state of being, it seems as if my life has been nothing but that moment, that damn moment of waiting; too much wanting and waiting have worn way my being, and I am always at the point before the door opens.'

"At the time I understood what he said but

didn't pay enough attention or didn't apply it to his situation. I just accepted his book with the fanfare of the moment."

Whatever the following manuscript is, it exists and will have a large effect because of its existence, a reason why I hesitated at the time even to try to publish it. And again, isn't it strange that even if the experience which he records is not real, or even represents reality, the manuscript itself has a real existence (shades of dreams, again). Even if all the following wasn't true, and he knew it not be to be true, its physical existence is actual and the effect will be. But then this type of reality is not only dealing with Jacoby's manuscript but his death. How many of us believe in a philosophy or religion which does not in fact have any validity in the real world, and yet just in the believing of it makes it real to us? Just the believing of a non-authentic philosophy affects our decisions, influences other people, and in fact has an existence of its own, not because it is innately true or real but just because we believe it. Maybe no real reason for existence, no true philosophy exists, but in believing in one and acting upon that belief, we give it a reality, an existence, and may be that is as true or real as it gets.

So how can I condemn Jacoby's manuscript or question its validity. If the manuscript validates its own existence, whether true or not, it should be published. I can see the influence of my reading it. Maybe I would not have made such a statement before, I don't know.

Anyway without any further ado, except to say

that my private title for the piece is _Onward into the Night_, rather than Jacoby's _A Stay at the Ocean_, and my only contribution to it has been to correct his punctuation and spelling. Neither of which Ike Jacoby was conscientious.

A STAY AT THE OCEAN

By Ike Jacoby

Aug. 10

> Awaking
> Awaiting in the blue
> Hazy inside and out

Aug. 11

Trying to break through the incommunicable prison to me. Trying to express what can't be expressed even to me. Trying to even just retrace the thoughts I have experienced which meant so much. The retracing is possible for me; but it is, at the moment, impossible to re-experience the thinking of them, to experience the emotional experience of the insight so that the thought will be vital, real again so they will mean something to me, so I can believe them again.

Forget yesterday and begin anew.

Aug. 12

A bird with no voice
Flies over the desert sands of his mind.

Aug. 14

Deserted planes of my mind,
Not finding what I once possessed,
Not being able to reconstruct the feelings or
the insights,
It was once a lush, green, fertile land,
Inhabited;
A land worth the long journey to get there.

Aug. 15

Where is my creativity? Has it flushed with the rest
of the shit? Was it manifested into another form
unknown to me? Or was it just never there?

Aug. 20

I have taken one step beyond my reality, myself and
am floating free.

Locked out,
Without the Key.

Ocean has ripped this soft shelled crab
From a tide breaker.

Back fins beat
In silt suspended water.
With no control,

My direction
Freed
From the responsibility of choice
Opens to unforeseen possibilities.

Aug. 30

Is the reality I see such a fragile thing that my
perspective, my way of seeing, could be altered by a
novel just read? Is any abstract reality real? Can we
know anything beyond the physical? And how real is
that? Our perception? How real is the reality which
I know? My conceptions of both the physical and
those which I overlay on that physical? Could one
who is dissatisfied with the reality he knows, break it
down to create a new one?

The answer would be no, if there is a pressing reality
beyond man's conception of it. No, if there is a truth,
a single over all Truth for man would just be ignoring
this Truth and just hoping to survive without knowing
it or may--- be in spite of it.

Yes, if there is no absolute reality but more realities

than the number of conceivers of those realities, ie. The Infinite (wouldn't the fact of The Infinite existing be the "Truth"?). Yes, if there is no single truth but a randomly changing reality, chaotically changing truths.

> Oh, to be in that flow,
> To change,
> To experience,
> And know.

But in both cases, wouldn't reality, at least to man, partially be man's belief in it. If there exists a single over all Truth and man doesn't know it and can't know it because we do not know the totality and can't know, for we are only such a small part and cannot lift ourselves out and look at it objectively, then man's reality, at least in part, is the speculation we make about Truth; his belief is a part of his reality. If there exists an Infinite, man's beliefs may be his reality in that maybe what man conceives as reality for himself is in fact reality because he conceives of it and all possible realities would exist in the Infinite. Just believing it would make it true. We, as a race of human beings, would have a total conception of reality, of our reality, which we would communicate to our young but yet, how many more realities could exist if we only believed in them?

Aug. 31

Isn't what I see, feel, hear, only a portion of that which exists? I can't really see what exists for that extends beyond my sensibilities. I am a limited poor soul. I can only see a certain range of the spectrum, only hear certain range of vibrations; my skin is only sensitive to certain intensities of touch, and it is from these limited sensitivities that I interpret what is and what it all means. It is from this partial set of information that I abstract my concept of reality.

Further still, since our individual sensibilities are different we see, feel, hear different things and interpret our different sensibilities differently and from all the different sensibilities involved, how could we share the same concept of reality? Our individual realities are concepts which have been constructed out of a brief, not quite complete perception and then we even in turn, project our conception of reality back into what we see, feel, etc. in the form of expectations, anticipations; our personal, changed reality then becomes the reality we predict.

It is amazing that we get along as well as we do. We not only function as individuals but as social units, and there is more of us alive than ever before. Our separate realities seem not only to be comnunicatable but functionable as well and are, or at least seem to be, validated by non-human machines and beings.

But then again, maybe our realities are not so different

because we are taught what is here, what to see, what to hear and what it all means. Our realities are formed before we have a chance to question it. It is all taught to us before we are old enough to think.

Sept. 1

Going back to Aug. 30, what if everything is infinite, and every interpretation works but of course what I am talking about is mainly the unknown which exists and will always exist in man's mind. But suppose we cannot make a wrong interpretation of the unknown because every possibility exists and just conceiving what awaits us beyond life makes it happen.

To clarify my question, is there an infinite number of valid conceptions because the non-physical reality is infinite? God is an Infinite Imagination? If this is true then each man's conception of the non-physical reality is as valid as the next, if it is as functional in the immediate physical reality.

Or maybe there is a reality beyond our knowledge, a real Reality, the Truth, and a part of that real Reality is the nonphysical reality, a unperceived reality, the un-thought of, the unknown. Not even the terms of this realm can be clarified, and yet every man has his interpretations, his conceptualization of this unperceived reality. In fact, many men in the past and present are saying that their conception is the true and the only conception. How could one prove that this unknown reality is correct, real? How could one prove that one's conception of the unknown and the actual unknown coincide? Would being able to live as though it were true be proof enough? No, many men in the past who've had contradicting beliefs, lived and died thinking those beliefs were true. Unless Infinite possibilities exist then one or the other of those people lived false beliefs.

Until one can unconditionally prove a single concept of Reality, I hereby declare a Holiday of Belief.

Maybe time could make the decision by an evolutionary process, i.e. the false beliefs fade out and the real beliefs survive; for unless truth and/or Reality change then only falsehood would change. Truth, because it is Truth, would remain constant and the false beliefs would die out and real beliefs will prevail. But could we base our lives on the beliefs which are still in existence? Which one? ones? Could we, or even would we, be able to see the answer if it did survive? The Truth would only have to survive, not the belief in it.

No. Each man's conception of the non-material Reality is as valid as the next person's, if it is as moral, functional, and compatible.... No, this is setting the standard too low. EACH MAN'S CONCEPTION OF THE UNKNOWN IS AS VALID AS THE NEXT'S IF IT IS MORAL, FUNCTIONABLE, AND COMPATIBLE. IF ONE CAN LIVE A FULL, MEANINGFUL LIFE BELIEVING ONE SET OF BELIEFS RATHER THAN ANOTHER? Because if reality is set, a single truth which none of us can escape and we can't really know it or if there is no set reality, what difference could it make what one believes?

I am not saying that there are no truths and that everything is --permitted for that would bring chaos, but what I am saying is that maybe there are no sets of truths, nor a Reality and so let each man judge the functionableness of his own Reality as long as he doesn't infringe on others beliefs.

Sept. 2

Let me see; let me organize the possibilities. 1) There is a set, single Reality, knowable and/or unknowable. 2) There is a multitude of realities. 3) There is no Reality nor a multitude of realities. 4) There is a single and a multitude of realities. All of the above may or may not be changing. LOL, the old quantum logic.

What do I mean by Reality? It is not a conception but The True Conception, the key that all Truths; that which exists beyond the conception of it, that which is not dependent on the conception; the Truth which encompasses the total.

A possible explanation of possibility #4 (There is a single and a multitude of realities.): if Reality exists then it could exist in the form of a single over-all Reality that breaks down into many truths, some which may be either knowable or unknowable.

A discussion of possibility #2 (There is a multitude of realities): if there is a multitude, this multitude is either infinite or finite. If there is a finite number of realities, they would not necessarily form a single, composite Reality, nor if there is an infinite number of realities would they have to form a composite truth except in the way or knowledge that there is an infinite number of truths.

A discussion of possibility #3: if there is no Reality or multitude of realities then all of mankind's beliefs are unfounded but at the same time true to the person conceiving them, ….. real for him?

Sept. 3

Does one know the Truth intuitively and only confuses his knowledge through questioning?

Can any non-physical assumption be make then proved or disproved conclusively? Can a jump, not counting the leap of faith, be made from the physical world into the non-physical through extrapolation, inductive reasoning, etc.?

Maybe individual and composite realities are the only realities which exist. Could I constantly be seeing Reality from different perspectives and not recognizing it?

I see the possibilities of choice of what to believe but not how to resolve the choices. Maybe I should ask the question this way: should one create a non-physical reality and /or seek it? Or let it be and just exist, be neutral to its existence? A more logical way of questioning: A) Should one just seek reality and not create at all? B) Should one just create? C) Do both? D) Do neither?

I reject B and D, for if one didn't seek Reality man would not progress in the realm of finding truth or truths if there are any. It would be taking a real gamble believing there are no truths. If he believed there are no truths and there are, then he would not gain in wisdom and/or knowledge and thereby not be able to make better choices. What would be the basis for discussions? How would we control our actions and direct our lives? On another man's conception? The conception which is passed from one generation to another? But what if truth was changing?

Further discussion of B: could one create a completely functioning reality independent of the one which exists? Would one dare to try? The unsuccessful attempt may be Icarus plummeting to earth. One could get to the point where a single event, a single truth would destroy all that has been created.

But if there is an infinite number of workable realities, would it be possible?

Discussion of A: if one did seek Reality and attained knowledge of it and it changed, one would again have false knowledge. But if Reality is changing and one conceived of one then it may change into the conception and the creator would fall into the new Reality. Or could one hook into the changing Reality: Oh, to be in that flow

> To know
> And go
> With the flow.

Discussion of C: could one take that which we know exists and try to guess and create the Reality then test to see if the creation is the Truth? Yes, C seems the best for if one just sought the Truth, and there was an infinite number, the seeking would be continuous and fruitless. Or if there were no Reality beyond man's immediate perception, one would be seeking nothing and not know it.

I laugh thinking about the possibility. How ironical if the Reality was that no Reality exists. Is it in the contradiction, the paradox, where the answer rests?

After sitting here and thinking about it, I have decided that I have not come up with any answer at all. I have a series of speculations, if not guesses, and a wish. I still don't know if there is a Reality or not, whether I should seek something I am not sure exists.

Sept. 7

Could an extreme case of disparity between the Real Reality and a conception of it be interpreted as insanity? Is the breakdown of my perception of reality, a sign of insanity?

That fear is probably the main reason why I am living in this house on this deserted beach. I thought that those friends of Margery's were trying to drive me insane, or at least we threatened each other's sanity, and came to the conclusion that either they or I had to be insane, and there were more of them than just me.

They thought they shined a light exposing my disorganized thoughts, the quagmire of my mind, and my fear of falling into the quagmire and then they acted as if they had. In that they were partially right, in that they exposed my fear of questioning my sanity, afraid I would find insanity, afraid that I would again be put away without any control over my being, afraid of again losing control, they forced me to retreat. They forced me to seek refuge here.

Now, I remember when the fear of insanity first began, when I was young and took that introductory course in Psychology. I found the symptoms which I had read about already manifested in me. Yes, that was the beginning. The symptoms were paranoia. After reading about it, I know I had it infested in me. For example, I thought that one morning about 2:00 when my wife was visiting her mother's, people outside my window were cursing me. We lived on the second floor, and they were yelling curses up at me from the alley below. Was I dreaming? Was it from smoking that pot and then falling asleep? Whatever it was, I was frightened and turned on the radio to drown out the voices. The radio talked to me and only for me. It lectured me then cursed me as the voices in the alley. Of course, I never told this to anyone.

But it was around then that my uncle threw me into the nut house. Of course I quit smoking pot and I think that made the difference, not the treatments.

It was also around that time, I became acutely aware that my wife was trying to get at me. I felt she was analyzing me, found me wanting, and then she was trying to destroy me, break me down, discover some secret about me and destroy me with the new found secret. I even thought that she was paid by the Psychology Dept. at school put me through a series of psyche experiments to find out if I were crazy, and I couldn't let her know I knew.

I never mentioned this to anyone, especially not her, out of my fear of being put away again without any control over what was happening to me, of getting electroshock treatments or even worse, a lobotomy - without my being able to stop it. So I kept my mouth shut. My fears grew in my mind and with no outlet. They were compacted in a too small a space.

After a while I tried to cure myself by saying that it was just my paranoia acting up when any singular incident occurred. I was seeing a gross exaggeration of what was really happening. In fact it got to the point where every incident that I couldn't understand, I would dismiss as paranoia. It seemed to be working for the number of paranoid type of incidents decreased. Even though I became satisfied with the results, dismissing the incidents, now I can see it may have been foolish. Paranoia was just a symptom of something. I was just erasing the symptom of paranoia, not the cause. I was not curing it but dismissing it. Maybe the cause of the symptom would and has manifested itself in anew.

Sept. 8

Lost in the fog.
Closed around me – without touching.
Can you see it also?
The external doesn't touch anymore.
The inside goes to meet the outside
To try to create a new reality,
A livable one.

Sept. 9

Maybe I should address my writing to the diary and start out each day, Dear Diary. But I know it's not to the diary I am writing; it is only a method to arrange my thoughts and besides, I write when the pressure in me is up, at any time night or day. I write when the need to express is at its greatest point and when writing is the only thing I can do to release. At some of those times I feel that it is poetry because I am just expressing my being, where I am. At other times I just express my thoughts to get them out so they don't repeat in my mind, again and again. Then I try to analyze and discover who I am, who would think those thoughts.

This need to express myself through writing is not unopposed. I have a fear of writing and defining myself and the reality too firmly and thereby closing myself off to possibilities, other possible visions. Could I eventually limit myself until I was unable to be anything but my definition? Unable to be anything but my attempted philosophical resolution to my own questionable questions.

Sept. 14

The question of my sanity keeps regurgitating in my mind. I thought that I had been building a mountain out of doubt so I quit thinking about it, but it keeps popping. I can now see that what precipitated my questioning was all the events of the last year, not just the existing doubt from college. It has been in every relationship I have had this year. The main reason for moving here was to get away from all those relationships, to be alone and sort out my self, to find out who I am without someone else's projection of who they think I am.

But I am enclosed in my loneliness and in my need to communicate, to express, to be understood. My need for someone to break through to me and my need to break through to someone else, for different realities to be shared and compared so that the "real"" will shine through in spite of the veil which seems to cover my vision.

There are times like now that I question why I question my sanity. I feel completely sane, but in re-reading what I have written, insanity and my questioning it have been the predominate theme from the very beginning. Maybe just the questioning of my sanity is a sign of insanity.

After first getting out here to this beach house, I tried to keep myself busy so thinking would be kept at a minimum. At first, the days filled me with chores restoring the place but then I felt the necessity to fill the days because the moments of the day were not enough to squelch my thoughts. My thoughts became so forceful that they had to be dealt with.

My questioning and fear drove me to write. Now I can see that it has been a question of my sanity all along. The earlier questioning about reality, though real enough, was either a manifestation of my fear in another form .... a sublimation, or an evasion of my real fear. Now I can see that not even I would accept the answers to the questions on reality, no matter how good the answers were, if the question of my sanity is still on the edge.

As I have said, this bout of questioning my sanity was precipitated into an active conscious state when Margery came to see me on Sept. 4th. Well, to begin at the beginning, at about midnight on the first of Sept.

Margery called. I was in bed suffering from insomnia as usual. She said she was coming out, that she had a weekend free and she wanted to see me. Her call was somewhat of a shock for it was the first communication I have had with anyone for over two months, since I have been here. I have, of course, been to town to make purchases but have never really met anyone there. The first ring of the phone exploded the silence which had existed in the house for over two months. For a while I didn't know what was happening. I couldn't figure out where the noise was coming from. Then when I figured it was my cell phone, I couldn't find it.

I hesitantly picked up the phone, and she was on the other end, alive, not just in thought, but talking to me. I didn't even listen to what she said; I only heard her talking. It took two or three minutes before I heard words.

Another reason it was a shock was because of the manner in which we parted company. I never expected to hear from her again. I thought it was a final fight. She knew I wouldn't call her. She knew I couldn't. We had been separated for a while, but I kept visiting her in her new apartment until one day she wanted me to leave, she ordered me to leave, she yelled, "Get out. Get out before I do something violent." Where could I go? All we knew were her friends, a bad situation for sure.

We had met at a concert one night during intermission

and found out we had a great deal in common. It was really quite beautiful, all of our discoveries about each other. We had seemed destined to meet each other, a perfect match, but then I started meeting her friends who I didn't like.

They seemed to be working on the surface, talking on the surface; we never got past talking on a superficial level. At the time I was seeking depth. They couldn't offer anything to me and I could give them nothing.

All this is a value judgment. What I should say is that we were in different places and couldn't offer each other anything. But then that statement is not really how I felt. I disliked them, who they were, what they were doing with their lives, and when they realized my dislike of them, they began forcing their selves upon me.

This is all an interpretation of what happened and not the actual events. What is worse about my interpretation is that I question my sanity. Maybe I should just recall an event as it happened, and maybe see it more objectively. But which event? Hell, of course it was more than just one event; it was a multitude. From that multitude I have to choose which one. I'll just continue my dialogue, my train of thought and see where it takes me.

Where was I? Oh yes, Margery's friends. They forced themselves upon me and then seemed to intentionally misconstrue everything I said. Or maybe there really was a communication gap. They were unable to communicate, or I was unable to understand. It seemed at times as if I were carrying on conversations with people who made no sense at all. The most extreme case was when Margaret and I weren't living together anymore; I went over to her apartment near the park. Some guy answered the door and said, "This is the most fucked-up mess I have ever been in."

"Hi," said a girl walking-up to us. I guess she was also going to answer the door.

"Why?" I said to the guy but not looking at him but at her. She didn't have a shirt on, only a bra.

"What?" she said, leaning forward to me as if her hearing and not the conversation was at question. I must admit, I wanted very much to grab her and hold her breasts and fondle her. I was missing having sex, obviously.

"Why did you say that?" I said turning to him trying to end some of the confusion and because I didn't want to keep staring at her breasts.

"This is the best conversation I've had all day," she said. I turned back to look at her and smiled. For some reason I said "Yes" not because I thought she thought that it was but because it really was for me. It was really only a whisper and wasn't meant for her to hear.

"How come?" she asked.

"What?" he said.

"She said she wants to know how come," I said.

"'No," she said, "I was questioning my statement not yours."

"Which statement?" he asked.

"I don't believe it," I said, and laughed.

Both of them glared at me, at first frightened

but then anger rose in their expressions.

"What? Believe what?" His blood shot eyes where squinty tighter and tighter with frustration.

"Where is Margery?" I asked wanting to clear the air.

"Who?" she said.

"What?" he asked and began to laugh.

I began to laugh and said, "Why do you think this is a fucked-up mess?" At last I thought we were communicating. I struck his shoulder and laughed harder at what I said. But either he didn't understand my laughter, thought it insulting him or something because he turned on me and said, "Are you fucked-up or something? You'd have to be nuts not to think it isn't."

"Why are you both saying what you are saying?" she asked. "This is not really the best conversation I've had today but the worst," and started to cry.

"I'm sure we can straighten this out. Don't cry." I reached out to her, but she didn't move closer.

"What's going on here? You started this. You and your damned questions. Why don't you keep your damn mouth shut?" He knocked my extended arm away.

I withdrew it and again began to laugh. What else could I do? Was it really me who was causing the confusion? "Why?" I said just audibly, to myself. My laughter had become a dry hysterical cackle. I don't know why I continued to laugh like that.

He looked as if he were going to hit me but instead ushered the girl down the hall with his arm around her shoulder. I stood there a moment trying to regain my composure.

The guy I had seen before but didn't know his name. The girl I had never seen. For a moment it occurred to me that it had been an act, put on for my benefit. At that time, Margery had some friends who were actors and actresses; most were working in improvisational skits down in North Beach and of course it was an act and I was the audience. Maybe every time that I have met her friends before it has been an act.

With that thought firmly implanted in my head I ventured further into the apartment. I looked into Margery's bedroom, the first room, on the left walking down the hall. The two to whom I had just spoken were petting passionately. She no longer was wearing her bra and his pants were dropped; he hadn't stepped out of them yet. He was fondling, one of her bare breasts and sucking on the other one. His other hand was fiddling with the snap on her trousers. Both of her hands were down his boxer shorts. Both were doing some heavy breathing, no doubt about it. At first I stood there aghast. I guess because they hadn't even bothered to close the door. A very expensive camera, lights, and a huge silver movie screen were occupying one wall of the room.

They were still writhing right there before me. More

than envy grew inside of me. He had managed to unsnap her pants, and they were pushed down exposing her see-through underpants. My emotion hit its peak; an erection was pushing hard, but I didn't know what to do. I couldn't just stand there watching. I closed the door. What else could I do? An act? I doubted it. I wanted it so much to be an act. A pornographic movie? It would not have made me so envious. Looking back now, it could have been a bra commercial, LOL.

But by closing the door the hall had darkened. I stood there adjusting to the change in light and trying to control my breathing. Noise from the living room penetrated my concentration. It seemed lighter down there so after everything had settled down, I slowly walked toward the light.

There was a crowd. It wasn't even three o'clock in the afternoon and a party was going on, or at least I think it was a party. People were gathered in groups of about five or six. I walked around looking for Margery then joined a group which I thought I would feel least alienated with. I had met a lot of these people and knew some of them to some degree.

In the group I had joined, a younger man named Jack was talking about something happening but after listening for a while I couldn't quite understand what. I had met Jack someplace before and didn't remember disliking him in spite of the strange circumstances, the strange party where we met. Many of the people at the party wore masks and were doing strange things but what they were doing seemed well organized. I mean the separate things that different people or groups of people were doing seemed to have been well worked out beforehand. But maybe my interpretation is faulty, and it was the kind of thing where you could join any group you wished and interact with them.

But what was going on here, now, I thought. I stared at Jack trying to understand. Why was he the only one talking? Why was he talking all? Maybe these were some kind of instruction groups. I listened to see if it was something like that. It seemed as if he were talking in some kind of code, but it wasn't a lecture of any kind. It was a description of something happening. Yes, he was still describing something, but what? Maybe I would have understood what if I had been there at the beginning of the conversation. He didn't seem to be letting up, and what he was saying seemed so intense I didn't want to interrupt.

Jack's lecture seemed to take a turn, and it brought me out of my thoughts. Again, I tried to understand him but didn't succeed. This time I didn't even pick up his train of thought; I couldn't follow how one sentence led to another. I couldn't find that thread which held his conversation together. Could it be me? The alcohol and bad drugs in my youth flashed before my mind. Too many, too young.

I had been there five to ten minutes and couldn't get

anything out of it. Everyone else seemed to be under-standing. Or were they just being polite? The scene in the bedroom flashed in my mind. Polite? An act? The situation wasn't unlike seeing the beginning of a complex movie which I entered in the middle of.

The moments I questioned my sanity were the most frightening; I felt threatened. Was his conception of reality so distant from mine that nothing could relate? Was one of our conceptions faulty? Why are these people standing around? It is one of those modern plays. Maybe the theme is a cocktail party.

Maybe they thought I knew what was happening and so nobody had to explain it. I stepped out of the group and looked at the whole room. All the groups seemed pretty normal. It was an early afternoon cocktail party with drinks in hand. Jack was still going at it without pause, so I walked across the room and tried to join another group.

Pretty much the same thing happened. After standing there for a while I realized I couldn't get into it. This group seemed to be talking too personally. Maybe they knew each other intimately. In contrast to the last group, this group was being polite. I assumed the pose of everyone else. I was politely waiting for a pause in the conversation so I could ask Margery's whereabouts, or where to get the booze.

An analogy of this group could be: they were all standing around holding cocktail glasses with their little fingers extended. I tuned the conversation out just slightly beyond my auditory perception and listened to my own thoughts, but then thought I began hearing my thoughts expressed by them. I listened closer; they were talking about me. They were using the term "she" for me, but it was about me.

I can now see that maybe I took the conversation out of context by only listening to phrases or parts of conversation then personifying and personalizing it, to the point where I thought they were talking about me. (What tricks an egotistical mind will play upon itself.) I swear that small- minded, two-faced people use this or these kinds of tactics all the time. I've heard them. But maybe that isn't true because then all of a sudden two of them who were exchanging small talk, turned and looked straight at me. It was a man and a woman talking back and forth without pause. Even after they turned toward me, their conversation continued. May-be I was misinterpreting them and they were talking to me and not about me? Maybe they really thought I understood their conversation, and they were having me join in? All the rest of the group was directing their gazes back and forth at the person speaking. It was not unlike a tennis game, that is, the head movements of the observers. Then when the guy was chatting about something, he smiled at me. I smiled back and made an affirmative gesture. There was always a little communication before when I had seen these people; I had always understood something of what they said, although nine-tenths of the time I was bored by it.

I caught myself falling into my own thought again.

Startled I pulled myself back into the immediate, then took a step out of the circle, stopped myself when I saw that the guy was still talking at me. "Nice meeting you," I said with a slight bow then started again to move away. Everyone looked at me after my statement. The man stopped talking for a moment then said the first statement which I thought I understood. "How long have you been like that?" My constant questioning of my sanity sprang to mind, and I flushed.

Now I could interpret that statement as meaning, how long have you been a hypocrite, but at that time I felt the blood rush to my face, and I turned and almost ran for the door. Was the communicational barrier real, and I really couldn't and communicate?

When Margery finally came up to the beach house, we should have talked in depth about that party, about whether she understands me, about communicating. But I when I mentioned I came to her apartment looking for her and she asked if a group of people were rehearsing. "Oh," I said. So I was just stupid not to understand what was happening. I dropped that conversation and again we talked about nothing important. The usual case.

I still can't get over the shock from the ringing telephone. It is still so vivid, more indisputable than our conversations. But yet, it seemed unreal. I had never heard it before. She was so distant five minutes before the call, only a reoccurring thought, only a slight pain in the stomach, but that phone call changed her into something real and the blast from the ringing-buzz into something unreal. My mind went from, "It can't be real," to "How did she get my number," but then I remembered the dramatic note I dashed off to her about moving up here to my Uncle's beach house and that if she ever felt different to write me. It was only after remembering that note that I began to hear what she was saying, and it was again as if we had never separated, that no time had passed between when we were living together and now.

When the phone noise went blank, the room seemed different. It was more material. While cleaning the cabin, I wandered around for two days touching everything, with the feeling of living in a more substantive world. But then she got up here and nothing happened. It wasn't even worth recording in the diary. It was the same old thing. We fell right back into our old habits. We did nothing new. Nothing had changed. We didn't even walk along the ocean front. That would have been new. The walk might have stimulated conversation but no, we did nothing but make love. I can't deny that I didn't enjoy it. I liked it. In fact I can truthfully say I loved it. It was making love and not just screwing, but after it was over, it was over. She slipped back into her thoughts, and I slipped back into mine. Mostly she lay on the couch with her eyes closed thinking; and I looked out the bay window at the ocean. There were times I wanted to do things that I should have said but I knew from the past that she wouldn't understand or didn't want to hear, so I didn't even try. I didn't want ...... No, I was afraid I couldn't communicate what needed to be said; I ..... I didn't want her to not come up here again, and I thought if I kept my thoughts to myself there would be a better chance of her reentering my life in a big way or at least coming up again.

The next morning when I awoke she was gone. I had slept as if I was drugged, a very deep sleep with no dreams. Probably the best since moving up here, which really isn't saying much. Was it just sexual for her? Reviving it, it seems so. It seems to be the same relationship we had for a month after she had moved out. Maybe it was only sexual before................and I was a fool to think otherwise. Another manifestation of insanity, me seeing things the way I want to and not the way they really are?

Where two people are concern, can there be a Real Reality between them or just a relative reality?

I just got up to get a cigarette and saw that it is after midnight so I should change the date.

Sept. 15

Maybe the increase in my creativity is due to me trying to intellectually rationalize my mental illness. Is it because I am pathologically abnormal that I am compelled to create or does my craving to know and my potentialities, drive me? I may be trying to discover something in my art and writing which doesn't exist. But I am happy when I am creating. (I am writing a couple of new poems.) I enjoy the excitement of exploring, seeing. Thoughts, ideas take form, but I wonder if I am really communicating them. To what degree? Is this a trip I will never be able to share? Am I going all the way out, changing me into an unrecognizable and an uncommmicable being? Am I cutting myself off from other human beings, my only hope of communicating?

I have just reread what I have written to see if it can be understood. I can see that my thoughts start on one subject, jump to another without finishing the first then to another subject without finishing the second.

If I were a skilled writer, it could be passed off as organic growth, but I not fooling nobody. It is that I am scattered. The drugs? My incarceration? Not my fault? My fault? There really is so much to tell, and as I start to tell it, more important information seems to pop into my mind, and I try to tell that. Is it my method of brainstorming? But as I reread I could see that so much important information has been skipped. In all the confusion it is hard to tell what is important in the information I have given. I can see that if my writing truly reflexes my state of being, I am in trouble. But why do I say if?

Where should I go from here? Go back, complete all the unfinished statements or just continue?
It's three in the morning and dark outside. Not even a

moon; I have reread again after having a drink of scotch. Relaxation had engulfed my body, but in the rereading an excitement has been stimulated.

Even if it somewhat scattered, it is getting put down. Seeing the confusion is a sign of hope. I also see the events with a different perspective. I have decided to just let the thoughts flow; record them, then analyze them and find if and where my insanity lies.

I wonder if reorganizing them would help or hinder. I would appear as if I were less scattered and maybe by doing it I would be disciplining my brain, or would this just be another deception?

The rereading revealed that I was going to talk about Margery's and our last meeting and not about her friends. But I got off on her friends, probably because of their threat.

Anyway, our last meeting. It was about two days before that rehearsal or party, or whatever it was, at her apartment. Why didn't one of those characters tell me what was going on? That would have been the polite, civilized thing to do. Maybe the whole idea was not to break character, no matter what. Or they thought I was a part of the scene. I don't know.

In any case, I had gone over to see her, and she was home alone. I tried to convince her that she should come back to me, if for nothing else but to escape the chaos in her apartment. She laughed, but then in a serious tone of voice, said it wouldn't work, that living together didn't work and that the relationship was finished. I had to admit that it was not the relationship of my youthful dreams, but I was happy in spite of the difficulties. I knew the relationship was on rock bottom, I had to admit that, even to her. There was no more newness. Individually we weren't growing with each other. We couldn't hold each other's interests. We had satiated ourselves with each other. We were a "habit," to use her words, each other's habit. The relationship really was only a sexual occurrence by this time even though she didn't say that nor do I think she wanted to admit it. But I realized it. The relationship wasn't much, but it was more than nothing, and it could get better. I believed we could make it work. We could change and thereby change the relationship.

But yes, we didn't hold each other's interest. Maybe to be more truthful, she held mine, but I didn't hold hers. Then again, why did she give up hope that it would get better? I was really stagnating. I had even given up reading which had never happened before. Not to place the blame, but I think that if the relationship was good, I would have been doing more than I was doing which was absolutely nothing. I only sat around worrying about her growing distant and about what she was doing when she wasn't with me. She was gone most of the time. That bothered me. It had gotten to the point where we were only seeing each other at nights, and sometimes not even then, and if anything made me go insane, it was those nights when she didn't come home.

At first when she moved out of the apartment, we continued to share sex then she said, "NO!" What did she gain by stopping the relationship completely? Her words were sincere; I believed her. Could she be in love with someone else? I directly asked her, but I don't remember her response.

"Do you think I am insane?" I blurted out almost involuntarily.

"No, that's not it. Really."

"Is your 'really' patronizing? Is there something you don't want to tell me?"

"Only that I wish you would understand, that for right now, it is over for me. I love you, but as far as living together, it doesn't work."

"Don't you want to make it work?"

"It won't work. We tried. Just admit it."

"Couldn't I make you want me again? It could get better. We can make it better, but you don't want it to be. Why? It's me. Isn't it? I know it is me!"

"It's not!"

"Can't I say anything to convince you?"

"NO! I need to get away."

"There must be something I could say or do to convince you."

"No," she said despondently.

I went up to her and began, playfully, attacking her body, ripping off her blouse. I forced her down onto the couch and was lying on top of her. This is when she began to yell, "Get out." She pushed me off her, and I landed on the floor. At first I was shocked, then her words themselves and the way she spoke them hurt me. I couldn't say a thing. Her words were a surprise and weren't a surprise at the same time. I had expected them, and this final break for a while, but when the actually occurred, I had acted differently than what I had expected, what I had planned. When I hit the floor and was stunned, I couldn't say anything but then I got mad and didn't want to say anything. I had thought I would argue, fight for her, make her want me; yes, by force if necessary. But when she pushed me and started yelling, I knew her well enough to know how she meant what she was saying, and it hurt. I suppressed all my feelings, all that I had planned to do, all that I could have said, and just turned and walked out.

It was some time later and when I was in a weakened-state of being that I went over to find her and found the party instead. After that I again rehashed what had happened at our last meeting and decided that I didn't want to be the one to try to make the reunion, and the only way to stop me was to leave town. It was too easy in a moment of weakness to go to her apartment.

It's dawn outside. The fire in the fireplace has long since diminished, and a chill has made me get a warm coat, but since I have nothing really more to say about coming up here, at least right now, I will try to get some rest.

Sept 17

I slept all of the fifteenth; up periodically, feeling so

badly and so tired that I forced me back to sleep. It must have been all the writing I did on the _____ I don't remember how long I wrote, but it didn't seem long. It all came out in a series of bursts of recall. The physical and emotional strain of it all was probably too exhausting.

I woke yesterday feeling stuffy. The sun was not up, but unable to fall asleep again I got up, made some coffee to clear my head. First I started a fire in the fireplace then the coffee. The sun rose behind my back as I waited for the steeping to stop. By the fire, I sipped. But neither the warmth from the fire nor the coffee could clear my head so I decided to walk to a beach down south of here, get some exercise, release some of the pressure that my sleeping couldn't handle, think about what I wrote and in short get out of the house and try to get out of me.

By the time I was hygienically ready with a sack lunch, and outside, the fire had burnt down, and the sun was full. The wind was still chilly, but I knew it was going to be warm later in the day, despite the constant wind.

The walk for the first two miles was completely un-eventful. I kept trying to force myself to think about what I had written, about Margery, about my solitude and if I were gaining anything from it, but I couldn't hold anything. I couldn't retain a single thought to its logical conclusion.

I had made this walk three or four times, and so knew where I was. After my efforts to think about my problems had exhausted, I didn't think about anything, but just felt the elements. The walk was pleasant, enough. Fog was close to the shore, but I knew as the day matured the fog would recede.

The foremost problem with the walk was the dried weeds. As I journeyed, the weeds crackled under my feet, stirring the dust and pollen which dried my nostrils. I know that it was the pollen and dust and not just the wind because later in the hike, the pollen and dust had stuck to my temples. At the time I took precautions against the dust from the underbrush by walking slowly, but I still sneezed often. Cause I didn't have an tissues, I blew my nose, like I had seen farmers in their field, by holding one nostril close, but almost nothing came out.

Knowing I had nothing pressing my time, I stopped various times along the way. In spite of myself, I did extend a little effort getting up that thirty degree incline before the last half a mile down, but never pressed myself to the point of exhaustion. Half way up the hill I stopped and ate an orange from my lunch because of dry throat and dry thirst. A breeze cooled my wet face. It was all peaceful enough, but I felt a certain emptiness, a loneliness.

I could be gone for weeks without loss either to me or someone else. There is no one to return to. Nothing awaits me. There is nothing to wait for. Years at work on something to believe in with nothing to show for it. I have nothing. I am nothing, without friends, without influence..... (I laughed out loud at this absurd thought, as if that is what I wanted, or thought was important, but my depressed thoughts persisted) ... and even without money. I am a nobody in a nothing world. What have I gained in all my struggles?

After feeling sorry for myself, I finished the incline and stopped at the top, viewing what I had seen before, a gradual descent through shoulder-high shrubbery. Even with the help of the moderate descent, this next part of the walk had always been the worst. It had always being a struggle to find a way because the bushes are so close together with no path that I had ever found. One has to guard himself against falling over boulders and large rocks protruding from the ground and at the same watch for branches which could hit one in the face. On one adventure, I had fallen into a giant hole, which frightened me more than hurt me. At the end of the decline was a ravine, a dried river bed of boulders and sand. Because of the trek through the dense brambles, I had never come out in the same place. But once at the river bed, the way was easier, still arduous because of the boulders on which I had a tendency to twist my ankles, and hot, dry sand, on which I always found hard walking, but mindless because I could follow the dried stream bed into the middle of the beach. And during this walk on the river bed, I could view the ocean. Both the vision and its emerging sound would pull me forward

After my sojourn and visualizing the nastiness between here and the river bed, I decided to find a new way down, closer to the coastline where I thought there would be less brush. I turned directly toward the sound of the ocean. I could not see if it were easier from the top of the hill where I was because of a huge mound of jagged rocks which protruded....as much as twenty to thirty feet in front of the coastline. I decided on this new way because the old way was both a struggle and boring.

The descent over the top was rapid: the terrain immediately changed from crackly weeds to bushes with red berries on them. The scrub was just far enough apart not to cause trouble, but the loose soil and the intense pitch under my feet was a little treacherous, so I held onto the bushes for support. As the dry leaves brushed against my face, I perceived the dry and crusted dust from the jaunt through the weeds.

The question of my decision, as the terrain began to drop more rapidly, flashed for a second through my mind, but so involved was I with every single step, that I abruptly faced a bare rock wall. Was this one of the protrusions I had seen from the top?

Am I trapped and have to retrace my steps? I walked down to where I thought I could see the shoreline. It was to my right as I face the wall. Was it truly the shoreline, a cliff above the ocean? I descended to see. Yes, a straight drop into the sea. I carefully retraced my steps up out of my precarious position of loose soil and rotten rock. My only other alternative besides returning the way I came, was to skirt down and around this mound of rock.

On the other side of the prominence, I again reached a place where I could see my destination, the beach. I had made a good decision to come this way. Only a cove stood between me and the beach. Because I had never seen the cove before I decided to try a descent into it and then traverse it and climb the twenty or thirty foot rock which separates it from the beach. The cove has about fifteen feet of brilliant white sand in the shape of an open fan.

The way began with a minor pitch, but the difficulty increased with every step. The loose soil turned into a sheer rock drop. I finally reached a place where I again was faced with a descend directly into the ocean. The way to the right was blocked by a stone wall which I didn't think I could climb. The cove was down under the wall. Turn around? Walking away from the edge I found a place to sit. Placing down the paper bag, my lunch, I could only think of how much trouble it had been to carry it.

I relaxed into the wall feeling the sun and wind on my face. The roar of the slightly distant ocean below drowned the sound of the wind. The waves pounding the cliff shoreline seemed constant and strong, but the chaotic pounding rhythm ceased for a moment, and I listened for the wind whistling in among the nooks and recesses along the shore. All the while, the sound was an underlying whistling hum. The wind always blew. I can never remember a day or night when it didn't blow. Another wave awakened the sound of the ocean, and I relaxed further into rock.

Yes, I can take my time. Endless days of nothing. My only discipline is writing and reading.

Mind drifts daily into the cosmos,
Unable to catch itself
And look into a mirror to find an identity.
Dreams seek themselves among the globular
clusters
To find the dreamer.

Locked out of my being,
Without a key,
Seeking both dreamer and dream.

Thoughts upon thoughts flashed through my mind, more than I could possibly remember, maybe more than I could possibly know in my life time. With no mental or physical watch, I didn't know how much time past as I sat, but it must still be early morning.

The crash of a huge wave startled me as if out of a trance. What time is it? No time. Today, tomorrow, what is the difference? Three hours from now or now? It doesn't matter. My life: a finality in the timelessness. Stupid but true.

I stood and stiffly walked over to the cliff. The thought of jumping made me laugh but looking over I felt the pain of the hit, another belly flop. I laughed again, but abruptly my smile disappeared with the thought of getting pounded against the rocks. Dostoevsky was right: it is not the fear of death that stops me but the fear of the pain of death.

Life and death struggle in existence,
Sometimes within one human being.
Is it that death dares
And we don't care,
··· enough?
An unconscious destruction built as an
opposition?
Original sin
Or the results of what has been?
Self hate?
Guilt?
Or just a mad debate?
A divine fate?
Or seeded by nature's necessibilities?

Is it wanted?
Is it needed:
For sure, the future unfolds
(And a fool can fare well).

I really didn't want to turn back and maybe there was just enough of the smile still on my face to say go on. I put my paper bag into the back of my shirt, tucking both the shirt and the top of the paper bag under my belt. I walked up and down the ridge to see if I could see a foothold but nothing   Then I did a terribly foolish thing. I lowered myself over the edge, trying with my foot to find a notch, a foothold. After three attempts with rests in between, I found what I sought. Slowly releasing one hand from the ridge, I tested indent in which my foot rested; then never letting one hand leave the rock, I sought a place for the other hand. Another pocket. I slowly released my second grasp from the ridge, and found a lower handhold. My one leg was tired, and I switched feet by putting all my weight on my new found handholds, another foolish move because only one had to collapse, but it worked; upon finding another foothold, I was on my way down. The grips became easier to find because the many ledges were more jagged the rest of the way down. When finally my foot touched the sand, a relief overcame me, an overbearing tension was released, lifted, as I sank into the sand. It was mostly mental; my muscles remained tight. There were cuts and bruises on my hands, arms and legs. I began shaking, not violently but as if I were cold. I wasn't.

It was a beautiful cove, towering walls curving around to a small opening to the ocean. A wonderful sandy beach from five feet near the opening to twenty to thirty feet where I had descended. I walked to the lapping surf to wash my cuts. The overflow of sand in my tennis shoes filled. So I stopped and took them off, rolling my pants legs:

577

"I grow old … I grow old …
I shall wear the bottoms of my trousers rolled."

The pain shocked my awareness. The water was so cold that it wasn't cold. Pain of my cuts, pain of the water on my feet and legs. Again the physical world had awakened me into the here-and-now.

I had only washed one arm when I heard the sound of a wave explode through the mouth of the cove. Good God......The spray from the wave hit me in the back as I ran, best I could in calf high water, to the beach. The bouncing paper bag in the rear of my shirt was ripping loose. I had to hold it in place cause I couldn't retrieve it without dropping it into the rising foam brine. I had reached dry land before the wave finalized on the beach, but the rising waters had still caught me and wet my pants to my calf. Once the wave had retreated back through the cover's opening, I threw the paper bag then me face first onto the dry sand. What if it would have caught me? Would I be soaked head down, or worse, swimming on the other side of the cove? Another wave roar through the opening, like an explosion. Too tired to do anything, my body remained inert, but my mind thought "what the hell?"

As I slowly pushed myself up with both hands and turned over, another crashed through into the cove. This one rode to my feet. Particularly large swells? I looked in front of me. The paper bag, sand then the cliff. Too exhausted and permitting the warmth of the sun to relax me, I allowed my body then head fall onto the beach and sank into a peaceful blank moment.

An exceptionally large wave crashed through the opening, for this one, compared to the rest of them, it sounded like a cannon shot from the gunner's perspective.

I took notice of the noise but didn't stir. What seemed like seconds later, the water hit my legs; I began to move but realized it was too late. I quit struggling to get up, and I rolled over, did a push-up, and just let it happen. Holding my head up, I laughed at my fate, then relaxed into the feeling of wetness surround me. The receding wave washed the sand from under my hands and feet making me question my place on the beach. With the water gone, prostrated face first on to the wet sand, all my front felt the uncomfortableness of the wet sand and trickling water. I rolled over still on the ground; not caring if I was completely wet, and looked at the blue sky. The wind on the wet shirt caused a chill, but within minutes I could feel my shirt drying, and again the warm sun on my face.

My laughter,
A message from my madness?

Know a laugh
That is not mocking,
Not cynical
But
A laughter of everything

About everything.
Reach into it
To have your ears cleaned.

My laughter. My only freedom? Hearing another wave, I scooted belly up further back onto drier sand.

"I should have been a pair of ragged claws
Scuttling across the floors of silent seas."

Another pound of gigantic wave breaking through into the cove. It was a little stronger than the last. The tide is coming in! A really high tide? I should have checked my tide book. Hell, I laughed,

Here I am in a cove with cliffs all around me, and the tide is definitely rising. The wind seems to have picked up. Am I trapped here through my own efforts? With Margery? In my life? Trapped and the tide coming in? I laughed again, and just let my thoughts flow in the shifting surf; the smaller waves lapping the sand; the wind on my wet clothes; eyes closed, feeling the earth roll on it axis.

I imagined a panoramic show of fifteen foot waves crash through the opening and pound the cliffs behind me. Of course, this was exactly what had created the cove. Then I saw a wave crash over me, the currents sucking me into the ocean, me clawing at the sand as it gives way under my body. Another wave so large and so far over me that I can hear it hit the shoreline before I feel the brunt of its force swallow me; grabbing for land as it slides from me: gasping for unwatered-air, swimming without effect, tossed and dragged under the water, seeing nothing but pain green light, feeling nothing but the burning salt sea water in my lungs.

My vision caused me to sit up and look at the mouth of the cove. I stood, undressed, letting the paper bag land in the sand, rung my socks of water, shook my clothing, placed them on the cliffs facing the sun, then found my abandoned tennis shoes and the paper bag. I forced myself to eat a sandwich, a candy bar, and an apple. I folded the bag and put it into my pocket before shaking my clothes and dressing. I walked to the end of the cove and surveyed what remained to be done. After walking backwards, gathering a mental picture of a possible route to what seemed like the top. Exactly where was my decent route? I sat down to digest my food, gathered my strength, and analyze the route I chose. With tighten laces on my shoes, without further hesitation I began the ascent.

During the climb, I was oblivious to everything except the placing of my hands and feet. I watched the path as a projected vision from across the cove where I had sat. My mind was focused on the planned path and its final completion.

Of course I had not projected far enough, and my vision had stopped at a false summit at which time I found myself unable to able to further my ascent. The climb must have been fifty to sixty feet not forty. I was exhausted; my muscles hurt. I was about forty feet above the ground and thought of jumping back onto the sand and starting over, but I didn't know if I could clear the rock below. The thought of bouncing off the wall and landing sideways, or worse, deterred me. Also, it looked too high. Even clearing the rock face and landing feet first could break my legs. I was just clinging to the side of the cliff. My toes were strained by the pressure of holding the complete weight of my body. If I could only have found a place to put my heel and relieve some of the pressure. My left hand was holding me close to the rock between waists and shoulder high, so I couldn't put any weight on it. My right was feeling for a hold, but every place I could reach was smooth, or with a little pull gave way. Rock crumbed, bouncing off the wall then onto the beach below. I couldn't hold on very much longer. I tried finding my last step with my foot to go back but couldn't, and I was in a too insecure position to keep looking. I couldn't balance myself without three contacts on the rock. I found a protrusion and began to apply pressure, but it too crumbled and fell onto a shelf below, bounced, and fell to the bottom. I almost lost my footing and fell with the stone. Quickly I changed hands and began searching. I found a ridge. My legs were giving, so rather than testing it, I just hung on. It held, and I grabbed for it with my other hand; now it was holding my complete weight. Pulling myself waist high, I hooked my belt over it. For a moment I dangled .. ...relief ...... no pressure on my legs and hands. The thought of the jagged stake-like-protrusion giving way, made me push on. While my feet were dangling in the air I tried to put my weight onto my right hand, the stronger of the two, while frantically searching for another hand hold with my left.

I found one. I switched my weight and was hanging by my left hand for a moment until my right hand found a secure hold. I unhooked my belt, pulling myself up until my feet reached the once waist high hand hold.

That was too close. My arms and legs were shaking again. I found another hand hold for my left hand and rested. Tears flooded my eyes. Everything for a brief moment became blurred, soft edged. A larger than usual wave exploded through the mouth of the cove, and I looked down. The wave expanding formed a fan pushing onto the beach and then making its final flap onto the bright cream shore. The fan was now a white foam echo of the wave, then only a distancing shadow dissolving into the sand. But my beach was gone, only ten feet of sand remained.

A surge of wellbeing filled my body, a feeling of strength. In spite of my precarious position, I felt secure. Glad to be alive. I looked up to find my next move, and in what seemed like seconds I was working my way through shoulder high berry bushes to the top. In a way I don't remember how I got there. I remember sitting, relaxing on the top, my body pulsating, pounding with life. I felt living with a new sense of awareness: I had chosen life rather than giving up. I had chosen to struggle rather than stay submissive on the beach.

A shadow of a bird pierced my consciousness. Glancing upward, about ten feet from me, motionless in the air, a sea gull, complying with the wind's demands, then motionless again, it ejected shit, resumed its flight, not with flap of wing but only a concentrated effort. Contorting body used the chaotically changing currents to further its journey. Head thrust forward, wind in wing, then an almost motionless glance at the cliffs, determining its speed. A darting thrust forward, diving, gliding upward again, working his way across the mouth of the cove.

Further out at sea, a duck dived off a huge island of rock, flying close to the ocean, beating its way northward. The duck began to rise in altitude, its flight lost momentum. The wind was too strong, and the duck gave way and flew southward.

I walked to the pinnacle of the hill. The gull now was just a white spot moving in the distance; it still complied with the chaotically changing currents fractured off the cliff's shoreline.

I sat on the top and watched gulls soar upward on what seems like different rungs of a ladder, spiraling upward. In a huge circle without a flap, they soar round and around, higher and higher. Are they using a whirl-wind to travel as high as possible so they could

584

coast landward or were they chasing a swarm of insects? Flowing with them? Controlling the elements? Could they soar too high? No, "no bird soars too high if it soars on its own wings."

I stood and surveyed the scene. I was standing above the unseen cove on one side and the beach on the other. Looking to my left I could see where I stood this morning before I made the decision to go that way. Further to my left, this whole shoreline was a large cove, the shape of a crescent moon. To my right I could see where the dried river bed emptied onto the beach and further up the shore, the top of the extension of crescent. I had never seen the dynamics of this shoreline before.

Also, these birds must have been around me all morning, but I was oblivious to them. Here is life, different from what I will ever know. What could their consciousness be? What is it to be a gull, flying up the coast to a certain point, landing, resting then flying with the wind, down again pass me, heading for the opposite wall of the beach, faster than I had ever seen a bird travel, gliding close to the opposite wall, body fully extended against the rock backdrop as it curved and went straight out to the rock island, where the duck began. It hovered above its landing and settled. Was it for fun that they fought their way up the coast? Just to catch the wind and come down again?

A single gull passed by my head, coming from the

land, flew on out past the island and out to sea. Where is he going? I envied him. He was free to go, with no limitations, but his own strength.

"The swamp pheasant in the cage cannot be high in spirit,
But the snowy gulls across the waves
Love each other even in dreams."

Freedom and the dream of freedom: states of being.

Without completely surveying the situation of my direction, I began my descent over the top to my original destination. It was a matter of not just giving up but not failing in an attempt. It looked easy enough to not give it much thought. It was just a matter of placing my feet in crevices or going around big boulders. I encountered a couple of faces where it was not as easy as it looked. It could have been dangerous if I didn't expend my utmost concentration, but after what I had already gone through, almost anything would be easy in comparison.

Approximately seven or eight feet above the sands, I fell. It wasn't because the place was overly difficult or dangerous, it was only that I thought it was easy going that I didn't need to concentrate and test my moves. The edge on which I was standing crumbled, and I fell onto the beach. After the initial realization of what had happened had passed, and finding me unhurt, my fright became a stupefying exhaustion. I was almost glad it had happened. It was a tremendous liberation. It had happened so fast that it was not the same type of release of intenseness as I had felt before, but more subtle, more encompassing. I was at my destination; the challenge was over; I had accomplished my goal, and was still safe.

My mind became blank to everything except the aches of my body but knowing that, every breath kept my body alive, I breathed deep and strong with a will to return, to be revived and ready I stood. The familiarity secured my being. I took my shoes off and slowly walked to my favorite place to sit, a sand dune where the whole beach could be surveyed. I sat as I had done many times before but this time was a different experience. Yes, this was a high tide, the most I've seen. On the furthest point south, the rock face protruding into the ocean fifty yards held the secret of the cove. I had seen and even visited this wall before: thought of traversing it, but it went too far into the sea, which was too deep.

The beach meant more to me. It was not only a feeling of possession but that I had earned the peace attained. I had won my moment on the beach.

I buried my, feet in the sand, and it was only then that I noticed a large piece of yellow foam riding back and forth in the waves. I kicked at it, and it broke into pieces. Disgusting. It was then I noticed the beach was covered with foam and small plastic pieces of Styrofoam. There must have been a storm in the past week, but then with every wave the ocean cleans itself of debris. The strongest waves in the highest tide push the debris far enough onto the shore that the ocean rids itself. Submerged objects are deposited where the currents can no longer carry, but in time the sea will break them down into smaller forms which will be caught in the surf and pushed to shore. Did man crawl from the sea or was he ejected? Thrown out of paradise?

Not wanted to see or think anymore, I stared into the ocean. It was beautiful. The dark blue ocean meeting the lighter blue sky. The swells rising in patterned sets of blue-green racing landward. Small puffy clouds floating in the same direction, landward.

I checked to see if I could still see the fog. I couldn't tell. I stared at the horizon line and my mind went blank. The sharp wind made my eyes water, but I didn't blink. I didn't even want to blink. My eyes were caught on the permanence of the line and at the same time entranced by the chaotic movement both above and below the line. I don't know how long I stared until my eyes fell and were caught by the waves patterned in sets racing landward. Some of the waves broke out at sea with loud thumps, white lather on the crest of the waves resembled herds of horses thundering landward, their white manes blowing. I followed an individual wave until it crashed onto the beach before me.

Back out at sea the chaotic random sparkles of light on a momentary calm surface drew my attention. A young lady once told me that those sparkles were stars sleeping during the day. I smiled and wished she was here to experience and share the day with me.

The thud of an off-shore wave breaking changed my focus to following a long continuous wave, its hesitation, then a long stretch of it pounding down. Another wave behind it, without hesitation continuously curled its way down the coast. I lost sight of it in a hazy horizon.

My sight follows another wave to shore and crashes with it onto the sand. Another smaller wave catches it and pushes it further onto the beach. Oscillating foam runs onto the beach then slides off, that yellow disgusting foam. "Feel the moment; don't judge it," I said out loud to me. "Know and become." I look up a little and watch the waves in their final hesitation. Every wave ends differently. The chaotic ocean rises in sets. Ordered sets break into chaos. A never ceasing chaos pounds the shores of order. All is motion, a never ceasing motion of inter-changing chaos and order, order and chaos. Yes, yes. Life beats against death. Death beats against life.

A seagull squalks for attention. I look up and see it is only three or four feet from me. I yell a happy hello. Almost as if to show what it can do; it begins to climb. It looks down on me to see if I am watching and squelches again. Its soaring upward makes me lie back. It looks down on me again but continues upward. I laugh at the marvelousness of it all. I laugh with the gull, the pounding surf, the wind. Soaring ever higher, in a calm where all life is wonderfully sufficient, where existence doesn't need further explanation, except that it is. Gliding on a harmonious moment.

All sounds exist as one sound and so no sound. Eyes opened wide without sight, seeing All and nothing simultaneously, soaring in the very calm of existence, in the very cause of my being, in the very cause of being. It is so simple that ONE CAUSE. Life! Existence! I know. I know. Something is greater than me and my life. I am only a small part of something great, a force, a power. I want Him to know I know. I want to give Him something, something of value, an offering, thanking Him for existence, for being. To thank Him for giving me the knowledge and the ability to attain the knowledge.

I begin walking towards the ocean. I am the only thing I have to give, to give of my self. What a small sacrifice. I am nothing but yet all I am all I can give. All I have. A seal raises its head out of the surf and barks. For a moment two beings face each other on the edge of their different worlds. I stop. It wouldn't sacrifice itself but live and carry its role to its final conclusion. My offering will be my life, not my death. Tears burst forth and I cry aloud; my convulsing body falls on its knees, and I pray.

The battle was over, only a scarlet sky remained, punctuated by a red, huge burning sun, two feet above the horizon line and descending into the barely visible fog or clouds. The sun seemed to grow larger as it descended into the clouds. It grew redder, then darkened and disappeared. Flash! Red, white sunlight sprang between the fog and ocean, just for an instant. The sudden brightening flash didn't dissipate, but existed in intensity, then it was gone.

Light was fading rapidly. I stood to leave. A pale full, white moon met me. It had risen above the hills behind me, seemly larger than the setting sun.

Could this be a reason for the feeling of harmony, a balance of forces pulling, and me soaring down the corridor between the two? I must come back here with a total eclipse of the moon. Whatever it was, I thought, with a moon like that, I won't have any trouble finding my way back if I follow the way I know. Rather than leaving directly, I walked the length of the beach and back. Where had the day gone? An instant had passed, and all had changed. It seemed like a minute had passed since I stood on that hill overlooking this ravine and yet now, it is a different ravine, a different world.

I stood looking into the moving shadows of the brush. The wind had picked-up and was blowing hard off the ocean. My body was chilled, so I began moving again, this time toward the house. I tired easily and sat many times in the brush and looked at the moon through the branches. The difficulty of the walk to the top of the hill was increased by deceptive light and shadows. At the top of the hill, I could now see the fog and clouds almost on top of me. The wind was strong at my side but for a moment, I couldn't push on. I sat, then laid back, my head away from the wind. Relaxed, mind raced reliving the day. Had it all really happened? The coldness penetrated my rest until it forced me to get up and move. Had I slept? I rose and immediately began walking fast off the hill, sometimes falling on unseen rocks and holes. Progress was slower than I anticipated or the fog was moving more rapidly than I had expected, for it was upon me a little over half way home.

Home, that was the first time I had referred to my uncle's beach house as home. The thought of the front door being opened and a roaring fire in the fire-place, hot tea in my big easy chair seemed to warm me for a minute. The pale fall moon was momentarily covered by the racing broken fog clouds. It gave the appearance of the moon running across the sky rather than the clouds racing.

Imagination covers reality and tries to make a more pleasant life. How real was today? Am I really changed? I felt the wind and the cold, that could not have changed. I look upward.

Oh, pale full moon,
Spinning above a light, rapidly moving, cloud cover,
Seems to run across the sky.

Is everything deceptive and temporal?
If only Maya gives life
I don't care.
Let me gaze at your beauty
Until death
Rips the image from my brain

Still I'll struggle
To seek vital, viable,
Possible truths to share.

How much is gained by a single soul lapping the infinite? A single soul thrown onto the beach of the infinite? A flash of the sun? A moment to know. A moment to live, radiate, even if the next is a mergence back into the darkness, oblivion. I don't care. It will be enough.

Yes, the feelings remain, though the experience now is but a memory. With the thought of getting to the house, I quickened my pace. I will continue to seek truth and reality, and it will be that struggle which will give me meaning. If reality is above my grasp, beyond my reach, I will again be that soft shelled crab, swimming in a system greater than my conception, but I will attempt to know and communicate.

The moon was completely covered by the fog and darkness enclosed. Still I pushed quickly homeward but I could feel my limitation. "How great is the darkness around me and how small I am." But now I can face this without fear. A search without fear. Seeking means to find a way through, a means not to escape, but illumination, if even just for a second, an instant of illumination in the myriad of time.

It was at that moment I knew I was going to try to record the day. Even though I knew that the record of my search wouldn't completely record the truth; I knew I was going to try. And yet even more, I knew that even though a record of my search would not always have its manifestation that my search would continue onward into the night.

Sept. 18

In writing and then rereading yesterday's experience, I can see I have made great strides. Toward what you may ask? An adjustment, an adaptation, an acceptance, an awareness. I am refreshed, revitalized by my experience. Even though this place, this beach house reminds me, pulls me back to who I was three days ago and re-awakens feelings I felt then, I can face them with a new energy, a new perspective. I am not as involved with me and my problems as I was then. I got out of my limited being. I identified with something beyond me, something even beyond the sea. The sea and maybe nature itself were only a part, a manifestation of His workings. What part do they play in the whole? What is my part?

I became submissive to His workings. Mentally I was purged and became receptive. I flowed in the stream, letting the stream carry me, but being at one with it. It was not by choice that I flowed. The currents again had ripped me loose. It was the tears which fell; it was the fall at the end of the climb; it was the fear of death which awakened me. All of these ripped me from myself. It was not by choice, no. How would, how could one make that choice? I was that duck forced off his course by a too great a wind.

I could see yesterday and I can still see that there are forces beyond my conception. Not even my doubt right before getting back here can dispel the knowledge I gained. The forces are both within me and without. The force within me is a will to live. It was awakened again and again within me and yet before two days ago I didn't know it existed. The forces without are those eternal forces which drive "All that is," the forces which keep it going; is that Reality? Did I, for a too brief a moment, experience Reality? I was for that moment larger than me and my life. In that moment of blank meditation on the horizon line, I fell back into the flow from which it All is derived. I know there is a Reality but many questions, too many questions remain. There are forces beyond my recognition, forces upon forces, of which I only glimpsed, a part? some? the whole? Could any of these forces have a conscious effect on an individual's life as we know it or can know it? Could any of them have a conscious effect on an individual's destiny? Are any of them conscious?

I know there is something beyond me, something that

will continue without my awareness of it, something that will continue when I am gone, some thing beyond my consciousness, perception, or conception. The Truth is in the All, in us, for we are part of the Truth. Yes, seed of the All is in us, for we are a part of it All.

I remember now that at the moment of recognition, after that moment of meditation, I thought of sacrificing something to this or these forces. I had nothing but my self. The thought of walking into the ocean occurred to me for that was all I had to give. But I realized that I would be sacrificing nothing. How could a part of the All be offered to the All, for it is already in possession and there are many other forces to which to make that sacrifice?

Sept. 20

I slept most of yesterday; exhausted, probably still wired from the day before.

Sept. 22

For the last two days I have rested and worked on the house. In case I decided to stay, I began winterizing it. I also chopped some drift-wood, so I would again have a good supply. Earlier in the day I went to the store and did my shopping for the week. My work on the diary was to reread what I have written, clarify the writing, elaborate it, etc. I did compose a poem as a reaction to my excursion.

The currents of the sea
Find restriction in the approaching land,
But a message of its magnitude
Rises in green,
Hesitates
Because of an offshore wind;
Its cap
Bellows into mist,
Then breaks into white lather.

Still racing landward
Foam rides the crest of its mothered force.
The sea's undulations,
Patterns in sets
Rise and break
With a seeming design,
But in its final thrust at the land,
It is chaos which reaches out
Roaring,
"I am master!"

Three gulls
Force their flight up the coast
Each following the next
Weaving a pattern to speed their journey,
Fighting the wind,
Then down
Close to ocean
Gliding in the smooth curl before the wave
Soaring birds lift

As wave disintegrates beneath.
Back down to ocean
Another wave to transport.
Northward, swiftly northward,
Diving, gliding, soaring upward again,
Diving,
Racing with the sea against the wind
To a school of fish trapped too close to shore.

The cries of a thousand gulls,
Ripping the sound of surf,
Signify the panic beneath the water.

Looking back down the coast,
More gulls weave patterns,
But now their flights have significance:
Life – Death.

My mind bangs on the door of all I see:
"Run with the moment; don't judge it
Find contentment through closeness:
Know and become."

The oscillating foam
Runs up onto the beach
Then slides off.
Merging into sea,
No pattern maintains.

All is motion,
Never ceasing
Chaos:
Real,
For no imagination could have created it.

Laughter lets me in,
A laughter as insane as the vision
Joins with ocean to become a single deafening
roar.
Soaring through the imaginary sea-wall
Constructed to protect and secure mind against
chaos.

Soaring
Where opposites meet
And opposition ceases:

Human souls lap the infinite:
Feeling harmony.

I am thinking of titling it "Freedom Through Chaos."

I can see now that the original version of my diary was written by pin-pointing places to get off and then just letting my mind wander. In the original, I just let my thoughts flow, recording what came out. When I lost tract, got lost in the thought, when the thought became too complex or when my thought drifted away from the original point or when grossly illogical jumps were made, skipping from one thought to another, seemly without connection at all, then I had to reread, pick up the train of thought, clarify or complete the thoughts.

(Most of my writing, especially notes, are handwritten. But my more extensive writing is on computers, like this. This diary started in a notebook but I transferred everything to this. One of the major problems is that it is so easy to erase, to write over. But I have recorded the original writing and my first thoughts as "Diary Supplement.")

The main reason for doing this is to clarify my thoughts to me. Also by doing this I am forcing me to think thoughts through and hopefully organize my life around these thought-out thoughts, rather than living the fragmented, ill formed thoughts.

In that I can see my own confusion and clarify it must be a sign of sanity. Unless it is clear to me and no one else. Would I question my sanity if I were insane? Wouldn't I just try to deny it? Maybe, maybe not. Maybe it is insane to question my sanity. Yes, it is the fear of being insane that makes me insane. I am paranoid about being insane. Phobo-phobia, I have phobophobia. Why? That is the question. Maybe it is only one symptom. Why do I have a fear of been insane? Could finding out the event, if it were an event, which caused this phobia, help rid me of the paranoia? Maybe it was not an event but a part of a complex defense mechanism, a part of the paranoia complex.

Was it just a case of paranoia that caused me to not understand at that party? Could I have understood if I weren't paranoid? If their conversation was too personal or if it were all staged, I wouldn't have been able to understand, for sure. But was there a possibility to understand and/or to interact, and I couldn't find it because I was afraid I couldn't? When that man and woman turned to me in the second circle, they must have thought they were communicating with me. Or were they putting me on? Trying to get rid of me.

Insanity must be an inability to adapt, an inability to function, an inability to construe that which exists and distinguish it from the non-existent. Insanity must be an inability to make workable interpretations and an inability to change the interpretation when it is not workable. All are types of rigidity.

My insanity is a generalize paranoia with different manifestations of paranoia exaggerated out of proportion. The generalized paranoia is natural. It is inbred in people. Probably it is an instinct that was necessary for survival. There exists a fear of extinction, with just cause. Those who had some forms of paranoia lived and reproduced; those who did not have it were killed. It would be stupid not to be paranoid about some people and some situations, to have a fear of the unknown, fear of change, a fear of pain. Yes, paranoia is not totally unfounded, but the extent to which I exaggerate it, it is. My paranoia can makes me into a nonfunctioning being. It stands between me and other people. Why does it exist?

I looked up paranoia on-line and it said that it is "a tendency on the part of individuals or of groups toward suspicious, and distrustfulness of others that is based not on objective reality but on a need to defend the ego against unconscious impulses, that uses projection as a mechanism of defense, and that often takes the form of a compensatory megalomania."

Do I have a mania for doing great or grandiose things? I am writing, that's for sure. Am I defending my ego against an unconscious impulse? All the rest makes sense, why shouldn't those two be true? But what am I defending me against? It is true that I feel threatened by other people? It must be that I am afraid my self-identity, my self-image, would be destroyed. Maybe I don't want to see me as I really am but as whom I wish to be. I want to live in the illusion I have about myself, not to be awakened. But what would I do if I didn't feel I was important enough to even write? Then what purpose would my life have? No, I had better not go to the other extreme and demean me, to take away all my self-confidence and my meaning to myself. Maybe if I just recognized the paranoia each time it occurs and know it for what it is; I could use it and at the same time dismiss it. Yes, use the energy created by the paranoia to some worthwhile purpose. Is this an example of my mania?

If my attempt to deal with problems greater than I can handle is an example of my mania and is considered insanity then insanity is our teacher. Grappling with questions beyond my ability, trying to grasp a system greater than me, are my methods to explore. No, I am not trapped. I have voluntarily jumped in. I am only trapped if I consider me trapped and exploring if I consider me exploring.

No, my attempting to solve grandiose problems is not part of mania. If men can either discover possibilities or invent working possibilities then who is to decide if someone's extreme state of being is insanity. Only when these extreme states are harmful, or the harm doesn't justify the reason, then could it be considered an insanity of concern. Could not an extreme state of being extend possibilities? Couldn't man extend the possibilities of man by achieving extreme states of being? Who would hinder such a quest? Whether or not the environment could accept or reject the extension, the achievement of the created possibility, remains a question. Maybe all men are insane to some degree: it is their individuality, their uniqueness. There is no absolute norm but only an abstracted norm from which we all vary to some degree.

All extreme states
Are insanity.
Didn't you ever doubt the rational?

Swimming in the chaos
Upstream
Gaining momentum.

The state of being which existed the other day along the beach still slightly remains. I am sure it would be considered insanity, for it definitely wasn't the norm. If it could have only lasted: A feeling of profundity, grandeur, for sure, a connection with the All. I am not afraid of entering that state again even if it is called insanity.

But then again, is all of this an attempt to rationalize my insanity, my illusion of grandeur.

Sept. 23

In rereading yesterday's insert, the statement "if man can either discover possibilities or invent working possibilities then who is to decide if someone's extreme state of being is insanity," made me question. Would inventing possibilities (a possibility being something that can actually come into being) be possible in a finite universe? If one accidentally invented (discovered) existing possibilities then the answer would be yes. But if one combined existing possibilities to create a new one, would it still be a finite universe, for example the possibility of god with the possibility of unicorn so that somewhere in the universe there exists a unicorn god or God which is a unicorn? The answer to this would still be that that possibility would exist in a finite universe because there would be a finite number of possibilities and therefore a finite number of combinations of possibilities. But if by inventing we mean create from nothing, not just putting things together to form a new relationship nor discovering, but actually creating from nothing, [the Universe. itself or an original idea (do original ideas really exist?)]) the Universe could not be finite because more possibilities could exist than already exist. We could add another to that which exists.

What really is the imagination? Does man have one foot in the finite and one in the infinite? Is there a fork in the road which is ultimately a final choice? I am in a finite functioning system; at least my body is, but what about my imagination, mind, spirit, soul? Did a part of my being touch the Infinite at the beach the other day? Obviously the finite does exist does the Infinite exist, that is the question. Finite systems in a Infinite   Universe.   Finite   systems   ying-yang combining to create an infinite system.   Another possibility is that they could both exist on a continuum as the relationship of the colors black - white. If we are encompassed by the Infinite then we are a part. If the relationship of Infinite-finite exists on a continuum then we could be at the point where both meet. If the relationship is that of separate equal opposites then we could be trapped in the finite unable to reach out or in some-way unknown to me; be able to break out. Or if there is no Infinite then we are trapped, probably, in depleting systems.
If I did experience the Infinite the other day then I either experienced a greatness beyond me or fell over the edge on the continuum or broke-out, of my finite bonds. Or what did I experience if there is no such thing as an infinite?

Of course there must be more possibilities than these, but I can't think of them at the time. Can any answers dealing with this question be resolved? It still seems now to only be a matter of belief. Could believing or disbelieving place me a continuum, draw me closer to the thin line which separates them or take me further away?

Questions upon questions still fill the fleeting moments until my brain gives way to blankness. So far to go but not tonight. I am going to bed.

Sept. 24

Margery called and is coming up tomorrow. This house is a mess. I just think I will celebrate the first day of autumn and clean house.

Sept. 26

It is a little after midnight of the twenty-fifth,

Margery is asleep, but I have to record what has happened today before some of it slips my mind.

It was lucky I did most of the house cleaning because Margery arrived at one a.m. on the twenty-fifth. While cleaning and getting ready for her arrival, I tried to figure a way to tell her what I wanted, to break the ice as were, to try to get some communications started again. I memorized what I was going to say. "I have been in an incommunicable prison in myself for years and am unable to break out. There has been so much to express that I haven't expressed, so many times that I should have said something but said nothing especially in the last year and a half. My attempt to write has been an attempt to break the chains. We have stopped communicating. We stopped sharing. I can see now that a great deal has been because we quit trying. If there is no growth nor communication, it will eventually destroy what we do have; something I don't want to happen but something that seems inevitable."

We had been sitting drinking tea, not saying anything when I blurted this out. When I finally got to the end, of course, I realized it wasn't all I really wanted to say but I didn't know what more I could say. Neither of us knew what to say. We sat and finished the tea, then Margery broke the silence. "I don't want it to end either."

What a shock her words were. Pleasantness filled my body. Then it occurred to me to let her read the diary. I printed it and gave it to her. I didn't explain anything to her before I handed it over, and I didn't give the beginning to her but starting with Sept. 9 which began after her first visit.

"Let's go to bed. I will read it tomorrow."

In spite of my fear she wouldn't read it, would think it was stupid, not take it seriously, not understand it, etc., etc., it caused a real break-through.

While sitting in bed in the morning, when she first

started reading she said nothing for a long while. I brought her coffee and went about my chores, at first straightening the room. I could tell by her face that she didn't know how to take it, then she started to relax. I didn't nor couldn't relax. I tried to imagine where she was reading, what she was thinking. I made breakfast and brought it to her.

Finally after about two hours she said, "Our differences are real. I would even go so far as to say we do have different realities. I can see, now, there is a difference of our perceptions. The difference particularly exists in who you think I am and who I think I am; and who you think you are and who I think you are. I didn't really see a lot of what you have said nor can I now, but at least now, I see how you saw it, whereas I couldn't before. But different people with different realities can live together without hate, misunderstandings, by understanding how the other person sees the world. I have a new respect for you and your world, your perspective, your quests, in your words, your explorations.

"I have always respected you and your mental probing, your questioning, your exploration of yourself and your art….."
"What happens when the realities clash as they did, and as they will? If both of us want this relationship and it continues, what will happen when we want different things, when we want to do different things?"

"That is kinda what you have said here. I think we were on the right track when we decided upon common goals that we both wanted and were willing to work towards. Then our differences can be an asset because we can have differing viewpoints on how to achieve the goals."

She again began reading. I felt good: everything would be all right. I had spontaneously said what I had said, not repeated my memorization! I had expressed my feelings to her for the first time in years. She was nearing the end, and I knew she had understood some of it. "Did you intentionally not record my first visit, immediately afterwards?" She laughed and said, "You know, after you questioned your insanity the last time we spoke at my apartment, I began to question it, but never before that. I dismissed your strange actions and talk as the pressure we were both going through. You exasperated, frustrated me. I desperately loved you but we couldn't even talk, much less face our problems.

"Without us being able to communicate, we constantly hit brick walls, and I had to back away. Maybe I should have stopped working so hard and focused more on us. But since both of us wanted our relationship, I thought it would work itself out.

"I didn't know you were questioning your sanity. I didn't know your feelings at all. Let me reread some of this."

She picked up the manuscript, thumbed through it and found the place she wanted to read. She read it and found another place. She stopped reading and with the manuscript still in hand, said, "You know what happened at the party, as you call it, was that I had a job interview, and Janet had a meeting with her actor friends. She must not have seen you or else she would have said something. I don't know what they were doing either. I never asked them. I didn't know any of this was happening. I wonder who you met at the door. I really didn't know things like that were happening." She laughed and picked up the manuscript again and began reading but stopped, drew a blank face and said in a serious tone, "I have a confession."

"I don't want to hear it, unless you feel you absolutely must tell me.'

"Fine I don't need to say anything. Really I didn't want to tell you because I knew you would judge it differently than I, but let me say that I didn't fully respect myself for my actions. I couldn't love him because I didn't respect him for loving me. I have thrown myself at many people who didn't love me … but this talk is in the past. Where have we been for these last two months; wherever it was, it wasn't together, but for me it wasn't as far apart as for you.

"You know thinking about what you picked out of our last conversation about me saying it just doesn't work, here," and she turned to it and showed me. "Well, those weren't the right words, the meaning was there but the meaning was taken out of context. The emphasis was wrong. If I presented myself incorrectly then I apologize. I tried to emphasize that we should try to live separately for a while because it wasn't working for me. I was unhappy, 'bored' was the right word, but bored with our frustration, and I didn't know what else there was. I wanted to find out. I didn't want to live together because I was afraid to do what I wanted and had to do, because I would hurt you and you would withdraw even further. It got so bad that I felt there was no sense in even trying to communicate. And when you kept badgering me, I finally blew-up, but before that I left with the idea that by leaving, things would get better, and I am sure I expressed it. I am sure I had said that I didn't feel the relationship was over for good. How could we have meant so much to each other for such a long time, and it be over just like that? You are the only person I have really ever loved, and you know, I have found I really do need what you can give me. I need the respect of myself which I have with you.

"I wish I knew why you had come up here, I could have straightened it out. It is stupid we didn't talk. I just assumed you were up here because you wanted to be, that you wanted to be alone and that was another reason for your silence. I assumed you thought that this was a better place for you than San Francisco."

"Yes, I thought it was really over and thought that my hope, that it wasn't, was a fantasy."

"Let's forget it and have lunch." We immediately began preparing food, but our conversation didn't cease. She pushed forward by saying, "Now I understand a great deal about you and what you think about our relationship and my friends.

"I was becoming close to some of them and since we are a couple, I am sure they wanted to include you. I would even say, some of them wanted to help. They probably thought you were too enclosed in yourself or something like that and wanted to bring you out."

I laughed and said very sarcastically, "And I didn't even give them a chance."

"They are a very close group. Most of them have been together for years. Most of them are good people and mean no harm. It is their way, probably which evolved out of encounter groups and acting groups. They are into psychological reactions to their acting.

"You know, driving up here, I was thinking how any relationship would probably have gotten to the point where ours did, that any relationship can close off the rest of the world if you let it. There can be the relationship and nothing else because you feel you don't need anything else. I can see now, even with Janet and her friends I was closed off to the rest of the world. When I first took my job as secretary, I hated it; it was below me, and I felt that I didn't need to meet any of the people at work. I was happy with Janet and Janet's friends because they had depth, but now that I have begun to meet my colleagues, found that I was just limiting myself. There are some good, interesting people at work. We all have to work, so that is not totally who we are. It was probably the meeting them and letting them to get to know me which has helped further me, get me my raise.

"I must admit, I blamed you for closing me off to the world. I thought it was your jealousy and that you were trying to possess me, have me all to your own. Yes, ... but then I realized that it was me."

"No, but I was to blame. I quit doing everything that was important to me to just try to be with you. I wanted you constantly. I wanted to devour you, to have you all to myself. I was afraid to let you get out, for fear you would find something better."

"But you shouldn't have tried to control me. I shouldn't have let you. That was my fault. I also knew, I didn't feel the intensity you felt and that worried me, but I was happy, and I do love you.

"Your intensity, your closing yourself off to life and other people is you, and either I should accept it or get out. It is up to you whether you can accept me as I am. I want to accept you, and think I can." Putting the food on the table stopped our conversation for a moment but after we sat, she resumed it. "Did that really happen on the beach?"

"I think it did. I might have romanticized a little but my feelings were as real as any feeling can be."

"Do you really want truth?" I nodded an affirmative reply. "Do you know what some of Janet's friends would have described what you have written in your diary?" She didn't want a reply and continued without getting one. "An ego-manic growing into a mythomaniac. That you want significance to be someone so badly that things could happen in your mind which really didn't happen."

"What would you say or what do you think?" I asked her. "That's more important."

"Some others would say you are a mystic and had a mystical experience, a form of enlightenment; if you experienced what you said you did."

"What do you say or think?"

"I believe in you and believe what you say."

Flashing back to my fear of paranoia, "What is a mythomaniac?" I asked meekly.

She smile then giggled, "Maybe a made up word. But I mean it as someone who is so aware of his actions and the effect of his action that he can use them to create a myth about himself and is intentionally doing so."

"I don't see how that could apply to me."

"You can't sit there and tell me you didn't know your effect with Janet's friends. Your mysterious departures, your esoteric statements, your aloofness; they couldn't know you; you didn't let them and so they began to build you as they thought you were."

"None of that was with intent. I didn't know my actions would create that, and still don't quite believe it. I only wanted to get you back and work on my art. All my actions are directed towards those two goals. I didn't give a damn for your friends and who they thought I was. I feel that I have only so much time. And I should spend carefully. Only I can decide on what and with whom."

"But that's the problem. You don't know the reaction to you, and you go through life without seeing that you have an effect besides on yourself."

"So I am probably an egomaniac and have to

admit it but not a mythomaniac."

She started laughing, came up to me and threw her arms around me and said, "You'll never change, and for your sake, I hope you never do," then kissed me on my cheek.

I whispered in her ear, while were still embracing, "I don't really understand you. I guess I never will, because what I said was serious."

"I'm not laughing at your statement but your egotism."

"Is my goal to be that artist, to be able to create a 'me' that everything I express, no matter what media, will be art.... Is that a grandiose idea? Do you think I am defending myself, my ego, from a deep seated fear that I am a failure? "

"People may consider you a failure because they don't know your work, your progress. They just see that you are not supporting yourself, that you are not famous. Don't let their projection on you determine who you think you are."

That was one of the more beautiful moments of my life or for sure in my relationship with Margery. Afterwards we did the dishes, made tea, refurnished the fire, then sat in front of the fire and talked until it was very late. She went to bed and I came in and began writing. Now I am going to turn in.

Sept. 27

Margery left today. Yesterday both of us slept very late. She woke about eight and let me sleep until she had a fire going and brunch ready. After eating and cleaning, we went for a walk down the beach.

While walking she asked me about a statement in the diary concerning my belief. "This is one of the many reasons I love you." I answered, "It is who I am around you, who you bring out in me. I know you take me seriously, you believe me; you really want to know about me." I put my arm around her and pulled her close then answered her question.

"My search into the unknown can be advanced by speculating, creating, testing. But these are not our only tools. As we increase our sensibilities and our knowledge, we will increase the quality of our speculations and creations and in turn our concept of reality.

"One thing which I have control over right now, if I recognize it, or since I recognize it, …. is my attitude, my attitude about the reality, my attitude about my speculations and creations of reality, and my attitude about other people and me. This is where some of our choices lay. We each live, project, create our attitudes. Only we can defeat ourselves in this aspect. "Still fate, or other forces beyond our control help determine our attitude, I know that. The excursion on the beach the other day helped change my attitude about life. My fears are no longer as strong; I am less afraid of either death or life. I can let go. I don't need to hold on to anything too tightly.

"I have felt my insignificance in the Universe and now

I have less to lose. In seeking the Reality, I feel I am seeking my God through creating, testing and discovery. Because of my experience on the beach, I feel I can come face to face with Him; I am not ashamed of me nor my life; I want to know Him and truly see my freedom and His control; I want to know that Reality."

Margery looked at her watch, laughed, and said, "Could this be a reason why we never resolve any personal issues?" and still laughing, "They are not as important as your Universal insights." She hugged me and kissed me on my cheek, then pushed me backwards so I almost fell.

When I regained balance, I smiled, but with her statement I wound down and stopped like a tin soldier beating a tin drum. And actually what I just wrote was an elaboration of what I said and what I wanted to say.

Sept. 26

Today, the twenty-sixth, Margery and I talked on the phone for hours, discussing whether we would return and live together. I had given up the apartment we shared together, and we would have to find another because I don't like hers. I want to live together again and so does she, but there is something holding us back. We both think there is something we don't yet understand about each other and ourselves. She says it would be a gamble, because of our lack of knowledge. She is more worried about me if it doesn't work than about herself. I want it and told her that maybe the only way of finding out is if we try. To me the possibility of what I want for the relationship far outweighs the possible hurt and pain at the end, if the end comes. It is worth the gamble.

The phone conversation ended by me saying to do what she thought best for herself, and if she wanted to gamble with me, I would love it. She called back three hours later and said let's do it.

Sept. 28

I slept very poorly last night. About three o'clock in the morning I couldn't stand lying in bed anymore, got up, walked down the closest beach, the one Margery and I had walked. In the daylight the ocean would have been green-blue waves but in the night, the ocean was a moving mystery of grays and blacks: force, power, rising and falling, crashing on the shoreline, spreading gray foam on the beach. The wet sand was alive with either radiation or light greenish blue fluorescent plankton that scattered with every kick of my feet. I dismissed the thought of it being radiation as paranoia and began to play with the wet sand. But the fluorescent phenomenon couldn't hold my attention or contain my thoughts. My mind questioned itself and what it wanted. Resolutions have been made to problems which I faced, but more questions remained.

Mind, will, imagination, what part do they play in

Reality? Can our will unlock the mind and let it see? A deliberate act of the will? Are imaginary images a part of the total Reality, or is reality a part of the infinite imagination? The Universe a small portion of God's imagination?

Could the full potentiality of the mind, the brain, be able to see Reality? Be at one with God's imagination? And death be the falling into the chaos of this imagination, free-floating.

Feeling that I can neither stop the questioning of my mind nor the decaying of my body, I continued down the beach. I walked until dawn, then turned around and started back. I know now that I must live more fully, and with more awareness. My search should not end even in death.

All alone I walked, but I began to feel the presence of Margery. Every step took me closer to the house and my return to San Francisco. When daylight was in the air, and the world was again white and various different blues, I sat down and stared at the horizon line.
Blanking my mind to my decisions and questions, blanking my mind to all and just letting the motion of the waves below the horizon carry me inward, hoping the ocean would clean my soul with every lapping wave, leaving the doubts and fears on the barren sands until my life is only the essence of being.

Entry II – Appendix

The following document was sent to me from Berkeley. I called the professor and we had a very interesting conversation. Ike, in his first couple of years at college, had taken as series of philosophy of art and two or three Aesthetics courses, in both departments. From what the professor has surmised, this manuscript was the culmination of those courses. Ike presented this paper to all of his current and past art professors and then used it as a business card when he entered new art courses. Undoubtedly, this is not the only version.

A Definition of Art

What is Art? What is an art object? One way to determine these definitions is to list all the categories to which art belongs then try to list all categories which belong to art; point to an observable fact and say, "This is art!" or "No, that is not art," stating why, based on inductive and deductive reasoning.

If one could do this for every object that one claimed to be art or for that matter for every object which exists then all objects would be categorized as art or non-art. Dividing all objects into art or non-art becomes a matter of deduction based on the categorical definitions derived by induction. This is to say art can be equated with objects, events, conceptions, and definitions, and if complete categorization were accomplished then we would, for a time, know what art was: mainly, all the objects, events, concepts, and definitions named. Of course, we would have to have an open statement so that more definitions and concepts could be added as the need arose; for what would art be without the additive, creative quality? It sounds simple enough but would this process be possible?

One must assume that perceptual terms would not have been developed unless consistent properties (physical characteristics) were inherent in objects. Also without consistent qualities (abstract attributes), one must assume that concepts could not be contemplated and/or discussed. Unless we perceived objects with these non-varying substances, properties and qualities, our language and indeed our thoughts would be awashed in total chaos. Our words would have fluctuating meanings, and we would have no anchor for our cognition. Therefore, if the word "art" has any meaning, one would assume that in the naming of these consistent properties and/or qualities which in their naming would define art. If one could find properties and qualities which only existed in art and in no other terms or objects, then in the naming of these one could define art.

Some of the properties which have been equated with art are "creations" or objects with form, techniques or style; or existence of an artifact showing human workmanship; or a unique manifestation, not replicated nor even possibly duplicated. Some of the qualities which must be explored are the aesthetic, beauty, knowledge, and significance.

All of these terms together, or any of them may be the consistent qualities of art. However, without defining aesthetic (which is discussed later) beauty, knowledge, or significance, it is certainly evident that each of these is not the single quality which defines art. For example, pieces of art are not necessarily aesthetic and beautiful, and yet other objects can be. Some art works were created to repel, to shock, and to repulse the viewer. Robert Morris' "Litanies" removes the aesthetic from the object. (Is this possible? Obviously it depends on the definition and his capabilities.) Nevertheless, Bosch's "Garden of Delights" is presumed to place the fear of God into viewers and repulse them at the same time. "Guernica" by Picasso displays the horrors of war. Some of Willem de Kooning's women and some of Francis Bacon's people are not beautiful and seemingly are not supposed to be. A great many Pop Art pieces do not attract the on-looker. Some Wassily Kandinsky's works push the viewer from the painting; much of German Expressionism (1900-1930) and Dadaism, to name a few, seem not want to give pleasure, not to want to draw the audience into the work but to smash some human horribleness into the spectators' faces. The history of art is thus filled with pronounced masterpieces which are not beautiful or aesthetic. Of course, the reader may take objection to any or even all of the objects and movements named but surely the reader must concede that not all art is either beautiful or aesthetic, and we need find only one piece of ugly and unaesthetic art which the reader accepts as art to disprove that these are not criteria. Then on the other hand, many objects and events are beautiful and aesthetic but not considered art: the planet earth, sunsets and other scenes from nature, pretty much all of life, automobiles, paper towels, packaging for a great many products. I have been meditating on a particularly pleasing clear, glass beer mug with "Alaskan Brewing Co." on it, which my niece gave me. I use it for coffee. She gave it to me, and I received it knowing this mug was not an art object but an advertisement. Returning to the main point, one would be hard pressed to prove that either beauty and/or aesthetics is an element essential to art.

The question of the existence of an artifact needs even more exploration than the above. If we accept the fact that artifact must be produced and that an artifact is an object showing human workmanship then Mel Henderson's 1970's fifteen search lights probing the San Francisco's night sky, a floor of lights one at a time in the Alcoa Building consecutively flashing on and then off, a moot synthesizer broadcasting from a popular radio station while people in parked cars up and down the hills in San Francisco flickering their car beams to its rhythm, and many more occurrences happening for thirty minutes throughout the city with the culmination of three search lights merging into one beam on a single engine airplane would not be considered an art object, much less a sculpture, for without even considering the question of unorthodox media, no "real" object existed. All productions of songs, dances, plays, concerts, in fact all living art forms could only be considered art in their concrete forms: scores, scripts, manuscripts, movies because no artifact by this definition was produced.

To concede this point would be to exclude the affect and the effect of the production. Many art pieces have been lost through destruction and because of their temporal form, but their effects may have continued through their influences. In fact, the presentations may have changed the concept of art, art's direction, at the time of creation, but no artifact was created. The whole argument concerning the production of an artifact rests on the definition of it. If artifact means the existence of an object then an artifact is not a necessary property of art. But if artifact is "something done" then an artifact is a necessary condition, for it can not be acquiesced that an unexpressed idea or concept is a work of art. If something thought or expressed is always something done then just by thinking or describing an object is art, another point which cannot be conceded. It must have taken form: be an arrangement and have a structure. Now however, if something expressed through a medium has an effect, then this is probably a giant step closer to a viable definition. All the same, it should still be recognized that even if an art object is accepted to be an artifact that artifacts are not always art. A computer may not be a piece of art although it is an artifact.

The question of knowledge is slightly different. All art does seem to convey knowledge in some manner. For instance, one can obtain a certain type of knowledge from almost any object contemplated. One can see how the product was constructed, the relationships of its component parts, the use of materials, and its place or connection to the rest of the environment. These are just a few examples of knowledge which can be gained. But the article contemplated doesn't have to be an art entity; it could be a moon-rock, and yet from every piece of art some type of knowledge can be gained. The capability to express or convey knowledge is an essential aspect of art, but other non-art objects convey information. Not only are knowledge of construction and knowledge of relationships conveyed but meanings, understandings, information, and even truths are examples of knowledge which art can bear.

This discussion of knowledge assumes a perceiver of the art presentation: either the artist and/or audience, a receiver and/or potential analyzer of the knowledge. This component, object and viewer, is approaching a condition necessary to define art.

And so, not only must we assume a viewer by which these are perceived but a conveyor, an intentional or unintentional expressor of that knowledge. We need a creator of the artifact who is the medium of the knowledge. Without venturing into the field of religion, it will be assumed that humans must be the originator of both. It will also be surmised that all knowledge and all artifacts are not created by artists, but artists are necessary to create art. Later in this paper, "artist" will be defined, but for now, if the preceding statements are accepted then we at least have a property, a quality, and a condition which define art. It is a formed artifact, a potential source of knowledge, and human-made (the creation of an artist). But so is this manuscript.

Therefore taking this argument further, if we were to say that art is a composition that an artist created with the intention (another condition) of creating a work of art then we would be hard pressed to disprove the creation as art, no matter what the result. Albeit, this statement raises a series of questions. Is everything an artist creates with intention an art object? What if the artist is dissatisfied and throws it away? Or could an artist, or even a non-artist, accidentally create a work of art?

These are interesting problems and will eventually be addressed, but more pressing questions need be confronted first, such as what do we mean by artist? Creating? Intention? It seems evident that these terms must be investigated before a satisfactory definition of art can be determined.

It must be emphasized before venturing further, many art objects possess all the qualities discussed (aesthetics, beauty, knowledge) and a property (form) plus satisfy the conditions (an intentional creation by an artist). Some people would say that all these together are the criterion of art. But as demonstrated this contention is not shared by the author. Beauty and aesthetics are qualities which may or may not be present in art.

If we assume that art is what the artist creates then we must assume that the definition of art is not an independent entity unrelated to humans to be researched and/or discovered, but that both the definition of art and the compositions are created simultaneously. The artist controls the definition of art by creating art objects which represent his/her concept of art or what art is to become. Every art creation that artists designate art could define art because the definition would expand as fast as artists create new conceptual objects. The concept of art, being a direct function of the artist, has changed and will continue to change as humans continue to evolve and find new concepts. This is to say that art has an open-ended quality; no single concept of art will be available for human's definition or even perfection; it is a matter of redefining through creating.

THE ARTIST

Who is this "artist" who defines and redefines art? The artist perceives external and internal phenomena i.e. events, emotions, concepts, etc., conceives an understanding and/or an interpretation, then expresses a new understanding or interpretation using a medium as a vehicle. To say that artists interpret and understand is to say that they consciously or unconsciously abstract, classify, categorize all external and internal phenomena then associate and integrate them with past experiences and present knowledge. The mind arranges the incoming information into a meaningful context by integrating it with the other senses and by associating it with previous sense experiences. This is to say that smells, tastes, feelings, sights, sounds, thoughts, concepts, etc. can enter the body through the senses and are abstracted into words and/or pictures and are associated with past sense experience then are expressed with or in a new relationship with insights, feelings, or any other additive that an artist can express through his medium. This sounds as if any human being writing or even speaking, with the medium being words, can be an artist.

The main difference is that the person has created of her or himself an artist. Artists are created with intention, which means the willingness to study, train in, and practice art. The people discipline themselves both physically and mentally for this endeavor. They learn to manipulate materials with a certain degree of skill; meanwhile, they create the perceptions, the perspectives, the cognitive processes of an artist.

However, the human mind does not need to abstract the incoming information for it to be categorized and classified. The raw sense experience can be recorded on the memory trace without putting it into words, pictures, or a meaningful context that the artist can comprehend. That is to say, the information can be recorded in the unconscious (As mentioned, this is one means by which the unconscious is formed; another is forgetting). The artist can suddenly be inspired and express something that he, at the moment, can not comprehend for the knowledge rested in the unconscious. The existence of the unconscious also explains how an artist may have set out to express an idea, thought, concept, or tension i.e. feeling, emotion, but unconsciously expressed something more or something other than what she/he wished. In accepting these creations as art, we have to conclude that an artist does not have to have created a specific art piece with intention. In addition, if artists continually practice their discipline, they are bound to make mistakes, and/or stumble onto something new, beautiful, expressive, aesthetic, and it will be the artists' prepared minds which will perceive the discovery, and the accident can become art.

Spontaneous art further exemplifies the preparation of the artist. An artist may work diligently for years drawing bamboo trees, and one evening, slightly tipsy, the artist may create the ultimate of the attempts. Or a poet may, in an instant of inspiration, conceived a poem in its entirety with no corrections necessary. In each of these cases both artists have without deliberate intention manifested an work of art. How and what then is "intention"? This is a question which needs a detailed examination, but we still need to define "creating."

CREATING

Conceptualizing in the mind is definitely a form of creating. But this does not distinguish an artist from a non-artist except for the training of the mind. Artists find materials which they can be manipulated then arrange and rearrange them and give them form. In most cases this unique structure represents more than the rearranged materials. Usually, the artist must let feelings and thoughts incubate so thoroughly that both become organically compressed, which then the artist directs into a medium over a sustained period of time (a form of intention). The achieved object can depict the artist's interpretation, understanding, feelings, and any additive which the artist wants to express. Artists can add meaning to subconscious impulses or unconscious intuition through conscious manipulation. The manipulating usually does not cease until the artist thinks the expression is finished, the added qualities exist. The completion becomes a conscious fulfillment of intent. The product produced is a compound built with its component parts, but once the materials are ordered the whole may represent more than the sum of its parts. The aggregate may represent a transcendent quality in the form of tensions, images, or concepts. A poem is not just words on paper nor is a painting just paint on canvass. All art has to represent something more than its component parts, if not in its purpose.

The tensions are created by the tonalities, the timbre, the complimentary and contrasting elements, the technique and style of the work of art. The images can be created by the forms or patterns of the line, notes, pigments, words, etc. arranged in such a way as to imitate something other than what it is. Associations created by the work of art to the physical or emotional sometime elicit images, which is to say that a work of art could elicit or awaken an image or emotion in the mind of the viewer by association. The concepts are created by the relationships of elements i.e. pigments, lines, words, notes, etc. and by the collection of elements and images in the art object as a whole and the art object in the environment. All of these are added ingredients which transcend the raw media.

To give some examples: In music it is the overtones, the harmony and dissonance of the notes and instruments together with their loudness and softness which create the tonalities and timbre and tensions. Whereas the tonalities and timbre are obvious in music, the images and concepts are more difficult to describe. An image can be a run of notes including the rhythm, loudness and softness. In the most apparent music, the images can be a melody imitating a pastoral scene or a breaking wave onto the shore. Although in music, especially contemporary works, the images are not usually as pictorial, but dwell in the realm of indescribable abstractions, emotions, and feelings. The concepts can evolve through the interplay of images either abstract, pictorial, or emotional. The concepts become the emotional content which the composer may have wished to convey or the final, overall impression of the completed work.

(The simplicity of these examples must be overlooked and forgiven for the sake of clarity.)

The tensions in literature are created by the placement of words as exemplified in poetry or by the plot, the ironies, the techniques, and style. The tonality of literature is create in the placement of words through technique and style; it is the mood, the tone of the work, the intensity of the voice of the author. The means by which images are created are at one time obvious and at the same time illusive and unexplainable. They exist from a description of an object to the building of a whole environment. In literature concepts are created by metaphors, similes, collections of words which create images, story line, or the "message" of the work.

In the plastic, graphic arts, the tensions are created by the loudness or softness of pigments, the relationships of pigments, lines, forms, images, concepts, technique and style, and even the subject matter itself can create tension. Images are created by the placement of lines, color, forms patterned in such a way as to imitate something. Images here can also mean emotional expression as in an abstract design. The concepts are created by the different relationships of elements and images involved in the creation. It can be created by the collection of these elements and images and by the object as a whole or its relationship with the environment. A more specific example of the latter could be an human-made object in the middle of a natural setting which expresses a human relationship with nature, a human's place in the cosmos. These qualities can be added intentionally with control or unintentionally.

Taking the question of creation without intention further: no people in any type of discipline could be fully conscious of all movement, motor skills, intent, meaning, implications involved in their actions and/or thoughts. Skilled tennis players in a tournament may not be aware of their stance, grip on the racket, placement in the courts, but may be conscious of things like the way the opponent strikes the ball, the movements of the other player and the strategy which this opponent implements. Mannerisms like stance, grip, and placement have become an unconscious discipline. This type of unconscious discipline can be present in holding the Chinese ink brush, the thickness of ink on the brush, and the stroke of the brush on the rice paper, as it can be present in the meaning of the words, rhyme and meter, form and placement of a poem on paper. It is present in the prepared mind and brain. As a discipline is practiced and aspects of it are mastered, artists will naturally refocus their attention, and spontaneity will occur in the mastered aspects. But as mentioned earlier, even the unmastered, out-of-control aspects, sometimes prove to have interesting results. Once the energy is directed and momentum is obtained, artists can be taken beyond themselves, and new unintentional creations can be achieved, sometimes something more than they expected. But, of course in most cases, the greater the mastery of the discipline and control of the intentions, the greater the control of the direction of the expressed creation. ("Intention" may also imply awareness of creating. One must know one is creating.)

The previous two examples of creation, bamboo and poem, are spontaneous art: although the intention of creating a specific art object is not present, the intention of creating art is present, consciously or unconsciously. But what if not even this type of intention is present? What if different people find objects which they consider art, and thereby it seems as if no intention of creating exists? Examining Picasso's bicycle seat and handle bars; a dog knocking over a paint container onto a canvass stretched on the floor, or finding a piece of driftwood and placing it on a mantel might answer these questions, as will in the same way Duchcamp's "Fountain."

In that Picasso arranged the bicycle seat and handle bars then placed them on the wall to resemble a steer or bull shows the intention of Picasso. Also in that an artist would see the spilt paint as art and, not only, not throw it away, but frame, then hang the canvas, it becomes art. In taking the piece of driftwood, or man's urinal, from its environment or context of a sand bar near an ocean or river, from a manufacturer or man's bathroom, and giving it special significance by placing it on a mantel, in a museum on a pedestal, then shows intention of the artist. The intention exists in that an artist intends for each of the objects to be viewed as art and treats them as such.

But do all four of the above objects satisfy the necessary conditions of art? Are these presentations really art? The arrangement of bicycle seat and handle bars intentionally creates an image of a steer, and although each of the component parts is not art, the combination through arrangement (creating) makes a new object or image, a transcendent quality. The separate and combined parts are a human-made artifacts, and, probably most importantly, Picasso arranged them. Knowledge conveyed may be not only that bicycle parts can create the image of a bull but that a classical cultural symbol, the bull and all of its connotations are represented in a non-classical, nonconventional medium, a medium which would not have been available to someone before the twentieth century. It is not only that the aforementioned concepts are conveyed, but many concepts, too many to mention here, are conveyed. Some of the concepts deal with the creative process or how an art object can be preconceived before the arrangement, and, of course, the concept of what is art. These concepts are the transcendental qualities.

The arrangement of materials in the example of the dog spilling the paint was neither preconceived completely by a human nor completely human-made. Only deciding to frame the piece and how the arrangement should be seen on the wall was conceived. The paint on canvas is not human-made but the canvas undoubtedly was primed and placed on the floor, obviously with the intention of creating art. The question whether the object is a human creation remains. If the artist were honest and entitled it "Dog Art," the viewer might understand its concepts, the reasons the artist exhibited it. It would not only be paint on canvas, color on color, but chaos (undoubtedly) on human-made order, nonhuman element on human backdrop, curves on square, etc. And of course, it could be beautiful and/or aesthetically pleasing.

The piece of driftwood has no arrangement of materials except that it was placed to view and is not human-made. The artist must have seen some quality, some significance, that she/he deemed worthwhile and wanted others to see this quality. Driftwood, the moment it has its added human significance becomes an artifact. As long as that significance is communicated and has effect, it is art. An artist sees a piece of driftwood and thinks, "That's beautiful....!" it becomes his or her exemplification of beauty. In that the piece of wood was removed by the artist from it natural surroundings and displays it, it gains a significance. Undoubtedly, it is placed on the mantel in a manner that others may see the beauty the artist saw. The same with Duchamp. By him placing the urinal on display and titling it, he gave it a significance. In both cases the found objects were arranged. The urinal could have been placed upside down on the pedestal; the driftwood could be standing on end.

Art has to be intentional in that it is a proposition. Art is usually offered for contemplation, to be believed, doubted, or denied. In that a viewer can participate with the art object either by adopting the statement or rejecting it, the object becomes an experience, a unique encounter.

First, to return to earlier questions: Would a non-artist see these objects in these ways? Would a non-artist treat the objects in these manners, i.e. treat them as art? Would a non-artist explain the objects and their treatment as the artist would?

In that artists do not have to direct energy or emotion into a medium, they must intend to do so. Artists could, on one hand, disperse their emotion or on the other hand produce with another type of directed intent. For example, screaming at the top of one's voice is not producing art, but directing one's emotions into a medium that depicts "The Scream" is producing art. As mentioned the intent of the artist also takes place after the object is complete and the artist decides whether the object is successful or not; whether the artist wants to place the object on display to be judged or not. Therefore, it must be produced with directive intent and displayed with conscious intent.

"The Fountain," when I saw it, rested in the Philadelphia Museum. Some authority, some expert must have thought it was art. Since then I have seen it in art books. Unless art is a conspiracy, we must accept it as art. But do we need to accept the driftwood on mantelpiece as art? What if the person who placed the wood on mantel is a questionable artist, a freshman as were? If we add one more condition to these presentations or any, I'm sure the reader will be convinced. The objects must function as art? Before exploring the function of art, some more terms need be defined.

TECHNIQUE

The technique which is incorporated in the tonality is the skill and control of the artist over the medium. It is the learning of the different relationships of pigments, tones, words, notes, etc. It is the skill involved in learning how to apply paint, how to organize the notes to create harmony or dissonance, how to hit middle "C" on a violin, how arranged words create a picture; it is learning how to create tensions, images, and convey concepts through the arrangement of the raw materials, how to organize the images, feelings and concepts to communicate what the artist wishes to communicate. It is an ability which can be learned and sometimes taught. It is what is perfected through practice. It is learning how to use the basic elements of the media and the potentials and limitations of the media.

STYLE

Just as techniques deals with the objective part of tonality, style deals with the subjective. It is the temperament of the artists, their individuality which all artists bring to their medium; their individual frames of reference, their viewpoints, their separate individual insights, their separate way of exploring their field, their special way of expressing, their interests, how they view art, how they feel at the moment of creating. In short, it is their psychological, physiological, philosophical, and spiritual make-up. An artist can not but bring this depth, a personal style to art. The artist has a different frame of reference not only because of personal individuality but because of a unique place geographically and in time.

The artist stands where no other person has stood both in place and time.

A work of art not only represents one artist's temperament but it represents the era in which the artist lives. Art can be either a conscious comment on the world in which the artist lives or an unconscious comment. Even if artists are not aware they represent their present-day existence, they do. All of us are products of our environments and educations. We react to our environments and educations, whereas artists also react to the existing forms of art. As artists become saturated with existing art forms, they will usually react against these forms and seek new vibrant forms with which to express. The artist's individual reaction to existing influences not only adds another subjective element to art objects but also adds to the objective elements, the choices. It helps to determine the artists' techniques, the media which are used, their goals including their field of exploration, what they want to express or communicate and so forth.

The field of art exists because it has served a purpose for the human race. Artists continuously produce in spite of a lack of financial rewards or even positive reinforcement[*] because art serves a vital function for them, as well. So why do artists create? And why do viewers participate with art objects? These will be answered when we define some functions of art.

FOR THE ARTIST

Art functions as a tool for the artist; it sometimes is a means by which to solve problems, a means by which to express, to explore, and to control. Art can be a resolution to a problem. The problems are either innate in art, in the environment, or they may be created. One query may be how to realize an idea, a concept, a vision, or an emotion and then materialize it in a medium. Using art to express one's self is a very mysterious process. It seems to be at one time connected with acquired skills and yet at the same time beyond any conscious attempt.

---

[*] These are inherent in art. For, artists on the creative edge can sometimes be misunderstood. Critics usually use their present definitions, criteria, value system to determine art from non-art, and good from bad art. But these artists are in the process of defining and/or redefining art. Their products are not necessarily recognized as good art much less sometimes art. Many times neither the created works nor even the artist is accepted into the field.

Artists express themselves, their states of being, and even others' feelings and emotions; they can express the moment as reflected through the artist; abstract thoughts and concepts; insights, interpretations, etc.

The artists can self-explore through expressing themselves and in turn explore human emotion. The result is usually an objective aspect which the artists can then analyze. Expressing then analyzing the expression, maybe expressing again from the analysis, choosing what they consider worth consideration are the ways and means which an artist may explore and direct themselves.

Art may be a tool to explore art itself: the possibilities of what art conceivably can become, and the definition of art at the immediate moment. A means by which to explore the definition of art is to study existing art forms, for example to imitate other artists. Art is a means to explore the manipulation of materials and their effects. It is also a means to study the evolution of methods.

Therefore another way that the artist can use art is to use it to control art itself. Art objects become a directory from which artists can choose to begin their explorations. Also, the development of art-forms reflects the development of the artists. Artists become artists through creating art and in turn create themselves. They can use their media to help break existing patterns of art and their own beings through imagining, creating a vision, building a fantasy then testing it in the environment, trying to make it real and thereby creating a new reality. In this way they not only directly help to control who they are but indirectly through the environment in which they live. "We are all a product of our environment" and in this case, our environment is a product of us.

For example, while working in a medium, the artist may create a mental state of being and when once expressed, if the object is new, it creates a new environment in which the artist lives. The artist may have recorded the flow of thoughts and feelings by directing energy into an art object, or she/he may have let them flow from the self, capturing the one's he/she thought were important, or the creator may have focused on sensations or thoughts and expanded them, worked on them, manipulated them until a new sensation, thought, or insight was achieved and expressed. By changing the environment the artists in turn cause a change in their reactions and relationships to their surroundings; this in turn causes new feelings, thoughts, etc.

Because artists place ideas, concepts, feelings in the world, they can be used as a tool to communicate, to effect change, and to create experiences in the viewer. The artist can force concepts and relationships, insights, visions, ideas, etc. into the existing environment and if the seeds hold and grow through their effects then the validness of the objects as art is tested. The test of an object as art becomes not only how it functions to the artist but its general acceptance and its effect, whether it opens fields of investigation or whether it continues to exist at all, either through its effect or in its physical manifestation. It would be very easy to say, great art has a great effect.

FOR THE VIEWER

Why do people participate with art? Why do they go to museums, poetry readings, theaters, etc. To experience is the explanation. In viewing art, a person may gain knowledge, a sense of history, an understanding of an artist through studying style, a comprehension of technique, a sharing of the artist's insights, feelings, perspective of the world, methods of thought, any transcendent quality which the artist intentionally or unintentionally added to the art work. The audience may seek art to awaken human qualities: emotion, thought, awareness. The perceiver can experience another world other than his or her own and gain understanding of herself or himself and their worlds through this experience.

The participator may seek and find pleasure, beauty, or aesthetic feelings (still to be discussed), but in seeking these, the viewer may be disappointed. So, are there no other qualities, properties, or conditions beyond the qualities the artist intentionally places into the piece? Does art have no intrinsic value beyond these stated functions, or can art not be valued for itself and not function as anything except art?

In the above four cases, Picasso, dog art, driftwood, and Duchamp, arguments can be created for the reasons the artists might have displayed these objects with the criteria of expressing, exploring, communicating, and controlling; and in turn, an argument can be created for why a viewer would judge each piece as art from the criteria of knowledge, pleasure, and communication. But why would either artist or audience want to?

As mentioned earlier, the test of an art object becomes not only how it functions for the artist, but its general acceptance and it effect, whether it opens fields of investigation or whether it continues to exist at all. If an artist examines a completed piece and throws it away, it was art because of its effect. But is it no longer art? And in the same way using the most tenuous example "Driftwood on Mantel Piece," once the artist with the explanation of why it is art is no longer present, is it still art? If nobody but the artist realized that it was art, and the artist is now dead, is it art? Without knowledge of artist's intention because no one saw him place the piece in its exact location on the mantel, how would anyone know it was art and not a piece of wood ready for the fireplace? The intent of the artist is usually found in the manipulation of materials. In fact it is easy to say that the signature of art is human manipulation. If the design of the object effected and still continues to affect many other works of art, then it was and still is art. If the object has been destroyed and no potential effect remains, no it is no longer art. It may be a memory, and it may have been art. Objects can be art at one time and cease to be art because of a lack of continued acceptance or effect. When objects no longer persist to function as art, and when they are destroyed or dissipate in effect, they are no longer art, i.e. driftwood burning in fireplace.

I still maintain in order for any object to be categorized as that object, it must have a consistent property or properties in common with all other objects in that category. If the consistent property is a function, then it must be able (have the potential) to function in that capacity. For example, in order for a chair to be a chair, it must be able to function as a chair, although it does not always, at all times, function as one. This implies that it must be able to function as a chair for someone on some occasion. Even if it never functions as a chair, but as a museum piece (too valuable to sit in), it must able to function as chair. In other words, it may have other functions and never actually function as it is supposed to, but it must have the potential to function as the rest of the objects in that category in order to be an object of that category.

Art must be able to function as art for the artist and the viewer. The potential for art to be a tool to communicate, to express, explore, and control must exist. Art must be able to be a source of knowledge and communication for the viewer. This is not to say that art must function either for the artist or the viewer at all times and in all places, but that if one sought these qualities, it must have the potential to be instrumental as described.

To restate the main previous question, are there properties which the artist cannot intentionally add to the object which are intrinsic? Form is such a property. In that all art must be an artifact, have human manipulation, all art must have form. Form can not be intentionally added or omitted although it can be intentionally or unintentionally manipulated.

The expression of an idea may loom so great in the artist's mind that the form is inconsequential; in fact the medium (another intrinsic property) may be inconsequential for the artist. Style is an intrinsic quality. It comes about with intention and/or control or just unconsciously as an aspect of the manipulation and thought of the artist. In that creating is an individual manipulating materials, characteristics of that individual must necessarily be incorporated into the art work.

Do intrinsic <u>values</u> exist in art for both the artist and the audience? If this is so, then by definition they must be present in all art. As with essential, inherent qualities, the values can not be added or omitted, but must automatically exist. The intrinsic values can lead to other values or functions (they may have the potential) but can be valued in and for themselves. At first one may think that maybe an aesthetic experience or quality could be an innate value but as discussed not all art has aesthetic qualities. Also an artist could intentionally try to add or eliminate this quality ie. Robert Morris. No, the value must exist for its own sake. It must be the experience of the art object for the sake of experience. For most artists it undoubtedly is in the experience of creating, and for the viewer, it must be in the experience of viewing. To say that it is creating for the sake of creating, or for the pleasure of manipulating would be wrong because creating is not at all times pleasurable. To say that the audience participates for the pleasure of participating would also be wrong because participating with art is not always pleasurable.

When a person accidentally places a hand on a hot electric stove, a reflex action will occur, and that person will involuntarily withdraw the hand even before realizing the burning sensation. This is an example of a raw reaction as compared with an intellectual response. With art objects, which are not easily identifiable as art, a long gap in time may exist between the felt immediate presence of the creation and the intellectual response because one does not know how to respond, and only after a lapse of time can one even make comment. It is in this moment before intellectual response where the intrinsic value rests. The intrinsic value is that individualistic moment of raw sense experience before the intellectual response and evaluation. It is the stimulation of the unique experience that is valued.

When artists realize something which they wish to share, or to express, explore or control, then the experience must be translated into a medium. It is no longer the original experience which the artist experiences through the manipulating of materials but a new unique experience. The artist has never created this production before, either physically or in the same state of mind, in the same space-time continuum, and therefore it is a unique challenge to express, to explore or control. When this singular experience of creating is finished, the artist becomes a viewer-critic and intellectually evaluates the finish work.

The audience in approaching an original work of art has a moment of experience which is unique to that moment. The moment exists because of the presentation. The viewer does not necessarily seek this instance because after it is complete and an evaluation has taken place, it may not have been deemed enjoyable or even worthwhile.

If in retrospect the viewer wants to experience the object and again confronts the manifestation, another unique experience is encountered. A changed person now sees it, if for no other reason but that one has seen the work and now seeks its.

In that each work of art is individualistic, art tends to promote this unique moment of experience more than other objects in nature, because the artist has presented it as an experience and with the knowledge and hope it will be experienced..

UNIQUENESS

In order to have this singularly type, challenged experience in creating and this novel type of experience in viewing an art object, each work must offer something all its own. For the artist it is a special type of tool, a medium through which expression can be conversed, and for the observers, it is a finished product presented for contemplation which contains the unique expression with the artist's imprint. The attendees seek this experience, knowing what they will find.

We visit museums knowing we will stimulated by unique creations presented by artists. We know the objects are displayed for some reasons. We place ourselves in its presence to experience its mysteries: what is it? why is on display? what are some of its qualities and values?

It is the individuality of each piece which separates art from the massed produced, the chair as a work of art verses the common kitchen chair. The original chair, as a prototype, might have qualified as an art object with the intention of the creator. But the ten thousandth chair off the production line is not art, no matter who created the original. We assume this, why?

The immediate response might be that no value exists in the ten thousandth chair except as a chair. It is not a collector's item. But then we must consider the ten thousandth "copy" of a Picasso print, signed and unsigned. Even the unsigned ten thousandth print has value to some. Qualities can be gleaned from the work. But without Picasso's authorization, his signature, do we know if his intentions were fulfilled by this particular print? Do we know if these are the qualities and values Picasso wished to communicate?

Another difference is that the original is engraved with the process of creation. One can, if one knows the language, read the working mind of the artist, see the mark-overs, the changes, see the subconscious and/or unconscious expressions slip through, even see the excitement, the moments of insight and inspiration. I once experienced a traveling Picasso print show in Denver, where different stages of development of the same print were displayed. Picasso's thought processes were more readily seen than I could have in just the finished print. I felt I was closer to understanding the process of creation of an artist.

The medium is usually a ready receptor of the manipulation, a magnifier of expression, and finally the record of the workings. The finished creation stands before both the artist and audience as a recording of the process. And an authorized piece says, "Yes, this is what I want to proclaim; this is what I want experienced."

So then why is the fifteenth print in a series of twenty considered art? The artist intended to create a series of twenty. For instance, artists if they know their medium will know when the quality of the print begins to lessen with each "take," which is to know their limit to preserve quality and/or value. Therefore, for various reasons, the artists designate a set number of end-works, then number, date and sign them. The whole twenty may be considered an art object.

If artists, as some printers do today, hire other skilled laborers to do the production work, are these products still art? It may not be a question of art verses non-art, but of who is the artist, or in some cases, artists. A production of an opera has many, many artists working for the performance.

One of my favorite past times is watching movies; some of which I consider art. Obviously the creation of the movie could have been art, but when I am in a movie theater or at home with my DVD, am I experiencing art, and not in some cases copies of copies? I seek movies which are considered masterpieces of art. I respond to some of them as such. But have I been fooled? Is this the same as viewing a forgery, especially if it is a very old movie? Reverting back, what is the intention of the artist? To fool, deceive? or to produce a creation from which copies can be created and viewed (hopefully) throughout the world? Has this object been created and set forth in front of the viewers as an object of contemplation? As an art object? Do the viewers seek and respond to it as art or just as entertainment? Even more subtly, the art work is not just the presentation but the audience's reaction to the performance. It is a different experience by myself at home verses in the theater. It may be that the art experience is not just the performance but the total "happening" of the event, the audience's response included. We still attend movie theaters in spite of the costs to experience the whole scene, not just the reproduced movie. Every night the performance is almost exactly the same, yet with the audience's help a unique experience can be acquired.